The Coward's Emblem

Book One of The Emblem Series

A.D. Guier

The Coward's Emblem

By A.D. Guier

ISBN-13: 978-988-8769-35-3

© 2022 A.D. Guier

Cover design by Emily's_World_Of_Design

FANTASY

EB160

All rights reserved. No part of this book may be reproduced in material form, by any means, whether graphic, electronic, mechanical or other, including photocopying or information storage, in whole or in part. May not be used to prepare other publications without written permission from the publisher except in the case of brief quotations embodied in critical articles or reviews. For information contact info@earnshawbooks.com

Published by Earnshaw Books Ltd. (Hong Kong)

1

It hurt like nothing else ever had. It *burned*. He had never known what it felt like to burn. Fire and heat had never been his enemies.

He dropped with a bone-jarring thud that could be felt for leagues around. The crust of the earth buckled and caved beneath him — beneath a body slighter and smaller than the size the crater deserved. Smaller and slighter than what he was used to: too thin skin and uselessly weak fingernails and blunted teeth in a jaw too narrow and short. The sound that escaped him was pitiful; a groan that wobbled and died moments after leaving his puny, soft throat. Aching and cold, *so cold*. His body curled tighter, his knobby elbows and knees worthless protection against the chill and wrenching pain.

Minutes? Hours? What felt like eons later, the sound of voices broke through the groggy fog in his mind. Shouts of shock and fear. The skidding of rocks and dirt down the sides of the crater to patter against his bare skin.

Skin? That's right. Skin.

And fingers. His fingers twitched against dirt. Eyelids. *Just one on each eye... I forgot how heavy and strange it felt.* Eyelids squeezed shut and feathery hairs fluttered against his cheeks until finally his eyes opened. Everything looked dim and flat. Blank colors lifeless without a pulse of life inside them.

More dirt and pebbles clattered around him, a cascade that

had him instinctively flinching away and closing his eyes again.

What have I done?

"Hey! Hey, you! Are you alive? Mamá! Get a rope or something, we need to get him outta here!"

"We don't know what it is!"

"It's just a boy! Get a rope, Mamá!"

There was a loud, irritated huff, but the sound of nearing footsteps pounded in his poor excuses for ears. He held back another pained groan, muscles cramping in every part of him. Everything was so dull. *Is it supposed to feel like this? Surely it hadn't been this bad before?* A hand touched his skin, and he couldn't help the quiet, feeble hiss that escaped through his teeth.

"What are ya, some kinda cat? At least you're alive. C'mon now, wake up," said that rough female voice in a oddly coaxing tone. It sounded like the stable hands soothing the spooked horses whenever he got too close to the fields.

"'m awagge," he mumbled, the words muddied and twisted around his too inflexible tongue. A scratchy, croaking voice, but young and high despite it. Too young. Too high.

Too human.

"Thank the Sovereign's luck. Let's get you up, yeah? Before someone less nice than me finds you," the woman suggested. Her hand returned; the roughness of her skin belied the gentleness of the touch.

"'oo?"

"What's that?"

The hand snuck its way around his bare shoulders and made him flinch and moan at the touch to the quivering flesh. How did they live decades with such a sensitive outer membrane? Ah yes. They had *clothing*. He needed some. Soon. Unless he died from pain before he could find some. Why did it hurt this much?

"'oo rrr yoo?"

"Huh? Did the fall knock your brain right out?"

He frowned, nose scrunching—where was scent? Where was the smell of dirt and pollen in the air, the body odor and sweat that would tell him everything about the stranger with the coarse hands and insistent voice? Forcing his unfamiliar mouth and tongue to work properly, he used the rest of his strength to painstakingly open his eyes.

Wide black eyes under thick bushy brows and a riot of dark curls in a dark sun-weathered face that was much younger than he had expected gaped down at him.

"Who're 'oo?"

"Who'm I? Who're *you*? You're the one that just ruined half my field!"

"Hamasssa." The name hissed between his teeth strangely. He licked his lips and tried again. "M-My n-name is Hamasa."

The young woman stared and her mouth moved. Maybe she spoke a name? And then darkness fell completely. Hamasa was unconscious before he could figure out what the stranger had said or could speak again.

2

A HAND WAS on his shoulder; a strong, wide hand that turned and lifted him with barely an ounce of effort. His body was hot, too hot, and he could hear the mutter of discomfort near his ear. But the hand didn't leave. It moved to wrap a wiry arm around his shoulders, jostling him awkwardly, to keep him upright. He winced and hissed through his teeth. The woman—girl?—cursed colorfully, but quietly, her movements ever more gentle over the bandages wrapped around him.

"Sorry 'bout that, but it's healing up real quick and we'll kick this fever out of you, no worries," said the familiar female voice. Her accent was thick, consonants clipped off and vowels rounder than what he was used to, but he could understand it a little better each time he woke to her coarse and lyrical voice at his ear. He hadn't been able to reply more than a few stuttered words, though.

"M-Mara?" he whispered hoarsely.

He struggled to open his eyes, but everything was so dark, whether they were open or not. Streaks of sunlight pierced through the dimness and made him flinch when he tried to look. Eyes closed for now. He was still half-twisted around, and he struggled to sit properly. He bit the corner of his mouth while the backs of his thighs and buttocks burned with a dull kind of agony against the mattress.

"Ay, almost. Mar*ya*," she corrected with a chuckle. "Here, lean on me. We're gonna try to eat a bit more today. Mamá made pojola."

His tongue flickered at the corner of his mouth. His nose twitched. Spices. Meat. Something starchy, like rice but not. This was the first time his food smelled unfamiliar. And interesting. Marya set the steaming bowl carefully on his lap, a comforting spot of warmth through the layer of brightly dyed wool, and she raised a wooden spoon to lips to blow lightly.

"Careful, don't drink too fast. It's hot."

The warm soup filled his mouth, and, for that blissful moment, the skin of his lips was hot and searing. The flavors rushed in and he recognized the taste of chicken, of garlic and onions, but most of it was as unfamiliar as the scent. There was a crisp tang of some spice and citrus-y burn of a fruit, and the blandness of not bread and not rice squeaked between his teeth until he crunched something like a radish but sharper than any he had ever eaten. He frowned in confusion as he chewed slowly.

But it was good, and not just for the heat. He peeked through his lashes to see pale broth filled with bright green leaves, small red-and-white radish slices, and bloated kernels of what looked like both rice and corn? All strangely unknown despite how long he looked.

"It's called hominy. Never seen it before?" Marya asked with a snicker when she caught sight of his puzzled frown. Hamasa shook his head mutely.

"W-We ate a rot-*lot* of rice," he admitted softly. His voice still sounded so wrong and his words came out stuttering and strange.

"Hmm, you don't look very Riyukezan to me. You're all dark like us Mekshi folk," Marya said, unexpectedly observant. He inhaled sharply, but she only lifted the spoon to his mouth.

THE COWARD'S EMBLEM

His eyes fluttered shut, warm broth slipping easy and delicious down his throat. He missed rice and the gritty, simple tastes of miso and do'hu, but all these flavors and spices were good, too. Made his mouth and lips tingly in a pleasant way that had him smiling despite himself.

"You're not bad-looking when you ain't white as salt and hissing like a cat," Marya teased. Hamasa sputtered and stared at her as she grinned and winked. "Don't you worry, I'm a professional. I don't flirt with my patients."

Hamasa's eyes dropped to the bowl. The smell of chicken had drool building in his mouth. Meat. "I should try to eat on m-my own," he murmured, cheeks burning red.

"*Ay*, is your fever coming back? You're getting too hot," Marya said worriedly. "I'll get you some water, but see if you can sit up without me."

Her arm moved slowly away. Hamasa tensed all over, determined to sit well. Marya gave him a once over. She then moved a bundle of woolen blankets behind his back, moving slowly as she packed them in, her mouth pulled tight when Hamasa winced.

"All right, there ya go. I'll be back. Eat slow."

His lips pulled up into a tremulous smile and he nodded once. When she left, the sigh slipped out of him involuntarily. He sipped methodically at the soup on his lap, pausing whenever he got dizzy or the skin on the back of his arms or shoulders pulled too tight. Outside he could hear Marya's voice rising, laughter bubbling, as she and her mother spoke. Thanks to his crash landing in their field, both women were constantly outside and coming back for meals covered in dirt. Yet somehow they smiled warmly whenever they caught his gaze.

He supposed his situation was more than fortunate. He should be dead right now, had all but resigned himself to it honestly. The second-most likely scenario should have been him being chased off this little plot of land with pitchforks to fend for himself naked and starving in a body relatively unfamiliar to him in the forest. The young-looking man shuddered at the thought of how *cold* that would be this far into autumn and without clothes. Instead, Marya and her mother had nursed him through the worst of his sickness, given him clean clothes and hearty, delicious food from their own scarce pantry and a warm, loaned bed to sleep in that Marya would not take back for herself. He had no idea why this tiny family had allowed him to stay or why they were being so kind.

The bowl was empty, the wooden spoon clacking against the shallow clay bottom. His lips and tongue still tingled with spice and citrus juice. Slowly, arms heavy and eyelids heavier, he set the bowl to the side and began to creep to the side of the bed. For such a small surface, it took forever to get his feet over the edge. Something wet and hot hung from his bottom lashes, and he sniffled. His bare feet touched the ground. Rug. Leaning forward, his entire back pulling at the motion, Hamasa looked over the side. Quite a few woven rugs covered a packed-down earth floor. The rugs, the clothes he wore, the blankets thrown over him; they were all so vividly colorful with dizzying geometric patterns.

Across the room, he could see the small hand-looms with yet another something being made. A blanket? More clothes, maybe to replace the ones they had given him? He plucked at the tightly-woven linen that covered his thighs. He had never worn anything like this. He was used to much thinner fabrics, slick and smooth as water, layers upon layers and wide sleeves, clothes that created long, thin silhouettes and tiny mincing steps. Trousers were for those outside. The ones who held swords and spears... Lances.

"What are you doing? *Danto!*" Marya exclaimed.

Hamasa flinched, then froze all over when the sudden action had his skin screaming. Marya was already rushing across the room, oddly thin and flat sandals flapping at her heels, while her mother shook her head and carried a wooden bucket to the small cooking area. Señora Garsia looked just like her daughter, or, well, the other way around; dark-skinned, black curly hair tucked under colorful kerchiefs or tied into a single long braid, and warm black eyes. They were also short and wiry with big, rough hands. The only major difference were the amount of laugh lines and creases at the corners of Señora Garsia's eyes and mouth and across her brow.

"M-my name is Hamasa," he corrected meekly as Marya checked over the bandages on the back of his legs and hips. She *tch*ed and glared at him. For a young woman mostly the same height and weight as himself, she was a force.

"Danto ain't a name. Haven't you heard it before?" she asked. At Hamasa's slight head shake, Marya grinned slyly. "It means you bumped your brain too hard. *Danto*, no smarts."

"Oh," he said, then attempted a smile. "I supposed I m-might have."

"I thought your accent was strange. You're from a big city, then?" Señora Garsia asked. She held a small clay cup in her hand that she handed over.

"Yes," Hamasa whispered. He sipped at what was obviously well water, the earthy taste of it now well and truly familiar to him.

"Our goats gave us plenty o' milk, so you'll have some with dinner," Señora Garsia said firmly.

Hamasa nodded and handed the cup back. Only to yawn a moment later, wide enough that he pressed a hand to the right side of his face and winced as pain lanced through him. Just over the apple of his cheek, something cool and sticky coated his skin.

His tongue flicked over his bottom lip before he remembered to use his nose; sharp, tangy, with that same strange cool feeling that mint created against his palate. Slowly, his fingers trailed through the sticky gel, barely missing his eye and ear as it moved upwards over his temple to his hairline.

"Makes ya look mysterious. All heroic and stuff," Marya said with a wink. It didn't quite hide the look of concern in her black eyes.

Hamasa's hand dropped to his lap. His fingertips glistened with the gel, little green bits mixed in with the clear fluid. It made his fingers sticky as he pressed them together, pulled them apart, again and again. He wasn't sure how he felt about his body, so fragile and unfamiliar, already marred with the mistakes that led him here. To this tiny family with concern-filled eyes and open hands.

"C'mon, brother, let's get you laid out," Marya's voice was distorted and hollow. Too far away to hear. But she was already turning him with strong, wide hands, laying him down on his belly. The bed smelled like goat's wool and that cool gel.

3

"That's it now," encouraged Señora Garsia—*Irmen* she had told him. "Just one more step, Hamito."

"H-h-*hamasa*," he stuttered. But he took one more step, braced his hand against the wall, and looked up with a wobbly smile and hot cheeks. He turned at the sound of cheers, and saw Marya in the doorway, a bucket of fresh milk in one hand and her fist waving in the air, as if his triumph were hers, too.

It had been a long week full of struggles and setbacks, and Hamasa couldn't help but laugh with his own sense of victory. The hut wasn't much ground to cover, but he had finished crossing the length of it twice on his own for the first time. The past few mornings, Irmen had taken to helping Hamasa out of bed, handing him a clean, soft rag and cool water to clean himself behind a woven blanket she held up and chatted gaily through. When enough time had passed, and he'd wet what skin was bare, he would give Irmen the word and she'd help him re-dress. He hoped she hadn't noticed how little he smelled. He neither sweated nor had much body scent of his own. He smelled more of this little home, of goat and alpaca wool, of coarse linens and well water and the heavy spicy scent of their cooking. It was nothing like the silks and precious metals and flowery perfumes of… of before.

Irmen came closer, her careful hands steadying him as he

sank onto a chair. Marya set the bucket of milk, quickly followed by a lumpy sack of produce from the small garden, on the table. As Irmen scolded Marya for putting something so dirty near where they ate and Marya laughingly emptied the sack into a large, shallow bowl, Hamasa looked it over, slowly frowning while trying to figure out what was missing.

"Oh, meat," he said suddenly. Marya and Irmen glanced towards him, their busy hands stilling in their work, and their expressions matching looks of confusion.

"What do you mean?" Irmen asked. Hamasa's gaze flicked between them, then down to their hands. He squirmed, grimacing.

"There's no meat this time," he clarified, eyes on his lap.

"Yeah, I guess you ate a lot more meat in that big city you're from, huh," Marya mused, picking up the bowl filled with fresh vegetables and herbs. "We havta be careful with how many birds and livestock we butcher. The milk and eggs are more useful than meat."

"I'm sure more meat will help you heal faster, but Marya is right," Irmen said apologetically.

"It's all right! I was, uh, I mean… The chicken soup w-was good," Hamasa protested quietly. He glanced up in time to see mother and daughter exchanging a look, Marya obviously biting the inside of her cheek. Her dark eyes danced and Irmen smiled.

"I promise more pojole soon," Irmen said at last, the laughter ringing behind her words. Heat spread across his face, down his neck, and up his scalp as the two women chuckled at him.

"You don't have to do that," he mumbled.

"You're a guest, and we like to treat our guests right," Marya said. She set down another large, empty clay dish in front of him and handed him a bunch of dripping wet herbs. "Why doncha help me with making our dinner?"

Hamasa sighed in relief, taking the herbs willingly. "Just tell me what to do."

"That's what I like to hear!" Marya crowed. She ruffled his hair high on the crown of his head far from his burns.

Hamasa let Marya boss him through the preparations, Irmen rarely interrupting—mostly to praise them both, or ask Marya to fetch something. A pile of cut vegetables and chilies, to which Hamasa discreetly added a few more, and herbs were waiting on his dish. His fingers tingled with the scent of spice and fresh and green, and his muscles felt pleasantly used. Hands were filled with so many tiny moving parts, and even holding that small knife made his fingers ache and his wrists burn after it was all done. Most of his cut produce was jagged and misshapen compared to the much larger amount that Marya had finished so expertly. She hadn't needed to concentrate on her hands, her mouth running and her attention bouncing between her chore, her mother, and Hamasa without a bit of hesitation. She swept the dish toward the fire pit and her waiting mother. Hamasa flexed his fingers and hands, turning them over and around, wondering how they could accomplish such a delicate task. With another quick glance at the Garsias, he licked at the pads of his fingers, his palm, his wrist. The flavors, the juice of the limón particularly bright, whisked over his tongue, the roof of his mouth, and down his throat.

"Not a bad first time. You might be a natural cook," Marya teased, moving on to her next chore. Hamasa discreetly hid his hands under the table and watched Marya wash the dishes and utensils they had used, dropping all the scraps into a bucket for the goats.

"I think cooking requires m-more skill than I have," Hamasa disagreed, smiling anyway. "I prefer the eating." Marya laughed.

"You'll be able to feed yourself, I can promise that much,"

Irmen assured him, wiping at her hands and standing. "It'll be one way to amuse you. Now that you're awake, I don't want you to be bored while Marya and I work outside."

"Ay, Mamá, you're right, remember when I broke my arm that time? I got laid up for *weeks*," Marya said, turning back to Hamasa and rolling her eyes upwards. Her whole body heaved the sigh. "Worst weeks of my *life*. How can ya stay holed up in here all day and not go crazy?"

"I don't have m-much choice," Hamasa pointed out dryly. He looked towards the window as Irmen swatted at Marya with a flick of her rag. The horizon burned deep crimson and gold. His heart clenched in his chest, his hands tightening unconsciously into fists, and his eyes traced the sun-painted wisps of clouds and found the dim glimmer of stars above the dark violet edges of sunset. "I don't know how not to, either," he whispered.

"I'm sure we can think of somethin'," Irmen said encouragingly.

He shrugged and met her earnest eyes with a bashful smile. "I'm sure any book you might have will be enough. I enjoy being ar-alone." His smile slid away when Irmen's mouth twisted to the side, eyes glancing away and pained.

"Books? We don't got books." Marya snorted loudly and crossed her arms over her chest. "I know enough writing for my own name, but that's 'bout all. Mamá?"

"No, I never learned. Your father could read a little, but only Mekshan," Irmen admitted.

"I've never learned to read Mekshan, only how to speak it," Hamasa said with a frown. "I thought anyone could be educated in Mekshi."

"Yeah, if we wanna travel across whole leagues to the nearest big city and learn how to write all Empire fancy-like. No one outside the cities use Riyugi. And anyways, most Mekshan stories are made for telling 'round the fire," Marya told him. Her eyes lit up and she clapped the side of her fist to her opposite open palm. She hurried over to the hand-loom, picked up a large woven basket, and brought it over to Hamasa to set it next to his foot. It was full to the brim with flat and lumpy but smooth layers of wool, and a wooden tool that looked a bit like a child's spinning toy. "You can spin!"

"You just want less chores to do," Irmen accused, turning back to the now-fragrant pot over the fire.

Marya rubbed the side of her nose and chuckled. "That's just a perk."

"I don't know how," Hamasa said, stroking his fingertips over the soft wool.

"It's easy. I'll teach you before dinner's even done," Marya declared, holding up a fist and displaying her flexed bicep. Hamasa didn't understand how her flexing would help with making thread, but returned her guileless grin regardless.

4

HAMASA SAT balanced on the fence around the Garsia homestead. Northern Mekshi was a rocky place, but the soil was good and rich among the stones, and the Garsias knew how to work the steep sides of the hills and mountains that made up part of their land with terraces and carefully dug ditches. The terraces cut into the hillside near their home barely cleared the top of the hut in height, and the largest and lowest area of the field lay around their little, pale tan adobe home. Across the field, which still looked distinctly bowl-like, Marya was cajoling and cursing at the single donkey dragging a small hand-plough that Marya directed. Dark, rich soil foamed around the dull blade like waves upon the beach. He frowned to himself at the memory of the sea.

"Ay, Hamasa! Don't stop yet! You've still got more paces before Mamá says you gotta rest!" Marya called over cheerily.

Hamasa smiled a little crookedly, and waved towards her. "You don't need to worry about m-me!" he shouted in reply.

The farmer began to whistle gaily and urge Idiot the donkey onward once more. *Danto* seemed to be a favorite word of Marya's. Hamasa's eyes followed the furrow and then past it. Most of their fence was gone, bits and pieces of charred wood jagged at the edges—what was left of the crater he had made when he fell onto their field almost three weeks ago. While he had been in and out of consciousness, and later spent days walking up and down the length of the hut and learning to spin thread, they had finished filling in his mess. Today, Marya was already beginning to sow gourds and barley for early winter harvest. A mixture of awe and guilt bubbled up in his throat as he watched his new friend work her land.

His jaw firmed and determination glinted in his brown eyes before he dropped to his feet and began to walk. Each step farther from the farm was stronger, steadier. He had made a promise to himself days ago. He would do his best to not be a burden on this kindhearted and generous family, and also to gift them with something they did not get easily nor often. Beef, or large livestock meat in general, was a luxury for these small northern villages, where wild grasses were tough and sparse and meadows practically nonexistent. Something Hamasa should have remembered before embarrassing the Garsias.

Sheep, goats, and alpacas were the most common livestock this far north and throughout most of Mekshi. But that was livestock. The mountain and forests were teeming with wildlife. Perhaps Hamasa was small, and his nails weak, and his eyes barely better than blind, but he was fast. A lot faster than anyone or anything would expect.

Unlike further south, or like the forests in the many, many books and scrolls he had read, the forests of the north were more scrub than anything. The scattered trees were tall, but the trunks were thin, boughs thinner. Dry yellow grasses and fallen twigs crackled under his feet. In autumn, the rainy days were fewer and far between even as it got cooler. As he got used to the way his body could move, how his arms swung for balance, and his feet leaned forward on his toes as he ran, his pace became faster, easier, more natural. It was almost as if he belonged in this diminutive form. His burns pulled and stretched and the wind whipped through his clothes and chilled his feverish skin. But he could ignore the discomfort and twinges of pain as he raced all but silently through the trees and around the low, spiny bushes.

Oddly, he *saw* it before he heard or smelled it, and he froze in the shade of a tree. Peering through the trunks, Hamasa watched a four-legged alpaca-like animal rip the greenest grasses out of the dirt. It was shaggier, with reddish-brown fur rather than white or grey, and its neck longer than the Garsias' goats. It was closely reminiscent of the Harenese dromedaries he had seen in pictures, but he remembered enough to know it was a huanaco, a wilder cousin to the alpacas domesticated by most of Mekshi. Its long ears twitched towards him. Wind whistled over stone and bush, whisking past his raised nose and unmoving body. Unable to hear or smell him, the huanaco continued to graze.

The heat of the sun warmed him, each movement of his muscles slow and precise, his steps carefully chosen. Usually he had to care about the sun, where precisely it hovered in the sky, where his shadow fell, how swiftly would he need to snatch; but now it was just the sound and the smell of him that mattered.

A shadow passed overhead. His eyes told him it was a cloud, drifting by on the wind, but he couldn't move. The shadow was darker and vast, so vast it had blotted the entire sky. The weather had been warm, even in the early morning hours when the ground had been shining with dew, but his dread had been icy and sudden. There hadn't been a roar. Only searing pain and the weight of something so large he'd been crushed, bowing under the burden, then *falling*

Falling

Screaming

A twig cracked under his foot. There was a patter of hooves. Rocks and dirt skittered down an incline. Hamasa fell onto knobbly knees and unfamiliar hands; this flimsy, cumbersome body wrapped him too tightly, not tightly enough, too exposed, neck bare, scars burning. Hamasa gasped, eyes so wide tears grew on his lashes, his arms and legs shaking, his back twitching and flinching and tensing over and over. He was so bare.

When he had finally caught his breath, when the chill had left his chest and his limbs no longer shook, he looked up to see the huanaco long gone. All that remained was a bedraggled bit of weed lying on the dirt, half-eaten. He had to struggle back to his feet groaning, moving stiffly to brush dirt off his borrowed trousers and tunic.

"I m-made a p-promise," he whispered to himself, clenching his teeth hard enough to hurt to stop his trembling lips. Perhaps stalking prey was not his forte these days. He would move fast, fast enough not to think. Not to remember.

It was a long while later, long enough Hamasa almost had to give up on his promise for another day and was trying to ignore the relief as he turned back towards the Garsias'. A shadow darted along roots and fallen leaves. The scramble of paws over dirt had him moving without thinking. Among the bracken and grey bark of the trees and dark brown of the dirt, the thing's fur had made it nigh invisible. It was under his clawed fingers, the snap echoing under his palms like a tree branch under his foot. Empty eyes stared up at him, its mouth gaping. He dropped the small animal with a cry and threw himself backwards. His shoulder smacked into a tree and he spun around from the force of it, fingernails clutching as he doubled over and vomited, shoulder burns screaming with pain, throat rasping. And the *snap* echoed in his head. His eyes stung, and his stomach roiled, but Hamasa managed to straighten and press his forehead to the bark.

"M-maybe... m-maybe tom-morrow... I'll just, uh, hoe the garden," he whispered, his too-hot face heating the wood under his skin.

He made his way back to his kill and knelt beside it. The mara was still warm, its fur soft and body lax. With the right sight, he would have been able to see what was left of its last heart beat, the hues of red and orange that made up all life fading to blue. His fingers smoothed brown fur and traced the fragile long bones of its legs.

"Shōkra'rak," he whispered, the words fitting in his mouth in a way Mekshan and Riyukezan did not. He cradled the small creature close to his torso the whole way to the farmstead. It took getting there, watching Marya's eyes light up seeing what he held, to remind him of his own hunger and years of hunting and meat-eating. Marya's cheers and excited anticipation for dinner had him trying not to smile or flush hotly.

"Wait 'til you try Mamá's grilled mara meat! She makes it the best! I can't believe you hunted, how could you even catch it?" Marya exclaimed, wrapping a sweaty arm around his drawn-high shoulders and giving him a little shake. "You're amazing, Hamito."

"Thanks," he muttered, head ducking and his whole body tensed to keep from flinching away. It wouldn't be right to cringe away from her freely given kindness. To make her feel bad when he had been hoping to repay her and her mother's goodness. He let Marya drag him inside, biting back a sigh of relief when her arm fell away and she took his catch within.

By the time Irmen's specially grilled mara meat and vegetables with tortiyas were finished, his stomach was rumbling. The scents and tastes of those enticing herbs and fresh meat dimmed the worst of the afternoon's horror. The sharp-smelling green sauce Marya gleefully covered the whole plate with was deceptively spicy. His nose and eyes stung, but he ate it all with gusto. It "all" being a small amount, but he had never tasted anything like it. He hadn't ever been this hungry his entire life, either.

THE COWARD'S EMBLEM

"We'll make a real Mekshan boy of you yet, city boy," Marya whooped, clapping his back proudly when he asked for more of the spicy salsa. Hamasa sputtered and choked and reached for the cup of milk Irmen scooted towards him.

"I hope you didn't push yourself today," Irmen said, although she was smiling as she spoke. He shook his head, grateful for his mouthful.

"He was walking upright and regular when he got back," Marya said after a large and loud swallow.

"You're going to choke, miha," Irmen scolded. Marya piled more filling onto the next tortiya whispering 'worth it' under her breath to Hamasa. "You should drink more water and go to bed. You're healing fast, but let's not push too hard."

Hamasa met Irmen's eyes and guiltily looked away. He probably *was* healing faster than he should.

"Ya gonna go huntin' 'gain t'moorer?" Marya asked, bits of cilantro and salsa falling from her mouth. Irmen sighed, rolling her eyes skyward, her mouth moving silently to '*Sovereign bless her*'.

"Uh, no. I thought m-maybe... uh, I could help in the garden," Hamasa murmured. His breath shuttered in his throat at the thought of hunting again.

"I'd ruther have more meat, but, yeah, you can help there, too," Marya said.

"It'll give me more time to make some winter clothes instead of being outside. Thank you, Hamito," Irmen said.

He smiled wanly and buried his face in the next bite.

5

MORNING CAME and went. After too short a time, and the garden barely weeded successfully, his back, his legs, his arms, his *everything* was quivering and flushed. In the end, Hamasa had spent more time gasping and splayed out over the dirt, arms little more than limp rags at his sides, than he did working. When they finally stopped for lunch, Hamasa guzzled down the entire wooden bucket full of well water. Marya, on the other hand, had spent the entire morning, which started before his, whistling and chatting between grunts, her entire body in constant motion. She had taken her coarsely-woven overshirt off in the afternoon heat, the sun beating down on the sweaty, dark skin of her bare arms and neck. Hamasa pushed himself up and stared at his own arms. Pulling up his sleeves, he saw the slight tan and almost pink of his underarms, the brighter pink scars high across and behind his biceps, and wondered if his frail body would ever look like Marya's. Or if he would ever work so effortlessly through the same arduous tasks.

He had never known what a human body was truly capable of until he could compare his fledgling, unfamiliar one to a young woman in her prime amid hard work like Marya. Fortunately, his healing had progressed so well during this third week at the Garsia farm that all that was left of the terrible burns was the pink skin that was still stiff and new. And only so obvious because of the natural brown of his skin. He sighed and sank back into the cool dirt, gazing skyward longingly.

The sun was the sort of warm that reminded him of his mother and of the Sun that shined in that far away place. It shined here in the flat vast of the blue, blue sky. A blue vastness broken by the occasional puff of white clouds and large dark predator birds that cawed their freedom proudly through the air.

He never thought he would miss the sky so much...

"I think this is as good as it gets. The soil's a bit rockier than I'd like, but whatcha gonna do," Marya said with a grin, thumbing at her nose and leaning on her shovel.

Hamasa jerked upright, grimacing, but it wasn't because of the burns for once. A hot, deep ache was in his every muscle. "You're *amazing*."

"Nah, Mamá says I haven't stopped moving since I learned how to in her belly," Marya joked. Her chin braced on her hands crossed over the top of her shovel, eyes curious and intense as Hamasa struggled to his feet and pounded on his shoulders with his fists. "You know I never did ask, what kinda spell didja blast yourself with anyway?"

Hamasa blinked at her, fists dropping to his sides. "W-What did I b-blast w-with w-what?" he repeated, flabbergasted.

"What?" Marya asked, just as bewildered.

Hamasa cleared his throat and tried again. "What did you mean about, uh, the blasting?"

Marya snorted. "I'm not stupid. No way can a boy drop outta the sky and *live*. You must'a been fiddling with some magic and it exploded right in your face. Everyone knows how much trouble them wizards get in."

Hamasa blinked even more rapidly. He had started to wonder why the Garsias hadn't bothered asking him questions.

"Yes, um, mage. I'm an apprentice mage from Riyushu."

"Yeah, like I said, not stupid," Marya said with a heavy eye-roll. Hamasa nodded and swallowed painfully. "Riyushu, huh? Explains why you don't catch every word we say and your accent's so funny, like Ma said. Riyushu's got that fancy Riyukezu talk. So, how'd you get this far north?"

"We..." Hamasa gulped and stared at his blistered hands. "We went up to San Yamarasu. The university there, there was special training," he said haltingly. He didn't know every university in Mekshi, but he knew enough of them, thankfully. Marya made a thoughtful noise. "It was a dare, but I didn't want anyone to get hurt, so I came out of the city some ways. At rea-least no one got hurt."

"No one but *you*." Hamasa shrugged. Marya rubbed her nose with a little frown. "So I guess you'll be going back soon enough?"

"No! I cant! I... I'm most definitely experred for this if they find out!" Hamasa said, a glimmer of truth in his words that lent his panic some credibility. Marya peered at him, then let out a gusty sigh.

"Experred? Expelled?" At Hamasa's nod, she continued, "Doncha got family down there? In Riyushu?"

"No," Hamasa whispered, eyes lowered. "I have no family now."

Silence fell, the bleating of goats warbling through the air. A moment later, the young farmer cleared her throat. Hamasa glanced up to see Marya's grin.

"So how 'bout we go into Elorra, the nearest village, for dinner? I know the best place for sangria," Marya said.

Hamasa slowly and awkwardly smiled, his nose scrunching. "I'd rike that." Maybe. He wasn't exactly sure if he would like sangria, but he did like how Marya beamed cheerfully.

THE COWARD'S EMBLEM

***

"Whaddaya mean you've never had sangria? *Everyone* drinks it! What else is there?"

Hamasa stared at Marya's back as the door to the local cantina swung inward under her hand. The question didn't make any sense. The past fortnight had passed without either of them drinking sangria. Of course there were other things to drink.

"Water. Sakki. Fruit waters. Tea. Mer- *milk*. Cow's milk, sheep's milk, goat's mi—"

"You don't have to be a know-it-all," Marya interrupted with a theatrical groan, eyes rolling upwards, wide mouth pulling up at the corners.

"I don't mean to be?"

Marya clapped her big hand to Hamasa's back chuckling good-naturedly, and led the way to the long wooden bar. They scrambled onto the high stools, both of them too short for their feet to touch the ground even if they stretched their legs and pointed their toes. The wood under Hamasa's hands was smooth and darkly stained with both age and care, and he ran a finger along the grain as his eyes scanned over the cantina curiously. The tables here, like the single table at the Garsias', were all tall, maybe hip high, with simple wooden chairs arranged around them. People lounged indolently, rocking on rickety chair legs and stretching their legs out beneath the tables. The few wooden dishes on the tables were large and flat, and the cups were large with handles to slip a hand through. He didn't see a single teapot in the entirety of the cantina. The only small cups were squat and made of cheap glass, occasionally filled with a milky clear liquid.

Everything, from the way these people sat to the way they spoke, seemed so... unrestrained. Behind the bar, a scruffy, shabbily-dressed man wearing a broad-brimmed hat pulled low over his eyes meandered his way towards them. Hamasa glanced towards the man with his heart beating too hard against his breastbone.

"What'll it be, Garsia?" the man drawled in a voice as slow as his languid movements.

"Definitely two sangrias and whatever Tonyo was told t'cook tonight." Hamasa gave her an odd look, and Marya grinned as she rubbed her nose. "Whenever Tonyo gets an idea for something special, it's usually the best thing getting ate all day."

The bartender, Vacero, scraped a hand over the patchy stubble on his face and finally said, "Tonyo's all over the chilaceles and grilled goat. Added some fresh peppers, so folk have actually been eatin' their greens in this den."

"Sounds great," Hamasa said at Marya's eager glance. He honestly had no idea what chilaceles was, but if the Garsias' meals had taught him anything, green peppers he loved.

"That's the spirit, Hamasa!" Marya crowed, clapping his shoulder with a friendly little shake. Hamasa smiled awkwardly, but preened somewhat at the praise.

Vacero's gaze went from laconic to dagger-sharp and back again so fast Hamasa almost missed it. A chill went down his spine. "Hamasa, was it? Not much of a Mekshan name. Haven't seen you here before, neither," Vacero said. Said leadingly in Hamasa's opinion.

Hamasa answered with his eyes resolutely on the grimy counter, "I've never b-been here b-before." He completely ignored the observation about his name. He really was a danto.

"C'mon, Vac, I'm *starving*," Marya said with a petulant whine in her voice. "What're you doing small talking?"

Vacero acquiesced with a tip of his hat. He sauntered away as leisurely as he had come, leaving the two friends (*are we friends?* Hamasa thought with a pensive frown) to talk alone. Their drinks appeared somewhere between Marya naming every patron in the bar and an amusing anecdote of the unlikeliest-looking old man who loved to dance on the tables when far enough in his cups. Hamasa was giggle-snorting his way through a glass of ruby red wine filled with slices of fresh fruit, the aches and pains of farming long forgotten, when two huge steaming platters of meat, fried beans, and green peppers topped with a fried egg were set in front of them. Marya eagerly snatched up her utensils, all but drooling, while Hamasa eyed his platter in bewilderment.

"There's no way I can finish all this," Hamasa said, a hand on his stomach. His surely much too small stomach. The first two weeks in his strange body had been mostly consuming soups, maybe some tortiyas and beans, but the Garsias didn't exactly make meals this large when they were living mostly off last year's harvest.

"'Skay. Wadeba yeh don' 'iniss dey give t'da pids," Marya told him through a bulging mouthful. Hamasa squinted at her, bewildered.

"I know it's not the cleanest bartop, but I prefer you not t'spray it with food," Vacero said mildly. Marya grinned sheepishly and shoveled another mouthful in. "If you can't finish what you've got, the pigs'll do it for you," he added in Hamasa's direction, his gaze on the the drinks he was pouring.

Hamasa nodded, and then took a more sensible bite, teeth clacking against the underside of his spoon. He was still clumsy with these strange eating utensils. Why didn't anyone out here use hashi sticks? He blinked rapidly as he chewed. Under the beans were more tortiyas, soaked to softness in a spicy, flavorful, red sauce. He met Vacero's eyes and said, surprised,

"It's good."

"Thank you kindly, sir," Vacero answered with a humorous twinkle in his dark eyes under the shadow of his hat. He looked back to Marya, leaning his hip against the bar after sliding the drinks down the bartop to some waiting patrons. "So you'll be wanting t'hear the latest from Riyushu?"

Marya perked up, black eyes glittering with curiosity. Hamasa sunk as low as he could on his barstool. His shoulders hitched around his ears and his hand methodically brought food to his mouth.

"Seems like the Shield of the Sovereign has got itself good and lost."

"*What*!" Marya exclaimed, spraying food over the bar and immediately choking. Vacero sighed and threw a cloth in her face.

"Missing?" Hamasa repeated, his lips numb and fingers curled into fists on his lap out of sight. It took everything in him to keep his gaze on Vacero without flinching.

"Missing. Took off t'face down a monster and never came back. Folks are saying the Shield got itself killed," Vacero explained bluntly, his eyes too sharp. Too keen.

"No chance the Shield is dead! The Sovereign'd know, wouldn't she?" Marya interrupted, slapping her hands down on the bar, rag already discarded. "What monster could kill the *Shield*?"

A tremor worked its way down Hamasa's spine.

"The Beast," Vacero said harshly. Marya's jaw dropped. "The Merciless."

Marya gulped loudly, throat clicking dryly before she forced out a chuckle. "But the Shield, everyone said it's the strongest, fastest, most powerfullest Shield in living history."

"And the youngest," Hamasa whispered softly. Vacero and Marya glanced at him and he grimaced slightly. "The Shield isn't half the age of the Shield that came before it. Maybe ress—*less* than a quarter."

"I had heard something 'bout that," Vacero agreed, stroking his scruffy chin pensively. "Garsia here *was* right 'bout something."

"Huh, what? I was?" Marya actually startled on her stool, then puffed up her chest, chin rising. "A'course I was! What was I right about?"

"That the Sovereign would know if the Shield was dead. I got word from a pal in Riyushu and it looks like half Her Imperial personal guard are gone. Whispers 'round the Capital is they're all lookin' for the Shield."

Hamasa's heart twisted while his stomach knotted and writhed. "The Lances."

Vacero tipped his hat at Hamasa with a humorless smirk on his face. "The famous ones themselves. Looks like the Sovereign don' think the Shield's gone for good. Nobody knows what happened 'tween it and the Merciless, but it's been more'n three weeks. Soon enough them Lances will be knockin' on the trees 'round these parts, seein' what falls out."

"The *trees*? I don't think a—" Marya started with a loud, incredulous snort. She broke off as Hamasa's platter scraped over the bar's surface. He clambered down to his feet, unable to even think about food let alone eat any more of it.

"I'm tired and this tark about m-monsters and, uh, Shields. I've *lost* m-my appetite. I'd, uh, I'd like to return to the farm and sleep," Hamasa told them with a small shake of his head and embarrassed, quavering smile.

"Ay, you really do look tired, Asa, and I can barely understand you. Let's get you back 'fore you fall out, yeah?" Marya said in true, kindly concern. She didn't even bother pointing out how bad Hamasa's affectation had gotten. Guilt flittered over Hamasa's ashen features.

"N-No, you don't have to do that," Hamasa protested shamefully.

"Stuff it, Asa. I'm not letting you walk all the way back alone. Uh, Vacero, do ya mind maybe giving me a pail or somethin' for this food?" Marya asked with a beaming, hopeful smile.

Vacero tore his somber gaze away from Hamasa. He nodded once as he picked up both platters. "The pigs'll be sore disappointed, but sure. It'll be extra if you don't bring 'em back."

As soon as Vacero disappeared through a swinging door, Hamasa headed for the exit. He couldn't be here a moment longer. He couldn't be in this village a second longer, not even the Garsias' farm would be safe for another day.

6

HAMASA PAUSED outside the door, eyes darting in every direction, sweat dewing his forehead. Hamasa wasn't always great at reading people, but it was obvious Vacero knew there was something off. If a squad of Lances came here, there was no telling what the sharp-eyed barkeeper might say to them.

Should he just... leave? Just start running down the Great Road that wound through the country? Keep running and not stop? He gnawed on his bottom lip until he drew blood and flinched at the sharp, unexpected pain. Hamasa wasn't really good at making smart decisions, book learning or not. But maybe worse than his bad decisions was his indecision, and that particular trait had him waffling outside the cantina. His borrowed sandals shuffled over the dusty road that would lead him to the Great Road, and his eyes unconsciously tracked the shifting crowd of villagers. Where could he even go? Further north, to San Yamarasu? Head to the nearest port city and get the first ship off Mekshi entirely?

The door behind him swung open, almost smacking right into his back, only for something to actually smack into his back a moment later. Hamasa grunted as he jerked forward, a hand on his shoulder barely keeping him on his feet.

"Whoa there, Hamasa. You trying to leave without me?" Marya said with a short barking laugh. Obviously a joke. Hamasa winced.

"I... I'm not feeling well," Hamasa hedged, warm hands rubbing against the rough cloth of his trousers. Marya squinted at him before her eyes widened in worry.

"You kinda look like you've been puking your guts out. Or you're about to. Let's get home," she said, patting his shoulder. Hamasa nodded miserably and let Marya lead him from the village, two battered tin pails swinging from one of her big, farmer's hands.

"I'm sorry I ruined your night out," Hamasa whispered, head hanging low.

"Hey, nah, Vacero was acting strange, and Mamá will be excited about the gossip, anyways. Lances coming *here*. She'll be coming into the village every day to wait for 'em."

Hamasa swallowed painfully. "Won't you be coming, too?"

Marya frowned. "What, and leave you alone? I can tell you don't like it here," she said, eyebrows rising when Hamasa skittered away from a passerby as if to exactly illustrate her point.

"That doesn't... I mean, I shouldn't be a factor, Marya. I won't be much longer, so while I appreciate your concern—"

"What d'you mean you *'won't be much longer'*?" Marya interrupted, voice rising and brows arching up.

"I can't stay here, encroaching on your family's hospitality. I should leave. Soon." Hamasa hissed the last word while dread crept down his spine.

"No chance! You 'sploded yourself with *magic fire* or something! You should stay as long as you need to!"

"And it cost you weeks of work before you could finish plowing! I'm just another mouth to feed," Hamasa argued with no small amount of self-deprecation. "I can give nothing back to the farm. I can barely weed a garden."

Marya stopped in the middle of the road, her iron-hard hand on his shoulder holding Hamasa in place and turning him to face her. Black eyes gazed seriously into brown.

"If you think my Mamá and I care about getting our money's worth more'n giving an unlucky boy help when he needs it, you haven' been paying attention. You ain't gonna make or break my farm, only how hard *I* work can do that. Got it, buddy?"

Hamasa blinked, eyes and nose stinging suspiciously. "Buddy? We're friends?"

Marya grinned widely and gave Hamasa a little shake. "Yeah! A'course we are!"

"Thank you," Hamasa choked out.

He reached up to rub awkwardly at his burning eyes. They stung like salt had been sprinkled in them, and his voice sounded wobbly and ridiculous. Weeping was such a useless act, but it also felt as if he were suddenly cleaner. Marya made an embarrassed sound low in her throat while Hamasa hiccupped the last of his few tears away. With his eyes closed, his other senses were minutely stronger, and, as he was pulling himself together, he picked up the sound of something frighteningly familiar.

The clanging of iron.

The stamp of hoof beats.

The snap of cloth in the wind.

Instinctively, Hamasa tilted back his chin and his tongue flicked over his lower lip as his nostrils flared. He could taste the salt of sweat and tears on his lips, but not much else. His nose was clogged with mucus, rendering any scenting his nose could have done utterly impossible. Not that he really needed it to know what was coming down the Great Road towards Elorra. Towards them.

"Hamasa, are you all right? You're whiter'n a ghost."

"We need to get off the road. Now." He snapped the words past lips that quivered, his hand clutching Marya's bony wrist tightly to drag them towards the dusty underbrush.

"Why? Calm down, you're gonna trip and take us *both* down, and the food, too!" She froze, jerking Hamasa to a stop. Her head turned towards the commotion down the road and Hamasa's stomach dropped. "Do you see that?"

Shaking his head mutely, Hamasa tugged harder to get off the road. Off the road and away from the small party of riders on huge, expensive horses and wearing outfits that glinted in the dark golden rays of sunlight. Above their heads, a cloth on a tall pole whipped in the strong autumn breeze. They finally got near enough to make out the iron breastplate they all wore, the bright trappings of the horses' gear in weather-beaten hues of silver and blue, and the banner on the pole: a silver lance on a field of blue.

"Óra," Marya said breathlessly, dark face flushed ruby and black eyes wide and glittering. "Lances of the Realm, knights of Sovereign Aneya herself. Hamasa, are you *seeing* this?" she said, swinging around her arm to lightly punch Hamasa's ribs. Unfortunately, she forgot about the tin pails in her hand and they thudded into Hamasa's gut.

A loud, involuntary groan followed the thud, and he doubled over, almost kneeling, one arm around his waist.

"Sorry, Hamasa! That was my fault."

"I know," Hamasa said through gritted teeth.

Where the Lances might have ridden past two nameless young farmers at the outskirts of nowhere, Marya's fumbling and Hamasa's pained sounds had them turning in their direction. Hamasa kept his head bowed, his arm taut around his middle and his other hand twisting in the loose fabric of Marya's tunic. *Just keep going by. Stop looking! Please, in the name of the eternal Sun, stop looking!*

Most did just that, unimpressed with two obvious Mekshan peasants. For a moment, Hamasa felt the tension loosen in his shoulders, his knees almost vibrating in place. Until a single rider halted a few paces away from where Marya and Hamasa stood. Silence stretched as Hamasa's heart stopped beating. The other Lances halted, too, calling back in puzzled voices to their comrade, but the words, in their too familiar language, were drowned out by a roaring in Hamasa's ears.

Saddle leather creaked and well-oiled steel rattled. Two, heavy, ironshod boots hit the dust and walked towards them.

"Who is this?"

"Who? Me? I'm just Marya, Marya Garsia. I own a farm up a ways with my mamá," Marya babbled, tongue-tied and giddy.

"Not you. Him."

Hamasa inhaled sharply, eyes closing, body too tense to flinch.

"A friend. Ha—"

"No one. I'm *no one*," Hamasa said harshly. "Sorry for w-wasting your time."

He shoved at Marya, ignoring her squawk of confused outrage, leading them past the too-nosy knight. There was a quick thudding of footsteps and he could feel the abrupt looming presence of a threat. A large gauntleted hand fell on the shoulder furthest from Marya, turning him away from his ally and towards the threat at his back. His heel spun over dirt and his vision sharpened with a clarity he had missed for weeks.

A stern-faced young man, a few years older than Marya, stood proud and straight-backed on the dusty road. His armor shined, but the leather of his gloves and boots was well-worn and supple from use. The helmet mostly covered his face, but the opening in the middle revealed oddly familiar and smooth-cheeked features glowing pink with warmth under sweat and made older by the fierce scowl and dark ageless eyes. Eyes that were wide with shock one moment and triumph the next.

"My lord."

Hamasa flinched and his vision blurred again, eyelids blinking rapidly. But he could too easily make out the knight kneeling suddenly and gracefully, helmet off and tucked under his arm. Inky black hair tied back neatly shined in the late afternoon sun from where the man bowed his head. There was an outcry from the squad, but Marya's reaction was much more distracting.

"What's he doing? Why's he bowing? Hamasa, a *lord*?"

"You should not be so familiar with the Shield of the Sovereign," the knight said with a displeased scowl up at Marya. Marya and Hamasa paled at the glance. "He is my lord or his Lordship."

"I am *no rord*," Hamasa snapped, hands shaking at his sides. He grimaced at the ill-timed impediment.

The knight made a puzzled frown at Hamasa. "It has been many years since I've seen you like this, but I would never forget. You are exactly who I think you are."

"The Shield? He can't even hoe a garden!" Marya exclaimed, both hands gesticulating wildly through the air. She barely missed thumping Hamasa with the pails again, but she *did* smack herself in the chest hard enough to wind herself.

"You hoed a garden?" the knight asked, incredulous and furious.

"Valerius, what is happening? You're scaring the squires again," spoke yet another knight. This one was tall, *very tall*, with blonde hair shorn close to his head, a honey-brown goatee framing his sweet-lipped mouth, and his pretty face still boyish despite a few scars on his cheeks and ears. He looked more from Harenae than from this side of the Ajul Mountains.

"It's the Shield. We found him," the knight, *still kneeling*, answered. His dark eyes returned to Hamasa. Again, somehow, he seemed familiar. The bile in Hamasa's stomach churned.

"He's alive."

Silence fell again.

"You think... you think this tiny kid is the Shield of the Sovereign, Kana'iro the Red?" the tall knight asked, hazel eyes on Hamasa's grey face.

Hamasa stepped back, stomach heaving, and abruptly turned to vomit into the dust. The bile stung his nose and scraped the back of his throat.

"Get away from 'im!" Marya bellowed moments before her arm wrapped around Hamasa's shoulders. It didn't escape his notice that she had put herself between him and the knights. "Are you all right? Hamasa?"

"I'm fine." Hamasa tried to smile up at Marya, only to gag and press his hands to his mouth.

"His name is Hamasa. That's neither Mekshan nor Riyukezan."

"Yeah, and the Shield's name is *Kana'iro*. That's not proof, ya block of wood!" Marya snarled over her shoulder. The first knight, Valerius, stepped forward, mouth thinning into a white line, eyes flashing. Marya stood up straight, shoulders squared, and glared right back.

The tall knight grabbed Valerius' shoulder, pulling him back and whispering in his ear. His jaw ticked and, with another glance at Marya and Hamasa, let himself be walked back to the group of knights whose voices rose as soon as he got close. Marya and Hamasa were finally left alone, kneeling in the dirt. Wiping his mouth with the back of his hand, Hamasa stared around Marya's torso at Valerius, watching as he calmly and steadfastly argued with what looked like every other knight in the small squad. The taller knight, who towered over everyone there, looked torn, his eyes darting between Valerius and the others and over towards Hamasa. Another man, not quite as tall, but as powerfully built and broad, was the loudest.

"I've seen the Shield like this before, none of you have. My word should be enough," Valerius said in a tone of finality.

"We all know how little your word matters when it comes to recognizing people, *Kaecus*. We've had to deal with that particular problem for the past five years," the shorter, disapproving knight retorted sharply.

Valerius actually rocked onto his heels, eyes flashing and mouth pulled into a thin, white line once more. The creaking of metal and leather from his suddenly tight fists had a few people edging away warily.

"Maryo, Valerius is your superior in every way, you can't speak to him like—" the tall knight began.

"Except he can't see mirda right. He wouldn't be able to recognize you if you so much as shaved your beard, Kelso. There's no proof that some peasant is the Shield and I won't be made a fool of in front of the Sovereign."

There was an awkward shuffle until a less aggressive but similarly stern knight stepped forward. "I'm sorry, Sir Kelso, but Sir Maryo may be right. Sir Valerius is an amazingly skilled knight with more than eight years in service, however... recognizing someone, especially one he hasn't seen in over a decade, is not one of his strongest skills."

"Let's get outta here before crazy tin can man starts brawling over your honor or something," Marya whispered, tugging Hamasa to his feet.

He had to hold onto Marya's arm until he regained his balance, but they managed to get away unnoticed. They ran through the sparse forest, neither stopping to look back. The moment they got to the farmhouse, Hamasa went straight for the well. Marya slumped next to him, dropping the pails of food to the ground and rubbing at her sweaty face. Hamasa washed his mouth out with water from the well and spat into the grass. Then, with a pained glance around the farmyard, he started towards the forest.

"What are you *doing*, idiot?" Marya shouted, exasperated. Hamasa almost smiled at the return of her favorite word, but she yanked Hamasa to a stop by the back of his shirt and he choked instead. "You're just gonna take off into the wilderness with nothing?"

"I haven't anything to take with me," Hamasa answered simply, eyes on the distant mountain range.

"You've got me! Friends, remember?"

Hamasa gaped at her. "Even after—"

Marya crossed her arms over her chest and rolled her eyes. "Even after some lunatic thought you were some lord or something? *Yeah!*"

Hamasa sighed, relieved to his very bones. "Thank you so m-much, but... but I have to go. They'll come here again. When they hear about the crater," He gestured needlessly towards the bare, shallow depression still all too obvious.

"We'll just tell 'em the truth. Your spell went wonky, and you blew yourself up," Marya told him with a reassuring smile.

Hamasa shook his head. "I can't."

Marya snorted loudly. "I know it's embarrassing, but you don't got a choice."

"That's not it," Hamasa tried again desperately, but with Marya's stern glare, he knew he would have to convince her this time. He wracked his brain for something believable. "There's a very good chance they won't believe me, or they'll take me back to Riyushu to face a trial. Reckre... uh, reckless use of magic, property damage, and human endangerment? They're very serious charges." And some of that wasn't even a lie.

Marya's eyebrows rose. "I ain't gonna blame you. It was an

accident. Why do they care?"

"It's how it works. Riyushu is built on proper procedures and protocols." Hamasa wrung his hands, his heart beating too hard as his eyes rose to the sunset. Twilight, and his window of escape, was closing in quickly.

"We'll go face 'em together."

"No! I can't go back!" Hamasa shouted, red-faced and panting. Even more desperate, desperate enough to choke and heave. Worry took over Marya's righteous indignation, and she helped Hamasa sit by the well, rubbing his arms briskly.

"All right, all right, we won't go to Riyushu. But you can't go off with a burr under your saddle. We'll leave in the morning. They'll be too busy fighting to come this way for awhile, I bet."

"We?" Hamasa wheezed. Marya nodded.

"We."

"No, but your mother, your farm—"

"Mamá can take care of this place on her own for a bit and I always wanted an adventure," Marya interrupted firmly, winking for good measure. The heaviness weighing Hamasa down lightened even while shame colored his cheeks. "We'll come back when that crazy Lance gives up on you. He looks like a real stickler, no chance he'd try to do anything on his own. His friends will be dragging him outta Elorra soon enough."

"You're sure?"

"Sure I'm sure." They shared a small smile. Then, Marya looked away and rubbed her nose. "All right, your lordyship, let's break the news to Mamá. We'll pack tonight and take off first thing in the morning. Didja have a plan in mind?"

"Not really...?" Hamasa admitted sheepishly.

Marya burst out laughing. "A'course not. We'll get Mamá to help. She travelled a while with Papi before they settled here. Before Sangsierpe."

THE COWARD'S EMBLEM

"I'm so grateful, Marya. If I could repay you somehow, I would," Hamasa said fervently, getting to his feet alongside Marya.

"I know, I know. I'll trade it in some day. Let's finish our dinner and get to planning."

7

He looks like a real stickler, no chance he'd try to do anything on his own.

More dangerously untrue words had not been spoken. Hamasa grunted and moaned, head throbbing and waist caught in an iron bar wrapped too tightly around him. He thought the blisters on his hands and the ache in his muscles after a full day of farming had been bad. It was nothing compared to the constant jostling and chafing a saddle created on his bum and inner thighs.

"You can become your true self," Valerius the *definitely doing something on his own* Lance said after the thousandth or so pained moan.

"I don't know w-what you're talking about," Hamasa replied through clenched teeth.

They were the first words they had exchanged all morning; it was well on to being noon. It didn't take a conversation to be kidnapped. No, all it took was Hamasa waking up in the middle of the night, woken by a strange noise. He had known, dimly, he should return to his warm bed and ignore any sounds, but there had been such an intriguing scent, sharp and fresh, that had dragged Hamasa out the door in a nightshirt and poncho — a newer gift from Irmen that he wore as often as possible; it was just so *cold* at night — loose breeches, and sandals he barely remembered to shove his feet into. Just after shuffling outside, a bag had covered his head and a hard thump had him out like a light.

The next thing he knew, he was waking up to Valerius at his back, a horse under him, and a barely beaten track in front of them through the trees. Hamasa scowled in remembrance of how easy it had been to capture him. And what had that scent been? It couldn't have been…

"I saw them."

Hamasa started slightly at Valerius' abrupt and nonsensical statement. He should ignore the knight, focus his scattered brains and plan an escape. Marya might be on their trail, so it was up to Hamasa to at least get free.

"Saw?" he asked instead. *I shouldn't have said that! Marya's right, I'm such an idiot.*

"Your eyes. I know I saw them. They were yellow, like flames."

Fear raced down Hamasa's spine. "That's ridiculous. Humans don't have yellow eyes."

"No, humans don't. Eyes like that, I don't need to see the rest of your face to know who and what you are."

"The rest of my—?" Hamasa's hands tightened around the saddle horn between his knees. "My eyes are brown," he said, firmly. He would not let his curiosity get the better of him again.

"Perhaps they are now."

Hamasa bit down on his bottom lip and forced himself into silence. Nothing good would come of keeping up this circular conversation. The Lance didn't seem to be much of a conversationalist, either. For the rest of the day—so long, too long—the only sounds were the steady thudding of hooves to hard-beaten earth. Occasionally, it was the rustle of leaves and unseen forest dwellers added to the near silence. Hamasa wondered if the native Mekshi forest sprites, chanaces, or the shy, crossroad-dwelling dende, were hiding among the trees somewhere. If he called out, would they help him? Would they even be able to tell what was hiding under his skin? Would that make it worse or better?

"We'll stop here."

Hamasa almost wept in relief at the announcement that came hours and hours later, the forest around them already long sunk into gloom. Most likely only the well-being of the horse travelling in the dark had prompted Valerius' halt. It was embarrassing and painful trying to get down, made more humiliating when the knight had to help Hamasa when he whimpered like an infant. The cold metal of his armor pressed against Hamasa's cheek, his large hands somehow gentle despite the unyielding grip on Hamasa's arms. He stumbled the moment Valerius let him go. Valerius stared inscrutably down at him, his eyes boring into Hamasa's and making him cringe.

"W-What?" Hamasa squeaked, cringing even more at the terrified sound of his voice. Valerius pulled out a short length of rope and tied Hamasa's hands behind his back, brisk and quick, but not rough. He bent down a second later, causing the smaller man to squawk in bewilderment, but he only hobbled Hamasa's ankles with another length of rope

Only.

"You're not what I remember," the Lance said at last after he got to his feet.

Who is this? Remember me from when?! Hamasa frowned, but his heart was already pumping at the first opening he'd had to press his story. "B-Because I'm not what you think I am! I'm not... I'm no one's Shield. I'm just m-me."

"Why are you talking like that?" Valerius asked, eyes narrowing. "You shouldn't be talking like that."

Hamasa's entire face flamed crimson, blood rushing up so

fast his fingers and toes tingled in a way that had nothing to do with the ropes. "I can't hepp how I tark!"

Valerius scowled darkly before turning on his heel and unbuckling various bags from the saddle of his horse without another word. Hamasa shuffled awkwardly, trying to convince himself not to feel—of all things—guilty. He wasn't the one pointing out how Valerius talked. Hamasa glanced around as Valerius unpacked, wondering: if he ran now, how far would he get? If Valerius didn't get on the horse bareback, then he had a chance. A bigger chance if he… didn't quite hold back his speed.

First, he would have to figure out the ropes. He had options that could help, but he really didn't want to use them. Not already. Not ever.

Hamasa settled against a tree and slowly slid down to the dirt. Everything in him told him to do anything he could to get away, to run and keep running. *It had been a mistake to stay with the Garsias as long as I had. A huge mistake,* he thought. His knees drew close to his chest and he leaned forward, trying in vain to get some pressure off his arms and shoulders. Watching Valerius, looking for the opportune moment, that should've been the most prevalent thing on his mind. Instead he dropped his forehead to his knees and squeezed his eyes shut.

What are you doing, Hamasa? Get up! You can get up, so do it! You only need a little—

But he was frozen, every muscle locked tight and shaking. Hamasa could still feel it; that overwhelming terror, the pain that scored its way deep into his flesh, the sound of his own screams as rushing wind tore his voice away.

I can't. I can't. I can't.

Breaths were coming too fast and choppy, brain spinning wildly in his head as sparks bloomed in the darkness behind his eyelids. He could hear his heart thundering too hard in his chest.

A slow flickering warmth crawled over his limbs.

A hand on his back, hesitant and unsure. "Your breathing sounds uneven."

Hamasa would've laughed, but he only wheezed breathlessly. There was a schnick of metal in leather followed a moment later by tugging and yanking at his wrists. The rope fell away. He dragged in air as if he were breaking through the surface of water and fell forward to brace himself upon trembling arms that burned with a strange tingling along his very nerves.

"Slowly, my lord. Breathe slowly."

"I-I'm—" *cough cough* " —n-not a rord!"

Valerius' hand patted his back without a word. He stilled, eerily tense, and Hamasa looked up with blurry eyes and drool at the corners of his mouth from choking. The knight was looking off to the side, through the growing shadows under the trees. Hamasa wiped at his mouth with his numb-ish wrist and Valerius got to his feet. He left Hamasa on the ground to go pick up his pole-arm. At one point, Valerius must have started a tiny fire while Hamasa had been not-so-silently panicking, and the flames glinted on the three prongs topping the weapon.

A trident.

Hamasa gawped at his broad back walking away from their temporary rest area, and he knew. He knew exactly who this Lance was now. Salt stung his eyes, disbelief making his breath stutter. No. There had to be a mistake. Surely more than just one Lance used a trident.

"Show yourself," Valerius commanded into the trees around them. Although he had removed helmet and gauntlets, he was still in his armor and was a fearsome sight with his trident in hand.

The woods here were neither very old nor very deep, but there was enough forest to create shadows to hide in. Hamasa struggled to his feet with his ankles still loosely hobbled—not even Valerius' steed was hobbled, Hamasa noticed in embarrassment. A branch crunched underfoot somewhere in the trees. His tongue flicked over his bottom lip, nostrils flaring, but he could only smell his own body heavily overlaid with horse sweat.

"*AAAAAAAAAAAAAAAHHHHHHHHHHHHH!*" A small figure wielding what looked like a long stick jumped from the shadows and swung with all its might.

Valerius dodged expertly, not even using his trident to brush the attack away. The newcomer held up the stick—a staff perhaps?—and went swinging feverishly at Valerius, despite being half Valerius' size and armor-less. Hamasa licked his lips and glanced at the horse, then edged closer without thinking it through completely.

"You giant bastard! How'd ya think you can just steal my friend? I'm gonna kick your tin pail gulo!"

"M-Marya?" Hamasa gasped, neck creaking he whipped around so fast to look again.

To indeed see Marya trying her best to wallop the beyond much better trained knight. There were already sweaty, dark patches growing under her arms and over her chest and back, and heavy rings under her eyes. Marya looked over at his gasp, attention broken for only a second, but it was all Valerius needed. With a move too fast to see or for Marya to dodge, he knocked the staff out of Marya's poor grip and flipped Marya over his shoulder through the air in almost the same moment.

Marya flew with a shocked yelp and thudded into a tree. Another thud to the ground had Hamasa wincing. He hurriedly hobbled towards his fallen friend, but tripped on his rope within a few steps. A strong arm captured him around the waist before he could hit the dirt.

"I know you're out there, too. She didn't chase us the entire day on foot," Valerius said to the trees, ignoring Marya's low groan and Hamasa's wriggling to get free.

The tall knight with the kind face walked into the clearing leading his huge horse. He stopped to hold out a hand to Marya. She huffed and brushed his hand away to get up alone.

"Valerius, what were you thinking kidnapping an innocent man?"

"Is it kidnapping if he's not a child?"

"It's not like you to split hairs."

Valerius and the tall knight stared each other down. Marya stepped forward, arms crossed, feet planted wide, and curly hair frizzing around her face and shoulders. Hamasa hadn't seen it free of the customary horsetail braid and was mildly surprised at the volume of it.

"Let him go. He's done nothing wrong!"

The long, silent gaze broke when Valerius glanced at Marya with eyebrows raised. "From what I understand, my lord appeared mysteriously in this area approximately three weeks ago. How would you know?"

"I haven't done anything! Just r-let me go!" Hamasa exclaimed, shoving at Valerius' arm and chest. It was like trying to move a mountain.

"Valerius, I know you think he's the Shield, but it doesn't make any sense! He's just a young man, a small weakly-looking one at that."

Hamasa wanted to be offended, but, well... He sighed and slumped over Valerius' arm.

"Whatever he looks like now, it's just a disguise. He arrived here almost three weeks ago, left a depression in the earth that could account for falling from the sky, he has the same name, and I saw his eyes, Kelso," Valerius gritted out, arm tightening

THE COWARD'S EMBLEM

around Hamasa's waist rather protectively. Hamasa kept his eyes on the thrice-cursed rope tied around his ankles.

"They're all coincidences, Valerius!" Kelso said, almost desperately. "You can't even be sure of what you saw. You forget faces the moment you look away. I've known that since we were pages together."

"Are you seriously thinking Hamasa, the kid who can't even cast a spell or hold a hoe right, is a dragon in disguise?" Marya burst out, jabbing her finger at Valerius and glaring ferociously.

Silence fell as his would-be-rescuers looked at Hamasa. Who, he himself knew with all too much certainty, looked pretty pathetic. Drool stained the sides of his mouth, his eyes were bloodshot and damp, and his face too pale and wan.

"You're a real bag of nuts in the head, arencha?" Marya accused Valerius, gaze flinty and pissed.

Hamasa sighed. "That's not a nice thing to say, Marya."

"I am perfectly sane. Hamasa is Kana'iro the Red, the Shield of the Sovereign, who went missing three weeks ago. I *will* take him back to the Sovereign and she'll know it, too," Valerius said firmly, tone hard and unflinching.

Kelso muttered under his breath and rubbed a hand through his hair. "I can keep the others from following."

"What!? You said you'd help me, not him! He's crazy!"

"M-Marya, please, don't make this worse," Hamasa pleaded from where he hung trapped in the crook of Valerius' arm. "You can't win this fight." Marya's nostrils flared.

"Valerius is not crazy, Señorita Garsia, which is why I have to let him do this. He'll keep your friend safe." Kelso met Hamasa's weary eyes. "I promise no harm will come to you in his care. If he's wrong, you'll be escorted to wherever you wish in every comfort the Sovereign can provide you." He paused and rubbed a hand over his sweat-darkened blonde hair. "It's not often he's wrong, though."

"And this gulero will be punished, right?" Marya demanded.

"If I'm wrong, they'll strip me of my title and of my position in the Lances."

Hamasa startled in Valerius' grip and stared, slack-jawed, up at him. Valerius calmly returned their gazes.

"You're m-making a m-mistake," Hamasa whispered, gaze dropping to the ground.

"I don't believe you! And I don't trust you to keep Hamasa safe. Not if you think he's some sorta *dragon*. I'm coming with you, and, as soon as you're proved wrong, I'll make *sure* you get punished," Marya said with a loud snort and eye-roll.

Hamasa honestly didn't know what to feel about this turn of events. Relief that Marya believed him without a doubt? Or guilt that the belief came so easily to her, and with so little evidence to support it? Hurt—no, best not go there. Not even in the relative safety of his own thoughts.

"That is not a good idea. Return to your home," Valerius told Marya.

"You can't tell me what to do!" Marya retorted. "I'm coming with you. For Hamasa."

"You don't have a horse. You will slow us down and make the journey more dangerous," Valerius argued.

"Señorita Garsia, maybe it would be best..." Kelso began slowly. Marya rounded on him and raised both her fists high. He quickly held up his hands in surrender.

"If she wants to come, I would ri-like her to come," Hamasa murmured, stomach squirming. He felt Valerius tense at his back. "She and her mother have been so kind, and she's uh... my friend..." He looked up hesitantly to meet Marya's eyes. She smiled at him, her fists falling.

"Fine, my lord. The girl comes with us. It'll be on your head if she's injured," Valerius said flatly. Hamasa flinched, stomach squirming more. Marya whooped.

"As I said, I'll keep the squad away, but you'll definitely need this if Señorita Garsia joins you. Here." Kelso threw a small pouch towards Valerius. At last, his arm dropped from Hamasa's waist to catch the pouch. Coins rattled. "Use my earnings to make sure they get what they need. It's a long journey, especially with only one horse and with these two who aren't accustomed to the road. Also, Valerius," Kelso paused with a lopsided smirk, "I know subterfuge isn't your style, but you should probably keep your armor and any crests hidden. You're a rogue knight now."

Valerius' stony features twisted into outrage that almost had Hamasa actually laughing. Almost.

8

VALERIUS HAD discarded his armor that morning as suggested, keeping it stowed in saddlebags and generously padded with wool and leather. Hamasa wasn't sure how he felt about seeing Valerius out of his armor. He was less intimidating, sure, and he was less protected from Marya's staff blows if they tried to escape—a staff that had obviously been her shovel at some point. On the other hand, Valerius could now move faster, so it would be harder to run. There was a chance his well-trained mare, Nerva, wouldn't listen to them over Valerius, either, if they tried to ride her away. Valerius hadn't bothered to hobble her the day before, or during the night, and had stood eerily still when Valerius saddled her and tied on his packs. A single click of his tongue against his teeth had Nerva lowering her head for the bridle, which didn't have a bit fitted between her teeth. Very well-trained. Hamasa gnawed on his bottom lip.

Although Marya had brought the bag she and Hamasa had mostly packed at her farm, it hadn't been packed well, if Valerius' dark scowl could be read properly. Seeing as they had a single bedroll, a few empty hide bags for water, and a mara's foot on a leather string "for luck", but not a scrap of food, Hamasa had a feeling he could read Valerius' expression that much. Marya snatched her pack out of his hands and glared at him.

"It's not my fault our plans got changed, is it?" she snapped at him. Valerius didn't even have the decency to look ashamed, though his scowl lightened.

"I suppose not. We'll continue on and stop for supplies at the first village," Valerius said, glancing towards Hamasa.

Hamasa's heart beat sped up, his stomach knotting. "Do you... you're not going to tie me up again?" he asked slowly.

"Only if he ties me up, too," Marya said with a few swift steps to Hamasa's side. Her hand wrapped around his wrist, and he barely kept from heating up at the unexpected touch.

Valerius' eyebrow slowly arched upward, his dark eyes moving from Marya's defiant scowl to Hamasa's wide-eyed gaze. "Do you approve of the plan, my lord?"

Hamasa blinked rapidly as Marya snorted loudly.

"Now you're asking my permission?" Hamasa asked incredulously.

"You said it, Asa." Marya barked a laugh.

For once, Valerius broke eye contact first. The muscle in his jaw pulled taut and his face turned away from them. "We agreed to travel together."

"'Cuz we had to, scrap pail. Didja forget you tied him up and threw him over your horse like a sack of potatoes this morning!?" Marya exclaimed, hand waving towards Hamasa and the horse with wide swings of her arm.

Valerius glared so darkly, Hamasa reflexively glanced towards the saddle to stare at the canvas-wrapped polearm safely strapped down. Marya took half a step back before she jutted out her chin and set her feet flat on the ground, as stubborn as old Idiot the donkey.

"I did what I must for the sake of the Sovereign's Shield. Her Imperial Majesty Ane—" Hamasa flinched, but luckily Valerius cut himself off quickly, black eyes flashing at Marya's loud, disparaging scoff.

"It's fine!" Hamasa interrupted desperately. After a sharp inhale, he smiled over at Marya, a tiny fleeting thing. But it had her shoulders loosening and her heavy brows relaxing. "It's fine, Marya. Sir, um, you have more experience of travelling than either of us." He met Valerius' gaze, wished he could understand how Valerius could stand so still and straight with a face as blank as stone. Hamasa's eyes quickly fell to his sandalled feet. "So, um, yes. I agree."

"Of course." From under the fringe of his bangs, he caught the sight of Valerius' bow, his hands flat on the sides of his thighs and face parallel to the dirt. Hamasa licked his lips and stared into the trees, the uncomfortable knot in his stomach twisting like irritated snakes. Marya snorted loudly and knocked her shoulder to Hamasa's gently. "If you'd mount first, my lord," the knight added, voice low and tight.

"Oh, yes..." Hamasa stepped forward, licking at his lips again and tasting skin instead of the horse sweat and leather tack right in front of him.

"I don't got a horse, so better not take off too fast," Marya said, pointing a threatening finger at Valerius. Hamasa froze with one hand on the stirrup.

"She's right," he said, stepping away from the mare. His shoulder bumped Valerius' chest, and he skittered away. Marya stared at him, but he took his place beside her. "You're right. You don't have a horse. I'll walk. With you."

This time his smile wasn't quite so fleeting, lingering long enough that Marya's surprised stare grew into a wide grin. Hamasa couldn't believe he had been so thoughtless. Was it because of his need to keep the knight appeased? Or worse, was it the 'my lord' that Hamasa couldn't help responding to?

Oblivious to Hamasa's half-disgusted musings, Marya was beaming as she thumbed at her nose. "Asa, you don't gotta do that."

"I... do *gotta*," Hamasa disagreed with a shake of his head. Marya snickered at his bad accent.

Valerius glanced between them, lips thinning. "The next village, how far is it?"

"Huh? What, Ristahe? Not far. Usually takes me and Mamá about half a day," Marya answered rather nonplussed. Valerius jerked his chin into a nod.

"You both will ride or we can put your pack on Nerva's saddle and we will all walk."

Hamasa and Marya exchanged matching incredulous glances.

"You're going to... walk?" Hamasa asked.

"I will not ride if you walk, my lord," Valerius stated. Marya snorted loud enough that Nerva's nearest ear twitched back towards them.

"Sure, it's not so unknightly of you to treat him like a sack of taters, but Sovereign forbid he walk while you ride," she muttered.

But while she spoke, she flipped the long tail of her hair over her shoulder and stomped up to the mare. She frowned at the stirrup, then, after much hopping and cursing under her breath, got her foot in and heaved herself up. She reached down for Hamasa, helping him get up on the horse behind her. Valerius gently straightened the saddle and the canvas-covered polearm that Marya's flailings had knocked askew. Already, Hamasa was regretting being remounted. His thighs and bum were still sore.

"You holding on, Hamasa?" Marya asked, reaching for the reins tied around the horn.

"Yes?" he said, hands cautiously settling on her waist. Hamasa's eyes caught on the reins hanging loose from Marya's hand. He wasn't sure if it would work, but... He glanced back at Valerius, who was fitting something into a saddlebag and not paying them any mind. "Marya," Hamasa whispered.

Marya glanced back at him, and he tightened his arms around her waist more solidly. She blinked, eyebrows rising, until he jerked his chin to the reins she held. Her eyes widened and she grinned, sly and eager. With a loud shout, Marya flapped the reins and kicked the mare's sides. Hamasa clutched at her tunic, gritting his teeth, as Nerva reared and jumped forward. From the corner of his eye, he saw Valerius stumble out of the way of hooves. Marya whooped and air whipped past Hamasa's ears and through his hair.

"We're outta here!"

"Where are we going to go?" Hamasa shouted as adrenaline pumped through his veins.

Perhaps everything would work out? They would leave Valerius and his dogged insistence and uncomfortable observations far behind, and Hamasa would be right back where he was yesterday: unknown.

A whistle, shrill and sharp, cut through the air. The wild pitching and reeling of the mare's gallop ceased with a suddenness that had both Marya and Hamasa jerking forward faster than Nerva's standstill. Marya yelped and lurched forward into the saddle horn, groaning and coughing as she clutched desperately to reins and horn. Hamasa thudded against her back and slid to the side, his precarious balance and poor seating proving themselves as he tumbled to the ground. His entire body rattled with the landing. Gasping like a fish out of water, he tried to breathe. He utterly forgot how it worked, how to drag it in, how his chest should expand, how to exhale.

"Hamasa!" Marya shrieked, feet flailing as she tried to get them free of the stirrups.

"My lord!" Footsteps raced down the Road, and Valerius was at Hamasa's side, kneeling and getting a hand under Hamasa's elbow.

Hamasa wheezed and coughed, flapping the dust away from his face and his body one giant bruise. Sun-blessed air filled his chest and he rose like an elder human, every bone and muscle and tendon working as hard as they could.

"I'm fine," Hamasa choked out. He shuffled away from Valerius' hand and lifted his poncho to wipe at his face.

"What was that?" Marya asked, running forward.

Behind her, Nerva return to them in a jog, reins dragging through the dust and saddlebags jangling and creaking. Valerius stood and wrapped the trailing reins around his fist.

"All the horses given to the Lances are trained to respond to certain cues. I suppose I should commend your effort," Valerius said. He looked Hamasa up and down and his tense jaw relaxed. "Would you like to try again?"

"No," Hamasa said. He grasped Marya's bicep, squeezing gently. She met his eyes, face dark under her heavy brows. "We tried. It failed. I would l-like to not fall off the horse again."

"Her name is Nerva, my lord, Senorita Garsia. The offer to ride is still standing, though perhaps I'll keep the reins," Valerius said wryly.

"No. No more horses," Hamasa said firmly. He dusted off his trousers and shook his head.

"Ay, if you say so. I don't like the idea of walking all the way to... wherever we're going," Marya said dubiously. Without warning, Valerius yanked Marya's pack, and she yelped and wriggled out of the straps when he didn't relent.

"This will be on Nerva," Valerius told her. Marya glared at him, rubbing a shoulder. "Or we can leave it here on the Road."

"Put it on the horse."

"Nerva." He turned to tie the last pack into place, stopping to murmur to the mare and stroke the ridge of her long nose.

"I guess he's not as stupid as he's crazy," Marya said, crossing her arms over her chest and kicking at the dirt.

"I guess not," Hamasa agreed. Valerius looked over at them, and gestured for them to go ahead. With a sigh, Hamasa trudged forward. Marya stuck her tongue out at Valerius as they passed, but the knight merely raised an eyebrow silently.

9

DESPITE HIMSELF, Hamasa almost enjoyed the walk. Early morning this far north was an unfamiliar kind of silence. Unfamiliar, but soothing. In the south, there had always been the roar of the sea. In the deepest hours of the night, when only the city guards walked the streets and most the citizens slept, there would still be the constant echo of the waves slapping against the shore, the sheer cliffs, the sides of wooden ships. Here, there was the rustling of the wind occasionally brushing through the sparse foliage and tree branches. The too-quiet pattering of wild creatures' paws or hooves on hard-packed soil and loose stones. And, of course, there was the huffing of the mare and the creaking of the leather saddle, the clicking of muffled metal, and the shuffle of their feet over the well-maintained road.

The Great Road was relatively new in the history of Mekshi, but it was more than four hundred years old. All those generations of wagons and pedestrians and beasts of burdens had stamped the already neatly cut and flattened road into something rather soft under Hamasa's leather sandals — another too generous gift from the Garsias. Marya wore leather sandals so worn down the straps had been replaced by rope and the soles were a size too large and obviously not made for her. Hamasa rubbed his fingers over the slick, shiny scars on the back of his elbow.

Autumn or not, by noon the sun was shining down hot and

bright enough that Hamasa was uncomfortable under his heavy wool poncho and thinner linen layers. Marya's face was beaded with sweat with tiny black curls clinging to her skin along her hairline. Not that it slowed her down any, her strides matched Hamasa's easily while she kept up cheerful chatter and gestures at the scenery around them.

"This place is gonna be full of wagons and traders and all kinds of people in just a few weeks, maybe days. The end of harvest is the biggest holiday until spring, we're not gonna be able to spit without hitting a man from here to San Yamarasu," Marya told Hamasa as they passed by a small pile of stones. She grabbed his arm to yank him to a stop. "Here, we gotta leave something. Ay, walking bucket, got something for the dende?" She turned to face the knight a few paces behind them, his hands loose on the reins as he led Nerva.

Valerius' eyebrows crept up slowly, actual confusion creeping over his expression. Marya rolled her eyes and gestured towards the little pile of stones. Hamasa's eyes widened.

"Oh! Dende! I've never met one. They don't go anywhere near the big cities like Riyushu," he exclaimed, eyes roving along the tree trunks and nose rising in the air.

"The what?" Valerius asked. He reached out with a hand, a short, quickly aborted motion, as Hamasa walked towards the treeline. Hamasa ignored him to kneel at the stones.

There was more than just the one pile. Most of the stones had been there a long time as well. Sun had leeched the color from most, and thin yellow lichen had grown like animal fuzz over the surfaces. One pile was shinier than the rest, the stones newer and painstakingly stacked to keep from falling too easily. *Bad luck*, Hamasa remembered with a small smile. No one wants to offend a trickster. Around the stones there were bits of mostly melted candles, some small shreds of paper and cloth, even a few lichen covered pennies. Leftovers of thoughtful gifts the dende hadn't needed. Food was the preferred gift, food they couldn't find easily on their own. Though, shiny things were appreciated, too. While Marya and Valerius argued over leaving silver or tin coins, or some of their meager rations, Hamasa perched on his toes, hand on his knees, eager eyes searching through the trees.

Normally his presence would scare such shy and small creatures away. But maybe now... wouldn't it be nice to meet someone who had lived on this continent for millennia? The dende's history was longer than his own, and longer than the history of the Riyukezan Empire. They had been worshipped as minor gods, once upon a time, and the local Mekshans still left shrines like these in remembrance. It was also just good manners and common sense. Hamasa hadn't even noticed his mouth moving as he explained this all aloud, eyes lit up and skin a soft pink. He turned excitedly to his left... and saw no one.

His voice stuttered and fled, throat catching.

There should've been blue eyes looking at him, silken black hair in a complicated mound of twists and loops, and glittering ornaments of blown glass tinkling bell-like against a pale cheek. His eyes fluttered closed, breath exhaling on a quiet hiss, as the hot northern sun beat down on his too-sensitive neck, as the rough linen of his tunic scratched against too-smooth skin, and the only scents were smelled. No taste of silk or lotus flowers or rice powder.

"Ay, Hamasa? Were you talking to me?" Marya asked, squatting down next to him, her arms crossed over her knees.

When Hamasa startled and turned to her, she smiled softly, dark eyes warm and patient in a way she only got when Hamasa's pain had been so high he'd cried. Reflexively, he brushed the heel of his palm under his eye, relieved to feel a dry cheek.

"I forgot... I forgot w-where I was."

"You can tell me, you know? What were you saying?"

"No, it's nothing." Hamasa glanced back to the series of stone markers. "You could tell me more than any of my old texts. What do you suggest we leave for them?"

"I dunno, maybe a good case of bad luck will get us away from Sir Face Stuck Like That," Marya grumbled, her warmth gone.

"I can hear you, Senorita," Valerius said stiffly. He knelt on Hamasa's left, who barely kept the instinctual grimace off his face. His fair skin and black hair was too similar to the vision of the girl he'd had moments ago.

"Señorita," Marya corrected.

"That sound is hard for me, too, Marya," Hamasa said without meaning to. His cheeks heated under Valerius' assessing glance.

"I know the circumstances are less than ideal, but it'll be easier for us all if you attempted cooperation, Señorita Garsia," Valerius said blandly, his pronunciation noticeably better. Marya scowled, but Hamasa reached over to tentatively touch her arm.

"He's right."

"... fine," Marya said, sighing roughly. "You're giving up too easy, Asa."

"What's the point?" Hamasa kept his eyes on the stones and clapped his hands together. His eyes closed and, rather more like a Riyukezan than a Mekshan, whispered a simple prayer for health and luck.

Marya whistled. "Sounds pretty, whatever you said, but they like silver or gold better."

"I am not wasting gold at a pile of rocks," Valerius said plainly. "Some potatoes or corn will have to do."

"And like *I* said, what are we gonna need so much gold for? Unless we're gonna buy a whole hostal in San Yamarasu, it's just extra weight doing us no good," Marya retorted. "They can get corn and taters on their own! If you're gonna leave food, it should be interesting."

Hamasa sighed and pressed his fingertips to his forehead as the two of them sniped over his head. There was a rustle among the trees and shrubs, but he didn't feel a breeze. Heart stuttering, Hamasa peered through his lashes. In the thin shade, a small figure peered back. He could just barely make out a hand with grubby, short fingers and a glittering eye. Just that glimpse and Hamasa could feel its curious glee, something wild and magical was looking back, and his heart leapt towards it. The leaves fluttered in a true breeze, and the light shifted, and the birch pale skin and protruding nose were exposed. Both eyes met his and it winked. Then, was gone.

A smile tugged up Hamasa's lips while his eyes stung. *She would've loved to meet you*, he thought towards the little figure in the woods.

"I don't wish to bring more notice on us than we must. Leaving gold on the side of the road is more noticeable than having a few coins hidden in a pouch."

"Then, a silver or two. Don't be so cheap, aren't you some rich noble's son?"

"... that's not untrue, but I borrowed most of this money."

"Sir Kelso will be repaid, whatever happens from here on," Hamasa finally interrupted. He leaned forward to kneel and find a suitable stone among the grass. Carefully, he brushed the dirt and grass from it and set it atop the newest stack. "Leave them a gold. I'm sure they'll like it."

"As you wish, my lord."

"Ay! Really? It's that easy?" Marya *tch*ed loudly, glaring at Valerius as he left to get the gold. She slapped Hamasa's knee, jostling him. "Next time, say something sooner. He never fights with *you*."

"He kidnapped me," Hamasa pointed out.

"Not actually a fight, was it?" Marya smirked and got to her feet.

Hamasa narrowed his eyes at her, his face burning red. Before he could rise alone, her wide, work-callused hand reached down. He grabbed it after a short, sulky moment, grateful for her help when his scars pulled slightly at the movement.

"We've already stopped. Let's eat now before continuing," Valerius suggested when he came back to set the gold down. It twinkled among the lichen and grass and discarded gifts, and the sight of it made something lighten in Hamasa's chest. The little creature he saw would find joy in it, he hoped. Valerius began to walk again towards the horses and said, "There should be a water source nearby. I'll find it swiftly."

"Good thing we're giving the dende a gift or we'd get lost trying to find it!" Marya called at his back. Valerius paused, then walked on to untie the bags. She snickered.

"You're playing with fire teasing a Lance like that," Hamasa warned, although his lips twitched.

"What's he gonna do now? Goat's already in the house, and he's too serious. Them that don't have humor are the easiest to rile. I can't help myself," Marya admitted with a shrug and an unrepentant laugh.

10

Ristahe was almost identical to Elorra, though, unlike Elorra, it was built on both sides of the Great Road. Farther from the Road, Hamasa could see the shapes of small houses and barns and fences, but most of the buildings were all but on top of them as they walked into the village. Shops lined the Road on right and left, and even more small stands with colorful awnings were squeezed between buildings. Most of the stands were really colorful woven blankets on the ground under bigger canvas or woolen blankets propped up on posts, all the sellers' wares laid out for display. The sun wasn't yet setting, but most of the stalls were empty, or close to it. Hamasa saw what was left of their daily harvests, some earthenware and pottery, woven and dyed cloths and fabrics, but Marya passed by most with barely a glance.

"The best things are getting held at home until all the big traders for harvest come through," Marya whispered to Hamasa.

"As long as we can find enough to get us to our destination, that doesn't matter," Valerius said, frowning slightly as he said it. He was eyeing a stall that sold blankets and warmer woolen items. The frown deepened.

"Yeah, yeah, whatever you say. Asa, look, candy," Marya said, steering Hamasa where she wanted to go. Hamasa glanced anxiously over his shoulder, but Valerius watched them go without stopping them. "How fast d'ya think he'd catch us if we ran?"

"Run where?" Hamasa asked pointedly.

Marya scowled. It lightened instantly when she saw the candy in bowls on the colorfully woven rug in front of them. A woman Irmen's age smiled up at them and waved them down. A small child was curled up next to her, sucking on their thumb and staring at them, especially Hamasa. Marya squatted immediately, pointing and asking a thousand questions about the bowls and baskets full of unrecognizable treats—small candies and sweets, as well as prettily frosted breads. Hamasa and the child stared silently at each other. It didn't take long for Hamasa to realize those wide, innocent eyes had found the burns across his right cheek and temple, the patches of missing hair behind his ear where there was more pink skin. Slowly, Hamasa lowered into a crouch and held out his arm. He turned it over to show more scars on there and the child's thumb fell out of their mouth.

"Does it hurt?" the child whispered. Hamasa shook his head, throat too tight and full to speak. The few people who had spoken to him outside the Garsia home hadn't asked, had barely paused to notice the scars. Although he had felt stares on more than one occasion, he had refused to acknowledge whomever had been staring. There was no avoiding a child who didn't know what was or wasn't polite. "Didja fall in the fire?"

"No. Not fire," Hamasa whispered.

"Pala! We don't ask about those things and we don't stare! I'm so sorry, señor."

"It doesn't matter," Hamasa assured her quickly.

"It does matter. I'm so sorry. Please, take a piece of anything, go on," the mother urged.

Hamasa stared at it all, completely lost. He glanced at Marya, then at the mother, then the child.

"That one," Pala said, pointing at one basket. There was a bread bun that looked rather like a seashell with bright yellow sugar topping. "That's my favorite."

"I like yellow," Hamasa told her awkwardly. Pala beamed.

The first bite was soft, all but melting in his mouth. It was also drier than he expected, but sweet. The sugar flaked around his lips and fluttered to the ground, making him flinch back and flap the crumbs away from the rug. The laughter that rang out from the others didn't feel at his expense, though, and he ducked his head to hide his own smile. Carefully taking another bite, hand cupped under the bread to catch crumbs, also helped hide his face.

"Never had conchan before, señor?"

"Did you say seashells?" Hamasa asked, staring at the bread. "Oh, I see. There's no filling in... conchan?"

"Filling?" Marya asked. "Do you put meat in your bread down in Riyushu?"

"No, sweet fillings. Like beans or peas..." Hamasa trailed off as the seller and Marya stared at him incomprehensibly.

"Beans are sweet?" Marya asked. "Whatcha growing down south?" Hamasa shrugged, brushing at his mouth, and Marya quickly pointed at the basket of conchan. "Let's get a bunch of those, and is that turron?"

Pala snuck closer to Hamasa, whose mouth was once more full of sweet bread and sugar that he chewed thoughtfully. The few times he had had sweets, they had been made with rice flour, with nuts or sweet pastes made from beans or peas. He couldn't recall anything like these seashell breads in Riyushu. Pala reached out her fist and opened it to show him a small, hard candy, brownish-orange in color and covered in orangeish-red sugar.

"For you. This is my favorite."

Hamasa's eyebrows rose slowly. "I thought the conchan was?"

Pala shook her head. "That's my favorite pastry. This is my favorite candy. It's tamarind."

Hamasa vaguely remembered tamarind being some kind of fruit, and eyed the sugar-coated treat dubiously. He hadn't been that fond of sweets before... but she was smiling at him so hopefully.

"It's my sorry. For asking about the fire," Pala added shyly, skinny shoulders hunching high around her ears.

Hamasa held out his hand without further hesitation. "In that case, I accept your apology. Thank you, senorita."

Pala giggled and licked at the sugar grains left behind on her palm.

Keeping his sigh inward, Hamasa popped the sweet into his mouth. And immediately regretted it. He slapped a hand over his mouth, eyes watering, coughing—hacking—in surprise. Marya leaned over to thwap his back briskly.

"You okay, Asa?"

"I didn't mean to! I just gave him candy!" Pala exclaimed with teary eyes.

"N-no, no, I'm f-fine," he choked out, dredging up a smile that he wasn't sure looked quite right. "I was expecting it to be sweet. It's good, it's..." He stopped and rolled the candy in his mouth, trying not to purse his lips at the unique flavor. "Spicy. I like spicy." Which wasn't a lie. He just wasn't expecting candy to be spicy.

Beside him, Marya was suddenly laughing, laughing hard enough to fall down on her butt. "I thought you were dying," she wheezed. Across the rug, mother and daughter were also giggling, the tears on Pala's lashes thankfully forgotten.

Hamasa rolled the candy around once more, frowning

curiously, making Marya and Pala burst into more giggles.

"Despite the first surprise, I do like them," he said decisively.

"Well, thank you, my lord, we Mekshan locals were hanging on the edge of our saddles for that," Marya teased, punching his shoulder lightly. Hamasa huffed in amusement and shook his head. And hoped she didn't notice the way his skin crawled at hearing her call him 'my lord'.

"What else haven't you tried?" Pala asked eagerly. Hamasa grimaced slightly, but her mother, who he had overheard Marya call "Señora Mandes", and Marya herself were already smiling in encouragement. Sighing, Hamasa pointed and Pala squealed excitedly.

When the heavy tread of a warhorse and knight came up behind them, Hamasa was sure he'd never get rid of the taste of sugar. It coated his lips and tongue and throat, his fingers were sticking together, and he had about five half-eaten bits of candy and pastries in his hands. Valerius stood over them, judgemental eyebrow arching high enough to touch his hairline, his eyes on the sweets in Hamasa's hands and the little girl trying to shove another one directly into Hamasa's mouth.

"It's our protector. Finally here to ruin the fun or will you try something, too?" Marya asked, sugar from her own pink-coated conchan all over her face and lap.

"I'm sure I need to pay for what's already been eaten before I can decide either way."

Marya actually ducked her head to hide a bashful flush to her cheeks. Valerius' eyes roved over the sugar coating everything, the small sacks filled with sweets and pastries, and the conchan half-eaten in Hamasa's hand. With wide eyes, Hamasa watched as the knight tied the reins around the saddle horn and knelt in front of the rug.

"I've never had Mekshan candies," he told them bluntly.

"Anything made with fruit? Nothing spicy."

"Yes! Lots of them!"

As the last of their purchases were paid for and Señora Mandes tied the bags expertly, Valerius leaned forward to lower his voice and speak. Marya braced on her hand to get closer.

"We shouldn't stay here long. The news I've heard from around the market hasn't been all good," he told the two listening closely. Hamasa swallowed what was left of his candy, eyes stinging.

"What do you mean?" he gasped painfully.

"The ones that've gone missing, yes?" Señora Mandes asked. Hamasa saw the frown flicker over her face, her brown eyes seeming darker, glimmering faintly... wetly.

"Missing? Who's missing?" Marya asked around her mouthful.

"The fairies. We know our forest friends aren't exactly the nicest every day, but they're friends and folk the same as us. We been asking for help from San Yamarasu for weeks, and ain't heard nothing back," she explained with a deep lines creasing around her mouth and the corners of her eyes.

"Fairies? Like... dende and añhana?" Hamasa asked. Beside him, Valerius covered his frown with his gloved hand, brows low and dark.

"Añhana don't live this far outside the cities. They like those fancy clean ponds and gardens," Marya told Hamasa, her own brows pulling low. "But chanaces and lohas run wild 'round here."

"But they take the animals most!" Pala burst out. She cowered under all four adults matching frowns, not realizing none of them were of anger.

"She means the ones that don't speak or look like people, anything with paws or feathers. Though, to be sure, there's always been animals, monkeys and parrots and the like that've gone missing. But the Others going missing, that's newer. They protect the forests and the rivers 'round here, but.. there's been less 'n less of them," Señora Mandes said, wrapping an arm around her daughter's shoulders and pressing her hand against Pala's temple. Pala nodded and sniffled.

"Some of those creatures are dangerous. They wouldn't disappear easily or willingly," Valerius murmured. His heavy hand clapped down on Hamasa's shoulder who flinched under the sudden touch. "We must go on, m... Masa."

Marya and Hamasa stared at him. Without meeting either of their incredulous gazes, Valerius hefted the silently gaping Hamasa to his feet. Marya scrambled after them, arms full of bags. Hamasa didn't get a chance to say farewells, barely even heard Marya yelp her goodbyes and thanks yous. He stumbled to match Valerius' long-legged stride with his wrist caught in the knight's grasp, glancing over his shoulder to see Marya struggling with the purchases and the worried seller helping her.

"What's your hurry?" Hamasa forced himself to ask.

"Whoever is taking these creatures, they are targeting those made of magic. How are they able to find creatures famed for their evasive abilities and stealth? If they can hunt them down, what will keep them from you, my lord?" Valerius said, scowl downright thunderous as he chivvied Hamasa faster.

"But I'm not—" Hamasa stammered.

Valerius froze. Hamasa hit his shoulder with a quiet oof, grateful for the chance to stop and Marya to catch up with them. Thoughts of Marya, of gratitude, of missing creatures, fell out of his head as Valerius stepped close and loomed closer. The smell of sweat and leather and candied fruit brushed over his cheek at Valerius' exhale. Hamasa was pinned still and unmoving under pitch black eyes, skin heating under his linen and wool layers.

"Do you know what brought you to me the other night? What that incense was?"

Hamasa's stomach sank.

"Not many know of it even among the Riyukezan families. It's made from an oil, from tree resin thousands of years old, from a country across the sea. Surely you've heard of dragon's amber."

Hamasa's blood pulsed hard enough to shake him, a drum beating in his temples, his wrists, the vein on his throat. His eyes darted over Valerius' face, those black eyes unyielding and burning on Hamasa's skin. Or was his skin heating? The scars suddenly pulled taut and painful. Valerius' grip twitched, then yanked away abruptly.

"What are you running off so fast for? You can't just leave me behind!" Marya exclaimed as she reached them. Hamasa startled, too dry mouth parting without a breath, eyes darting from Valerius' wooden expression and Marya's concerned one. "Asa? What's—?"

"We need to continue on." Valerius turned back the way he had been going. His hand, the one that had held Hamasa's wrist, flexed at his side.

"Asa?" Marya whispered, creeping closer. She winced a bit, shuffled the items in her arms, and reached to press the back of her hand to Hamasa's forehead. "Are you feverish?"

"N-no."

He smiled weakly at Marya's frown. Then, he hurried to follow Valerius and Nerva. Staring at Valerius' tense back was easier than meeting Marya's kindly concern head-on.

11

As they left the village's outer limits, sunset burned the sky orange and peach and pink. Hamasa had to pause to stare, wide-eyed and somehow elated, at the disc of pure molten gold among the tapestry of clouds. Twilight's deep indigo already bruised the edges of the sunset, but the Sun still shined over the northern mountain ranges. Beyond that horizon was the land he once called home. Wind rustled over the road, brushed over his bare face, and hair tickled his flesh. Inhaling sharply, he flinched inward, cringed away from his skin with nowhere to go.

Surely you've heard of dragon's amber.

He shuddered, body prickling as little bumps tightened his skin up and down his limbs.

"You cold?" Marya asked, looking over her shoulder at him. Her cheek bulged around marzipan, making each word thick and strange. "You've got goosebumps."

"No, not that," Hamasa said quickly.

Fortunately, there was a loud commotion preventing Marya from asking further. The three of them looked back as what looked like every citizen of Ristahe flooded the Road or leaned out of windows and doorways, to cheer the newcomers riding into the village. The sound of hooves echoed against the front façades of the buildings on both sides of the street, but there weren't any banners snapping in the air, barely even a rattle of metal. The three women that rode into town didn't gleam of any armor, but they were bristling with weapons—bows and spears and swords. Unlike most of the Lances, none of the women Hamasa strained to make out were Riyukezan. Two of them were darker than Mekshans, skin in hues of ebony and rich brown; one had dark copper hair left unbound and in clouds of thick curls. They smiled or waved when entering the village, interacting in a way the Riyukezan militia, the Arm, never did.

And then Hamasa realized what he was seeing: they weren't riding horses. At their waists, their bodies smoothly transitioned into the bodies of horses. Cabadonas, the horsewomen of Mekshi.

"Órala, do you think they're in the Salvatropas?" Marya asked eagerly after choking down a large swallow.

"I'm sure not every cabadona is," Hamasa said pointedly.

"But maybe they came to help, that's what they do, help people all across Mekshi," Marya argued, shaking his arm excitedly.

"Help people?" Valerius repeated with a low snort. "They're making their own laws and calling it help. My lord, we should move on."

"Whatcha gonna do? Tie him up and throw him on your horse in front of the Salvatropas?" Marya asked with a glint in her eye that made Hamasa shift awkwardly.

"The law should be enforced by the Sovereign's word and only that," said Valerius shortly.

"Riyushu is real far away and Her Imperial Highness could use some help," Marya said. "Didn't you hear Señora Mandes? They've been trying to get word from a real city for weeks. They don't exactly march up and down the Road helping all the folks that need it. They help the cities and the students in those fancy schools. We're lucky if we see any soldiers when they go one city to the next," she retorted. Another short cheer had her looking back at the three cabadonas speaking with a small group of Ristahe villagers wearing the nicest and most colorfully woven ponchos. "The Salvatropas, though, they move fast. They care 'bout the little towns."

"They have no one to answer to, only themselves. If they cross the line, who can control them or put them on trial?" Valerius pointed out, scowling, lips pulling tight at the corners. "They are knight, council, and Sovereign, but if they make a mistake, if they hurt or kill an innocent person, they disappear into the wild."

"They're not *killers* who run off into the trees afterwards. They *save* people! They give money or food to villages with bad harvests, they help raise buildings and fix towns broken down after bad storms!" Marya listed off, hands waving through the air. She paused, pursed her lips, and finally blurted, " And yeah, they find or fight off criminals, sometimes bringing in bounties, but people don't, I don't know, pay them to go off and kill people they don't like."

"You're hopelessly naive if you think they don't do whatever they want and call it helping," Valerius said sharply.

Marya inhaled through her nose, face burning red, fists clenching tight. Hamasa set his hand on her arm. She glared at him, and Hamasa quickly moved his hand.

"Whatever points b-both of you have," Hamasa started, cringing back when Valerius also glared down at him. "It doesn't matter. They're magical like those going missing around here. It makes sense they would come if they heard about it," he said. A small thrill raced down his spine despite how awkward the moment was. "I wonder if we could meet them."

In Riyushu, Hamasa had met añhana in the garden pools... somewhat. They more enjoyed splashing in the fountains and making the wind chimes in the maple trees dance rather than talking with people. After the dende sighting that afternoon,

Hamasa had been hoping he would meet more Others, many of who preferred the wider open spaces of the north. He just didn't think it would be so soon.

Marya clapped her hands and nodded once. "I'm going to meet them."

"How? Are you just going to walk up to them?" Hamasa asked, glancing between the group of cabadonas, Marya, and Valerius.

"Yeah. Exactly." Marya flipped her long hair back, squared her shoulders, shook out her large hands, and stomped into the village.

"Senorita Garsia!"

"Señorita," Marya called back. She wended through the crowd, disappearing among the cheering and chattering people.

Hamasa licked his lips and glanced at Valerius. The knight met his gaze, and, with a deep inhale, pinched the bridge of his nose.

"You want to go after her," he said after a moment.

"I should go after her."

"Lead the way, my lord," he said with a gesture for Hamasa to pass by.

"Not a lord," Hamasa muttered, but he walked past with swift steps.

The leader of the Salvatropas, stocky with dark skin, darker hair in dozens of thick long braids, and colorful bands wrapped around her bulging biceps and braided into the coarse mane down her back, lifted her flat nose to the air. Her front hooves struck at the dirt restlessly before she lowered her chin. And met Hamasa's gaze directly. He stumbled to a stop, dust collecting on his toes, and watched as she slowly smiled at him. As if she could see a secret.

Then, her eyes roved past him and fell on Valerius. Surprise pulled her eyes wide, eyebrow arching and lips parting, until she grinned toothily.

"Look here, my friends, we have a real warrior among us."

The leader stepped forward as the villagers around her parted quickly. Her two other companions turned their way, startling as they caught sight of Valerius. As Marya had mentioned before, Hamasa looked more Mekshan than he was. He blended in, downright nondescript when most of his scars were covered. Valerius, on the other hand, was decidedly not nondescript. He was taller by almost a full head with broad shoulders and much fairer skin than a typical northern Mekshan, or even most southerners. Although Mekshans also had dark hair and eyes, Valerius' hair was sleeker and left to grow longer than the local custom, and his eyes were so black they were barely discernible from the pupil and made even darker by his fair skin.

The cabadonas continued forward to stop in front of Valerius and Hamasa. The two others got a look at Hamasa; their eyes widened and they exchanged quick glances and crooked smirks.

"I'm Sitlal," the leader introduced, nodding her head at Valerius. His eyebrows rose, jaw tightening slightly. "You don't like us Salvatropas, southerner?" she asked, though her grin was already more of a thin smirk.

Valerius' tense jaw ticked, the muscle standing out in sharp relief. "It's not my place to like or dislike citizens of Mekshi."

"Maybe he doesn't approve of us," one of other cabadonas teased.

"The Salvatropas is a rogue group of warriors, who work outside the word and will of the Sovereign. It is not for you to—" Valerius began, voice slowly rising in pitch and heat. A rumbling snort and hair-raising whicker interrupted him from the unnamed cabadonas. The three shuffled in place, their hooves cutting into soft sand.

"It's unimportant now," Sitlal said sharply. Her two companions stilled, though their tails still whipped behind them. "Would you be willing to speak privately, Riyukezan?"

Marya forced her way out of the crowd, stumbling a bit, and glanced between Sitlal and Valerius with eyebrows high. "You wanna speak with him?"

Sitlal glanced down, lips twitching and quickly smoothing flat. "From your tone, you know him."

"You could say that," Marya muttered, crossing her arms and glaring their way.

During this, Valerius had his eyes on Hamasa. Hamasa licked his lips, glancing towards the cabadonas and at Valerius' impassive face. Although, it wasn't quite as impassive as usual. The corners of his eyes were tighter, an almost invisible crease formed between his eyebrows.

"It's probably about the missing Others," Hamasa said quietly.

Valerius nodded once. "I thought the same. I want to get you out of this place, but I should at least hear them out."

"Oh good," Hamasa sighed, a small, surprised smile growing. "I think so, too."

Valerius' eyes darted over Hamasa's relieved expression, that slight crease easing away. His head tilted forward, not quite bowing, before he strode towards the Salvatropas, Nerva at his heels and that scowl back on his face. Marya ran past him, grinning widely and starry-eyed, and grasped Hamasa's hands.

"C'mon, they're waiting for us!"

"What if Valerius said no?" Hamasa said, laughing lightly.

"But you wouldn't say no," Marya said.

He couldn't reply, not with her dragging him almost right off his feet. Not that he had anything he could say to that, either.

12

THE SALVATROPAS led them off the Road and further into Ristahe to a rather large and walled ranchita. The courtyard was swept clean, a single slender dog sleeping under a vibrantly blue jacaranda tree overflowing with blooms. On the porch that wrapped around the courtyard on three sides — the fourth side being the entrance gate — were several chairs and tables, one laid with a game board and a bowl of black and white stones. Hamasa stared at it, wondering who in this home played a traditional Riyukezan game. Marya dragged a stool to the edge of the porch and straddled it, hands between her knees as she leaned towards the cabadonas stopping just in front of her. Valerius stood to the side, Nerva's reins still wrapped around his fist. Hamasa glanced between everyone, then shuffled his way to the small table with the *go* board, picking up a black stone to roll between his fingers.

"As I said earlier, I'm Sitlal. This is Eluya," Sitlal began, gesturing towards the cabadona on her right. The other cabadona had a much paler, golden body covered in freckles, and her hair was an untamed mass of coppery brown. She stared at them, fair brows touching and green eyes lingering on each of them heavily. "And this is Tepin," she finished. Tepin grinned and waved. Like Sitlal, she had dark brown skin and a not-quite black lower body, but her head was shaved smooth with a dark blue tattoo in the shape of a wren mid-flight over her crown. "I'm sure you've heard the news of the missing Others. Am I right in thinking you're a Lance? You don't wear the armor."

Valerius nodded, jaw taut. Hamasa's heart clenched, his fingers curling around the black stone in his palm.

"Are you here to look for them?" Marya asked breathlessly. Sitlal's frown broke, a smile escaping when she caught Marya's excited, flushing face.

"We are. There's been a group of poachers in this area for years, and recently they started collecting more dangerous prizes. We found them near here, but we have a small problem. We are outnumbered," Sitlal said, the confession dragged out of her as her eyes closed and her brows scrunched together tightly. Tepin snickered.

"Huimitl warned you," she said. Sitlal snorted and shook her head, turning to glare at her friend, who just smirked back.

"How much are you outnumbered?" Valerius asked. Hamasa and Marya stared at him, but he very carefully kept his gaze on Sitlal.

"There are around a dozen with dogs." Sitlal tched loudly. "And they managed to set up camp inside a temple. It'll be impossible for us to sneak up on them while they're inside that, especially with dogs. And most likely a mage, or bought spells."

"Why's that? I mean, why do you think that?" Marya asked, frowning.

"Because of the Others."

It took a moment for Hamasa to realize that had come from him. And everyone was staring at him. He ducked his head.

"They can't be caught without it," he muttered.

"Exactly. And if they have bought spells, or worse, a mage, while encamped inside a temple, then it'll be impossible to sneak up on them on four legs," Sitlal said.

"We could use two legs, it's not that hard for us," Tepin added cheerfully, "but it'll make us weaker, we don't want to run in with less than half our strength and no magic. Cabadonas aren't great with spell casting, either, and what little we can do, we won't be able to use as two-leggers."

"Why not just wait for them to leave? Are there too many exits to watch?" Valerius asked.

"Temples only have one." "Temples only got one door."

Hamasa and Marya both replied at the same time. Marya stared at him, and he waved his hands at his sides nervously.

"You continue! I only know from reading! And what's left of the ruins down south. You'll know better."

Marya rubbed her nose and then shrugged. "You're right. There's only one door, up at the very top of the temple. Probably why you can't get in easy, all them stairs," Marya said, looking up at Sitlal, who bowed her head in agreement.

"We could wait. We did send for more 'tropas from the main camp and perhaps the next camp the poachers set up won't be quite as defensible. However," Sitlal paused, grimacing. "The idea of leaving those creatures in there, magical Others or mundane, any longer than we must doesn't sit right with us. It could become a siege if we can't get it done right."

"A siege could result in even worse outcomes for the creatures," Valerius said flatly. "Seeing me meant your plans could change."

"But what outcomes are they heading for now?" Marya interrupted. "Where are they taking them?"

"To the cities, child," Sitlal said, sounding soft and kind, but one hoof struck hard at the dirt. "San Yamarasu is only a few days travel north and there are plenty of Riyukezan and Mekshan nobles willing to pay for… pets."

"Pets?" Hamasa whispered. "But northern Others are to be left alone. There are so many more Others down south that enjoy cultivated gardens and human homes. There are laws protecting the Others from forced domestication since the last Sovereign."

"There will always be the rich flouting those laws," Eluya said shortly. "It's not just us wild folk that ignore the will of the Sovereign."

Valerius' nostrils flared, black eyes flashing as they met Eluya's vivid green.

"Let's not annoy the one whose help we're trying to get," Sitlal suggested mildly.

"The Lance isn't the only useful one," Eluya retorted. She didn't look at him, but Hamasa's skin pulled tight. He set the black stone in his hand in its bowl, willing the creepy crawling feeling down his back away.

"Three. Three of us can help you," Marya said. She shoved to her feet and stood, arms akimbo and legs shoulder-width apart. Valerius held up his arm to hold her back.

"We don't even know the plan yet," he said, eyes on Sitlal. She nodded, but some tension was already leaking from her shoulders.

"The idea is for you to get close enough to the temple and keep hidden. About half of them leave for more hunting around twilight, and we can make sure they don't return," Sitlal said. "But there are always at least five or six in the temple. If you can get inside and past them, you can let the prisoners out."

"Don't return?" Hamasa echoed, licking his lips quickly.

"We're not killers if we don't have to, friend," Tepin said, smirking.

"It's a simple enough plan," Valerius said, his hand loosely curled over his mouth.

"We've got enough brains and brawn to get us in there, no problem. Asa, can help us with magic, right?" Marya agreed, grinning over at Hamasa.

"I— What? Pardon?" Hamasa startled and gaped at her, jaw dropping. He hadn't expected "we" to include himself.

"You gotta know at least one spell or two that can help. Let's save some magical creatures from poachers."

Hamasa swallowed hard, eyes darting from Marya's bright, glittering eyes, to Valerius' typical frown, to the cabadonas that all smirked so knowingly at him. His eyes caught the dark blue wren on Tepin's scalp and an inkling itched at the back of his mind.

He licked his lips and smiled weakly. "Sure?"

"My—" Valerius broke off quickly and tried again immediately. "I have to disagree. You two should stay in the village. I can take care of this myself." Eluya's derisive snort was barely covered by Tepin's snickers. "It's not safe."

"There's gonna be at least six of them in there!" Marya exclaimed, waving her arms in the air. "You can't go in there alone!"

Valerius raised an eyebrow. "These are trained hunters. You're a farm girl with a stick."

"Listen up, you—" Marya started, stomping towards him, her index finger raised and her eyes aflame.

"Marya," Hamasa said quickly as he raced forward to grab her arm. She huffed loudly, still scowling. "Valerius, Marya's right. You can't go alone. I m-might…" He glanced towards Tepin and the blue wren tattoo once more. Tepin smirked, eyebrow rising. "I might have an idea."

Marya crowed and pumped her fist in the air. Valerius scowled, eyes on Hamasa, hands curled into fists at his side. Hamasa gulped hard and shrugged with barely a twitch to his shoulders.

13

EACH STEP WAS careful and slow, but Hamasa winced at each crackle and crunch beneath his companions' feet on either side of him. Valerius didn't seem to notice how heavy he was, even with his natural grace without his armor to hold him back. Marya was louder and more obvious than Idiot the donkey hauling a plough through a rocky field; slapping branches away from her face carelessly, huffing through her nose when she had to hurry her pace to keep up with the much longer-legged knight, her feet stamping over twigs and dead leaves even though her sandals were made of paper-thin leather. Neither were great at subtlety in their personalities, so perhaps Hamasa should've expected it in their way of walking.

However, they were trying to sneak inside a camp of a dozen poachers. Poachers who were good enough to not be caught for several months, if not years. Just a moderately quiet scout without the aid of magic or glyphs in the forest around their camp would be able to hear them coming. He winced again as Marya tripped slightly and kicked a stray pebble against the trunk of a nearby tree. Valerius turned to frown at her and Marya glared back as red bloomed over her face.

"You should've stayed back in the village with the Salvatropas."

"No way. I'm not completely useless and I'm going to help,"

Marya snapped.

"You're not exactly quiet y-yourself," Hamasa said, stuttering and trailing off into silence when Valerius faced him with eyebrows pulling low and tight.

"Pardon, my lord?" Valerius asked, tone mild but jaw ticking. Marya snickered behind her knuckles.

"You're loud. You're *both* loud," Hamasa whispered, staring at his feet. His toes curled and uncurled against the smooth leather of his sandals.

"Well, then, you go ahead, little mouse," Marya teased.

Hamasa flinched at the word leaving Marya's lips. His eyes had watched her mouth move, but his ears heard another voice. Deeper, raspier, echoing through the wind in a language that hissed and rattled in his bones.

Valerius' frown broke, eyebrows rising in surprise when Hamasa let out a low hiss. Marya stepped forward, hand brushing his linen-covered shoulder, and her mouth opening around words of concern. Hamasa ducked away from her touch. He had left his poncho in the care of the Mandes twosome, the colors much too vibrant for a task requiring stealth. Without the layer of bright wool, his skin was too exposed, too bare, with only its single layer of linen. He pulled up a tight, small smile, feeling the thin skin around his eyes crinkling.

"Watch my feet. Stay back at least a full adult's length before following."

With that, Hamasa stepped past them. He didn't look back, didn't so much as glance the knight's way as he passed him. As he had asked, they waited silently before continuing after him. He kept close to the trees, slipping shadow to shadow, eyes darting over the ground to avoid loose debris and bushes. The breeze that made the trees dance overhead made the darkening shadows and his own low-crouching body movements blend together. He was one more wild animal, there and gone again.

Behind him by several paces, Marya and Valerius were moving better. Not so obviously loud. Fewer twigs being snapped at least. The break in the trees came suddenly, and Hamasa almost forgot to lean into the tree's shade. His jaw dropped and his body fairly trembled as he inhaled sharply.

The structure wasn't unfamiliar, but it was startlingly beautiful and intact. Made of dark grey stone and built to resemble the mountains around them, the centuries old temple sat in the midst of a very large clearing. Its base was wide, half or more of Ristahe's Roadside market could fit inside. The sides of the temple were blocky and square, unnaturally so, showing the care and craftsmanship of the ancient Mekshans that had painstakingly carved every block. Each terrace was slightly smaller in square-size, building upwards to its narrowest peak. On this side, there were no visible stairs, but he knew there must be on one side. Steps narrower than a foot, taller than the typical adult's shin bone, at least three steps per layer, all leading to the top where an opening into the temple's sanctum lay. He counted nine layers, another number divisible by three, and grinned in a giddy kind of triumph. He knew it had to be nine. Three by three. Three by nine. Powerful, indeed. The texts all said so, of course, but he had never seen it in person.

A hand fell on his shoulder and he flung himself away. Thudding against the slender trunk of the tree beside him. One hand with flat and useless nails curled outward cut through the air. Marya stared at him, eyes wide and hands up, and Valerius right behind her, holding her from where he had tugged her back and away from Hamasa's aggressive motion.

"Oh, oh Sun. I'm sorry, I w-wasn't—You startled m-me," Hamasa gasped, heart pounding and blood boiling under his skin.

"Yeah, I see that. Did... did you just try to scratch me?" Marya blurted, eyebrows jumping up to disappear behind her mop of curls.

"Um." Hamasa glanced away and hoped the breeze would cool his skin before he set the tree behind him on fire.

"Perhaps becoming lost in thought while we're tracking a band of poachers is a bad idea. This close to their hideout, they're sure to have lookouts posted," Valerius said smoothly.

Hamasa swallowed and nodded. "There's none... none over here. At least not now. There aren't any recent tracks or signs of anything not fauna."

"Fauna? You don't know 'idiot', but you know *fauna*," Marya said with a little head shake and a smirk. She stepped closer to him, but very carefully didn't touch him when she peered towards the temple a league or more away. "How are we gonna get close enough without getting seen? There ain't any cover."

"We can circle the perimeter for now and see if there's another way."

Hamasa was already shaking his head as Valerius spoke.

"The grounds of all Mekshan temples are kept cleared, there won't be any brush to use for cover. There could be magical traps or scouts anywhere around here. The more we travel around, the more likely we'll be seen."

Valerius scowled. "You're right. Even waiting here until full dark has its own disadvantages or could get end in them finding us first."

"So that's it? We can't just give up!" Marya protested. Hamasa glanced at her, and then away, licking his lip quickly.

"Subterfuge is not our strong point as a team. Not right now."

"Again with the university talk. Just say I'm louder'n a herd of donkeys," Marya told him with a crooked grin.

"Well... you don't bray."

Marya snorted.

"You said 'not right now'. Do you mean the idea you mentioned before?" Valerius asked, arms crossing over his chest.

Hamasa bit his lip and looked toward the temple in the distance. "Um, yes. I'll need some time and space."

"Oh!" Marya slapped a hand over her mouth to muffle her volume. Hamasa sighed. "You're gonna use magic, ain't ya?" she whispered loudly.

"Of a kind. Do you still have that mara's foot?"

"The mara's foot? You asked me to bring it, so..." Marya patted at her trousers and carefully unrolled the woven band that kept them up. The mara foot fell to her palm; she quickly put her clothes back to rights and rolled her makeshift belt tightly. Hamasa reached out for the foot and gave her a quick flash of a smile. "You finally gonna tell me what my lucky mara foot's for?"

"Some creatures are born with magic, of magic, really. They can pull it out of themselves with the right amount of will, focus, and incantation. The more of all three you have, the clearer and more powerful the spell," Hamasa explained, glancing towards the temple one last time and then moving further into the trees. He spoke quietly as he walked, knowing Valerius and Marya were right on his heels. "But humans, like the shamans of Mekshi who built those temples hundreds of years ago, used the ambient magic of the natural world. It's more ritual than incantations, and requires more time, but it could work for us. It harnesses the elements themselves, calling upon what they considered gods, personifications of those elements." He stopped at an area with the least amount of underbrush and carefully began to clear the ground.

"Dragons are the physical manifestations of the elements. You don't need such rituals to cast magic," Valerius said. He squatted at Hamasa's side and frowned as Hamasa stroked his hand over the dirt to check how smooth it was.

Hamasa's hands stilled, dust caking his fingers and hovering over the ground, and he stared at Valerius. "Who told you that? About dragons?"

"Kana'iro the Red."

Hamasa stared with eyes slowly widening until the scar tissue on the side of his face pulled painfully. Valerius stared mutely back. His black eyes were heavier than stones, flat and unyielding. It didn't take long for Hamasa to look away as shivers twitched down his back. Marya was gaping with shining eyes at Valerius and didn't seem notice Hamasa's silence. Soon, though, she began to frown.

"If you've talked to the Shield, then you should know Hamasa isn't who you're looking for," Marya told Valerius with a frown made darker by the thickness of her brows.

Valerius' heavy gaze broke. A stifled gasp brushed against the back of Hamasa's teeth, trembling past his lips with barely a sound. Keeping his eyes low, he focused on his hands rubbing compulsively against the rough linen of his trousers.

"Perhaps you should understand that I've met the Shield and therefore I know exactly who Hamasa is," Valerius finally said.

From under the shadow of his bangs, Hamasa watched Marya's flickering expressions as those shivers raced down his spine again. She braced her hands on her knees, eyes darting from Valerius' too-serious frown and Hamasa's down-turned face. Her mouth pursed, twisted to the side, and parted around a rough, shoulder-shaking sigh.

"Stubborn donkey," Marya muttered, using a colloquial word Hamasa knew was much ruder than simply 'donkey'. Judging by the taut line of Valerius' mouth, he too recognized the Mekshan word.

"I should keep my attention on the temple. I do not want us to be caught unaware while we wait for the ritual," Valerius said, moving to get to his feet.

"Wait a moment. I need you and Marya," Hamasa said.

He reached out with a hand, not quite touching the now-dust-marred white cloth of Valerius' kimono sleeve. Despite the lack of the slightest pressure, Valerius had stilled immediately, eyes on Hamasa's hand. With a sudden jerk, Hamasa's hand dropped. Marya came towards them at Hamasa's words, eyes on her feet as she skirted the edge of the small circle he had made. It had the diameter of about his arm length and was clear of any twig, pebble, or grass.

"Whatcha need, Asa?"

"Um, blood," Hamasa said absently, staring at his hand. He looked up at the silence that followed to see Marya stumbling to a halt, eyebrows once again flying high up her forehead. Valerius' expression mirrored hers almost exactly. He turned the words he'd said over in his mind and grimaced. "Just a bit? It sounds worse than it is. I think saliva or sweat could work as well, but the shamans were recorded using blood most often, and since this sort of magic isn't used much these days, not even in universities, I think it w-would b-be..." He broke off to breathe in deep and end his worsening stutter. "I think it would be best to stick to the recorded practices."

"Don't tongue tie yourself. I trust you, Hamito." Marya squatted next to him and held out her arm, wrist bared, the side of her mouth curling down and eyes averted.

Hamasa huffed a sigh and gently took her index finger. "I'm not going to cut you open, Marya."

She huffed a quiet chuckle, shoulders rising towards her ears. When she stopped moving, Hamasa pressed the still sharp nail of the mara's claw to her finger, pricking hard enough that blood welled up and stained fur and nail alike. When he moved the claw away, it had barely been wetted. Marya popped her finger in her mouth and grinned incredulously around it.

"That's it?"

Hamasa nodded, smiling shyly back. "Should be."

He lifted his own hand to his mouth, using the slightly too sharp point of his incisor to cut into the soft pad of his thumb. It was easy enough to let a few drops of blood fall on the claw from that. Licking at the cut on his hand, he turned. Valerius had already pricked his thumb with a small, slender dagger that Hamasa didn't even know he had. Silently, he held out the mara foot for Valerius to hold his hand over.

"Do you require my assistance for anything else, my lord?" the knight asked, casually slipping the dagger into the wide black obi around his waist.

"Ah, no?" Valerius' single eyebrow rose. "No."

Valerius nodded once, then stood and walked farther into the trees. His footsteps didn't so much as disturb a fallen leaf, although he still had too much weight at each step. But better. Much better.

"So, what happens now?" Marya asked eagerly and shuffled closer, interrupting Hamasa's musings.

"I have to call upon a specific divinity, but I think it's more about drawing in the natural element that the ritual needs. The divinity is just the focus," Hamasa said, snapping back to attention and balancing carefully to begin scratching lines into the dirt with the bloody claw.

"Hm. Doesn't sound like you believe in the gods."

Hamasa turned to Marya, eyes wide and a hot churning deep in his chest. "I didn't m-mean to imply —!" he began, only to swallow his deluge of apologies when Marya smirked and patted his shoulder. The touch was swift, without lingering, and it had tension in his back and neck unknotting at the return of her casual affection.

"I'm just teasing, you really are so easy to rile up," she said with a snicker. "There's a reason all them temples are empty, have been empty a long, long time. We mostly stopped believing before the Riyukezans came with their dragons and blew down what was left of the old ways."

"It was only one dragon," Hamasa pointed out, though he smiled. "And not all of them blow typhoons into existence."

"Yeah, the last Shield was kinda known for his fire-breathing," Marya said matter-of-factly. Hamasa ducked his head, hoping his hair was long enough to cover the sudden blanching of his face.

"I'm sorry I struck out at you," he said quickly, gesturing back the way they came. "I... uh, I've never seen a temple so intact. L-like this one. It was startling, and I couldn't help getting lost in my thoughts earlier."

"Ay, was that it? You were gazing at that temple so much you didn't hear me coming at you? You're a weird one."

"I like to read, and I've read a lot about them. The old rituals and the shamans of old Mekshi," Hamasa explained, once again drawing swift, straight lines that softened into curves at the beak of the old divinity he drew.

"Didn't think those fancy magic universities taught old Mekshan magic," Marya mused, scratching at her cheek.

Hamasa's hand slowed, then continued. "Some do. Rarely. Most of what I know is from personal study."

Marya nodded and lapsed into silence while she watched him work.

14

SOON ENOUGH, the movements of his hand quickened, sure and steady, as the portrait formed in the dirt. Centuries ago, before dragons flew over the horizon and brought with them a fleet of displaced nobles, a ritual like this would look different. Perhaps drawn on stone with vivid paints mixed with the blood of the magic caster and the affected subjects as apprentices stared on breathlessly, hoping one day they might also harness the magic from the very air they breathed.

There would have been a price paid; pieces of gold or precious stones, foodstuffs that priests and shamans were too revered to reap themselves. The portrait of this divinity, with its harsh angles and impressive wingspan, was an overly stylized portrait of a dala. In the years since, dalas and dalos, cabadonas, dende, and so many other magical creatures were no longer believed to be gods or descended divinities, instead they were neighbors and friends united throughout the years of war and peace. But it didn't make the magic now less potent. It was a focus for the ritual, that's all. His fingers, where he clutched the slippery smooth fur of the mara's foot, fairly vibrated with each stroke. Marya's voice faded. The too heavy foot falls of the knight disappeared. There was only the scratch of the claws in dirt. The whistle of the wind that swept over the circle though not so much a particle of dust was disturbed.

For the first time since he woke in that crater, a stranger's face hovering over him, Hamasa fit in his skin. Magic swept down his naked arms, tickled the nape of his neck, fluttered at his hair, and he felt whole. It wasn't from inside him, but it was magic. Shadows pooled in the lines of the figure he'd drawn, a tall body neither feminine nor masculine, with feathered wings arching high to touch the shape of the moon with the very tips of the longest feathers, the head a heron's slope with barely a neck and the beak slender and sharp. A dala, creature born of magic and air and Mekshan soil.

"Whoa," Marya whispered. "You really are a mage."

"Anyone can use this kind of magic," Hamasa said, blinking himself back into the world and smiling at his finished glyph. The afternoon sun shone down on them hot enough for Marya's hairline to be dotted with sweat and bright enough that the hints of red in her dark hair glowed auburn, but the shadows lingered in the edges of the portrait. "It draws on the magic inherent in nature, as I said before. It's elemental. Those university mages, the Others like the dalas and cabadonas, they're born with magic inside them. They draw from within. These rituals draw from the outside. Seeing Tepin's tattoo reminded me of this particular divinity, though the bird is not quite the same."

"I can't tell much difference between birds," Marya said with a laugh. Her hand hovered over the portrait of Guanabánoch, ancient divinity of night and shade. "So I could do this?" she asked.

"It's not as easy as drawing in the dirt, but yes. With learning and practice, you could use natural, ambient magic," Hamasa said. His gaze traced her profile pensively, taking in her parted lips and wide eyes, and he tilted his head. "Do you want to?" Marya turned, an eyebrow cocking as the gleam faded from her dark eyes. "Want to learn how?"

THE COWARD'S EMBLEM

She grinned and shook her head almost immediately, surprising him. "Nah. I like using my hands more'n my brains. It's interesting, but the way you just pushed everything out, like you couldn't hear me talking and your hands were moving on their own almost. I dunno if that's something I'd be good at. 'Sides, getting stuck in some big school with a bunch of rich braggers who wanna be Riyukezan and forget where they come from, nah, I wouldn't like that." She rolled her eyes and huffed stray curls off her face. "I always thought one day I'd be like my Papi. Join the Arm soldiers and learn to swing a sword around."

"You're strong enough to be a soldier, a great one," Hamasa said. Marya beamed brightly. "But if you change your mind, you can always try casting. There are plenty of mage soldiers. You have plenty of... of brains." He stumbled over the compliment awkwardly, face overheating.

Marya grinned and then looked back at the portrait. "I know that one. Guanabánoch, right? They always had the best stories, especially the scary ones. I liked it when my Papi told Guanabánoch's stories when it was storming and real dark and spooky. That's the best time."

Hamasa smiled and wrapped his arms around his knees, barely keeping balanced on the balls of his feet. It had been a long time since he thought on his own childhood and all he left behind. So many of those memories had ended with pain. Hearing about Marya's childhood was refreshing, even comforting; a reminder that memories could be good and warm. Footsteps approached and Valerius had returned, dark eyes flickering towards the figure in the dirt, and the two friends squatting at the edge of it.

"There's been movement at the temple."

"What?" Marya scrambled to her feet, unconsciously stepping away from the perimeter of the spell. "Are they leaving?"

Valerius shook his head and looked down at the spell circle

again. "Perhaps they noticed that."

Hamasa licked his bottom lip with a slight frown. "If they have spells guarding their hideout, it's likely some of them can detect other mages or spells in the area. I should've thought of that."

"What now?! The whole point was to be secret!" Marya hissed, stomping her foot.

"The whole of point of *this*," Hamasa said with a wave at the spell, "is to keep the secret. Go on."

Marya stared at him, at his gesturing hand, and at the spell. "What?"

"It's a stealth spell. Why do you think I called on darkness? It'll be strongest once it's truly night..." He trailed off and glanced to the west horizon; it honestly wasn't that long until then. "It should hide our trail and presence. It needed your blood so the spell can work on all of us. Get into the circle."

"Ay, this is crazy," Marya muttered under her breath. With a short exhale through her nose, she stepped into the circle and all but disappeared from view. Turning his head, he could make out the rather insubstantial shadow of her, flickering more fully into view as she waved her hands in the air and stared at, no, *through* her limbs. Hamasa sighed in relief.

"I'm a ghost!" Her voice echoed oddly, weak and thin.

"Oh, good. It worked."

Marya's shadowy arms flailed more wildly in the air. Valerius grabbed Hamasa's elbow, hauling him to his feet. Hamasa yelped under Valerius' scowl.

"It worked?"

"It worked?!" Marya's wispy voice crackled.

"I've never done this before!" Hamasa said defensively.

Valerius scowled harder, his glittering eyes as terrifying as a hawk's, and Hamasa cowered a little lower. Without another word, Valerius stepped into the circle. Hamasa stumbled in after him since the bigger man hadn't let go of his elbow.

The circle beneath their feet broke, the portrait not so much fading as much as abruptly gone. Wind rustled over Hamasa's feet, grit and leaves scattering across what had been the spell circle. He held up his hand to stare at the flicker of shadow and sunlight where his skin should be. When he stepped forward, there wasn't a sound. His loose tunic didn't so much as flutter as the breeze curled around him. The grip of Valerius' hand and the five points of pressure where his calloused fingertips dug in briefly were an anchor. Reminding Hamasa he was real. Solid. Not a dance of shadows beneath the sparse canopy.

"How long does it last?" Valerius asked. It didn't sound like him. The deep baritone of his voice lost in a trembling whisper.

"As long as we don't step into full sunlight. Or firelight, I suppose."

"So we stick to the trees? How does this help us get closer to the temple?" Marya asked incredulously. Her hands fluttered past his arm, then latched on with an obvious desperation. Perhaps she too felt unreal, his solid arm an anchor like Valerius' hand was to him.

"We come from the east," Valerius said. "The temple's shadow is already at the treeline. We won't need any tree cover."

"Yes, exactly. We just walk through the shadow," Hamasa said, surprised and staring in the direction of the knight's voice.

"But the stairs are on the north—" Marya broke off. Both her hand twisting into the linen of his tunic and the pressure of Valerius' fingers around his elbow tightened at the same time.

Hamasa raised his nose and licked at the air as voices grew near. Before he or Marya could speak again, Valerius was dragging them through the trees. As if they were some strange chain of humans about to dance around a fire, they remained linked while stumbling with an eerie silence through the trees. Although the path was winding, backtracking and slow, Valerius invariably led them around the east side of the temple.

As Marya had been in the middle of pointing out, the steps to the entrance were carved into the north-facing side of the temple. However, the temple was built in gradually decreasing layers, creating almost natural stairs onto every side of its surface. The actual stairs had been hand-carved to fit a foot more naturally, but it didn't make the rest of the temple impossible to climb. It would stretch the limits of the spell. Near silent as they had become, they still made some noises. But it was possible. Especially the darker it became.

The trio lingered under the trees as close to the edge of the temple's clearing as they dared. The small group of searchers broke through the treeline from where they had been when Hamasa cast the spell. Spindly-thin dogs pranced around the small group of people, whip-like tails low and heads lower. It was easy to see the dogs were acting strangely, as far as they were, almost opposite the league-wide clearing. Their snouts rising to the air and dropping to the ground continuously, they pranced and slunk around in circles, many of them breaking away from the group to run back to the trees. A few of the poachers snapped or shouted, their words indistinct despite the volume, and the dogs all but crawled back on their bellies, ears flat and tails dragging through dust. One dog went through this whole cycle at least three times, desperately trying to find their scent trail, or figure out exactly what their scent trail was, until its master cuffed it around the head. The dog cringed away and joined the pack rushing towards the temple.

"Guleros," Marya snarled from the shadows on Hamasa's right. "I shouldn't be surprised, them being the kind to sell living creatures like toys, but I just hate seeing someone hit their own animal like that."

"We'll tie his ropes tighter," Valerius said, so close to Hamasa's ear that it was almost loud. His voice cracked like flint striking iron, and Marya responded to it with low chuckle.

A few more people came down from the temple, whistling. The searchers on the ground met newcomers in the middle of the clearing. A few held obvious crossbows in their hands or had bulky knapsacks slung over a shoulder. In the next minute, the group broke. Only two people and a few dogs headed up the temple steps while the majority of the group and most of the dog pack disappeared into the dim woods to the north.

"When we walk into the shadow, we should become even more invisible than we are now. There's a chance we won't be able to hear each other. I don't know how strong or how deep the spell is," Hamasa warned as they stepped towards the temple's shadow where it met the treeline.

"Right. When is it time to jump on all these money-licking poachers?" Marya asked. The wispiness of her voice didn't quite cloud her eagerness for violence — and justice, Hamasa hoped.

"We need to stay out of sight until all the cages are unlocked and the cabadonas arrive," Valerius said sharply, voice crackling. Marya huffed at Valerius' obvious annoyance. Hamasa could clearly picture her eyes rolling.

"Stay out of any direct light. It's not true night yet, the spell will break," Hamasa said, innards twisting uncomfortably, licking his too hot too dry lips.

"Yeah, yeah. Let's go beat some gulos!"

There was a soft thud of wood to palm, and Hamasa barely made out the swing of her shovel-turned-staff. Valerius had left behind his polearm, but, remembering the dagger he'd had hidden in his obi, Hamasa was sure he wasn't defenseless. Hamasa himself was content being the focus of the spell, something he would need all his concentration for. His hands flexed ineffectually at his sides, useless nails at the end of his tensely clawed hands, belying his own inner thoughts.

The whisper of loose cotton over Hamasa's arm and the dim, leaf-patterned outline of Valerius' broad shoulders passed by. Immediately swallowed into nothing at all when the knight stepped into the fast-thickening shade. A large, soothingly warm hand wrapped around his.

"We can't let rust pits be the hero."

"He's not even wearing—" Marya had already pulled him forward, the hardly-there silhouette of her staff and barely restrained curls melting into shadow. Hamasa sighed with a smile tugging at his mouth.

Without the familiar weight and calloused roughness of her hand holding his too smooth, too soft hand Hamasa would've had no idea she walked a step ahead of him. He couldn't hear her steps, her breaths, couldn't taste the heady scent of adrenaline-fueled sweat. Maybe it was just as uncanny to her, or moreso, as her grip convulsed every other moment to reorient herself. To remember he was there.

The temple grounds were barely an echo of what they once must've been. The smaller shrines that mirrored the monolith at the center were worn down by the elements. Their sharp, stone edges had been rounded by age and wind and wild animals using them as scratching posts, shelters from winter and summer storms, or to help them shed their fur or build their nests. They were musty with the odor of years of use, although no animals burrowed there now. Not with humans and domestic hounds to scare them away.

The central temple wasn't much different, although it looked more imposing. More intact. As they began to climb, using only their free hands and sandalled feet—mistake, huge mistake, bare feet would be much less dangerous, by the Sun, Marya's sandals were tied together with rope—Hamasa noticed the first terraced layers of the temple were as worn down and riddled with signs of animals and precocious weeds as the smaller shrines they had passed below. About midway there were less signs of use, the edges of the shelves sharp and rough, worn down only by the air and water and age. He realized then, obviously, why this temple and other northern temples like it still stood so tall—it was the stone itself. Unlike the south, where most the natural stone was relatively swiftly eroding lime- and sandstone, this was much more enduring granite. Of course. He brushed his fingers over the pitted dark grey stone, mentally wondering the cost of hauling granite blocks this massive far enough south for a temple. It would also explain the lack of embellishment. What was left of the old monuments down south were studded with shells and coral, even precious jade pieces had been found in the rubble. None of which were to be seen here.

An insistent tug broke his reverie. Once again Marya brought him back to the here and now. Grateful she couldn't see the sheepish duck of his head, Hamasa struggled to keep his body from flushing with embarrassed heat. Who knew how far ahead Valerius was by now. Hamasa shouldn't be holding them back anymore. They needed to get in and prepare for the cabadonas' arrival. Night was sinking in its claws over the mountains and forests, and the cabadonas would ride out soon. Ristahe wasn't so far away that he could afford to dawdle and ruin their plan.

At the top, the temple suddenly flattened. The night breeze was sharper here, cold enough to feel truly like autumn. The door set into the stone opening was made of wood, crudely and newly made. The crooked, unsanded slats were still sticky with sap when Hamasa set his hand to it. He felt an arm brush past his, felt the wood give under his palm, and quickly grabbed a loose sleeve. The texture was too fine to be Marya, and her hand was still in his and hanging behind him. Valerius. The pressure let off and Hamasa knelt to peek through the latch hole. Inside, he could make out the flicker of torchlight, the mutters of voices as a figure passed his very small line of sight. He jolted back, shoved Valerius away from the entrance, and dragged Marya back with him.

The door opened and a man stepped out, a small cigarillo clamped between his teeth. The door swung slowly shut, scraping over hewn stone and coming to rest crookedly in the doorway. Again a slight breeze whipped over the temple's peak and the man cursed quietly, cupping the glowing red tip of his cigarillo and, for a moment, his face lit up. A southerner, weather-beaten and swarthy, with a pale smudge of a mustache under his nose making him look older.

Then, there was a thump. His body jerked awkwardly, as if something had fallen onto the back of his neck, and his eyes widened. The cigarillo fell from his slack mouth and he soon followed. Already unconscious. Before he could hit the ground, he was... frozen. Slumped and hanging in midair, held up by shadows. Shadows that dragged him around the corner of the peak. Marya's hand squeezed briefly around his and Hamasa wondered what she felt: awe? fear? excitement? Some combination of them all?

Hamasa only felt cold. He wasn't even sure if his spell was the reason why Valerius' attack was so silent. A single blow like that, that was true skill. He would never stand a chance against Valerius unless he did something drastic.

He took a deep breath, squeezed Marya's hand in return and warning, and entered the temple slowly, carefully, his heart pounding painfully against his sternum. He was sure he had heard at least one other person immediately beyond the door.

When they slipped through, nudging it a little more open, there was a single woman sitting in a chair with her feet propped up on a pack. She held a small curiously curved knife, nimbly and expertly shaving a small block of wood. She glanced up when the door opened and slowly began to frown.

Marya's hand fell away, and a shadow flickered along the wall. The woman glanced towards it, her grip shifting on the knife as confusion twisted her expression. Her head jerked to the side with an accompanying loud thud, and she fell in a huddle to the ground. Hamasa rushed forward, the shadows flickering wildly, the outline of his hands pressing under the woman's jaw. Relief left him on a silent sigh at the barely perceptible pulse. He was suddenly jerked out of the torchlight by a hand on the back of his tunic. Valerius again.

Hamasa glanced down at his hands, hissing between his teeth, but they were cloaked in shadows again. Invisible. She had fallen to the outer edge of the torch's shine so his spell remained thankfully unbroken. When he made no move to push away or jump back into the light, Valerius let him go and the unconscious woman's body began to slide towards the door. Hamasa turned away, slinking deeper into the shadows beyond the circle of torches, heart hammering. It was too uncanny, too grotesque, to watch a body dragged like refuse over the ground and to be tied up outside and out of sight with the other man. There was a quiet tap on the wall near him. He cautiously reached out until the back of his hand hit an arm. A few fumbles and Marya's familiar grip was back.

15

When the door closed again and was latched with an unseen hand, Hamasa bared his teeth and tightened his jaw. Then, he led Marya down the dim hall. It sloped gently downwards, the walls rarely opening into small rooms without windows or other exits. Most were empty and fetid with the odor of wild animals and must, as well as a strange dry smell that could only be air that had been kept closed in stone for years. The deeper they went, the less Hamasa could smell of animals that had encroached on this forgotten place, but that odd scent of old, trapped air and stone lingered. It tasted more like a cave than a building.

The path finally opened into a massive chamber, so massive that the few torches set atop standing poles couldn't light half the space. A large slab of stone sat at the far wall directly across from the bottom of the stone ramp. Most of the torches encircled this stone altar where packs and various items lay scattered over the surface except in the middle. According to texts and what Hamasa could vaguely make out, there was a shallow depression carved into the stone. Around the edge of the bowl would be various symbols in reoccurring patterns—the world made flat around the sky. Maybe traces of old blood were there, but that didn't seem likely. The shamans were quite meticulous in the texts. They wouldn't have wanted the wrong casters affected by the wrong spells. Most likely the old magic lingered, the layers upon layers of spells creating a feeling, a general sense of something there, when nothing in actuality was. And even these poachers, with their disregard for the freedom of creatures that had once been revered in this very place, edged away from the middle of the altar.

Hamasa counted five humans lounging around the altar, all chatting casually, their voices echoing in the cavernous room. Their dogs were crowded around their feet, gnawing on rawhides or hanks of thick rope. One was sleeping, its body stretched out flat and tongue lolling as it snored. He glanced around, looking for the captured creatures and froze, horror squeezing at his chest. He didn't need to feel Marya's hand clenching around his to know what he was looking at. Metal cages were stacked along the western wall, more than a dozen. Most contained only one creature, some carried two or more, but all were roughly the same size. A few cages were smaller and made of thin wires so closely braided that they were almost mesh. The tiny winged bodies within were silent, not even a buzz or chitter when one of the poachers walked past. Viciously sharp-toothed and winged lohas, smaller and more dangerous cousins of the dende called chanaces, and an extremely rare and beautiful winged páhalebra, the sight of which made Hamasa gasp out loud, grateful for the silence of the spell. He dragged his horrified gaze away, taking in the few mundane creatures like golden furred monkeys and rosette-spotted jaguars caged among the Others. All of them were curled into spaces much too small for them and drugged into manageable stupors. Their bodies were too lax, all of them too quiet. Either there were more spells or the more mundane use of drugs.

Marya and Hamasa hurried to the cages, neither tugging the other in their identical reactions, and almost colliding with the man walking back towards the altar in their haste. Hamasa knelt in front of the first cage, and his eyes locked on the sinuously beautiful and glittering coils that looked black as pitch in the gloom of the páhalebra inside. The wings, about an entire grown man's arm length in span, fluttered restlessly, and the páhalebra's tongue darted in the air. Could it taste his scent, could it tell he wasn't like those poachers? That he was a friend? Hamasa shook his head to clear the unnecessary thoughts and looked closely at the lock. It was a hanging padlock, which would be easy enough to break, but... He gently traced the edge of the lock. All the hair on his head rose, his skin pulled tight into gooseflesh. Where he touched the padlock there was a hot fizz of static lightning.

Locking spells. Of course. No common cage or lock could keep lohas contained, and páhalebra were as notoriously difficult at being caught as lohas were. What had they used to catch one in the first place?

"Ay, that thing is trying it again. Is that lock gonna hold all the way to Róntraih Porto?" a woman asked while walking towards the cages.

Hamasa was yanked away and behind the cage before he could flinch. One of Marya's arms, wiry and strong, wrapped around his chest, holding him against her. He couldn't hear the pants or wheezes, couldn't hear if she were cursing a mean streak, but her heart was beating so hard he could feel it against his spine, and her arm was shaking, her grip painful around the ball of his shoulder. For her peace of mind, he kept perfectly still, holding his own breath as the woman who had spoken neared the cage.

"It'll last. It ain't our first job," a man drawled, passing out playing cards to the remainder of the crew.

"Yeah, but we never had a páhalebra before. They're clever beasts."

The páhalebra hissed dangerously, its sadly cramped wings

fluttering and the dry slither of its scales scratching against metal and stone.

"Get away from it. It'll start bashing itself against the bars again if you rile it up. Let's get this game on."

The woman grimaced at the winged serpent that was glaring up at her with a balefully shining golden eye. "Sooner we leave the dirty sticks, the better," she muttered as she turned away.

Hamasa let out a silent sigh, Marya's chest shuddering with her own sigh behind him. Her arm loosened and he crawled away, then reached out and found her hand wrapped tightly around the shaft of her old shovel handle. It was, sadly, time to wait some more.

Hamasa looked once more at the páhalebra, and jerked back. Its head had risen, its wings spread as far as they could, and those golden eyes were looking right at him. It was waiting for him. Wondering why and how he could sit there, free, and do nothing. Hamasa swallowed hard, looked towards the altar, the pack of dogs and poachers, and then back at the páhalebra. It waited, feathers brushing the sides of the cage. There was loud thuck and the whole cage rattled and the the páhalebra flinched, twisting around and hissing. On the floor outside the cage was a boot. A *boot*.

"Settle down," another woman called over.

Hamasa squeezed Marya's hand and dropped it, then crouch-walked his way around the back of the cages. There were whispers of movements, interested chitters from the lohas, deep drags of breaths from the chanaces as he passed them. If they couldn't exactly see him, they knew he was there. Using their magic. Covered in what had been used in their name long ago. Of course they knew he was there. Maybe from the moment he walked down that ramp.

While most of the poachers' packs and equipment were on the

altar with them, not everything was. A wagon with burlap sacks and discarded ropes was resting in a corner. Probably to haul the cages. Although the air felt damp and heavy with age, the air inside the temple was actually dry. Dry enough that licking his lips was like rubbing sand on wood. He set his hand in the midst of the burlap and ropes and dirty bits of hay. Each and every bit of it flammable.

And let the heat come.

It bubbled up from his belly, spread through his veins, rushing fast and elated and free at last. Not quickly squashed down or restrained to a mere blush or fever. It burned through him. And then the burlap, rope, and hay began to smolder. Smoke began to rise around his unseen hand.

"Do you smell that?"

There were dog whines and snorts, a skitter of claws and shuffling of boots on stone.

Hamasa set his second hand amidst the flammable debris and pushed hotter, and hotter still, through his too soft palms. A spark rose, and another, like lightning bugs they fluttered around his wrists and arms and then a lick of flame. Just that one slip of real fire and suddenly the whole foul, awful cart, seeped in the misery of the captured, was burning. A bonfire in the middle of a cavern of stone. Hamasa was already slipping away, knowing the light of the fire was tearing apart the shadows covering him. He closed his eyes, desperately reaching for the cleared mind he'd found in the woods. Remembering the feeling of soft mara fur and grit. He couldn't let the spell drop. If it fell from him, Marya and Valerius could still use the element of surprise.

"What the—"

"It's on fire!"

"We can see it's on fire!"

"What are the dogs doing!?"

THE COWARD'S EMBLEM

Hamasa opened his eyes, his shaking hands clasping and unclasping in front of him, willing the telltale heat to ebb. The whole pack was rushing towards him, teeth bared around snarls as they searched out his scent. Only for the front of the pack to skid to a stop, then the whole pack, their noses lifting and falling, their bodies cringing away with whines.

"*Go*," Hamasa whispered in neither Mekshan nor Riyukezan.

With yelps and whines, they raced for the ramp, falling over themselves and knocking into the legs of their masters to run for the outside. One hunter ran after them, cursing and yelling colorfully. The remaining four beat at the cart with their coats, their shirts, spare trousers, one even tried emptying a waterbag over what was already an out of control bonfire.

"What the dragon's tit is going on here? A cart doesn't just burst into fire outta nowhere!" a man wheezed, dropping the ruined coat and stepping away.

"Someone's—" The woman broke off to cough, carelessly dropping the waterbag in her hand, the cured hide of it making a strange *schlop* on the stone. "Someone's in here!"

"Whoever set off the alarm glyphs earlier," a second man said.

The last man, who had held a coat long since dropped and smoking faintly on the ground, rubbed at his face and opened his eyes. To look directly at Hamasa, who was pressed against the stone wall and staring back wide-eyed.

"What the—"

"Ah..." Hamasa's breath squeaked in his throat. All four faces streaked with sweat and soot were turned towards him now. Firelight flickered over their expressions of disbelief and fury. "Um?"

"You little—" The first man to see him was the first one to move. He strode towards Hamasa with long-legged strides and reached for the sheath at his hip. It wasn't a sword, by the shape or length of it, but it was definitely a sharp pointy object that Hamasa did *not* want anywhere near him.

He scrabbled over the stone, nails scratching and sandals slapping his heels. Just as he managed to get fully standing, Valerius stepped into the ring of torchlight behind the poachers. The knight looked right at Hamasa, face thunderous.

"Sorry!" Hamasa shouted stupidly. Thankfully, it made the four poachers pause. The man with his wickedly sharp long dagger frowned.

"Did you just say 'sorry'?"

This time, Hamasa saw Valerius slip silently forward and chop the nearest poacher on the back of the neck with the side of his hand. The sudden grunt, and the immediate thump of the man's body to the ground, had the poachers looking over their shoulders, bewildered shock pulling their eyes wide and their jaws dropping.

"He was talking to me."

The three spun completely around, the woman letting out a loud squawk of a curse, but Valerius was already on top of them. With a speed Hamasa didn't even know humans were capable of, Valerius struck out with the flat of his hands, knocking away punches as if they were mere branches of a trees in his way, and ducked low, simultaneously sweeping the feet out from under one of them. Marya materialized abruptly, her stave clutched in both hands, but her run aiming for Hamasa. He rushed to her, forcing her to skid back and spin around when he grasped her sleeve. They ran around the worst of the fight, Marya muttering curses while barreling towards the cages and the creatures excitedly waking from their stupors. They clawed eagerly at the air between the bars or at the padlocks, ignoring the jolts of lightning or sparks of flame depending on the lock spell all while screeching and yowling.

THE COWARD'S EMBLEM

Hamasa slid over the stone on his knees, catching against the side of the nearest cage.

"How do we unlock these stupid things? I don't think we got time to search for a key!" Marya exclaimed, letting out a little scream when the jolt arced up her arm.

"Go for the mundanes. The animals without magic. Those locks should be magicless, too. Hit them. Bash them. Whatever it takes," Hamasa said, frowning at the magicked padlocks, one in each of his hands, and ignoring the sparks that flew around his palm. Inside, the chanaces — two in one cage, three in the other — backed away as much at they could, snarling and spitting at the lock.

"Bash it? A rock, or a... right," Marya raced away.

Without the shadow spell, it was even easier to call heat. Fire against fire was... messy, inelegant, but it would be fast. His palm heated, the locks glowed ruby red, and there was a *pop* inside Hamasa's mind. Iron melted between his fingers and he yanked the locks off.

The chanaces slowly crawled out, the torchlight falling over them so Hamasa could see them clearly. At first glance, they looked more like human children than anything else. Tiny little humans whose heads and noses were too big and their ears pointed. Then, they bared mossy green teeth and their eyes gazed up at Hamasa. Fathomless and dark, like the shadows that had gathered in the lines of the Guanabánoch portrait. Shadows pulled from under the trees and the passing of clouds. Although they were awake, their movements were sluggish and they crawled more than walked, spring-green soles of their bare feet showing.

Hamasa grabbed the next lock and Marya came back with a knife, the hilt heavy and thick and wrapped in leather. He yelped aloud, jerking back his hand.

"What happened?" Marya asked, hesitating at the largest cage. "Is it okay to just... let out a jaguar?"

"It's fine, I'm fine," Hamasa snapped. His eyes narrowed at the locks on the lohas' cages that fizzled with lightning rather than fire. It hurt in a way the other lock spell hadn't.

"I wouldn' do that, kids. Jaguars don't play nice," warned a low, rough voice with a heavy accent Hamasa couldn't place.

Marya and Hamasa spun around. Marya held out the knife on reflex, her jaw tight and her bushy brows lowered. The man in front of them had a blunt, heavy-ended club barely bigger than the man's hand — a sap — in his grip; the streaks of soot and sweat and the bloody swell of his fattened bottom lip made him more a wild animal than a man.

16

"Come any closer and we'll see who plays nice," Marya spat.

Past the sneering and bloodied poacher, Hamasa watched as Valerius drove his elbow into the other man's chest, only to then grunt and fall forward as the woman slammed a crossbow across his back.

Hamasa's attention snapped back to the man with the club standing right in front of him. Almost negligently, the sap arced through the air and the knife in Marya's hand clattered to the ground. She clutched at her wrist with a bitten off shout, and Hamasa dropped, cheek to stone, as the sap whizzed over his head. He kicked at the man's knees, only for him to move away easily and kick at Hamasa's stomach, a lot more successfully than Hamasa's flailing. He gasped, tears springing into his eyes at the pain. By all the Sun's light, he hated pain. He was so weary of it.

Fingers dug into his hair, pulling him up, and Hamasa snarled, lashing out with his fingernails. They scored across a stubbly, sooty cheek, dragging up welts over the sunken expanse of the man's thin face. Hamasa dropped back to the ground with a loud curse from the man, and he stared at his hand, eyes wide and lips shaking.

He had... he had done that. He'd tried to...

A boot cracked against his ribs and Hamasa gagged, bursting into messy, silent sobs against the stone. He'd... he could've... He didn't even feel the next kick.

Though, maybe that was because Marya had let out a

warrior's scream and leapt on the man. Looking up through blurry eyes and wetly tangled lashes, Hamasa stared as Marya grabbed each side of the sap and tucked it under the man's chin, shouting wordlessly as she yanked it back, hard, against his throat. His fist connected with her cheekbone, but she merely growled like the jaguar she'd tried to free, tightened her short, bow legs around the man's waist, and yanked again with all her considerable strength. His head snapped back under the sap, there was a sickening *crack*. And his legs gave out, his knees smacked to the stone, and he slumped back, Marya falling to the ground under him with a wheeze and groan.

Hamasa crawled over and, with shaking hands, pushed the dead body away. Marya stared up at him, black eyes too wide and her face ashen under her tan. Slowly, he helped her sit up and she looked down at her hand. The one still clutching the sap in a white-knuckled grip. With a small, quiet cry, she dropped it. They watched it clatter and then roll a short length away.

"I did that," Marya whispered. Even though the shadow spell was gone, her voice was reedy, thin. Nothing like Marya. There was a loud thud, a broken off shout.

"Valerius?" Hamasa gasped, spinning around.

The knight was already tying the two others back to back in a complicated series of knots. Both unconscious. Another shadowy lumped showed where the first poachers was left lying and tied up alone. Valerius met Hamasa's eyes across the room. Then, he glanced towards Marya, who was still staring at the dead man near her toes.

"Finish the job," Valerius said, voice clear and echoing. Emotionless.

Marya flinched as if struck and sniffled. "He's right. They might come back. Dunno if the Salvatropas are out there yet," she said grimly. She hesitated only a second before picking the sap back up again. The heavily weighted end of it was banded in iron. A lot easier to use than a knife hilt.

Hamasa looked back at Valerius. The knight nodded once and picked up a dagger. The same dagger that had almost stabbed Hamasa earlier. He swallowed hard and crouch-walked his way back to the lohas' cages. Which were swinging open. The chanaces were nowhere to be seen, and the jaguar was already gone. Marya looked around wildly, her hand on the top of its cage.

"Let out the monkeys, Marya. The jaguar is safe," Hamasa said, his smile weak and trembling. Marya blinked at him, and slowly returned the smile, though it didn't reach her eyes.

"All right." In the next second, she began to pound on the lock as the monkeys screeched sleepily.

Hamasa crawled to the last cage, where the páhalebra waited with golden eyes and drooping wings. "Hello, friend," he whispered. It nodded, feathers rustling.

He reached for the lock, braced for the lightning, and gritted his teeth through it. Heat against fire might be inelegant, but heat against lightning was painful. A thousand cuts against his palm, and the heat make the blade dull rather than sharp. Not exactly helpful. As hot as he could make his skin, this was pushing the limits, edging up against a fine line between what was natural and too much. Deep inside his chest, there was a wound. An emptiness. And he was poking at it, prodding it, threatening to rip it a little bit deeper, wider. And then the spell on the lock burned with a eye-searing flash and the iron melted with ringing drips to the floor. He tugged the padlock off and the páhalebra slithered from its cage.

In awe, Hamasa watched it wend and wind its way through the air, stretching its full wingspan. The torchlight limned its scales, showing how subtly beautiful its deep blueish green body truly was. Tiny, clawed fingers tugged at his ears, his hair, and a loha fluttered right in front of his face, distracting him from the páhalebra. The tiny vain things always wanted all the attention, and Hamasa laughed, wincing and hissing as they inspected him closely.

"Too small, it doesn't fit, where are your wings, poor thing," they chattered and giggled at him, all their voices melding together inseparably.

His laugh broke off.

"Hamasa? What are they doing?" Marya asked, creeping closer. She had an armful of drowsing monkeys, their long golden brown tails falling over her arms like untied obi.

"They're doing what they do best. Teasing," Hamasa said with a quiet sigh. They all chittered giddily, one so close to his ear he flinched. They also liked to bite, and who knew when their little bit of restraint would end.

"Should I... help?" Valerius asked uncertainly from somewhere behind Hamasa.

"No, it's fine. They'll get bored — oh," Hamasa broke off as the long, sinuous páhalebra draped gracefully around him. The lohas scattered, hissing their annoyance and inventive curses that made him very glad Marya couldn't understand them. The páhalebra's wings fluttered, Hamasa's hair dancing and his eyes squinting against unsettled dust. After a long, silent moment of those golden eyes gazing at him, the páhalebra slowly, deliberately, raised its jaw.

Páhalebras looked like serpents, but they were armored like dragons, with thick scales that were deceptively supple and sleek. The only weak spot, the spot that could kill them, was just behind the jaw, where the scales were truly thin and smaller than Hamasa's smallest toenail. The scales there were a brighter, bluer blue than any where else, and, when he placed his shaking fingers there, warm. Incredibly warm. His nails scraped gently. The páhalebra dropped its head and gazed at Hamasa.

He swallowed hard and slowly lifted his chin. Needle-like teeth pressed to his throat and those wings spread wide. Hamasa shuddered, eyes closing against the sting of more tears. This pain wasn't physical like before. It was *longing*.

And then the páhalebra was gone, undulating through the air like the Storm Dragons of old Empire.

"What... in the name of the Sovereign was that?" Marya demanded.

"It said thank you." Hamasa got to his feet and dusted off the knees of his trousers. "If they're not back already, then the cabadonas must be outside waiting for us."

"We can only hope. No one planned for a sudden fire," Valerius said dryly. Hamasa's ears burned and he ducked his head.

"I w-was improvising..."

"Some improvising. How'd you get the fire that big so fast?! And what spell melts locks? You gotta teach me that one!" Marya said with a wide grin. "That's useful."

"It is," Hamasa agreed edgily.

Valerius hefted the lone poacher over a shoulder and grabbed the other two where they were tied together to drag them up the ramp. He got a few paces, Marya and Hamasa right behind him and Hamasa wondering how he could help as his vision went spotty and his balance wobbled, when the sound of footsteps echoed down from the corridor. Valerius' feet slid over stone, his stance widening and lowering, and raised the long dagger he had apparently decided to keep. Next to Hamasa, Marya raised her stolen sap, expression set and pale.

A vaguely familiar woman with a shaven head and blue wren tattoo stepped into view.

"Well, looks like you did clean up. Good job, Señor Lance," the woman said with a mocking grin complete with an Imperial salute—a double-tap of her fist to her heart.

Valerius scowled, his stance dropping with the dagger. "Your help is unnecessary."

"I see that now. Though, leaving a body to rot in here is bad for the magic," the woman—no, cabadona—said after a quick look around. Marya stiffened at Hamasa's side, a tiny click in her throat audible only to her and him. "Gotta let the forest have that."

Valerius grunted and dragged the unconscious poachers up the ramp. The cabadona made just enough room to let him pass, grinning when one of the prisoners groaned. Hamasa and Marya hurried after him, suddenly desperate to be anywhere else but there.

"Too bad his face is always like that. He'd be good breeding stock otherwise," the cabadona said with a rather over dramatic sigh.

"Only if 'good breeding stock' means a pain in the butt," Marya muttered darkly.

"I'm pretty sure that was a joke, Marya. Cabadonas don't actually steal men for breeding," Hamasa told her, shrugging a shoulder awkwardly. He didn't know why his skin suddenly felt too small.

"Huh. Well, he does fight good. Let one get past him, but he didn't even have a weapon. Would be nice to fight like that," Marya said, her voice dropping low and pained. She looked down at her armful of monkeys. "I hated 'em, all of them, for hurting these little guys and all those others. But I didn't think... I didn't think I could kill someone so easy."

Hamasa glanced over at her. All the torches were behind them, and with nightfall outside there wasn't any stray sunlight to help see her expression. But he didn't think he needed to.

"You did it because you had to. You helped me, maybe saved me, pretty sure my ribs were one more kick from broken. You were brave," Hamasa said softly. He reached out to pat her shoulder, affectionate and brief, as she often did for him. There was a quiet sniffle, but she didn't disagree. "Thank you, Marya. Is your wrist...?"

"*Ay*, it's still sore. I couldn't even lift one of these little guys with it, but I'll be fine in no time. Just need a wrap. Oh, mirda, my shovel," Marya groaned, head tilting back. "Maybe that Salvatropa will bring it back up with the rest of the stuff?"

"I'm sure she will," Hamasa reassured her, patting her shoulder one more time.

17

Marya's wrist wasn't completely broken, but it wasn't exactly not broken. Fractured, the village healer said. Marya's wrist was then set with a thin stick carefully shaved and shaped, and then wrapped tight. Tight enough that Marya complained to Hamasa that she couldn't feel her fingers. They left the village healer's home, Marya still wiggling her fingers with a grimace and one hand around her bandaged wrist. Outside, they saw Valerius with the Salvatropas and those same colorfully, well-dressed villagers—and a few gawkers listening in.

"You're sure they won't be able to escape?" Valerius asked one of the villagers. The man shook his head.

"I assure you, Señor, Tenienta, there will be multiple volunteers on watch. All of them our strongest and armed," the villager explained.

"We both made sure they were unarmed and tied up tight, they're not going anywhere, Riyukezan," Sitlal reminded him. She grinned toothily, looking more like a jaguar than a cabadona. "At least, not until I drag them into San Yamarasu to face the Sicho's justice myself."

"The Sicho?" Marya asked as she and Hamasa stopped beside her.

"Yes, the Sicho in San Yamarasu is the voice of the Sovereign's will in most of the northern region," Sitlal answered. "His wealthy

THE COWARD'S EMBLEM

peers may be the buyers, but having the criminals thrown in his face means the Sicho will have to enact the Sovereign's justice on them."

"And you'll be paid for each one you bring in," Valerius said dryly. The villagers muttered under their breath, a few looking daggers at him, the others mostly uncomfortable or confused.

Sitlal only laughed. "If you'd like to drag that sorry lot to San Yamarasu and get the bounty yourselves, it'll save me the trouble. You've more than earned it."

At Hamasa's side, Marya shuffled awkwardly. When he turned, she grimaced and muttered under her breath, "I dunno if I want anything like money for it." Hamasa hesitated before knocking their shoulders together, making her smile over at him slightly.

Valerius' shoulders squared, his jaw tensing and chin rising. "I am not a bounty hunter," he said—almost spat.

Eluya scowled from Sitlal's other side, one hand stroking the smooth, curved wood of her shortbow as she glared at Valerius. Tepin, still on two legs, leaned hard against Eluya's side.

"Neither are we, Riyukezan," Sitlal said. Although she smiled, the inflection on the word Riyukezan was a warning, her dark eyes glinting. She wasn't announcing his title in front of all these villagers on purpose, and Valerius' spine somehow managed to straighten more, arms crossing over his chest. "Bounties are a side benefit, not the goal to the Salvatropas."

"She's already refused our own meager offers for a reward," one woman villager said. "If you would like to be paid, Señor, the offer will be extended to you."

Valerius stared at the woman, lips thinning. Hamasa rushed forward, setting a hand on Valerius' arm. "N-no, thank you, Señora. No reward. We were happy to help."

"Our friend calls it being honorable," Marya said with a sly grin. "It's one of his few good traits."

The village woman's slight frown eased and she smiled at the two. "That's very generous of you, but there must be something we can do to repay you. All of you. I'm Eleni Loparrez, the village head. Let Ristahe show you our gratitude."

"Just a comfortable place to sleep would be enough, Señora," Sitlal assured her.

"Your offer is kind and we appreciate it," Valerius said, slowly frowning as he spoke, dredging up the politest words he knew. "However, we should really continue on."

"You wish to leave?" Señora Loparrez said, rather aghast. "We really can't allow that! It's so late and you're so young, and this one is injured. You'll stay and let us thank you. I insist."

"Insist... on thanking us?" Valerius repeated, eyebrow lifting.

"Not used to peasant hospitality, Riyukezan?" Eluya sneered.

Sitlal rolled her eyes before smiling down at the villagers. "Señora Loparrez, we would be honored."

The woman, Loparrez, pressed her hand to her heart with a relieved sigh. "I'm glad to hear it. None of us would feel right if we let you young'uns disappear into the night without even a bit of dinner. Tenienta Sitlal, I know cabadonas don't usually sleep inside..."

"Just an awning and some blankets will do. Though, Tepin wouldn't mind a bed for the night."

"It'll make a nice change," Tepin agreed, stretching her arms over her head.

"The Loparrez ranchita is more than large enough for all of you," Señora Loparrez said graciously. "Follow my son, please, and my family will bring you everything you need."

A young boy, black hair falling over his face and dark eyes wide and staring in awe at the Salvatropas, ran forward. He tugged at his ear and grinned, brown cheeks rosy. "I'm Mateo!

THE COWARD'S EMBLEM

You can come with me."

Marya stepped up, pulling Hamasa behind her. He tripped behind her with a glance towards Valerius. The knight fell in step beside Sitlal, silent and scowling. Mateo led them back to the same walled ranchita they had used for their private talk hours ago. Every doorway was filled with wide-eyed people, many of them children. A few older children were stringing up square-ish paper lanterns of every bright color imaginable — mostly red and yellow and blue — with interesting cut outs. When the candles inside were lit, the shapes revealed more clearly the flowers and dragon faces, a pearl struck through with lightning, dancing lohas and flocks of stylized birds in flight. Hamasa paused under a bright red lantern, the face cut into it not the usually depicted Empire's Grey, but a Red dragon; face long and thin with spikes cresting the head and stylized flames erupting from the open maw and falling around the edges like snowflakes.

Swallowing hard, he forced his eyes away and found his seat beside Marya. Valerius followed soon, sitting beside Hamasa with his hands clasped over his knees and his back ramrod straight. Over and over, the Loparrez family, and many more besides, came up to them with questions and praises and thanks in between huge platters of food. The cabadonas stood near the jacaranda tree, Tepin sitting against the twisted old trunk with her human legs sticking out awkwardly in front of her. A small interchanging group of teenagers and a few elders spread out over pillows and low stools while playing instruments or singing. The strumming of the vihuelas and guitarróns, the bright clatter of spoons and castanets, the high sweet whistling of ocarinas in the shape of birds and horses all joined together in beautiful, heart-thumping harmony. Listeners clapped or tapped their feet and kept up conversations, while still more continuously brought in and took out platters and jugs.

Although the music was lively and the people kind, Marya remained quiet beside Hamasa. She only really spoke when someone spoke to her first, pulling out a beaming smile as she answered a question, and sinking into pensive silence as soon as the interaction ended. She didn't even eat much, picking at most of it with a spoon, wrinkles crossing her forehead and her brows pulled so close together they made almost one line.

"Marya?" Hamasa murmured. She blinked and raised her head sluggishly. "Are you tired? You don't have to force yourself to stay awake for this."

She blinked again. Then she grinned, sudden and bright, and shook her head. "No, Hamito, I'm not sleepy. Just thinking too hard. Didja try the chiles reyenos? I thought you'd like that."

"I liked it!" Hamasa said enthusiastically, trying not to let his relief show when she smiled wider. "It should be spicier, though. I thought it would be."

"It's spicy enough," Valerius said. "You can have this sauce they gave me. I won't eat it."

He passed a small clay dish full of fresh salsa closer to Hamasa's plate. This time, Marya actually laughed, small and quiet enough to be a giggle. Immediately, her shoulders drooped and she slowly got up from the table.

"I think I'll go talk to Sitlal and the other Salvatropas. Do you think you can handle Big and Mean by yourself?"

"Mean?" Valerius repeated with a frown.

"I'll be fine," Hamasa said quickly. Marya nodded and walked towards the jacaranda tree and the group of people surrounding the cabadonas laughing and chatting gaily. He frowned at Marya. Her shoulders were still slumped, her pace slow and trudging. "Do you think she's all right?" he couldn't help asking Valerius.

"The healer said it won't take long. Maybe we can find a potion in a larger-sized village soon," Valerius answered. He set aside his spoon, and the half-full platter, and went for the large basket of fruit instead.

Hamasa stared at him uncomprehendingly. Valerius had already cut several slices of fresh guava, the white meat of it glistening with juice when he finally noticed Hamasa staring at him. Valerius frowned and held out his dagger with the slice of guava on it. On reflex, Hamasa took it, but merely held it and watched Valerius cut the next piece.

"I meant emotionally," Hamasa said at last. Valerius' hands froze.

"I don't... I'm not skilled in that area," the knight said haltingly.

"You don't think she looks or sounds sad?" Hamasa asked, looking towards her. She did look a little lighter where she stood speaking to a group of Loparrez family members, but her hands were still, her movements contained, not gesticulating or making huge sweeping gestures. She didn't even speak loudly.

"I've never been good at telling how someone feels. Facial cues especially are beyond me," Valerius admitted. "My guess, if she isn't acting herself, is that it's a reaction to what happened at the temple. The man that died."

Hamasa nodded. "Yes, I thought so, too. It was awful." His gaze dropped to the dripping fruit in his hand.

"If she thought speaking to you about it would make her feel better, then she would speak to you. Otherwise, she needs to work through it on her own," Valerius said.

"I don't like that, but even if she did talk to me, I wouldn't know what to say," Hamasa said, laughing ruefully. He slipped the guava into his mouth. "Could I ask you a personal question?"

"If you must."

Hamasa snorted, quickly ducking his head. "You said you can't read facial cues well. And the other Lances called you

'Kaecus', that means blind one, doesn't it? And everything that Kelso said—"

"Faces mean nothing to me. They haven't my whole life," Valerius said, tone short and clipped. "It was easier, as a child, because I didn't know anything was wrong. I didn't have many people in my life, either, so I didn't have many to confuse or forget. Becoming a page really showed me how blind I was."

"Sorry, I shouldn't have asked," Hamasa whispered, cringing guiltily.

Valerius sighed and held up a hand. "I have no secrets from you, m..."

"Masa?" Hamasa prompted, huffing under his breath. He glanced around the courtyard again. A number of children had slumped into adults' arms, half-asleep or snoring without a care. The music was quieter, soothing, as a young man played on the last ocarina. "Gatherings like these must be hard."

"They don't happen often," Valerius said.

"They don't?"

Valerius shook his head and began cutting guava slices again. "Most Lances don't leave Riyushu. The few who do are only away for short missions that need to be done efficiently and swiftly. There's no room to make friends." As he spoke, he took turns passing a piece to Hamasa or taking it for himself. "Civilians see us walk by, they might wave or stare in awe. For the most part, Lances lean into the awe. It builds a distance. We can't be held back by personal emotions, we serve first and last."

"The Riyukezan way is detachment," Hamasa said quietly. "There's such a difference between Riyushu and everywhere else in Mekshi. It's two completely different worlds. Maybe the Salvatropas have it right."

"Personal attachment blurs the thin line between justice and vengeance. The Arm and Lance of the Sovereign should strike without bias or anger," Valerius recited in a tone without any inflection.

Involuntarily and so suddenly he couldn't stop it, Hamasa laughed out loud. "There always will be bias. That's how humanity works."

"Humanity. Saying that as an impartial observer?" Valerius asked.

"No!" Glancing at the knight, then quickly at the table, Hamasa heated all over. "And that distance m-might, uh, prevent some bias or vengeance, but..." He swallowed a lump in his throat and looked around the courtyard, the strings of lights and the comforting, welcoming strangers. "It means you miss all of this."

Valerius snorted softly. But he didn't argue again. When Hamasa gathered up enough courage to look, Valerius' eyes were on the Salvatropas. His hand curled over his mouth, brows lowered, but overall he was relaxed with a heavy-lidded and sleepy gaze. Hamasa ate the last slice of guava and got up. Valerius jerked upright, standing to attention while Hamasa stood. The heat was back, burning Hamasa tomato-red, and he skittered away from the table.

"Don't do that!" he hissed at Valerius. They headed towards the jacaranda tree with Valerius a few steps behind.

Marya jumped up when she saw them, a much easier and more real grin on her face. Sometime during the dinner, someone had woven fallen purple jacaranda blooms into her long, unruly braid and her lips were stained red by some kind of fruit. As soon as Hamasa got close enough, Marya swung an arm around his shoulders and tugged him close.

"Get bored with that one at last?" she asked, smirking up at Valerius.

"Just tired. And wondering if you're okay?"

She rubbed the side of her nose and cocked her head to the

side. "Ay, I guess. Thanks for asking, Hamito. Now, stop your fussing."

"We had a good talk. And I hope you remember it well, Marrita," Sitlal said.

Marya nodded, hand dropping and her smile with it. Replaced by her lips pressing together and a slight crease across her forehead. "I will think about it. I really will."

Valerius and Hamasa stared at her. A young man dozing near the tree, one hand loosely wrapped around a mango, sat up suddenly.

"What's goin—you goin' t'bed?" the boy slurred drowsily. Hamasa finally recognized him as Mateo.

"I didn't realize you were waiting for us," Hamasa said, eyes wide. Mateo grinned and shook his head like a wet dog.

"I asked to! C'mon, I'll take ya and I can go to bed, too," Mateo said eagerly, getting to his feet and yawning so widely Hamasa could see all his teeth.

"Until the morning then. Thank you again for you help," Sitlal said, raising a mug towards them.

Marya waved happily, Hamasa rather timidly. Valerius made a simple short bow.

18

MATEO LED them into the house through darkened halls lit by a single candle the young boy had stolen from a porch table on the way in. There were vague shapes of wooden slats hanging on the walls, the carvings on their surfaces too bathed in shadows to make out. The flickering pin-drop of candlelight made the vibrantly painted walls come alive—pink, yellow, red. Hamasa was so enamored with the colors, the designs of tile floor under his feet, he completely lost track of the turns. Luckily, it wasn't too far before they stopped. Hamasa yawned again while they waited for Mateo to open first one door, duck his head inside to look around, and then again at a second door.

"One room for the señorita and one for the señors," Mateo said, waving at the two doors in front of them.

"What!? No!" Marya exclaimed. She slapped a hand over her mouth sheepishly, but reached out with the other to drag Hamasa closer to her. "You sleep alone, buckethead," she said more quietly.

"I will not let Masa out of my sight."

"Please, not now." Hamasa sighed.

Mateo tugged his ear, glancing between them, then shrugged. "Ya got two rooms. I'm goin' to bed now." He gave the candle to Hamasa as he walked past and away.

"Marya, we won't leave without you tomorrow. It'll be fine,"

Hamasa said quietly. Marya glared at Valerius, nose scrunching. "You let me have your bed for weeks. Enjoy sleeping alone in a real bed again tonight."

"Fine. But!" Marya raised a finger to point right at Valerius' nose. "If you try to steal Hamasa again, the Salvatropas will help me find you."

"Understood." He opened a door and peeked into the room. He nodded once and then stepped back to let Hamasa enter first.

"You can go ahead. Wash up. I wanted to talk to Marya a bit. Oh, here, take the candle," Hamasa said handing it over. Valerius' eyes narrowed before he bowed, took the proffered candle, and stepped into the room. When Hamasa turned back to Marya after the door closed, she was leaning against the wall, her face almost completely in shadow. Only the flickering lanterns outside made any light, filtering through the cracks in the wooden shutters.

"You want to know what's going on?"

"If you'd like to tell me," Hamasa said. He set his back against the wall next to her, sliding down slightly to bend his knees, hands tugging at the hem of his tunic. The Mendes family still had his poncho, unfortunately. "Was it... Is it the man? From the temple?"

Marya sighed and brought her braid around to the front. She picked at the small flowers there, crushing them between her fingers as she plucked them free. The sweet, heady scent of them filled the small dark space between them.

"Yeah. I didn't know how to feel, and maybe I still don't, but I thought they musta killed before, right? I wanted to know if it gets easier," Marya admitted. "Didn't think Valerius' 'I'm better'n everyone' attitude would help, either."

"Does it?" Hamasa asked. "Get better?"

"No."

"Good. I'm glad. It shouldn't be easy," Hamasa said fiercely.

THE COWARD'S EMBLEM

Marya startled, fingers stilling on her hair, crushed petals falling from her head. With words stumbling over themselves, he hurried to add, "I don't think you were wrong, Marya! You did what you had to. But I wouldn't want someone like you to ever kill easily."

Eyes shining, Marya sniffled. She rubbed under the corner of her eye and half-chuckled. "Yeah. Yeah, I don't want it to, either. The Salvatropas don't kill, either. Not really, not if they don't have to. They don't normally do bounty hunts, either. But those poachers, they were stealing *Others*."

"I'm glad they took on a bounty hunt this time," Hamasa said. Marya nodded. "Did they help you? Do you really feel better?"

"Yeah. They, um, they said that sometimes, to be a protector, we have to learn to make the call. To do what we gotta to protect. We just need to know we tried our best, and did what was right, and hope next time the ending won't be so... so terrible."

"Do you... Do you want to? Keep going on? Keep trying your best?" Hamasa asked, eyes darting over her face.

She reached over, the last flowers in her hand scattering across the floor, and gripped his hand in hers. "I want to protect people. I want to help you. Everyone's talking about war, and if it comes, I'll be fighting in it just like my papi did." Hamasa's hand jerked in hers, heart leaping to his throat. "Protecting a friend from dying or killing strangers in the Sovereign's name... at least I know who I'm helping here."

Hamasa stared, mouth dry and lips trembling. Marya's half-cocked smile, neither happy nor sad, black eyes unwavering, cut through him. He squeezed her hands in his and forced his mouth into a tiny, quavering smile.

"I'm so glad I ruined your farm and not someone else's," he blurted. Marya laughed, curling towards him. They leaned against the wall, laughing softly, hands clutching too tight. "I'll go get the candle—"

"Don't bother. I'm gonna go straight to sleep," Marya interrupted with a hand up. She pulled away and shook her head hard enough any remaining flowers showered down. He knelt down with her, sweeping them into their open hands and dropping them out the nearest window into the courtyard. Marya bumped Hamasa's shoulder with a fist. "Sleep well, Hamito."

"You, too, Marya."

She slipped into her dark room, and Hamasa crossed his arms on the window. Settling his chin on his arms, he gazed into the courtyard. Only a few people were left, yawning and cleaning up, tables and chairs being taken away. Lanterns slowly being blown out and brought down. The cabadonas still sat by the jacaranda tree, woven blankets thrown around their shoulders and over their horsebacks. Instead of being shown to a room, Tepin remained with them and lay on a blanket on the ground. As if feeling his eyes, Sitlal turned towards him. She tapped her fist to her heart twice, and bowed. Bile burned and Hamasa pushed away from the window so fast he almost got dizzy. He retreated to the room, slipping in and closing the door with a quiet sigh. Inside, the candle, barely a stub now, sat flickering on the low table. Valerius sat on the edge of the bed, hands on his knees, eyes closed, wearing a fresh set of clothes. He looked up, and stood quickly.

"You didn't have to wait," Hamasa muttered. He tiptoed across the room to the bucket of water and clean rag waiting for him.

"I was about to come out and find you. You'd been silent a while," Valerius said.

Hamasa paused mid-wring, water dripping down his wrists. "Were you listening in?" he asked, horrified mostly for Marya's sake.

"Of course not, my lord. Just listening for voices."

Hamasa gnawed on his lip, then continued wiping down what bare skin he had showing. Lastly, he changed out of his dust-covered clothes to go to bed. It wasn't until he was lying straight and stiff as a board, that he realized he'd be sharing the bed with Valerius. The knight sat on the edge, hands on his knees again, then leaned over to blow out the candle. It smelled like soap and wool and linen and candle smoke, and Hamasa squeezed his eyes shut, as if it would block out the scents and the thoughts together. Valerius didn't move.

"Can you sleep like that?" Hamasa asked, peeking open one eye.

"No."

Hamasa stared into the darkness, frowning. "Are you going to sleep?"

"Of course not, my lord."

Hamasa huffed and sat up. The bed shifted as Valerius moved slightly. Silence. Hamasa leaned his head against the wall behind him and exhaled heavily through his nose.

"My lord?"

"Are you going to watch me?" Hamasa asked wearily. "While I *sleep*?"

"I'm not going to sleep on the same bed as my lord."

"I can't sleep with you just... just sitting there," Hamasa said, pulling his legs up and wrapping his arms around his shins. The bed shifted again and blankets rustled. "Are you lying down?"

"Yes, my lord."

Hamasa squinted. In the darkness, he could vaguely make out the shape of the knight reclining beside him. Also, he sounded very annoyed, his usual tone whenever having to agree with Hamasa. He crawled back into his side of the bed, grasping a pillow filled with beans and wrapping his body around it.

Closing his eyes, it was easier to hear the near silent sounds of Valerius' even breathing, the voices outside that faded to nothing, the steady thump of his own heart beat, until at last he fell asleep.

***

The dawn in the northern Mekshan autumn was a golden thing. It lit up the forest, the mountains, the great winding Road, and the sky overhead with streaks of gold so pure it reminded Hamasa of the páhalebra's steady, unending gaze. The poachers, kept unconscious with a simple draught until they could be brought to the nearest actual city, were tied up and slumped together on a cart bought from Ristahe, trading for anything the poachers had once owned that the Salvatropas hadn't claimed for themselves. Although they had only waited until dawn to leave, the Salvatropas were already antsy, hooves (and bare feet) cutting through sand, tails whipping through the air. Valerius wasn't much better. Sitlal, the leader, cantered to them, her hooves and tail giving away her restlessness as she shuffled in place.

"Did you think about our offer, Marya? There's always room in the Salvatropas for a fierce one like you."

Hamasa's head jerked up and his jaw dropped. "W-what?"

"They offered, last night," Marya said, rubbing the back of her neck, cheeks ruddy. "They don't only ask for cabadonas in the Salvatropas."

"My small unit now doesn't have a human or... Other... but that's by chance. Bad luck, really," Sitlal explained with a nod. "Our mage, a dala, remained behind at the main camp and I foolishly thought we'd be able to handle this without fuss. Which our fearless leader laughed at."

"She's always right," Tepin said, smirking ruefully. She

shifted the saddlebags thrown over her shoulders awkwardly. She was still in her two-legged body and it didn't seem to fit her after an entire night wearing it.

Hamasa tried not to utter another sound. He wanted to be happy for her. Marya deserved an offer like this. She was fierce and brave. But if she joined them, he would be alone with Valerius. Trying to figure out how to not get dragged all the way to Riyushu without someone getting hurt. Probably himself. He glanced towards the knight. He was standing by Nerva, his arms crossed over his chest and his narrowed, disapproving gaze on Sitlal. The cabadona had already noticed and was smirking unrepentantly at him.

Marya tossed the tail of her messy braid over her shoulder. "I think I gotta help Hamasa now. He needs me. Maybe one day I will. If the offer's still... uh, offered?" she said with a little chuckle.

"Hm. I'm sure your friend does need your help," Sitlal said, eyes sliding towards the one in question. Hamasa shivered under her cool dark gaze. It passed over him a moment later and she smiled at Valerius. "You were most helpful, Señor Lance. I would make the same invitation, but while humans are welcome, men certainly are not." She chuckled, her teeth baring.

A single eyebrow arched up Valerius' forehead. "I appreciate the spirit of your offer."

Sitlal's head tilted back in a laugh that ended with a piercing whinny-like sound. "I thought I knew your answer, but I wanted to give you a gift regardless. The offer to join us will always stand, Marrita." She held out a spear to Marya with a smile. Marya took it with one shaking hand, her bad arm pressed to her chest as if she were about to salute. "We noticed the weapon you left behind in the temple wasn't suitable for a warrior. Perhaps the Lance will teach you how to wield this properly. In service of your friend."

Hamasa frowned at Sitlal's sly smirk in his direction.

"A real spear? Not just a shovel?"

"Ah. A shovel. I suppose I lost that bet," Sitlal murmured.

Luckily, Marya was too busy spinning the spear in wide arcs around her. Even with her left hand, her movements were deft and sure. How often had she pretended that old shovel was the spear she carried now? Her eyes shined, mouth parted on a wide grin that lit up her face.

A warrior in the making, Hamasa thought with a sad smile and his chest constricting. She should go with them.

"We owe you a favor, and the Salvatropas hate being in debt," Sitlal said, interrupting Hamasa's thoughts. He looked up in time to see her cut a braid from her hair. It was tied with a leather string dyed bright red, a single copper bead around the end of it. She tied off the other end with the red leather, and then gestured for Marya to hand up the spear.

"You don't owe us, Salvatropa. We only did what Her Imperial Highness would have requested eventually," Valerius said, eyes on the braid she was twisting around the shaft of the spear under the iron tip.

"That's why I'm giving her the gift, Lance," Sitlal said with a loud snort. Valerius glowered, and Marya grinned at Hamasa.

"What about Hamasa? He's not a Lance," Marya pointed out.

"There's nothing I could give your friend he could not give himself," Sitlal said. She tied off the braid and met Hamasa's eyes. There was a challenge in her gaze, the tilt of her chin, the utter stillness of her hooves and tail and ears.

Hamasa broke her gaze first, tucking his hands under the borrowed poncho he had reclaimed from Señora Mandes a short time ago. Sadly, Pala had not been at the stall, fast asleep in their home somewhere in the village.

"If you need us, follow your spear," Sitlal wrapped her hand around it, covering the braid she'd tied there with her large, dark hand. Her eyes glowed blue. Hamasa's heart hammered, mouth dry, skin flushing hot. It wasn't the same hue, too dark, but it was blue. "What once was mine, shall find me again. Wherever you go, whichever way you roam. Just call to me, and it will lead you."

There was a *snap*, inaudible but for in his bones. Then, the spell settled and the blue was gone. Hamasa stared as Sitlal's hand moved and the simple braid remained. Looking unchanged. *Seeming* unchanged.

"We'll meet again, Marya. Lance. Friend."

Hamasa startled, eyes rising, and watched Sitlal bow. Behind her, the two others bowed in sync, and Hamasa wondered sourly if they practiced that. If their smirks were anything to go by... probably. His heart stuttered and tripped in his chest, and the cabadonas ran past them, even Tepin could keep pace—though they weren't running full speed yet. The few villagers that were awake raced down the Road after them, waving and cheering. The crowd swept the trio along with them. Some villagers stopped Marya to ask her about the spear, the braid, the offer to join the Salvatropas. Many of them congratulated her, or called her a fool for not racing away with the heroes right then. Marya only laughed and bloomed under the attention, rubbing at the side of her nose and flipping her curls behind her shoulder.

19

VALERIUS AND HAMASA managed to slip out of the crowd easily enough while Marya continued to say good-bye to the people of Ristahe. Perhaps Nerva's bulk and dangerous hooves helped them escape, but Hamasa was grateful regardless. Valerius stroked a hand down the line of the mare's face, whispering quiet Riyukezan words. Hamasa leaned against the saddle, picking at the edge of leather.

"I should've told her to go," Hamasa said.

"If she wanted to go, she would have," Valerius replied.

Hamasa scratched at the leather a little harder, frowning. "You really don't know her. Or maybe you don't want to."

"You could help explain."

Hamasa glanced up, watching as Valerius fed Nerva a sliver of dried apple. A brief, there and gone again, smile crossed his lips when the mare almost shoved him off his feet looking for more.

"She's like you."

Valerius met his eyes, absently patting Nerva's neck and waiting.

"Stubborn."

Valerius sighed. "We're not the only stubborn ones." Hamasa looked down at the saddle under his hand. "But I'll keep that in mind going forward. She's like me."

Hamasa moved away from the horse, turning his back on both of them. He didn't want the knight to see the amused smile he couldn't hold back. Marya running up to meet them couldn't have come at a better time.

***

The distant sight of the Salvatropas was gone in moments, and the blur of Ristahe was lost behind them not much later. Instead of continuing north towards San Yamarasu, Valerius turned west at the first fork a few hours after leaving Ristahe. Hamasa ducked his head to hide his smile under the fringe of hair when Valerius tossed Marya a gold coin without her asking first. She placed it at the small dende shrine at the fork, clapping her hands together and bowing her head like Hamasa had done the day before.

Other than the usual scatter of small villages and bigger trade towns, the largest city west of San Yamarasu was Róntraih Porto Cuidat. The fastest way to get down south to the Capital was taking a ship from there, Hamasa knew, and it made his pulse jump as they headed towards the lowering sun. Going west, the landscape began to change before the sun had set. The scarce forest was behind them, only low shadows smudging along the ground. The larger, more ominous shapes of the Ajul Mountains loomed further behind the hazy treeline. Now it was flat, grassy plains, the unending expanse broken up by low hills and occasional short, slender trees. After a brief rest for lunch, they managed a few more leagues that afternoon. When twilight reached over the horizon, they broke off a short ways away from the Road into a field and set camp near a stream. The ground sloped gently down to the water, the few short, wide-topped trees hiding even Nerva's bulk from sight of the Road.

Marya had kept ahold of her gift, the spear from Sitlal. She had absently spun and swung it around during their slow trek, carefully using only her left hand, gazing pensively at the pointed tip and the copper bead tapping against the wooden shaft. Even now, after they had set up camp and finally sat down to rest, she laid it across her lap, stroking up and down the smooth wood. At that moment, Valerius' large hands stroked over Nerva's back, gentle and soothing, checking for burrs or ticks, or whatever it is one did to take care of a horse, Hamasa wasn't quite sure. He barely knew how to ride one, honestly, but he could tell how docile she was under Valerius' careful examination. He couldn't help but remember the fleeting smile that had made Valerius seem as young as he truly was while Nerva tried to sniff out more treats.

"He didn't retie my ankles, or my wrists," Hamasa muttered. Marya glanced at him and he shrugged. "I thought he might now that we're back on the Road and we know the Salvatropas are out there."

"Someone thinks highly of himself. Think I can't get past you, Sir Valerius?" Marya said with a little shrug. She flicked the copper bead and grinned at Valerius when he scowled in their direction."What kinda name even is that?"

"Harenese," Hamasa said quietly.

Marya stared at Hamasa, then at Valerius. She tilted her head and squinted at Valerius a little more closely. "Huh. I was wondering why you were so big. Everyone always says the Riyukezu are shorter and smaller than Mekshans most the time, and you look Riyukezan, with the hair and everything, but if you're from some Harenae family, no wonder you're so tall."

"I am Riyukezan," Valerius said, coming to sit across the small cooking fire. He sat like one, kneeling with his feet tucked under his butt. "But I am Harenese, too. My family, it's an old one. From before the first war."

THE COWARD'S EMBLEM

"Never heard of an old Harenese family." Marya prodded at the embers of the fire with a stick, frowning slightly. "But I never could keep up with all those southern Mekshans, who rebelled and who got killed and who got some land and a fancy House."

"The first of my House *was* a southern rebel at first, one of the many old Mekshan wealthiest families that fought to keep their power and lands," Valerius told her. "We became Harenese later."

"So you're actually a noble!?" Marya exclaimed, gaping at him.

"My family is of the nobility on both sides, yes," Valerius said, mouth twitching at the corner. "After my Mekshan ancestor surrendered to the Stormwrought and helped rout the last of the rebels to push them into what became Harenae."

"If a giant Grey dragon showed up outta nowhere and blew in a typhoon in the middle of the dry season, I'd probably surrender, too," Marya said with a wry smirk. "I never been down that far south, but my mamá and papi have, and they said there's still whole cities buried and lost forever, especially in the southeast near Harenae."

"Mizukoro the Stormwrought wasn't known for her patience or her mercy," Hamasa said softly, trying not to shudder. All this talk about war was making his heart race and his skin heat.

"But Mekshi became a better place because of the Empire, my papi always said. Big paved roads, better houses and bigger ships for trade, and more universities, too. Guess it wasn't so great for those people back then, though," Marya said with a shrug. She glanced at Valerius. "But shouldn't you have a *Mekshan* name?"

"My ancestor gave it up and he would have everything else, but he married a Riyukezan noblewoman, which saved him some credibility. My father always told it like a love story, but my mother always told me it was a lot more political. It was a way for the Riyukezan woman, who normally wouldn't inherit, to have some power in this new country and the Sovereign and his council wanted an easy way to stabilize the border. Having someone who knew the area but couldn't usurp the shaky Riyukezan power made sense. They chose our House name after the alliance was sealed."

"I guess your mamá's probably right, but I still like your papi's story better. A lovely Riyukezan noble falling in love with a brave Mekshan warrior? That's the kinda stuff people like to hear," Marya said, grinning and leaning back on her hands. She immediately winced and lifted her left arm, listing to the right awkwardly.

"We should train," Valerius said, eyeing her grimace.

Marya stared at him and held up her bandaged wrist. "With this?"

"Yes." Valerius got to his feet and moved to the pile of their belongings. "In the Lances, we train with both hands. It'll be easier for you to learn the same if you can't rely on your dominant hand."

Marya's eyebrows jumped up high. "Why are you helping me? You think I won't knock you silly given a chance? I'm gonna try and get Hamasa away from you no matter what." She sat up straight and crossed her arms over her chest.

"Marya, don't make trouble," Hamasa said.

"These roads can be dangerous, and my priority is my lord's safety. Knowing you have something with which to protect yourself is one less thing for me to worry about," he said simply as he picked up his trident.

Marya blinked. Then, her head fell back as she laughed. "You're such a gulero!"

"Yes, I suppose we are both quite stubborn," Valerius agreed mildly. Hamasa dropped his face to his hands, trying desperately not to laugh or groan.

"Now, see here, ya bucket of loose nails," Marya got to her feet and stomped up to Valerius. She stopped right in front of him and shoved a finger to his breastbone. Hamasa was really glad Valerius had taken the armor off, because the thump of Marya's finger to his chest meant it would've hurt her if he'd still been clad in steel. Valerius' eyebrow went up, his eyes dropping to her finger. "I'll protect myself and Hamasa. And I'll do my damnedest to get us away from *you*, too. No matter how funny you get."

"I'm not trying to be funny." Valerius' dark gaze looked her up and down, lingering on her arms and legs, the road-grimed bandage around her wrist. Marya's dark cheeks flushed red. "You look sturdy," he said at last. Marya bared her teeth like a jaguar and Valerius took one step back. "Try it."

"Eh, what?" The wind dropped from her sails as she gaped up at him. Valerius' feet shifted minutely, his trident spinning in a lazy circle until he rested the butt end of it on the ground by his boot.

"You said you would... knock me silly, was it? Try. Use the spear."

"I'm not gonna hit you with the spear!"

Valerius raised an eyebrow. "You can try."

Marya huffed angrily and held the spear up and to the side, her good hand clutched around the middle, more like she was about to swing an axe than use a spear. Hamasa made a small noise, then quickly covered his mouth with his hand. Marya turned towards him, eyebrows rising.

And Valerius' hand was suddenly on the spear's shaft high above Marya's hand. She let out a yelp when he yanked her off balance, twisting the spear so quickly that she had to let go, fall, or get her shoulder popped out of socket. Her knees hit the ground, hard, and Hamasa hurried forward. His hands gripped her shoulders as she gritted her teeth and hissed. She knocked Hamasa's hands away to struggle to her feet on her own.

"Again! I wasn't looking!"

"Always look!" "Keep your eyes on me."

Hamasa and Valerius glanced at each other, Hamasa glancing away in the next blink. Marya stared at him.

"... Common sense?" Hamasa said hesitantly.

"Ay!" Marya shouted, shoving at him. She snickered, though, while Hamasa wobbled on his feet. Her one arm was a lot stronger than it looked. "You're right, I guess." Valerius held out the spear and, after a pause, Marya snatched it back to hold it the same as before. "Again?"

Valerius shook his head. Marya's face darkened, mouth wrenching open. Hamasa made a small noise, interrupting whatever rude thing she was about to say.

"You're holding it wrong," Hamasa whispered when she rounded on him.

"I... how can I hold it wrong? Ya whack like this, yeah?" Marya asked incredulously, swinging with all her might, bicep bulging under the loose sleeve of her tunic. Hamasa winced away from the wide arc of it. As she twisted through the swing, Valerius moved again. His one arm lifted to block and hold the spear in place, keeping Marya turned away and off-balance. Then, he tapped lightly at the back of her neck with the side of his other hand.

"That could be a dagger, a sword, or any other melee weapon," Valerius said calmly as Marya cursed violently. "A well-placed blow here can knock a man down."

"And you'd be dead," Hamasa added.

"Or unconscious," Valerius said.

"Like at the temple," Hamasa said, remembering those two

men. Valerius nodded.

"Huh." Marya looked between the blank-faced Valerius and the fidgety Hamasa. "All right. Show me."

Hands up and flailing awkwardly, Hamasa stepped away. "I'll r-leave it to the Lance. Lance. I... uh, I'll look for wood. Um. For the fire. And feed Nerva?"

"Don't wander too far, my lord," Valerius said with a small bow. The butt of the spear smacked his back. He turned with a scowl to see a smirking Marya twirling her spear lazily.

"Always look."

While Hamasa shuffled along the small creek under the bare trees searching for loose branches and twigs with one hand holding Nerva's reins, he could hear the grunts and thwacks and frustrated yells (Marya's) coming from behind him. A few times, unbidden and unwanted, he thought: *I have the horse. I'm far enough away, perhaps I could* — But then Marya would shout, sometimes triumphant, mostly exasperated. Once there was even a laugh, the carefree bright one that made Hamasa remember the long but comfortable days of recovery on the Garsia farm. He couldn't leave her behind when she had chased after him, refused to leave him, was determined to protect him from the 'crazy Lance'. Hamasa sighed and leaned against Nerva's withers. The mare's neck bent awkwardly around to lip at his sleeves.

"Right, dinner time." He smiled and patted her neck and began to lead her back to the camp site, his paltry bundle of twigs and broken down shrubs under one arm. His nose scrunched at the smell of himself and, with another pat at Nerva's neck, set the wood aside. "After something like a bath. I tas—*smell* like you. No offense."

Nerva didn't seem to be offended and took the chance to search along the stream bank for the greenest grasses. Meanwhile Hamasa splashed in the frigid water and tried his best not to overheat himself to compensate. He couldn't forget the feeling of that wound inside him, and how close he'd come to nudging it wider. He had to be more careful.

He finally returned to the camp and saw Marya leaning heavily on her spear. She was soaked with sweat, but grinning as Hamasa walked closer. Valerius wasn't nearly as winded, nor was he sweaty. He did, however, look younger than usual, his frown gone and something soft around his mouth and eyes. Hamasa looked away so quickly his neck creaked. Valerius shouldn't be so distracting. If Hamasa were truly honest with himself, his biggest problem wasn't the destination Valerius was aiming for. It was exactly who Valerius had turned out to be. Hamasa glanced to the trident lying near the packs, its brass finishings gleaming like gold in the firelight. The spear clattered to the ground next to it and Marya walked towards him.

"Oh, a bath. Great idea," Marya said, beating at Hamasa's back hard enough he gasped.

"You did well, Garsia. Don't forget to—"

"Watch my center, I know," Marya rolled her eyes at Hamasa. "Who knew my stomach muscles were so important." She leaned in close to murmur, "You gonna be okay while I wash up?"

"Of course. I think... I know he won't hurt me," Hamasa admitted with a slight duck of his head.

There was a quiet inhale and Hamasa flinched. Valerius stood at Nerva's head, one hand stroking her nose, his eyes on Hamasa.

"Didncha mother ever teach you not to listen in?" Marya huffed. She sauntered off with her things, glancing over her shoulder one more time.

Cringing away and eyes on the dirt, Hamasa sidled around the Lance to the small fire pit. It was easy enough to pile what he had found with what was already next to the stone circle. He slowly fed the thicker branches into the fire, watching as the wood caught and flamed higher. He looked down at his useless, blister-marked, soft hands, their pink palms and chipped, blunt nails and five fingers. Remembered the cart burning and the shadows scattering. The snap of the man's neck and Marya's ashen face when he rolled the limp body away. His lips pressed together. It was harder to remember the páhalebra, the violet and grey feathers and golden eyes. The warm scales as blue as the veins in his human wrist.

Steps approached and slowly, so slowly, as if approaching a skittish animal, Valerius crouched next to Hamasa. The distance between them was barely an arm's length, but Hamasa felt every handspan of it. Silence yawned in the space between them.

"I won't," Valerius said quietly. Hamasa stared harder at the flames. "Neither you nor your angry friend, I will keep you safe. You know the vows of a Lance."

"I'm not your Shield," Hamasa retorted hoarsely. "But I know the vows of a Lance. You would die for any citizen of Mekshi."

"I would fight for Mekshi and any citizen within it," Valerius disagreed softly. Hamasa glanced over at him. The long tail of his hair lay over his collarbone like a forgotten ribbon. The flames, small though they were, made his eyes gleam like onyx when he met Hamasa's gaze. "I would lay my life down only for my lord."

Hamasa flinched and looked to the fire again. There was too much weight, too many expectations, in those fire-lit onyx eyes. Behind them, Nerva's ears twitched. Hamasa's head tilted up, eyes squinting and nose high, mouth parted. Just barely, a flap of cloth in the breeze, the sound of… voices? Hamasa stood, Valerius beside him, one hand already reaching for his shoulder.

But the sounds were gone and Nerva dipped her nose back into her canvas sack of oats.

"My lord?" Valerius asked, frowning. Hamasa dodged his

hovering hand.

"I'm not your lord." He slunk away. After finding a low stone half-buried in grass and lichen, he sat with his arms around his shins and eyes closed.

20

Some time later, Hamasa hadn't bothered to keep track of time, Marya fell with a thump and sigh on the grass beside Hamasa's rock. Rather than her usual chatter, she allowed the quiet, taking out their things to set up for sleeping without preamble. After setting out their bedrolls, she dug out her mostly empty sack of marzipan and munched, eyes on the the stars emerging over their heads. At Nerva's soft whicker, Hamasa looked up to see Valerius emerge from the shadows. He dropped his eyes to his knees again, face too hot under the fringe of his bangs when he realized Valerius was coming back from the stream, his upper torso bare, his hair loose and shining with damp. He shouldn't notice or care that Valerius was bare to the waist or that his hair clung to the lines of his neck and collarbone like shining threads of black silk. He almost missed the string of fish the Lance carried towards the fire.

"Ugh, he thinks he can just walk 'round like that, with his stupid fish, and think he's better'n us," Marya muttered, viciously tearing into a piece of marzipan. "Don't he know there's ladies present? That's me, I mean," she added quickly to Hamasa, "I'm ladies."

"I didn't take offense being called a lady, even indirectly," Hamasa said with a fleeting smile.

Marya chuckled under her breath and took another large

bite of marzipan. When she swallowed, she cleared her throat. "Should we, I dunno, be planning an escape? How many chances are we gonna get like this?"

Hamasa gnawed his bottom lip thoughtfully, but shook his head. "We don't have horses. Even if we manage to get away, he'll be on our trail within minutes. I don't know this area well enough to find a place to hide, Marya."

Marya frowned, then bullsnorted her irritation. "I don't know this road much, either. Mamá and me usually sell our harvest to the caravans that come through. I've never been this far west. I think if we get to the city, we can escape pretty easy. It's huge!"

"Which city is it again?" Hamasa asked, chewing on his thumbnail rather than his lip.

"Róntraih Porto Cuidat." Ah, yes, that was familiar. Hamasa pictured the map, eyes narrowing as he dredged up the half-remembered details. "Stupid name. I guess some noble did it. Nobles really like to name everything after themselves. You don't see the Sovereign doing that," Marya said with a judgmental little sniff.

Hamasa looked over at her curiously. "You really like the Sovereign."

Marya puffed up her chest, smirking proudly. "A'course! She's the most beautiful and smartest Sovereign in the whole world. They say she's got eyes like the sky, 'cuz of her dragon blood."

"Dragon blood?" Hamasa repeated, the side of his mouth lifting incredulously. "I didn't realize it was so broadly talked about."

"She's so young, too! They say that even for a kid, only seven, the Sovereign was the smartest and wisest Sovereign we've ever had, *and* she has magic like no one has ever seen before!" Marya continued eagerly.

"She is one of a kind," Hamasa said quietly. Blue eyes and black hair. The smell of lotus and burnt rice tea. His hands curled into the loose folds of his trousers. "Unlike anyone else."

"There's a reason why you swore your allegiance to her," Valerius said from where he stood in front of them. Both friends yelped and flinched away. Marya recovered quicker than Hamasa and rolled her eyes at the knight. Valerius smoothed his hair out of his face and sat within arm's length next to Hamasa. He, thankfully, had replaced his kimono—with another pure white linen kimono, how did he keep them so clean?—tucked and folded into his hakama and obi. He pulled a leather string free from around his wrist. "Her grandfather and the Scarlet Dread Shield were the most powerful Chosen Pair in history since the Stormwrought and the First Sovereign. An era of true peace and widespread education."

"Until the War happened," Marya said with a pained grimace. "My papi came back with pieces missing, and I don't mean half his leg. It was like he'd never left the battlefield, waking up in the dead o' night, screaming and hollering... and crying..." Marya rubbed a hand over her eyes.

Valerius' mouth tightened. "Sangsierpe should never have summoned the Merciless. I've seen what's left of that country, the black rubble the Beast left behind and the poisonous mists. Before it came Mekshi's way."

"The Scarlet Dread died the day the Merciless entered Mekshi," Hamasa hissed, eyes flashing though the fire was too far to reflect against them. "He died to protect his Sovereign and a child was Chosen in the place of a hero."

"Hamasa?" Marya stared at him, heavy brows drawing together at the outburst. His jaw tightened as he looked away. "People have wondered why Kana'iro didn't Choose the Sovereign's father, or mother, or anyone older. Do you think the

Shield was wrong?" Marya asked quietly, so quietly the crackle of wood in the fire pit almost drowned her question.

Hamasa stared at his knees, the bumps of his knuckles, the sheen of scar tissue on his arms that peeked out from the fringe of his poncho.

"Maybe..." he whispered. The word dragged out of him like shards of glass. It tore his throat, his lungs, what was left of his heart and the edges of the brokenness inside him. He closed his eyes, swallowed the glass and pain. "Maybe."

"I saw him when he first came, when he bowed to her that day seventeen years ago." Hamasa felt Valerius' eyes on the side of his face, but he refused to look. "He saw in her what no one else did. It wasn't a mistake. You are not a mistake. You are the Shield—"

Hamasa got to his feet and walked away. He didn't look back to see the flabbergasted face Marya would make, or to try to decipher whatever stoically-controlled expression Valerius had. He didn't care how rude it was. He didn't care what they thought about his actions; he couldn't listen anymore. To Valerius' certainty, his belief in something that didn't exist anymore. *The Shield was dead.* The sooner that courageous and strong Sovereign realized it, the sooner everyone in this Sun-forsaken country realized it, the better.

He knew the layout of Róntraih Porto Cuidat rather well from his studies. He would manage to get away, from Valerius and Marya both, and take the first ship out of Mekshi. To anywhere else. Except the remains of Sangsierpe where no one ventured anymore. He would hide out in Harenae itself if it weren't for the Green dragon guarding the would-be King. Someone that old would sniff his magic out the moment he stepped foot on their only shore. There were the Dreikstan Islands to the far south, the distant continent of Pansa in the north, the old country of the

THE COWARD'S EMBLEM

Riyukezu, Osekai, so far west it became east.

Branches snapped and leaves rustled. As usual, their footsteps were too heavy. With a gusty exhale that shook his chest, he turned, ready to face Valerius the Stoic or Marya the Disappointed. Only to see the tall yellow grasses swaying in the wind. The light of the campfire was a pinprick in the distance and he frowned. He hadn't realized he had walked that fast or that far.

"Looks like you dropped your Lance, Kana'iro the Red."

A chill swept down his spine. He spun around, overbalancing slightly and wobbling on his feet. Two men melted into being from the shadows of the trees. There weren't even that many trees around here! He stumbled back, his flight response kicking in with its usual gusto. But the man with short hair and a broad, smirking grin was fast. So fast it had Hamasa shouting aloud as he jerked back and fell to his butt on the grass while Señor Smirk loomed over him.

He wore studded leathers dyed ruby red, gilt in gold and black, and dusty from travel. A bronze cuirass was molded to fit his broad shoulders and slender waist, shaped to mimic the musculature of his stomach with heavily padded shoulders broadening his silhouette further. Bronze clasps held a blood-red cloak long enough that the hem brushed his calves. His legs were bare under the hanging leather straps of his armored-skirt, and the bottom of his long tunic was the same length as the padded under-armor. Leather sandals, with thicker soles and more straps than the Mekshan style, were tied around his shins. A broad but short sword hung at his waist. The other man wore an outfit much the same, though his long, pale hair was tied back in a braided horsetail and a crossbow was held easily and familiarly in his hands. Already loaded and pointed at the ground near Hamasa's head.

"I'm n-not who you think I am!" Hamasa stammered, crab-walking backwards on his hands.

Their garb swiftly recognizable now, he knew exactly who these men were. That man's sword, the gladius, was a specialty of a certain legion of fighters; Harenae centurions, the most ferocious and well-trained army in the world. It was said their training was facing down venomous beasts and surviving weeks in the hottest pits of the Harenese desert, that tiny nothing territory in the south of Mekshi that was trying to be something. Their centurions had gone a long way to building the reputation the self-claimed King and Commander of Harenae wanted now to take advantage of. Before the unrest had grown in recent years, Riyukezan and Mekshan Lances alike were trained in the punishing Harenese sands and the seedy, ramshackle port towns alongside hard-eyed Harenese soldiers, desperate to prove themselves for the chance at true Imperial citizenship. Over the years, Harenese ranking systems, weapons, and some of their armor styles were adopted by the Lances. Until the desperation soured to resentment, and the resentment into violence, culminating in the Imperial patrols and Lances-in-training being attacked in broad daylight, but no witnesses stepped forth to name perpetrators. The territory began to call their culture their own, no longer Mekshan or under the Empire, and never Riyukezan — they were of Harenae.

"I think you're exactly who I think you are," the smiling one said.

Hamasa's mouth was too dry to retort, if he'd been brave enough to try. *Why do the scary ones never believe me!?* he thought desperately.

"I'm a Prefect Tribune Officer of the Harenae legionnaires, Gaius Tarcinius Varro. You are my prisoner, Kana'iro the Red, to be taken to the King of Harenae," the centurion, or prefect officer as he'd introduced, said with a glaringly bright and confident grin.

"He isn't a king," Hamasa replied dumbly. *So dumbly! What did I just say?!* he shrieked inside his own mind. Gaius' confident grin twitched.

The centurion reached down to grasp Hamasa's arm, yanking him to his feet and then gently dusting him off, like a father to his son. Hamasa bristled, squirming away and doing his best scowl.

"I'm n-not who you're roo-looking for, so r-*let* m-me go," he stated, exasperated and terrified at once.

Gaius glanced at his crossbow-wielding companion. "You're sure Eztal's token didn't lead us astray, Flavius?"

The pale-haired man nodded. "The pulse is weak, but it *is* reacting to his presence." He said it hesitantly, fair brows lowering.

"What is it?" Gaius asked, swiftly looking back to Hamasa. His gaze dragged slowly up and down Hamasa's body, making him feel exposed in a way he hadn't since Marya had woken him in the crater weeks ago.

"The token was trying to lead us an opposite direction at one point."

Gaius looked away from Hamasa, who gasped and slumped forward as if he been released from a too-tight web. Gaius frowned at Flavius. "That doesn't make any sense. Unless it tracks all dragons?"

"Do I look like a dragon!?" Hamasa shouted. He eeped at the combination of Flavius and Gaius' identical glares.

"There's one way to find out," Flavius said, stepping forward and lifting his crossbow. "In this body, he can still use some of his draconic abilities. He'll show himself with the right impetus."

Hamasa shivered, shuffling backwards as the crossbow levelled between his eyes . The cool emotionless gaze of the flaxen-haired man cut right through him. Gaius raised his hand and carefully lowered the crossbow to point at the ground.

"We don't have time for that. The Lance and his squire will follow soon enough and the King prefers him alive. I don't want to have an accident. We'll trust in Eztalpali's token for now. We can always release our little friend if it proves faulty. Although, I very much doubt it. There's more to our timid friend than meets the eye, isn't there, Kana'iro?"

Hamasa shook his head desperately, but the man only laughed.

"You can come with us the easy way or the difficult way," Gaius said next.

"I w-won't come with you," Hamasa replied, eyes darting towards the fire in the distance.

"The difficult way. Fantastic." That disarming grin returned. Before Hamasa could blink, Gaius darted forward. Hamasa cried out, pinwheeling backwards, but his wrists were caught and yanked forward. Metal cuffs clicked ominously before he could blink. He had barely seen the man's hands move. The runes on the metal glowed bright pink. And dimmed immediately.

The three of them stared at each other in confusion.

"They shouldn't have stopped glowing—" Flavius broke off as a loud, screeching approximate of a war cry shattered the night air. Birds burst from the tall grasses and Marya jumped in, swinging her spear like a mallet and knocking the crossbow towards the ground. The bolt released harmlessly into the dirt.

"Flavius, grab the—" Gaius hissed between his teeth, sliding his gladius free not a moment too soon. A familiar, deadly trident struck at his neck, prongs sparking against the sword's blade as he knocked it aside.

Valerius stood there, rage etched into his tightly-drawn features, and wearing only his linen kimono to protect himself from Gaius' attack. They must have left camp without knowing there was trouble and Valerius hadn't gone back for his armor. Hamasa's heart shouldn't have thumped so hard at the thought. Valerius was still going to *force* him back to the capital against his will. He still refused to *listen* to Hamasa.

Valerius rushed forward, his trident swinging and blocking like a quarterstaff in close combat against Gaius' lightning-quick attacks with the short blade. Hamasa stumbled back, mouth gaping in awe at the fight, until Marya's yell drew his attention away. Flavius had kept ahold of the crossbow, but was using it like a melee weapon, dodging Marya's mostly-untrained, one-armed swinging effortlessly. At the first opening, Flavius lashed out, smacking Marya across the face and sending her tumbling to the ground.

"Marya!" Hamasa exclaimed. He ran without thinking, bursting forward with inhuman speed and his head ducked low between his shoulders. He threw his whole body into Flavius' side before the man could set a new bolt to his crossbow. Both of them hit the ground with a grunt and rolled over the dirt.

"Flavius, take the dragon and go!"

"Oo leab 'im *alode!*" Marya shouted, blood pouring from her mouth and dripping from the cut on her cheek that was already swelling. She scrabbled over the dirt to grab the fallen crossbow. Hamasa, seeing Flavius reaching for it, grabbed a handful of loose dirt and threw it at his face. The centurion cursed loudly and wiped at his eyes, just in time to see Marya swing the crossbow and smack Flavius across the face.

He went down hard.

"By the Sun..." Hamasa whispered.

"Did I... did I kill again?" Marya gasped, equally horrified and dropping the crossbow like it burned.

He knelt woodenly and reached to press his fingers to the

centurion's neck. Marya inhaled sharply, and Hamasa's eyes fluttered shut. "He's alive." Marya pressed the back of her hand to her mouth to stifle the sobbing gasp.

"Get out of here!" Valerius bellowed furiously between swings of his trident and dodges from Gaius' gladius.

Hamasa and Marya exchanged looks.

"Let's go, Asa," Marya whispered, the words heavy. "This is our chance."

Hamasa paused. They could snag Valerius' horse and gallop away before he had a chance to call her to heel. It was a *real* chance. A chance to escape with no one more hurt than they were already... Valerius would be distracted enough by Gaius, but he'd be okay... Right? He met Marya's eyes, saw the spear returned to her hand and the copper bead flashing in the moonlight over her head. She held out her hand, the one with the bandage and splint, and nodded. His hands clasped the thickest part of her forearm, the cuffs on his wrists clanging together, and her bicep tensed as she pulled him up.

And they ran. The camp they'd left minutes ago still glowed orange with fire, the dark shape of Nerva, their escape, tossing her head near the glow. A few seconds. They had run maybe a few seconds when the short, bitten-off shout of pain drew Hamasa to a stop.

That was Valerius.

"What are you doing? Let's go!" Marya urged, grabbing Hamasa by the cuffs and yanking him.

Hamasa's feet stuck to the ground. "I..." He met Marya's eyes, resigned and terrified. "I can't leave him."

"Why not?!"

Honestly, there wasn't a good answer. Valerius had kidnapped him. Thrown him over a horse and tied him up like a kill after a hunt. He refused to listen to Hamasa's many protests and had tossed Marya, his first and only friend, like a ragdoll.

But he had also taken one look at Hamasa's frail, pathetic body and seen a *dragon* underneath. He believed wholeheartedly in a hidden something inside of Hamasa. He had run into a fight under-protected and weary from at least two days of walking beside Hamasa out of some strange idea of honor and respect. Made more tired by the Salvatropas' request to help save innocent creatures despite Valerius hating everything about their vigilante idea of justice. How could Hamasa leave behind a man that believed so blindly and faithfully in the very idea of him? Who chose to uphold a vow to protect every living creature that needed his help? Who even tried to teach Marya to fight when she threatened to use what he taught against him?

And then there was the boy. The boy that saw the Shield Choose a child and didn't see it as a mistake. The boy that refused to believe a dragon could be wrong almost two decades later.

His heart thumped hard and his mouth dried. But his sandals were turning over dirt, grass whipped around his bare arms and legs. How could he let Valerius die if he could try, even a little, to help? He couldn't run if it meant someone else would be hurt. Not if it meant Valerius could die.

The limp body of the mara under his hands. The dead man rolling onto the stone. The wind whipping past him as his body shrank and his skin burned.

"Seriously, Hamasa! You idiot!" Marya shouted at his back.

He was running, a knife twisting between his ribs with each gasp. Terror made his breath shudder and his vision darken, but he kept running at the two figures exchanging blows. One side of Valerius' torso was stained pitch black. The pitch dripped sluggishly to the churned dirt, spread like a grotesque flower over his side and stomach. Something burned in Hamasa's chest, his vision sharpening, every blade of grass around him detailed and concise, every drop of sweat on the men's faces and arms standing out clear and bright in the moonlight. They glowed red in their exertion, hearts pumping scarlet in their chests. With a loud shout, Hamasa raised his arms and jumped, too high for his weak, human legs, ignoring the sudden piercing pain lancing up his arms, pink lighting up the planes of his young-seeming face and the stretch of scars across his cheek and temple. Gaius turned in time for his eyes to widen and a smile to break out over his face—

"Kana'iro the Red."

—and then the confounded cuffs smashed across Gaius' face, the runes glowing brightly. His shout became a scream of pain, and Hamasa couldn't catch himself. He thudded onto Gaius' prone body and rolled through the dirt and grass, screaming and sobbing at the burning around his wrists.

"Hamasa!"

"Hamasa! YOU IDIOT!"

Everything went black even as his wobbly lips curved upwards. *I didn't run away...*

21

HAMASA WOKE UP with a groan and, once again, trapped against Valerius' chest and, again, on a horse. Unlike the first time, this was not a gentle saunter through the woods. Nerva was sprinting, the rocking and jerking of her under him making him instantly motion sick. Was this what a ship voyage would feel like? His eyes popped open and he struggled to turn, to look around and get his bearings in the dark, until Valerius let out a pained hiss at an unfortunate elbow strike.

"Marya?!" Hamasa demanded in dizzying concern. Or maybe he was still dizzy from the galloping pace. He hated human travel.

"Right here, Hamito. You all right? You went down hard," Marya asked, her words heavy with concern yet a little thin in the rushing air. Hamasa rolled his head sluggishly towards Marya's voice, and blinked. Marya was on a horse. A beautiful silver horse.

"Horse?"

Marya grinned and winked. "Stole it from those bastards. They still have another if they can catch it. Found out Valerius ain't just a bastard to me, he's kinda a gulero to everyone." She sounded a little impressed at this, but Valerius merely snorted loudly.

Hamasa tipped his head back to stare cross-eyed at Valerius' chin. "You're hurt, aren't you?"

"It will hold for now," he said shortly. At the sheen of sweat over his face and the deep grooves around his mouth, Hamasa knew that it may be holding, but it wasn't painless. Not in the slightest.

"We need to stop. You need to rest," Hamasa protested, trying to gingerly twist around to see the wound. The arm around him tightened.

"You'll make it worse. Stop moving."

"We can't stop, Hamasa. They'll be on us in no time. We have to keep going."

"We need to find a place to hide then!" Hamasa countered.

"Where? It's all flat nothing 'round here," Marya said, throwing her arm around them. The Ajul Mountains were far behind them, flat, grassy hills stretching out in all directions ahead as they continued to gallop west.

"I'll be fine. We need to make it to a town and we'll lose them there," Valerius muttered, his breath hot and choppy against Hamasa's ear. Something warm and wet pressed into his back and the arm around him loosened minutely. Hamasa's eyes widened. *He's bleeding again.* "Thank you for your concern, my lord."

"Not a r-*lord*," Hamasa whispered, feeling useless, especially with wrists still trapped in the cuffs. They must not have had enough time to try to find the key. Or there hadn't been one. They *were* ensorcelled. It would probably take another mage or a dragon to free him.

A shiver of awareness ran down his spine and his tongue licked the air instinctively. Of course he couldn't smell anything other than horses and blood, but he could hear a whistling. With a quick "hold on!" at Valerius, he grabbed the reins and tugged Nerva to the right. A bolt shot past them.

"Mirda!" Marya shouted.

"Marya, get out of here! It's probably trained to come to his call rike Nerva!" Hamasa called over.

"But Hamasa—"

"Go, now!" Valerius interrupted. Marya's mouth tightened, but she nodded and dug her heels into the horse's sides. Like a bolt from a crossbow, the steed took off, hooves churning up dirt and stones from the road.

"We have to face them. Nerva can't outrun them with two on her and after so little rest," Valerius said, grunting under his breath as he lifted his trident on his good side.

"You can't fight them ar-alone!" Hamasa disagreed, mind whirring with... with nothing. They had no choice. Even if he would've chosen to use his inherent magic now, he couldn't thanks to the ensorcelled cuffs. "What do we do, what do we do, what do we *do*?" he chanted. Another whistle and Hamasa steered Nerva sharply to the left, the bolt passing close enough to Nerva's eye to spook the mare into loping faster with a shrill whinny.

"Let me off and I'll slow them down. You can draw even with Marya and keep going," Valerius said decisively. "You need to go back to the Sovereign, my lord. Whatever you do, get back to Riyushu."

"I thought you weren't crazy?" Hamasa yelled over his shoulder.

"My lord, they're right behind us," Valerius retorted, twisting at the waist with a wince that Hamasa could feel.

"You are not going to die!" Hamasa said, tears burning his eyes. *I saved you. I saved you. I won't let you die now!*

"Hamasa," Valerius murmured. His hands tightened around the reins and Nerva slowed. Hamasa clenched his eyes shut, wishing he could shut out the sound of Valerius' softly resigned voice. Ignore the painful thump of his heart at the sound of that voice saying his name.

It really is him. Did she *send the Lances for me, because of him?*

"Kana'iro the Red, come with us and I'll let the Lance live! He'll bleed out if you don't stop now." Gaius' voice was thin and reedy from wind and distance, but clear enough to hear and yank Hamasa out of his own wildly churning thoughts. Valerius twitched at the sound, but the centurion was too far for the knight to make out the exact words. Unlike Hamasa, who felt each word like a physical blow.

"I won't. I *won't*," Hamasa chanted, teeth clenching.

A blast of freezing air startled Nerva into rearing, mane whipping Hamasa's face and hooves striking the air. Hamasa threw himself against Nerva's neck and clung tight to Valerius' arm wrapped around him, fingernails digging into the meat of his arm to desperately hold him in place. Valerius had instinctively kept hold of Nerva's reins himself, otherwise they would've fallen off together. The dampness spread over Hamasa's back and he gritted his teeth to hold back terrified tears.

There was so much blood.

"Looks like you're out of luck, Kana'iro! Our ally is here," Gaius called.

"No..." Hamasa looked up to where the huge creature hid, shadowed cleverly by clouds. His mouth spread into an awestruck grin, lips parting in giddy relief. "No, that's not your ally," he whispered.

"My lord, what—?" Valerius actually sounded anxious.

An enraged draconic scream rent the air. The clouds shredded around a plummeting body that shined silver in the starlight. Not black. Not green. But icy white. The dragon's wings spread to slow the descent, a screech proceeding a whirlwind of snow from an open maw. The two horses whinnied high and terrified, and Hamasa wheeled Nerva around in time to see a wall of ice steaming with cold blockade the road behind him and cut the centurion off.

"We'll find you again! I'll make you come with me next time, Kana'iro the Red!" Gaius shouted from the other side of the ice wall.

The sound of hoof beats rapidly retreated as icy air blasted over Hamasa's and Valerius' back. It buffeted Nerva several steps forward and had Hamasa and Valerius leaning over the saddle horn with matching groans. Shivers wracked Valerius' body, but Hamasa felt his own body's heat surge higher to combat the unnatural cold. Luckily, the runes on the cuffs didn't register it as magical. Yet. If he got too cold, it would probably counteract eventually.

He didn't think it would be a problem, though. Not when the gleaming White dragon soared low and coasted to a graceful landing. It turned, sinuous and catlike, wings tucking close to the glowing body, tail whipping over the road. Delicately clawed feet picked over the dirt until the dragon stopped just in front of them. Glowing blue eyes met Hamasa's. Abruptly, the dragon stood rampant, wings extending so wide they filled all of Hamasa's vision, almost blocking out the night sky. Just as beautiful as Hamasa remembered. Tears sprang to his eyes from sheer, overwhelming relief.

Icy wind whipped over them as the dragon roared. Nerva neighed high-pitched and screeching, the whites showing in her rolling eyes, but Hamasa and Valerius' sure hands on the reins kept her in place. Hamasa was smiling, widely and recklessly, heart thumping in painful joy until the sound of hoof beats jarred through the frozen air. Hamasa's throat tightened and he wheezed between his teeth. Then, he realized from what direction they came.

"Hamasa! Valerius!" Marya shouted, reining the stolen horse

to a halt on the other side of the dragon. She was far enough away Hamasa couldn't make out her expression in the night's darkness. "Sovereign's curse, this is a dragon," Marya gasped. The silvery stolen horse shuffled in place restlessly, but didn't try to run or rear back. A horse used to dragons.

"We told you to keep going," Valerius called out, too tired and in pain to sound irritated. Or stay in the saddle.

Hamasa let out a cry, twisting and grabbing at Valerius as the bigger man slumped and slid to the side. But with cuffs and his position and his puny human strength, Valerius' tunic slipped through his fingers and he fell with a horrible thud to the ground.

"Valerius!" He scrambled off Nerva's back, carefully rolling Valerius over and cupping his face in warm palms. "Valerius?"

His eyes darted over Valerius' torso and inhaled sharply. His heart stopped seeing how much the knight had bled out during the chase. It soaked through his kimono, past the waistband of his hakama to his thighs. He was so pale in the moonlight, he looked blue. Fear clawed at Hamasa's chest as he pressed his hand to the darkest part of the stain, grimacing at the squish and resulting groan. The knight didn't wake.

"Eternal Sun, help him," Hamasa choked out past numb lips.

The dragon cocked their head and, with a shimmer, shrunk into a much smaller human body. Clothed with very thin layers, and barefoot. The dragon's hair was almost as white as the scales had been, but, similar to Hamasa, the dragon had the same brown skin, mottled with patches of white, and a slender, whip-thin frame.

"Hamasa? You need to explain!" the now humanoid dragon demanded.

"Hold up, *you* know Hamasa?" Marya asked. She jumped off the stolen horse to hurry forward. The spear swung in a swift arc to stop and horizontally cross in front of the dragon's chest.

The dragon looked down at the staff, and slowly the dragon's gaze travelled up to the hand, and then the girl that held it. Inhumanely glowing blue eyes met hers. She gulped and her arm shook. "Don't you try and steal him, too. We got enough problems, dragon."

Hamasa tore off Valerius' kimono to bare his chest, not caring enough to listen to them. He gagged, the back of his wrist pressing to his mouth, at the sheer amount of blood and the grotesque hole in Valerius' side. There was so much blood he could taste it. It coated the back of his throat and tongue; a sickening mimicry of honey.

"You're either very brave, or very stupid," the dragon said dryly. "I'm not going to steal Hamasa. I have no need of that. He's my lifemate."

"Lifemate?" Marya repeated dumbly.

The dragon rolled gleaming blue eyes, the pupils slitted like a cat's, and an inner, translucent eyelid blinked vertically. Marya yelped and stumbled back. The dragon walked around Marya to where Hamasa pressed blood-soaked cloth to the wound, sniffling. As the chill wrapped around him, Hamasa glanced up, eyes wild and desperate.

"Help him, *prease*."

The dragon sighed and touched Hamasa's face. This close, Hamasa could see the patches of white were very faintly scaled — not quite human skin. Like Hamasa, his features were masculine.

"This is what happens when you play with humans, Hamasa. I told you that twenty years go."

"Arash, please," Hamasa whispered. Arash sighed again.

"You're much better at this. Fire heals better than ice." Hamasa stared mutely, lips pressed into a thin line, and Arash held up both hands. "I didn't say I wouldn't."

Hamasa backed away, dropping the ruined clothing and

kneeling with his bloody hands clutching Valerius' uselessly. Arash's nose wrinkled in distaste, but he lifted a hand and grew a single, long, silver claw from his finger. He traced a few lines of curling letters from right to left into the mess of blood on Valerius' torso. The words flashed bright white and then sank into his skin. Hamasa licked his lips, but all he tasted was salt and snot and blood.

Arash tilted his head. Narrowed his eyes. Then, he leaned down and blew over the wound. Ice frosted over the torn flesh, crusting and solidifying like a scab.

"The tissue and muscle inside the wound has knitted together, but my spells can only do so much. I focused on the worst of it. He needs human care or a more suitable mage—" he side-eyed the teary Hamasa "—very soon. That ice bandage will prevent his flesh from re-healing if left too long."

"I'm..." Hamasa lifted his arms to show the cuffs.

Arash's eyes flared so brightly blue, it left sparks in Hamasa's eyes when he blinked. "How did you allow this? Did those filthy mortals I chased off do this? I'll tear them apart!" Arash snarled, already half on his feet, his nostrils flaring and tongue flicking over his lips.

"Just help m-me get them off and we can go to the nearest town. Valerius needs help."

Arash growled savagely, eyes still burning, but nodded nonetheless. "You'll have a lot of explaining to do, qal'bi."

Hamasa flamed bright red and held up his cuffed hands. Arash rolled his eyes. He leaned down, eyes flicking up to meet Hamasa's, and breathed over the bespelled iron. Frosty air swirled over the cuffs. They glowed a rosy pink under the sheen of ice, then shattered like struck glass.

"Now that's done, *what in the world is going on?*" Marya yelled, hands thrown up in the air.

22

HAMASA SAT ON the small wobbly stool and peered anxiously at Valerius' pale features. The blood-replenishing potion the local healer had coaxed down the unconscious knight's throat had already drastically improved his color, but not enough in Hamasa's opinion. The ice patch had been melted off and a simple, nonmagical stitching had taken its place under fresh white bandages. There was only so much they could afford between a farmer, a dragon fresh from the other realm, and a man who had fallen naked from the sky two weeks ago—almost three now. In other words, they only had the few coins Marya had saved from previous market days. Hamasa had put his foot down when Arash and Marya had suggested going through Valerius' bags for more coin. Valerius could always pay them back when he woke, but they didn't have the right to go through his belongings. Hamasa had too many secrets of his own to be unconcerned with anybody else's privacy.

Hamasa didn't hear the door, nor the approaching footsteps that came after. Marya set her hand on Hamasa's shoulder, startling him out of his reverie, more startled than he should have been. What kind of guard did he make that he didn't even notice Marya walking in?

"He won't get better any faster with you staring at him. Come down and eat 'fore you're the one knocked out on a bed," Marya suggested. With her gentle tone and kind smile, she looked and sounded so much like Irmen, a part of him quaked. He had never missed a mother—hers, his own—more than in this moment.

Hamasa hesitated, eyes flicking over Valerius' slack features. He truly looked his age for once, so young and breakable. Hamasa's hand on the bedspread twitched, aching to reach out and touch his pulse—something he had done too often already. Hamasa was hungry, but in that way where his weak human body needed it while his mind rebelled wordlessly and strongly at the very idea of food. Although, perhaps he rebelled more at leaving this tiny windowless room in the cheap hostal they had found. The door reopened and a familiar chill crept up Hamasa's spine. He got quickly to his feet, ignoring Marya's irritated grumble, to tuck the thin blanket more securely around Valerius' broad shoulders.

"Why haven't you slunk off to bother someone else?" Marya asked, glaring at Arash as the human-looking dragon walked in.

"Because I don't plan to," Arash said, not so much as deigning to look at her when he replied. "Hamasa, we need to speak privately. Now."

Marya snorted loudly and messily, arms crossed over her chest and dark eyes narrowed. "We appreciate the help with Señor Frowny over there, well, Hamasa does. But whatever you want with Hamasa you can ask in front of me, too. Right, Asa?"

Hamasa couldn't help but smile, guilty and fond at once. Marya, always his champion, whether or not he deserved it.

"Actually, Marya—"

Marya's jaw dropped a second before she interrupted, "Really!? Hamasa, this... this dragon called you his lifemate! Do ya really know him?"

"I... I do know him," Hamasa said, sighing softly. Marya sputtered speechlessly. "But I'm no one's r-lifemate."

Arash's eyes squinted, the bright blue flinty and making Hamasa grimace.

"I don't... what?" Marya asked.

"Please, stay here with Valerius, won't you? I'll return soon and we'll go downstairs for dinner together," Hamasa suggested with a wibbly smile. Marya scowled, but flopped onto his vacated seat with a huff.

"What I do for friends, ay," she muttered, glaring at Valerius.

Hamasa led the way into the hallway, gulping nervously as Arash followed right on his heels. The chill of Arash's gaze was heavy on the back of his neck all the way down the stairs and through the common room until they finally made it to the moderate privacy of the stables. Hamasa's tongue flickered, tasting the faint tang of blood on his shredded bottom lip as the smell of hay and horse dung assaulted his nose. He was almost glad he couldn't smell better — A hand latched around his bicep and spun him around. Arash was right in front of him, walking him back with quick, shuffling steps until he was pressed too hard against the nearest stall.

"There's no one in here but us. Where is it? Where is your rohh?" Arash asked roughly, one hand spread wide over Hamasa's wildly and painfully beating heart. "Your *human* should be keeping it safe!"

"It's... it's gone," Hamasa whispered, shame burning in his stomach. Soon, Arash would know his true weakness, how low he had sunk. Despise him for it.

"How could she let this happen? You never should've trusted some mud ape. It doesn't matter, I'll get it back and we'll never come back to this place again. Was it that Beast, the Merciless? Do they have it? I'll tear them apart," Arash hissed, teeth sharpening as claws grew from his fingers.

Or not, because of course, his oldest and dearest friend's

first conclusion was one of rage on Hamasa's behalf rather than assuming the worst of him.

Hamasa quickly shook his head. "*No, Arash, calm down,*" he said in a language that was smoother than Mekshan, lyrical, and guttural. It flowed from his lips easier than any language he had spoken in years.

Arash's eyes closed as he inhaled slowly and deeply. On instinct, Arash leaned forward and his forehead pressed to Hamasa's. The touch was so familiar, so much like *home*, that Hamasa's breath left him in a shudder. His whole body shuddered along with it and his eyes slipped shut. Arash's hands were cool and dry on his arms, tucked up under the edges of the poncho he wore, and the scent of sky intermingled with the taste of ice and snow. Hamasa breathed in quick, gulping breaths, tasting it like mint and cilantro and limón.

"Arash," he whispered, hands wrapping around Arash's wrists. "*You're here.*"

"*Of course I'm here. As soon as I heard the Merciless was back, in this disgusting wet place, I came,*" Arash explained in the same language that had calmed him down.

"It's not disgusting, Arash," Hamasa protested, though his lips twitched upwards despite himself. Arash would always be Arash. The White dragon rolled his eyes, scoffing. "*You can't... You can't go after the Merciless, Arash. You can't.*"

"*I can't without you at my side,*" he agreed. His nose brushed over Hamasa's and he stepped away. A part of Hamasa was abruptly bereft, wanting to bring back the familiar affection he'd missed. But the words struck and his pupils dilated.

"No, Arash. Not with me at your side," Hamasa said, shoulders lifting to his ears as his gaze dropped to the vividly colorful weave of his poncho. "My rohh is gone because I couldn't..."

THE COWARD'S EMBLEM

Arash started, one foot stepping back, and his eyes widened. *"They did come after you. I wasn't sure—You got away, you lived, Hamasa!"*

Hamasa squeaked in shock as Arash pulled him forward, his arms clutching tight around Hamasa's frame. There was no gentle, icy brush of wings, the embrace only half of what it could be, but enough. Hamasa blinked rapidly, gradually relaxing into Arash's hold, eyes closing when he felt Arash shudder. It was more than enough. His forehead thumped to Arash's collarbone.

"I couldn't sense you, Hamasa, or your soul. I was so scared I was too late, that you were already dead. What have you done, my heart? Why did you come here?"

Hamasa felt guilt knot itself in his throat. "A-Arash, I..."

The dragon pulled away and shook his head briskly. His hands cupped Hamasa's face and his glassy blue eyes met wide brown. *"I meant it twenty years ago and I'm offering it again. Come home and Fly with me."*

Hamasa's tongue felt too heavy in his mouth and stuck behind his teeth. He could only shake his head. In his mind, a picture of Marya upstairs, arms crossed and heavy brows tight and low, glaring at Valerius. Trusting him to come back. The golden eyes of the páhalebra as it waited for Hamasa to break his inaction, to save them. The prick of sharp teeth at his throat in thanks, the scrape of his nails over vulnerable, soft blue scales. Most ridiculously, all but wildly, he pictured the unconscious Lance on the tiny bed in the hostal. He remembered that bravery he had held in his heart so fiercely for one glorious moment. He had saved someone's life, more than once, in this pathetic, weak body. He had never gone back, had never chosen to fight over running. This time he had. Was it Marya's brazenness, or Valerius' faith? What had they given him that had inspired him to be, and do, so much?

How could he leave them?

"I can't, Arash. I...I'm sorry," Hamasa said hoarsely. He looked anywhere but the dragon in front of him. As if the sight of dirty hay and indifferent, shaggy-furred horses were significant.

"You're making a mistake," Arash replied just as hoarse and quiet, disappointment in every strangely lyrical word he spoke in Mekshan. "This isn't where you belong. You're lying to them, even to that filthy monkey who thinks she knows you. You belong with me. You belong with your mother. Don't you miss us?"

Hamasa pushed Arash back, breathing heavily. "That's not fair! You can't tark ab-bout my m-mother, Arash!"

Arash smirked thinly, but there was a tightness around his eyes and mouth. "You were doing so well. Now you can't even get your own mouth to behave. What makes you think you belong in that body? In this world? I can protect you so much better than these apes."

Hamasa shook his head, arms clutching around his body. "I don't w-want to b-be... I don't want to be protected. I just want to be reft arone. Left alone," he spat out the words angrily, rubbing at his cheeks furiously. *Why were they wet again?*

Arash sighed and ran his hands through his hair. "You can't be left alone if an entire country is on your tail, Hamasa. Too many people already know who you are—"

"Róntraih Porto. Just help me get to Róntraih Porto Cuidat. Don't tell Marya or... or Valerius," he whispered the name despite himself, and his hands twisted around the hem of his tunic out of sight. "I can get away in Róntraih Porto Cuidat if you help me."

"You want me to keep your identity a secret, despite the fact everyone knows except for that moronic female," Hamasa's mouth wrenched open to protest, but Arash rolled right over it, "and you want me to distract a trained knight with *Riyukezan* blood, so you can escape in a crowded city to, what? Go hide in a hole like a scared rat? Without a rohh and two different countries and a beast hunting you?" Arash asked, incredulously.

"Yes," Hamasa hissed, lurching forward to clasp the front of Arash's tunic. "Please, I know I've disappointed you, and it's asking too much, but I can't go back to Riyushu."

"And you won't come back home. You don't…" Arash's eyes closed, some pained emotion drawing his features tight. "You don't have to Fly at the solstice, Hamasa. I would never force you. I'll take you where it's safe and never ask again, I swear."

Hamasa flushed brightly and looked away. "I… I couldn't face my mother. Not any of them. Not as I am. But thank you."

Arash extracted Hamasa's tight grasp on his clothing. Hamasa started forward, desperate, but swiftly held himself back and let Arash go. It was his right to say no. It was asking too much of him after everything Hamasa had done to hurt him. He watched, hands twisting in the hem of his tunic again, as Arash began to pace. Arash hissed between his teeth, hands flexing and tensing at his side. The horses joined in watching him, snorting, heads turning to follow him as he paced a line through the hay and dust. Abruptly, he stopped in the middle of the stables, and finally groaned out loud and stared upwards.

"Fine!" Arash spat. Hamasa jumped in place. "I will accompany you to this Róntraih place, but once there I won't help you get away. If you get caught again, that's it. You're coming back home with me. With or without your rohh, deal?"

Hamasa licked his lips, but nodded gratefully. He could prepare, maybe use a bit of human magic again when they got to Róntraih Porto. He would definitely be able to get away. From everyone he had ever disappointed.

"Thank you, Arash. Thank you."

"Don't." Arash broke off with a rough scoff. "Don't thank me, Hamasa. I'm doing this despite all logic and reason. I'm going to help you leave me again. So don't thank me."

He turned on his heel and left the stables.

Hamasa watched his back and the shame burned like acid in his stomach. It was fast becoming a familiar feeling.

23

AFTER DINNER, which was passed in a mostly awkward silence filled with confused looks from Marya, they headed towards the stairs. The food sat in Hamasa's belly like a stone and he already regretted forcing down the little he had eaten. It had all tasted like sand. All the peppers and salsa that Marya had added with gusto and poorly forced zeal hadn't been enough to change that. The common room was filled with a mix of farmers and merchants, at one corner, a dalo sat on a low stool, crimson red feathers blazing under the flicker of torchlight. His hands moved through the air, casting shadows on the wall as he told ancient Mekshan tales to wide-eyed children. Once, Hamasa would've been just as enthralled, eager to sit among them and hear a tale he'd read a thousand times before.

It's not the same on paper or scolls! Their history is meant to be told as a story, Anneki. How can we truly learn it if we don't learn it their way?

A trill of laughter echoed in his head, drowned out by the unabashed glee of real children. Hamasa stumbled on a step, hurriedly righting himself and catching Marya up on the next step. She glanced over at him, eyebrows rising, but said nothing. At first.

"Hamasa, I know I should say we should just go," she blurted, voice low and fervent. "But... it's getting real dangerous. Those men from Harenae, I never coulda protected you. There are too many people who think you're the Shield, no matter what we do or say."

She was right. And if he were a better friend, the friend Marya thought she had, he would tell her the truth. Tell her about the promise he had forced Arash into and invite her to join.

Long ago, his mother said he was a terrible liar. His stumbling and stuttering gave him away every time. Now, in his unfit body and with a clumsy jaw and tongue, his speech was unhesitating. His eyes watched each step, placing his foot carefully and precisely. "You're right... we'll be a lot safer with them."

"I'm right? That easy?" Marya stared at him and scratched the side of her nose. "Exactly! We'll get to Riyushu and the Sovereign will see you're not the Shield and send us wherever we want! Maybe to a different continent. We can have a new adventure, maybe a little bit safer with no one hunting you anymore."

"Marya, are you sure you should? You don't need to follow me that far. You don't know me. Not really."

Rather than answer, her heavy gaze bore into his and her hand gripped his shoulder. She wasn't just looking at his face, she was looking through him, her mouth tipped up in a wry little smile. His heart squeezed painfully. For the first time, Hamasa wondered how much Marya believed and how much she pretended to believe for his sake. A loud crash from inside a room down the hall had them both jumping, Marya breaking into a stilted laugh.

Then, Hamasa realized what room it had been. He pushed past Marya, his sudden and inexplicable suspicions put aside. Marya yelped in surprise, only to curse under her breath when Hamasa flung himself into Valerius' room.

"What are you doing?!" Hamasa blurted, halting mid-step and gaping at the sight. Marya peeked around the doorjamb and muttered 'idiot'.

Valerius scowled over at them so darkly the friends flinched and stepped back. The Lance exhaled loudly through his nose, his hand flat on the wall to hold himself up. What little color had returned to his face had vanished, leaving behind a grey tinge to his tight features. His black hair fell damp and thin around his face and throat.

"Where are we?" His voice sounded so rough and ragged Hamasa's mouth went dry in sympathy.

"We made it to the nearest village and hired a healer," Hamasa replied, wringing his hands anxiously. "It wasn't much, so you should really... lay down."

Marya stared over, eyebrows springing up to her tousle of curls. "Yeah..." she agreed slowly. She dragged her eyes away from Hamasa to Valerius. "What he said. The only reason we made it here was 'cause of this idiot, so maybe listen to him," she said derisively.

Valerius managed to frown even harder; if looks could kill, the two of them would have been dead ten times over.

"What?" he rasped, eyes darting between them.

Hamasa let out a small sound, tongue dragging over his lip. He couldn't smell it, but a bright red stain was blossoming on the white bandage on Valerius' side. He was across the room, frowning in concern, before he could even think it through.

"You need to lay down right now," he ordered, hands already on Valerius' arms as he gently nudged the much bigger and bulkier human towards the little cot. "It's not very comfortable, but it's all we have now. You're making the wound reopen."

Valerius stared down at Hamasa's determined expression silently. Without further fight, he let Hamasa guide him back to the bed and fuss over him. Marya rolled her eyes and huffed in the background, but refrained from speaking. Barely.

"The centurions? The dragon?" Valerius asked, lifting his arms obediently so Hamasa could pull the thin blanket up his chest and tuck in the edges. He was sitting up, his back braced against the wall, but the lines on his face weren't so stark from pain and some color had returned to his ashen cheeks. Hamasa peeked under the blanket to look at the bandage. He hissed at the sight, but the spots hadn't grown too big.

"You mean Hamasa's lifemate, right? Everyone's thinking he's a dragon, why not a dragon's lifemate," Marya exclaimed. Valerius scowled, eyes darting between Marya and Hamasa as the latter sputtered indignantly.

"I don't have a lifemate!" Hamasa retorted shortly. He glanced away, arms crossing over his chest. "Arash is a friend I've known a very long time. Like a sibling."

"Maybe remind him of that. I don't think he agrees," Marya said with a crooked little smirk. Hamasa's mouth worked open and closed wordlessly. She turned to Valerius and narrowed her eyes at him where he sat mute and frowning. "Now you're awake, can we use some of your coin to get another room? I ain't sharing with you and that icy lizard. It's like getting stuck outside in the worst of winter just being near him."

"Marya!" Hamasa managed to force out. She shrugged at him, hands rising.

"You didn't pay for this yourselves?" Valerius asked, glancing between the two friends currently having a silent, yet intense battle of frowns and grimaces across the room.

The battle of eye contact ended with a loud scoff by Marya. Hamasa carefully kept his gaze anywhere but directly at Valerius. As if Valerius' uncharacteristically messy hair and the wall behind his head were fascinating. There hadn't been any need for Marya to mention it. It wasn't as though Arash would sleep indoors. The idea was ridiculous. She obviously wanted to shame Valerius.

"We did. Hamasa wouldn't let us dig through your things," Marya told him when Hamasa refused to speak.

"Take what you need and whatever you already spent. You shouldn't spend your own money on this. You're the Shield of the Sovereign, my lord," Valerius said, directing the last bit at Hamasa.

With a cringe, Hamasa got to his feet carefully. Valerius winced at the movement of the cot, and Hamasa glanced towards him, guilty and worried. When Valerius' dark eyes met his, he swallowed hard and dropped his gaze to the floor. "We'll take a little more for a better potion, and dinner. You should rest," he advised quietly.

Marya rolled her eyes and promptly rummaged through the saddlebag at the foot of the bed. It felt awkward, the very air in the room tense. Hamasa couldn't help looking back, Valerius still staring at him, neither frowning nor smiling. His injury had made his features wan and strained, but he still looked young. Much younger than Hamasa had realized these past few days. There was a sudden motion, and Hamasa startled, looking up to see Marya tossing a small purse. It sailed too hard through the air, thudding into Hamasa's chest and knocking the wind out of him before it fell to the ground with a clatter of coins.

"Uh, oops?"

Hamasa laughed a breathless, choppy thing. Marya joined him, chuckling and rubbing the side of her nose bashfully. Hamasa snagged the purse, grateful for the break in tension. For Marya to look more like herself. And for Valerius' eyes to be off him.

"Sorry, I forget how strong these arms are," Marya said.

"It's all right. It didn't hurt much," Hamasa said with a shake of his head and a brief smile. Marya chuckled again, and, strangely, let Hamasa pass her towards the door. "I'll come back with your dinner soon..." he said slowly, eyes jumping from Marya to Valerius and back again.

Marya waved him on. "Ay, go on. I'll be right behind you."

Hamasa frowned, but stepped outside, and then just beyond the doorjamb. He leaned back against the wall with eyes closed to help focus on the voices in the room. It was ridiculous, eavesdropping like a naughty human child, but why would Marya would linger behind to talk with Valerius?

"I really can't tell what's going on in his head, can you?" There was a long moment of silence. Knowing the amount of expression with eyebrows alone those two could make, Hamasa wasn't too surprised. Nor was he surprised when it broke with a loud sigh from Marya. "Ay, I'll go get me and Hamasa a room. I still don't like you, and if I didn't need your help keeping him safe, I'd leave your gulo behind so fast. So don't stop being useful," Marya warned.

Hamasa slumped against the wall and smiling despite the heavy burn in his stomach.

"Thank you for the notice," Valerius replied, gravelly and low.

Marya's patience wouldn't hold long, especially with Valerius. Hamasa darted away on light feet. The longer she didn't know, and the more she defended him, the worse the burning in his stomach got. It reached up with sticky claws to his chest, scraping at the inside of his ribs. It wasn't right. He knew it. He knew he should just tell her. But the thought of losing her trust... Behind him, Marya's stomping footsteps were already echoing all the way down the hall. He jumped the last two steps and hurried to the bar. A drink she might not have tried before would make a poor bribe, and a poorer placation on his conscience, but Marya would appreciate it regardless of his intentions.

THE COWARD'S EMBLEM

***

Hamasa stood at the bar and watched Marya across the room where she lounged back on two legs of a chair next to a table full of strangers. She was already finishing her second mug of the local beer, what they called michalad, cheeks flushed and grin wide while happily chatting with mix of grungy local farmers and eagerly listening young people. Everyone liked stories of Salvatropas this far north, and Marya was a storyteller with gusto. No matter where she went, Marya could make friends. Something Hamasa both benefited from despite himself, and something he envied. None of those new friends had even realized how much information they had given away, earnestly laying out their woes and complaints to Marya's sympathetic nodding, only to be further rewarded with her entertaining stories.

Thankfully, this little town of Lomadera didn't have much going on but high taxes and winter coming too fast. Worries about the last harvest being cut short was the worst of it. When the children had left for their homes, the storyteller had taken out a shallow dish and begun to sing for coin. At the familiar chords of a song on the vihuela, Marya dropped to all four legs of her chair and whooped. Now that Marya had joined in with the rest, singing in Mekshan too rapid and colloquial for Hamasa to comprehend completely, it was easy to discreetly make his way upstairs, balancing earthenware platter and mug on a wooden tray. He stopped at the topmost stair to listen to the unabashed singing and loud cheers to a well-known and beloved song. Well-known enough that he recognized it, had heard it sung and danced to in the streets of Riyushu itself.

He mouthed the words to himself—most of them, anyway; it was a fast-paced song with rollicking lyrics, some of which he didn't understand—and knocked at Valerius' door. Abruptly, the pleasant buzz was gone, replaced with concern when no sound came from within. Heart thumping, he hesitated one more moment, then slipped into the room, the tray in his grasp tapping the edge of the door. It wasn't quite pitch black inside, but only a single candle was left burning. Slumped against the wall and sitting at the head of the bed, one hand brushing against the trident he must have fetched after they had gone, Valerius slept. His eyes didn't so much as flicker beneath his eyelids when Hamasa toed the door shut.

Relief and a small bit of bemusement had Hamasa's shoulders slumping, a quiet huff escaping him. Even here, safe and unknown in a room in the middle of nowhere Mekshi, Valerius was vigilant. Sleeping with one hand on a weapon and probably aggravating his wound as well.

Hamasa snuck his way towards the bed, setting the tray with the steaming bowl of black bean soup, fresh tortiyas, fruit water, and a little glowing red bottle on the table. A difficult and expensive find out here in the hills—not quite the 'sticks' nearer the mountains where villages rarely had a mundane healer. He hadn't stopped Marya from getting another bottle for herself when they'd gone back with Valerius' pouch. Hamasa stood at the side of Valerius' bed, feet shuffling over the floorboards and his teeth gnawing at his bottom lip as he wavered in his indecision. Should he wake the weary Lance to make sure he ate, or leave him to wake on his own and hope it didn't get too cold? He glanced over at Valerius' profile and...

Hesitated.

Slowly, carefully, Hamasa sank onto the edge of the bed, ignoring the little chair he had used before. Valerius' face was lax, his hair like silk thread against his sharply-angled cheek and brushing the hollow of his throat. Again, Hamasa saw the young human man he actually was. Unguarded. Like the little boy he had almost forgotten about.

"I remember you now," he whispered sadly. He reached out, his trembling fingers brushing soft hair away, tucking it behind an ear. "I'm sorry I forgot, Emerens."

In a move that would put a snake to shame, Valerius' hand struck. Snagged Hamasa's wrist. Hamasa let out only the thinnest beginning of a shout, but another broad calloused hand covered his mouth and his world tipped over and upside down. The thin mattress thudded against his back and air whooshed out of his lungs unbidden. His legs were pinned by the heavy weight above his, and the hands over his mouth and wrist were as inflexible as iron. Soft silken hair fell around their faces but neither of them moved to brush it away. Involuntarily, his skin flushed red and hot from his head to his toes. Where he held Hamasa down, the palms of Valerius' hands slicked with sweat.

Salt burned against Hamasa's lips, and he stared up with wide eyes at Valerius' hazy glare. Valerius' face tightened, eyes darting over Hamasa's face and down to his collar, to jerk back up and squint at Hamasa's right ear. Slowly, he raised his hand. Fingers that felt strangely blunted brushed over Hamasa's skin. As if they weren't touching skin.

"My lord?" Valerius asked, raising his hand from Hamasa's mouth as his expression cleared.

"Ah. Um. Yes?" Hamasa squeaked. He gulped and willed his full body blush to go away. It didn't work; in fact he was certain he got hotter when it finally sunk in Valerius was touching his scars. "I... dinner. I brought dinner."

There was a long moment of silence and both of them staring silently at each other. Hamasa finally looked away, licking his lips. He still tasted like salt. Valerius rose up on his knees, moving to sit on the edge of the bed. As soon as Hamasa started to sit up,

Valerius was there, gripping his elbow and helping him. They glanced at Valerius' hand and immediately jerked away from each other at the same time.

"You said my name."

Hamasa cringed and jumped to his feet. "I didn't get too much," he blurted, grabbing the tray so quickly everything rattled. He yelped and wobbled, desperately balancing the tray and spinning around to hand it over. He shoved it right into Valerius' chest. The knight grunted with a slight flinch and grabbed the tray and Hamasa's hands on both sides to keep him still.

"Thank you, my lord. I've got it."

"I..." Hamasa almost bit his own tongue. His fingers twisted together until he realized what he was doing and shook them out. "I'll go. You eat. And sleep. You should sleep."

"My lord—"

"Please call me Hamasa," he interrupted. Valerius' lips pressed together. "I don't... I don't like it when you call me that."

"I don't know how comfortable I am with that," Valerius said. He frowned down at the tray, then set it on the bed. "We can compromise."

"Compromise?" Hamasa repeated incredulously.

"Tell me how you know my given name."

Hamasa stepped back, blinking quickly and licking his bottom lip. Turning away, he covered his mouth with a hand and searched for a way out. He could scramble past Valerius fast enough to get to the door, but the window was closer... how high was two floors?

"You know for the same reason I know yours, Hamasa," Valerius said. "Why do you insist on lying? We both know who you really are. We both have the same memories of that first year in Riyushu, and the summers in Saig'shu with Ane—"

"Why are you so sure it's me? Why are you so certain that I'm the Shield?" Hamasa broke in. He flung out an arm, gesticulating up and down at his... everything. "Rook at me! *Look* at me! Listen to me! I can't even talk right half the time! I'm not... You're wrong. Whoever you think you remember, you're wrong."

He panted, chest heaving, his eyes stinging as they stared too hard at Valerius' feet. They were bare. He could see Valerius' toes. And it was suddenly the funniest, stupidest thing about this long, long day. Hamasa clapped a hand over his mouth. But the giggles and snorts escaped him, squeezed out between his fingers and around his palm.

"This is crazy. You're crazy," Hamasa wheezed, hiccupped, and gulped for air. Air that wouldn't fully fill his lungs. It shuddered out of him before he could get enough. His brain was woozy, vision spotty, and he gulped faster. His body temperature rose and his breath whistled past his teeth.

Suddenly, he was in darkness. Soft, comforting darkness. His eyes slipped shut and he fell to his knees with a gasp that rocked his whole body forward. He clutched the blanket hard enough to hear the coarse over-washed and over-beaten wool creak in his fists. Hamasa pulled it closer and it was warm, so warm, and his eyelids burned red.

"Is it better now?"

Valerius' voice was muffled, but close by. Hamasa nodded mutely, inhaling slow and deep, exhaling slower.

"Why won't you just leave me alone?" he whispered hoarsely.

There was the sound of moving, of settling near by, a grunt of pain that had his small dark hiding place blazing hotter. The shame was sinking its claws in again.

"When I was a boy, when Aneya was only Anneki and my closest cousin, who was closer to me than my actual sisters, I was there when her father died. I watched as her and her mother's hearts broke, but their family was already fighting among themselves, ignoring their grief. The war was finally over, but my cousin, my sister,... I thought she would disappear into her sadness and she would be gone. And then," Valerius paused, and when he spoke Hamasa could hear the smile in his words, and goosebumps slid down his spine. "There you were. You were everything I imagined a dragon to be. Shining gold and red and fierce, and I was terrified of you. But you walked straight to Aneya, and you bowed to her, and I knew there would be hope for us again. And for Aneya, who I thought I'd lost. You changed everything that day."

Hamasa sniffled and shook his head.

"The next day, I saw you walking next to her. You were small, and thin, and so *normal*. Nothing like a dragon at all. Just another human boy. I didn't realize it then, but you did that for her. So she wouldn't be scared. So children like me, and all those people in awe of you, wouldn't be so scared."

"That sounds like an assumption," Hamasa forced out. A sound, not quite a chuckle, came from Valerius' direction.

"It is," he agreed.

"If you haven't noticed, a lot of people in Mekshi are short with brown hair and brown eyes. I look like everyone else."

"That's not what I see. Hair and eye color, what kind of nose or chin someone has, none of that means anything to me," Valerius said. Hamasa remembered their conversation in Ristahe and the ironic honorable name of 'Kaecus'. "It's the way you hold yourself, the way you walk and duck your head. You always looked like you were trying to make yourself smaller, but you never forgot how big you really were. You wear your body like a disguise."

Hamasa pulled the blanket down. Valerius sat next to him, legs crisscrossed with one knee up high enough for him to rest his arm on. The bandages wrapped around his torso were cleaner, fresh, and badly tied — most likely because he'd done it himself after Hamasa and Marya had left the room. His hair was still loose and lying over his bare shoulders. Just barely, Hamasa remembered a boy whose face was more pudge than jawline and dressed in Imperial lavender. With a shiver sliding down his spine, Hamasa looked away.

"You need rest. Marya is waiting for me," Hamasa said, getting to his feet and rolling the blanket into a sloppy fold.

He lifted his eyes, licking his lips, then quickly looked down at the pile of wool in his arms when he saw Valerius' face shutter. Just like that, his fleetingly open expression was hidden behind the stoic mask of a trained Lance. He lifted the wool from Hamasa's arms and moved towards the small bed. In his wake, Hamasa's whole body chilled.

"Saying nothing is better than a lie, I suppose. My lord."

Hamasa winced that the short, too formal bow Valerius made, at the harsh, taut lines of his jaw, at the simple 'my lord.' "We'll see you in the morning."

"In the morning."

24

HAMASA SLUNK out of the room and tried to ignore the shivers. It wasn't far to the room he and Marya would share. In fact, it was maybe ten paces away. His teeth were all but chattering by the time he slipped into the dark room and set up a pad of blankets on the ground. He curled into a small ball under the scratchy wool, eyes squeezed tightly shut, and rolled everything around in his brain. Arash's sudden appearance, Marya's unconditional friendship... Valerius' years-long devotion to an ideal. Hamasa let out a gusty sigh and flipped onto his back. He stared up at the ceiling while flashes of torch- and firelight lit it up with each opening of the main hostal door.

A door opened, and the light spread across the ceiling from the opposite direction before darkening immediately. A few curses and loud bumps, and the wide, tallow-yellow, stub of a candle near the bed caught fire. The quiet thumps of feet on wood came closer, and he gazed unblinkingly into Marya's upside down face.

"What are you doing?"

"Lying down. In bed," Hamasa answered, nonplussed.

"That is not a bed. That is the floor. Git up, idiot," Marya said with an eye-roll.

Hamasa pushed up onto his hands, watching Marya walk towards the actual bed and kick her sandals away. Her hair was wet, face shiny, and he realized she must've washed up downstairs in the public baths. He should probably remember to do that before the smell of horse sank into his bones. Hamasa tucked his knees close to his chest and rested his chin on top, his arms around his shins.

"You want to share the bed?"

"A'course I wanna share the bed. I promise I don't kick." She paused, eyes squinting into the middle distance. "I don't think I do. I did when I was a little'un. Mamá said I kicked her right outta bed one time. But that was one time and it was a long time ago."

"I don't. Kick that is," Hamasa said. Marya grinned. "But are you comfortable with that?"

"You're the one who doesn't like being touched sometimes. So, I should be asking you that. I'm used to sharing beds. In the winter, it's warmer than sleeping alone," Marya said. She pulled a leg up, almost mirroring him when she set her chin on her knee to meet his eyes, her toes curling and uncurling around the edge of the thin mattress.

"I'm not your mother, Marya," Hamasa said with a sigh, heat rising to his face. "In Riyushu, it's not often that unmarried—"

"Wait, wait, slow down," Marya snorted, holding a hand up and waving it in the air wildly. "Are you asking if I'm scared you're gonna, what, ravish me or something?"

"Ravish?" Hamasa echoed, voice rising as he gaped at her. "I wouldn't ravish anyone!"

Marya burst into laughter, throwing back her head and falling to the bed with a painful thump. He watched, incredulously, mouth twitching upwards, as she literally rolled back and forth, heels kicking in the air while she guffawed.

"I don't know if I'm more offended by the first assumption, or this reaction," Hamasa muttered, smiling wider and gathering his blankets and single pillow.

"You? Ravish me?" Marya wheezed. She pushed upright when Hamasa got close, rubbing the tears out of her eyes.

"Maybe I should be worried about the other way around?"

"No, no, you're safe with me, O Ravisher of Maidens," she said quickly, snorting loud and pig-like a second later.

"Marya."

"No, seriously." She dragged in a heavy breath and scooted over so he could sit next to her. She even patted the mattress a few times. He rolled his eyes and perched at the very edge, eyeing her, waiting for what came next. "You're not my type, Hamasa."

"Pardon?" He felt his head tilt to the side, frowning slightly. "Type of...?"

"Man. Hm, boy?" she corrected with a critical eye.

"I'm older than you."

"You don't know how old I am!"

"Oh," Hamasa blinked and stared at her. "I don't."

She grinned and knocked her shoulder against his. "Eighteen. I'll be nineteen soon. This winter."

"Winter? You're a winterborn? I can't believe it," Hamasa said, shaking his head. "You'd baffle so many Riyukezan matchmakers. They believe very much in birth dates and seasons, down to the hour and minute you were born, dictating a lot of someone's personality. You're nothing like a winterborn."

"That's a bunch of silly Riyukezan shimsham anyway. We don't believe that up here," Marya said with a shrug. "But I always told Mamá I shoulda been born in the summer."

"I'll celebrate your birthday in the summer for you," Hamasa offered. Marya grinned. It was then he noticed she hadn't moved away, leaning naturally against his side. Awkwardly, with a small grimace, Hamasa struggled with his arm and got it around

THE COWARD'S EMBLEM

her shoulders. She snorted again.

"That's why you're not my type. I need someone who's better at hugging."

"I would say I'd practice, but then it sounds like I want to be your type," Hamasa said with a frown. "I have a feeling that I'm nothing like a person you'd be romantic with."

"So proper. 'Be romantic with', can't you just say, love? Or maybe lust? Lusting after someone is real easy, that's for sure," Marya said thoughtfully. "That has more to do with types than love does."

"Do you think love... that if you loved someone, it wouldn't matter what type they were?"

"Exactly."

"I still don't understand types," Hamasa muttered. Marya chortled and sat up.

"A type is just what things you like about people. My type would be..." Marya tucked her legs crisscross and stared upwards. "I guess someone tall, dark, and got interesting eyes. And their hair can't be too short. I gotta be able to put my hands in it, yanno?" Marya said, holding out said hands and making grabbing motions in the air.

"And if they're a male or a female, or human or not, that doesn't that matter?" Hamasa asked quietly. Marya cocked her head to the side.

"No. I don't think so. I mean, I wouldn't go out and date a dende. It's a little different when they're more creature-like? But there was a dala once. She was the most beautiful woman I'd ever seen and she told the most interesting stories with all sorts of different voices. I gave her a flower and asked her to marry me. She told me if she ever came back when I was all grown up, she'd say yes, but for now, she'd just appreciate my flower." Marya grinned, rubbing at her nose.

"How old were you?"

"Seven or something. What about your type?"

"Of course," Hamasa chuckled and plucked at the bed. Marya's bare toes snuck over and poked at his shin, and then did it again. He ducked his head. "I know. I'm thinking."

"Think faster, I'm tired. You know buckethead will make us get on the road again as soon as he wakes up. Ay, and your big icy friend will be back."

"I've never fallen in love. Or asked someone to marry me," Hamasa blurted. Marya's toes retracted and disappeared under her knee. "Not even lust. Not really. I don't think." He frowned, remembering how awkward he felt watching Valerius tie back his hair or lean over him. *Was that...?* Hamasa shook his head. "I've never thought about it. Or wanted it."

"But Arash—"

"Arash has his own ideas. I have mine."

Marya fell back on her hands, whistling quietly at his short outburst. "Is it because he's a boy?"

Hamasa frowned. Marya's eyebrows rose to her hairline. "Of course not. Arash is a dragon. He doesn't have to be a human male if he doesn't want to."

"*What?*" Marya leaned forward, jaw dropping. "He could... he could be a she?"

"If he wanted. Dragons choose their human form. He could look like anything he wanted. They also normally only choose their gender when they've found their lifemate. They can live to be thousands of years old, so things like breeding and sex and gender, it's all..." Hamasa licked his lips, frowning a little harder. "Ephemeral?"

"Effawhat?"

"Ephemeral," he repeated slowly, smiling as Marya repeated it to herself. "It means something like brief or fleeting. Maybe something lovely that passes quickly by, the life of a butterfly or a perfect dawn." Hamasa flapped a hand. "Ephemeral."

"Huh. Nice. But I gotta ask. If he wants to lifemate with you, wouldn't he choose a body you would like?" Marya asked. Her eyes widened and she thumped a fist to her opposing palm. "Oh, you don't know what you like."

"Yes. I suppose he chose what he did because he thought I would like it. Imitation is the sincerest form of flattery, especially when I have no… types he could choose," Hamasa said. He blinked in shock when Marya burst into raucous guffaws again, twisting and falling to press her face into the blankets. It barely helped muffle the sounds she made. "Marya?"

"He looks like you," she gasped raggedly, her face burnt red. "Because he doesn't know what you like."

"Um. Yes. I assume." Hamasa wondered if she also needed a blanket cave. If it weren't for the laughter between the wheezes, he would've thought she was having a panic attack.

"I need to sleep. I'll never stop laughing if I'm awake enough to think," Marya said.

She crawled past Hamasa, who turned to watch her go, bemused and smiling. She flopped with a loud oof and kicked at the blanket to get under it. Hamasa got to his feet to spread the extra blankets over the bed. A moment later he got under the blankets next to Marya, closing his eyes to listen to her shuffling and mutters and constant heartbeat. There was a quiet huff and Marya twisted around. With a lot less flailing, Hamasa turned onto his side and met her eyes. Through the threadbare wool, the flickering candlelight dyed Marya's face in zigzags of pink, black, and yellow. She grinned, wide enough her eyes creased in the corners like her mother's did.

"It's like having a little brother," she teased.

"I know I'm older than you," he retorted with a scoff. Marya opened her mouth, ready to ask, but he cut her off. "I... I have a question for you." He licked his lips, heart thudding.

"Yeah?"

"Why... why are you here?" he murmured. Marya's eyebrows rose. "I mean, why are you helping me? Why do you *care*?" Valerius' answer hovered at the edge of his mind again, rising up with the claws and bile in his chest. "Why did you follow me?"

"I told you. I wanted to help—"

"No, but... why? I'm not nice, or kind, or special. I'm not your *type*," Hamasa interrupted. Marya huffed through her nose. "So why are you here?"

Marya's hand smoothed over the mattress, stopping just by his. Their smallest fingers touched.

"Because I was waiting for you. Or something like you, and then you fell from the sky and I knew it was you," Marya said simply. Hamasa's eyes darted over her face, and she smiled thin and timid. Like another person—like *he* had taken over her expression. "I grew up thinking I'd be just like my papi one day. A soldier, or, even better, a knight. Sometimes I'd dream about finding the Salvatropas and travelling Mekshi helping out folks like my family. But then my papi died and my mamá needed help. No one could teach me how to use a sword, or a spear, or a shovel-stick," Marya explained, breaking off into stilted chuckles.

"And then I fell into your field."

"Yeah. I think Mamá knew, too, as soon as I found you. She knew I'd follow you when you were better, find that adventure I always dreamed about. Maybe I'm... Maybe I try so hard to help you, 'cuz I feel a little selfish. Just using you as an excuse to be a hero like my papi was," she whispered, burying her face into the pillow as her fingers curled into a fist.

Hamasa hesitated, then lay his hand over her fist, thumb

brushing the side of hers. She peeked out at him to answer his soft smile with a wibbly one of her own.

"You're not selfish. You're the bravest, kindest person I know. Besides your mother."

Marya laughed. Her hand loosened under his, twisted around, and entwined their fingers together. He twitched, hand instinctively drawing away from the oddly intimate feeling of her bare palm against his, but he held it there. Tightened his fingers around hers.

"If being selfish is giving up everything you've known, chasing after a person you barely know to help them, believing in them when they don't believe in themselves, the whole world should learn your kind of selfish."

Marya sniffled, blinking so fast her eyelashes fluttered, and she burst into laughter again. She pressed her face against the pillow. "I'm not special like that, you're crazy."

"You are. You *are* special. Thank you for being my friend. I don't have a lot of those. Just Arash. And you."

Marya squeezed his hand, sniffling again a second later. "We need to get you more friends."

"I like the ones I have. Any more sounds exhausting," Hamasa said, dryly. Having more people to talk to? To answer to? To learn facial cues and likes and dislikes? …to disappoint… Hamasa grimaced and Marya laughed.

"I'll make a lot of friends, and I'll share 'em with you. You don't need to spend too much time with 'em then. Just a little."

"I can do that. Probably."

She nodded, curls falling onto her cheek and spilling over the mattress, and she snuggled closer to the pillow. Her heart beat was a metronome in his head. Her hand warm and comforting. The smell of wool bleached by days in the sun and the faintest traces of lavender and herbs reminded him of Elorra. Three weeks of being no one. Just a youth in need of help, and two women kind enough to give it. If he closed his eyes and listened to her breaths, tasted the wool and linen and warmth under the blankets next to her, he could almost imagine Irmen humming by the fire, spinning yarn until he fell asleep.

25

The ride to Róntraih Porto Cuidat should've taken less than a week, but it felt like twenty. That was a slight exaggeration. Only slight. The days dragged under Arash's constant, barbed insults at both Valerius and Marya, Marya grumbling under her breath and snarling back at Arash, and, somehow, Hamasa back on Nerva several times throughout the trek with Valerius at his back and Valerius' arm around his waist. Valerius spent time teaching both Hamasa and Marya how to sit properly in the saddle, and Marya had begun to blossom. She rode the stolen silver horse as if she were born to it, grinning whenever she could pitch into a gallop, balancing on the balls of her feet in the stirrups, long, messy braid streaming behind her. But Hamasa barely endured the rocking and lurching with silent grimaces, rolling his eyes at Arash whenever he smirked up at him while loping easy and swift beside the mare.

It didn't help that Valerius had an arm around him to keep him in the saddle most of the time, and, unbidden, the worst images rose unceasingly in Hamasa's mind's eye. Trapped beneath Valerius' hands and knees, the taste of sweat and skin on his lips, dark eyes hazy and unfocused. Going back into Valerius' room after that had been the greatest exercise in self-flagellation he had ever participated in, and Hamasa was excellent at self-flagellation. He had burst into Valerius' room as soon as he'd answered the knock, only to fidget and pace around the small space while giving Valerius his breakfast, asking after his condition, and looking anywhere but directly at him. Then, he had raced off the minute Valerius replied — not that Hamasa really heard any actual words, only heard the easy and not-pained tone of the knight's voice — to spend the morning next to Marya, picking at his eggs and beans and trying not to make eye contact with anyone. As if what had happened had left some sort of mark that anyone could see if they only looked. Valerius coming down fully dressed and moving as naturally and gracefully as ever had been a relief.

Until he had ended up on the damn horse.

Nothing had happened. Not really. Valerius had refused to believe Hamasa wasn't the Shield. Yes, there was the childhood remembrance of the first years after the Shield Chose the Sovereign along with some insinuations thereof, but Hamasa had deflected that. Bluntly and badly. However, that was basically their every interaction thus far.

So why did it feel different now? Was it because of what he had let slip out? Was it Arash joining them and making obvious Hamasa's connection to dragons?

The terrain was rougher and rockier the further west they got, the wide grassy hills exchanged for low rocky plains and scraggy shin-high brush and cacti. Wild mara and quail leapt away at their approach. Occasionally they caught sight of a large, orangeish-wooled huanaco having ranged far from the mountains in search of more food, and Arash would launch upwards with a rush of icy air. He hated any food to be cooked, and their offerings of dried meats, chunks of white cheese, and tortiyas had offended him the first time they'd offered.

After one such unannounced departure, Marya watched him go with a noisy snort.

"So munching on bloody, hairy huanaco or goats is better'n what we stupid monkeys eat," she muttered under her breath.

"The man we'll meet in Róntraih is a selkie. He only eats raw fish," Valerius commented mildly. One of the first things he had actually said all day, causing Hamasa to startle in his seat and Valerius' arm to tighten in response.

Marya scrunched her nose. "Fine, but he's still a mirda bucket."

Hamasa frowned in confusion. "I've heard that before, what does it—"

"*Shit* bucket," Valerius said in Riyukezan.

"Marya! He's my friend, too!" Hamasa protested while Marya cackled. "And how do *you* know that word?" he asked, twisting to look up at Valerius.

"Most of the militia, and the Lances, are Mekshan. Of course I know the worst slang and curses."

"But you don't use 'em. C'mon, Wally, say gulo."

Valerius stared at her silent, one eyebrow rising. Marya snickered, ducking her head to smother it in her horse's mane.

"*Wally*," Hamasa whispered, horrified and amused.

"Please, don't encourage her, my lord."

Marya straightened in the saddle and cocked her head to the side. "You know," she started, dragging out the words, "you still haven' told us how an ice dragon is your friend, Asa. Or why he says y'all are gonna get married or whatever."

"It's p-personal," Hamasa said. He quickly turned to stare between Nerva's ears and down the wide straight road ahead. The presence of Valerius was *too much* at his back. "We're not getting married and he knows that."

"Why don't you wanna marry a dragon? I mean, he's a shit bucket—"

"Marya," he sighed wearily.

" — but he ain't a shit bucket to *you*," Marya said with a smirk. "Wouldn't any mage wanna have their own pet dragon? It'd make you as strong as the Sovereign."

"I doubt Arash would be anyone's pet," Hamasa said dryly. Valerius scoffed so quietly that Hamasa almost missed it. "It's tradition for only one dragon to Choose an Sovereign in a country. That is why the Riyukezu are in Mekshi at all."

"So... how he'd meet you? Are you secretly the Sovereign's brother? Are you a secret love child of one of the Sovereign's parents?" Marya asked, leaning so far towards them that her saddle began to slip. She yelped and hurried to right herself as the horse under her snorted and tossed its head.

"The Sovereign's family is above reproach and gossip, Señorita Garsia. You shouldn't jest about their personal lives, especially when it's untrue," Valerius interrupted. Thankfully. Because Hamasa could only stare, slack-jawed, at Marya's bright eyes.

Marya stuck out her tongue at Valerius. "You're no fun. How would you know if it's untrue? It's not like you've met them."

"I grew up at court." Valerius' hands tightened around the reins so tautly Hamasa could see the tendons at the back of his hands standing out in relief.

"You met the *Sovereign*?" Marya asked squeakily.

"The Valerius family have been related to the Imperial Riyukezu bloodline for several generations," he said.

"There's not many Harenese families that can claim that," Hamasa said. Valerius grunted a vague affirmative.

"What!? You're a prince?" Marya shrieked. Both horses snorted, their ears lying flat and their heads tossing at the sound.

"Of course not. My family are barons. We've guarded the border between Riyushu and Harenae for five hundreds years."

"You're a baron?"

"No, I'm a Lance of the Realm," Valerius told her. "My family are barons."

"Can't you be both?" Marya asked, eyebrows flying up.

Hamasa wanted to correct her, but something stopped him. Some barely there thought he couldn't quite grasp. Something that made his hands shake and guilt rise. What wasn't he remembering? He scowled at his hands wrapped around the saddle horn, and scoured his brain.

"No Lance can inherit land, title, or property. When I was knighted eight years ago, I gave up my inheritance. My sister will inherit, which pleased my mother. She never understood why a son should inherit. It's not how things are done in Harenae, and Saig'shu, my family seat, hasn't had a male heir for several generations. I rather broke tradition being born first," Valerius explained. Hamasa peeked over his shoulder to see that almost smile hovering at the corner of Valerius' mouth. "My mother prefers things done her way."

"Ay, that's how you can tell Harenese used to be Mekshan. Passing down the mother's name is the smartest way," Marya said with a smug little nod.

"Riyukezans usually don't. Other than the Sovereign, who is Chosen by a Shield, most titles and inheritance will pass down through the father," Hamasa explained, but his mind was still on Valerius' confession.

He just... gave it up? For Riyukezan nobles, the inheritance and name is everything. Even with an old Harenese name, the pressure by his Riyukezan father would have been immense, maybe more so for a border baron... He frowned, stomach churning, mind whirring.

Marya's mouth twisted dubiously. "But how do they know it's really the man's child?" she asked, effectively breaking through Hamasa's musing. "It's not like *they* push the baby out. Are they so sure they put it *in*?"

Hamasa snorted and slapped a hand over his mouth in mortification. Behind him, Valerius was shaking. Hair fell over Hamasa's shoulder and there was the briefest moment of pressure at the back of his head. The slightest sound escaped on a rush of breath against the nape of his neck. Hamasa's eyes widened, shocked.

"Asa, he's laughing," Marya crowed. "Óra, that's the saddest, tiniest laugh I ever seen."

Goosebumps trailed up and down Hamasa's arms at the quiet chuckle tickling his gradually heating skin.

"You really shouldn't tease him like that," Hamasa admonished. His skin could do whatever it wanted, he wouldn't pay it any attention.

Marya grinned at him and rolled her eyes before urging her horse into a gallop. Hamasa watched her ride ahead, shading his eyes with a hand as something moved in the sky. A shadow passed as quick as a fish down a stream, and Arash swooped down from the clouds, his scales blinding. Marya stood up tall in the saddle, throwing her fist in the air and whooping eagerly, whooping again when her horse whinnied.

"Careful, you'll burn Nerva if you get any hotter," Valerius warned, nudging Nerva into a faster-paced canter.

Hamasa stilled, and, stupidly, his temperature rose instead of fell.

"You didn't tell her you could still be Sovereign. Being a Lance doesn't take you out of the running for that," Hamasa blurted, his mouth throwing the words out as fast as possible.

Valerius hummed under his breath. "It doesn't matter. Her Imperial Highness is younger than I, and Sovereigns live many years longer than a normal human. The next Sovereign won't be Chosen during my lifetime." Hamasa closed his eyes, squeezing them shut so tightly his scars ached. His teeth creaked, almost cracking, as he gritted them. *Don't say anything. Don't think anything,* Hamasa recited inwardly. "Hn. It seems we're stopping."

Hamasa blinked his eyes open and saw Arash coasting in lazy circles lower and lower to the ground. Marya was already on her feet next to the silver horse, waving in big, exuberant arcs over her head.

"Thank the Sun." Hamasa sighed, shoulders slumping. "If I never ride a horse again... um, no offense, Nerva," he added, leaning forward to pat her neck.

"Luckily, my lord, Nerva isn't offended," Valerius said, gently reining her to a stop.

Hamasa frowned, half-turned around. "Was that a joke?" He managed to catch a glimpse of the Valerius' side profile as the knight dismounted effortlessly. He was very obviously and suspiciously not meeting Hamasa's eyes.

"Of course not, my lord." Valerius threw the reins around the saddle horn and held up a hand for Hamasa to take. "You'll be stiff," he prompted when Hamasa hesitated.

With a mental sigh, Hamasa gave in and grasped the proffered hand. He had spent hours riding with the man—holding his hand for a few seconds wouldn't make it worse. His whole body protested when he tried to dismount, a whine hissing between his teeth just getting a leg over the mare's broad back. He lay over the saddle, one hand grasping leather, nose pressed to the barely padded seat, feet dangling over the side. Valerius' hand let him go and rested on his lower back instead.

"Did you forget how to do the rest?" Valerius asked. This time, the amusement was so obvious, Hamasa didn't need to look. Ignoring the urge to kick, which would probably miss and use too many pathetically abused leg muscles, Hamasa hissed.

"If I say yes, will you leave me here?" he asked under his

breath. Valerius' hand was *there*, on his back, and Hamasa pressed his face to the saddle so hard the threads dug into his skin and his nose bent flatly to the side.

"What did you do to Hamasa!?" Marya demanded.

Valerius didn't bother replying. "Slide down, I'll catch you."

"No," Hamasa retorted sulkily. He inhaled sharply, gripped each side of the saddle, and jumped down. Sheer, stubborn, force of will kept his knees from buckling. Triumphantly, he glared up at Valerius, who bowed slightly and stepped back. Hoping he didn't look too bowlegged, he strode to where Marya was standing and watching them.

"You walk like an old man," Marya said, disabusing Hamasa of the idea he had any dignity left.

"Thanks, Marya."

His shoulders heaved in a sigh and he looked to where Arash was balancing on three legs, one taloned claw in a loose fist. Hamasa hurried to him, already smiling at the ethereal glow of Arash's dragon form. Steam wafted off his scales and minuscule flurries glittered in the sunlight. Arash lowered his head, stretching his neck forward. Hamasa reached out and gently held Arash's face in both his hands, stroking upwards to grip the gracefully arching horns growing from above each eye ridge. Vapor hissed where Hamasa's palms touched the smooth, silvery-white face plates, so neatly and perfectly fit together not a single seam could be seen. His forehead pressed to the smooth plate between Arash's eyes. The chill rippled down his spine, soothing the worst of the aches and pains. Too soon, Hamasa stepped away with a grateful smile.

"Thank you," Hamasa said, standing a little taller. A whirlwind of snow and ice buffeted his clothes and hair, and Marya cursed colorfully as her horse reared back. The fleeting blizzard ended and Arash stepped out of the circle of frost flowers already melting on the sun-warmed sand.

"Any time, qal'bi," Arash said, grinning cheekily. Hamasa's face heated and he shook his head. Arash hissed through his teeth and shoved a quail into Hamasa's hands. "Dinner. For you to cook." His lip curled with disgust before sauntering away.

Hamasa stared down at the quail in surprise. Marya edged up behind him and mirrored his stare.

"Is that how dragons flirt?"

"What? N-no! Flirt? No one is flirting," Hamasa protested.

"I'm better at hunting than Hamasa," Arash said casually, flopping to the ground and stretching out onto his back. "If I wanted it to be a gift, I wouldn't give him a single bird."

"Listen to him brag. Maybe he'll bring a whole flock next time," Marya said, rolling her eyes. Arash's mouth curled up crookedly; he didn't bother to deny or agree. "And Hamasa is a good hunter all on his own. He hunted for me and my mamá." She led Hamasa to where Valerius was clearing grass and brush away for a fire pit.

"It's all right, Marya. Arash likes to hunt, and he is better at it," Hamasa said. "He can fly."

"Hm, true..." She stopped and squinted at Arash. "Lizard-brain, are you shorter?"

Arash closed his eyes and tucked his hands behind his head. "Am I?"

Marya braced her hands on her hips and tilted her head to the side. "I'm sure you were taller'n me yesterday. You're shorter now."

"And?"

"Ay, just answer a question *right*, you giant lizard!" Marya stomped her foot.

"I'm taking a nap. Go away."

Hamasa ducked his head to hide his smile when Marya let

out a wordless shout mangled around an irritated groan. She grabbed Hamasa's elbow to drag him with her.

"What happens if we set his icy butt on fire?" she spat furiously.

"You'd need a very big fire," Valerius answered as Marya and Hamasa approached. His eyes darted towards Arash, and then back to the duo. "You hoed a garden and hunted, my lord? Your list of skills increase daily."

"Hunting was easier than hoeing," Hamasa said. He stopped, remembering the sound of the snap, and looked down at the quail in his hands. "In some ways."

"New skills, plucking feathers and prepping the meat. Let's get to work, I'm starving," Marya ordered. She led him a little farther past the fire pit.

"After lunch, we'll practice some basic defensive fighting. Both of you," Valerius warned them. They looked back in surprise.

"Both of us?" Hamasa repeated.

Valerius nodded. "Róntraih Porto is a rough city. You should be prepared."

"Why can't I just swing my spear at 'em like you already been teaching me?" Marya asked.

"If you want the city guards or militia on you within seconds, the spear is conspicuous enough to get it done," Valerius said mildly. Marya made a face at the back of his head as soon as he started moving nearby rocks into the beginnings of a circle.

26

QUAIL WAS a lot tastier than Hamasa expected, but that might have been due to hunger. Even just riding was exhausting and had whetted Hamasa's appetite beyond what he was used to. Arash had grumbled about sharing it, but Marya ignored him with a beaming smile. With it was a few more stiff tortiyas and a few ears of corn they had roasted still wrapped in their husks. Hamasa had liked it all, and felt satiated, but he couldn't help but remember the spices the Garsias had used in every dish, no matter how small. He remembered the fresh crunch of green vegetables, too. Maybe they would find a hostal or cantina with new dishes to try in Róntraih Porto. He wondered idly what Mekshans did with seafood, Marya would have plenty of… Abruptly, he cut the musings short. He might not have a chance to try something new with Marya.

As Hamasa sat cross-legged on the ground, hands clasped on his lap, he refocused on what was in front of him. Marya and Valerius stood across from each other, both down to a single layer of clothing, sweat darkening their collars and armpits and trailing down Marya's face. Marya nodded, mouth tight and eyes on Valerius' over-exaggerated and slow movements. Even though they did this multiple times a day, it was still odd to see Marya so serious and not talking back at Valerius' every word and command.

Then, he moved. If while mostly asleep he was snake-like, a fully awake Valerius moved like lightning. There was no excess movement, no flair or embellishment. Marya managed to shuffle back, arm rising automatically to knock his first jab aside. His second fist aimed for her cheek, and she ducked under it. When she stood up, her elbow thrust into Valerius' lower chest. He grunted aloud, feet shifting over sand and his arms moving to grapple her. She wrapped her wiry arms around one of his biceps, shoved her shoulder into his breastbone, and, teeth gritting, heaved him over her head. Although she finally managed the throw, she shrieked in surprise not even a second later as she went tumbling with him, dragged by the back of her shirt in his fist.

Arash chuckled as dust flew. "She's a lot stronger than she looks. Didn't think a human that small could lift something twice their size like that."

"What all humans can do is impossible to learn in a single lifetime," Hamasa murmured. "There were so many stories of gallant knights and human mages accomplishing these impossible deeds, but the more people I meet, the more I see, the more I think some of those deeds aren't so impossible after all. Marya is another person meant for a hero's destiny, I can tell."

"Heroes don't always live happily ever after," Arash said with an ugly little twist to his mouth. "In the end, humans suffer. Humans die. All they'll do is drag you down with them."

"Dragons die, too," Hamasa whispered, eyes closing, jaw tensing. The same tired argument, over and over again.

"You're not your father, Hamasa. You don't need to try—"

"I don't want to talk about it, Arash," Hamasa said.

"It's been twenty—"

"Seventeen!"

Hamasa dug his fingers into the dirt. In front of them,

THE COWARD'S EMBLEM

Valerius and Marya looked over, startled at the sound of his warning snarl. Marya was once again under Valerius' torso, working on her footing to compensate for Valerius' weight. They disentangled, Marya stepping towards them until Hamasa got to his feet and dusted off the seat of his pants. Arash's head tipped back, frowning with his eyes closed.

"Hamasa, please sit down. I'm not going to let you run away," his eyes opened, gleaming in annoyance, and met Hamasa's, "not yet."

"It's my turn," Hamasa said, raising his chin and walking towards the two wrestling.

"If you're willing, my lord," Valerius said easily. His eyes honed in on Hamasa's face, eyes narrowing somewhere around the corner of Hamasa's mouth.

"I guess I could use a rest," Marya said, eyebrows rising. She plucked her tunic away from her chest and flapped it to cool her sweaty skin. Glancing towards Arash, she frowned. "Are you...?"

"Yes."

She looked between the two of them again. Finally, she nodded and walked past, patting Hamasa's shoulder as she went. Hamasa licked his lips and turned to Valerius.

"Are you going to teach me to throw you, too?" he asked, tone sharp.

"Hn," Valerius crossed his arms over his chest. "Hit me."

The sudden order startled Hamasa out of his black mood. His eyes widened, hands awkwardly hanging by his sides. Just... hit him? He stepped closer, eyes darting over the relaxed set of Valerius' shoulders, his expectant gaze, the rising of an eyebrow as Hamasa hesitated.

"You're not going to give me any advice?" Hamasa asked. He licked his dry lips swiftly. Valerius shook his head.

"I want to see how fast you are."

For a challenge, it wasn't much of one. Not that Hamasa responded well to most challenges anyway. He pressed his lips tightly together and lowered his body, feet spreading further apart and knees bending. From all his sideline observations, he knew that using Valerius' center of gravity against him was his best bet, the way the knight was obviously teaching Marya. The difference, or one difference of many, was that Marya was surprisingly stronger than she looked, and definitely stronger than Hamasa. Strength had never been something Hamasa had, especially not now. Valerius didn't so much as shift when Hamasa readied himself. That was not a good sign... Sighing inwardly, Hamasa leapt forward.

Vaguely he heard Marya's gasp, a shocked whoop that choked and fell silent.

Hamasa was fast. It was what he was good at: being small and fast. But somehow, despite how swiftly he had flung himself forward, Valerius had stepped out of Hamasa's path, snatched Hamasa's extended wrist, and his other hand had gripped the back of Hamasa's neck, fingers pinching nerves that sent terrified shivers down his spine.

"For someone pretending to be human, you don't do it very well," Valerius said quietly. Hamasa cringed out from under the knight's hand, only to be tugged back by the iron grip around his wrist. Slowly, Valerius raised Hamasa's hand between them. While no longer quite... clawed, his fingers were still spread wide and curling forward slightly. "Humans don't have claws. Not even long fingernails can rend like a dragon's talons."

Hamasa swallowed. "I don't kn-know—"

Valerius used his free hand to carefully bend Hamasa's four fingers in towards the base of each, then curled his bent fingers into a tight fist. The thumb Valerius tucked over Hamasa's knuckles under his palm. After he was satisfied, Valerius set his hand on Hamasa's chest and pushed him up straight, and then, using his feet to push Hamasa's here and there over the ground, positioned Hamasa to be mostly facing forward, his left shoulder a little more forward and his fist near his cheek.

"Raise your other fist—watch the thumb, under the palm. Hn. Now, raise your fist by your other cheek. Try to always keep a fist near your face to be ready to block or protect your eyes," Valerius instructed. His words were low and blunt, but mellow. A voice that neither praised nor condemned. In a way it was soothing, and Hamasa's twitches and nerves ebbed under the quiet monotone of Valerius' simple commands. He shoved down on Hamasa's shoulders, ignoring the surprised yelp, to bend his knees into something not quite a crouch.

"This isn't how you fight. You used the flat of your hands," Hamasa said twisting his fists back and forth to look at them. Valerius sighed and yanked his fists back into place.

"I was using a different style of fighting that requires more finesse and experience. You can't throw a punch yet. You can think about style some other time," Valerius said dryly. Hamasa scowled up at him.

"When you jab, which is a straight quick punch, you need to turn your wrist so that your palm is parallel to the ground," Valerius continued to explain. He gently guided Hamasa into an overly slow jab. While one arm was extended, Valerius reached under to slap Hamasa's other elbow. "Keep it up." Hamasa hissed and raised his fist a little higher. "Good, try again. This time, when you jab, move your body with it, turning on the ball of your foot to put some weight behind it."

Hamasa frowned. Valerius demonstrated, once slow, and then fast. So fast Hamasa blinked and stared where Valerius' fist had jabbed across and then back right in front of him. With hard exhale through his nose, he jabbed forward, his foot slipping over the ground and his balance tottering.

"If only humans had tails!" Arash called as Hamasa flailed wildly to stay upright.

"Where's your tail, frosty?" Marya snapped.

"Ignore distractions," Valerius ordered, tapping Hamasa between the eyes with a finger. Hamasa cut a sharp glance up at him, but re-positioned himself as taught. Valerius hummed. One hand cupped Hamasa's shoulder to hold him still and Valerius nudged his back foot further forward. "There, your feet were too far apart. Try again."

"I'm just hitting air. Shouldn't I be hitting you?" Hamasa asked.

A quiet scoff answered him. Just as Hamasa gritted his teeth to try the jab again, Valerius came around in front of him. Hamasa stared incredulously. Valerius held up his hands, palms open and flat in front of him.

"You're right. Your right fist should punch my left hand. Go," Valerius ordered.

Hamasa's fists clenched, but he paused. "Are you going to move your hand?"

"Of course not. My lord."

"Stop calling me that," Hamasa muttered. Then, squinting and jaw tense, Hamasa struck. His knuckles hit Valerius' palm with a resounding smack, his body just barely twisting and his heel up as his foot balanced on the ball of his foot. Valerius smiled, a real smile, and pulled his hand away to shake it. Like Hamasa's punch had hurt. Even a little.

"That's it. Remember to bring your fist back immediately. Do two jabs, right, then left."

Hamasa grinned, actually baring his teeth and his body heating. "I did it?"

THE COWARD'S EMBLEM

"Yes, you did. Somewhat. We still need to strengthen your core," Valerius said, holding up his open palms again. Hamasa blinked at him.

"My core?"

"Your stomach!" Marya shouted.

"What?"

The flat of Valerius' hand cuffed him around the ear, and Hamasa sputtered and scrambled back. Valerius, the gulero, merely stared at him. "Stop being distracted, my lord."

Hamasa scowled and raised his fists. "Fine." He could handle a few days of learning to punch and strengthening his stomach. It shouldn't be too hard.

By the end of the thirty minutes, Hamasa decided: no. No, he couldn't. He was wheezing, every muscle trembling, his skin searing hot, and his core felt weaker. He usually didn't notice his stomach unless he was hungry, and now he wished he didn't have an abdomen. His ears rang from the constant cuffing of Valerius' open palm wherever he let his guard — or his fists — down. And though he had punched Valerius' hands what felt like a thousand times and his usually pale palms were bright pink, the knight barely shook them out as he eyed Hamasa impassively.

"You're fast. We can work with that."

Hamasa grimaced at Valerius' back and fought the urge to stick his tongue out like Marya. Arash and Marya came up, Marya clapping his shoulder and Arash bracing his arm on Hamasa's head. Hamasa groaned, drooping under their weight, minimal as it was.

"You did good, Hamito. That was almost a compliment," Marya teased. She quickly pulled her hand away and shook it out. "Ay, you're burning up, but you haven't sweated a drop. How do you do that?"

"You looked ridiculous," Arash told him, ignoring Marya completely. "But it was really cathartic seeing you punch him repeatedly."

"It looked more cathartic than it felt," Hamasa muttered. Marya burst into laughter, slapping his back. Hamasa grunted and fell to his knees.

"Ay! Hamasa!"

"I knew this was a bad idea," Arash said. His icy cool hands lifted Hamasa up under the armpits like a particularly lazy cat. "You're a reader, not a fighter."

"I've never been more aware of that in my life," he agreed. He blinked as Marya tucked herself under one arm and Arash did the same on the other side. Between Marya's beaming smile and the chilly comfort of Arash's arm around his waist, Hamasa huffed a small laugh. "Thanks."

"You'll be a fighter in no time," Marya promised.

"It'll take a lot of time," Valerius disagreed.

Hamasa glanced up, frowning, only to interrupt himself before saying a word with a loud groan. The knight had already finished buckling Nerva's saddle back on her and he waited at his mare's side for the trio to approach.

"Not more riding!"

"We still have a long ride to Róntraih Harbor," Valerius said. He held out a hand to Hamasa. Hamasa considered it. Walking while every muscle shook like a newborn kid's, or suffering on the back of a horse that did most the work for him. Sighing, he extricated himself from Arash and Marya and grasped Valerius' hand.

"If I fall asleep and fall off, it'll be your fault," Hamasa warned. It was easier, with all his practice, to get his foot in the stirrup, but actually heaving himself up made every quavering muscle protest in unison. Hands on his waist lifted him off the ground, and he scrabbled to grab the reins and throw his leg over in time.

"I won't let you fall, my lord," Valerius promised.

Hamasa looked down and met Valerius' eyes. The moment stretched out, silent and heavy, and Hamasa's hands involuntarily clamped around the leather straps in his hand. After everything, after days of wanting to be anywhere else, after the past thirty minutes of hoping he could punch hard enough to make Valerius wince for *once*, Hamasa's heart thumped too hard in his chest. He tore his gaze away and shuffled forward in the saddle so Valerius could swing up behind him.

27

"I SEE IT! That's Róntraih Porto, right?" Marya crowed, standing as tall as she could in the stirrups and shading her eyes to squint.

Hamasa peered the same direction and, sure enough, caught the glitter of the distant bay. He had to blink away the spots as the late afternoon sun bounced along the surface of the sea. The huge city sprawled out suddenly in front of them, the rocky fields sinking down into the bowl of the harbor. Houses of stone and wood with flat roofs covered with plants and clothes flapping from drying lines were nestled claustrophobically close together. Winding labyrinthine roads and streets twined between every building, barely wide enough for the wide caravan wagons that rattled down cobbled and dirt streets alike.

The most amazing part were the colors. Almost every building was brightly and vividly painted in shades of teal, yellow, red, white, blue, even occasional pops of orange or purple. It was nothing like the drab wood and clay buildings of the villages they had passed, nothing like the golden-wood walls and low, porcelain-tiled eaves of Riyushu. The buildings got bigger — and less colorful — the closer to the water they got; becoming huge warehouses and outposts for the myriad of traders from all over the world. Not even Riyushu had the same trading traffic Róntraih Porto Cuidat saw on a near daily basis. It was known for welcoming all kinds of peoples and Others, all living in close quarters with special laws and protections. It was also known for its tariffs—or lack thereof—for ships and caravans entering the city. Which resulted in the population being a diverse mix of Others and humans, as well as different races and their cultures from around the world.

As they neared the slope down into the city, the mostly empty road they had been following gradually filled with people. Weather-beaten wagons of families hoping for work in the city and caravans of goods from all over Mekshi. Sailors leaving their villages to return to the sea that beckoned them for one last expedition before the winter storms began. Rich folk that came to see their goods come ashore and their coffers filled, maybe checking on a ship's captain who might be taking more than their due. Hamasa watched each face as they passed with an eager curiosity, the dozens of stories possible with each person flitting through his mind.

"So this is what passes for civilization for you mud-wallowers?" Arash asked, unimpressed and eyebrows high. Hamasa sighed.

"Are you trying to make yourself unlikeable, Arash?"

Marya snorted loudly. Arash smirked unrepentantly at Hamasa.

"It's just so easy to rile them, how can I resist?"

"Aren't creatures that live several millennia above such pettiness?" Valerius asked.

Hamasa and Arash's eyes met. Hamasa had to quickly duck his head and bite his lip. Meanwhile Arash threw back his head to crow with laughter.

"Firstly, I'm not even four hundred. Older and wiser dragons would consider me barely out of my egg. And secondly, you obviously only know dragons by the fatuous stories made up by people eager for coin, not honesty. Dragons have spent millennia *mastering* pettiness. What else is there to do when you live that long?" Arash retorted, chuckling and wiping at his eyes.

Valerius grunted softly. Hamasa glanced over his shoulder to see the disappointed and pensive frown on the knight's face. He looked put out at the mere idea that dragons could be petty and childish. At the mere idea that dragons were as flawed as the rest of living creation. Hamasa turned around quickly, his amusement trickling away.

They made it into the city with perhaps an hour to spare before nightfall. There were only a few odd looks at Arash's easy running between the two mares. In a place like Róntraih Porto, there were enough Others that the looks didn't last long. The roads through most of the city were well cobbled, Nerva and the stolen horse's hooves striking sparks as they trotted. Several people in brightly dyed clothes purposefully walked these avenues with large straw brooms, bowing or blowing kisses for each coin handed over as they swept. Instead of going for a cantina or hostal, Valerius led them straight through the dizzying streets to the wharves. Through the warehouse district, the roads were even narrower, the cobbles cracked and dull, some missing. Not a single one of those brightly garbed sweepers was in sight.

Valerius continued to steer them towards the sea of masts looming over the warehouses without pause. Hamasa's heart began to speed up, his mouth drying, as those masts neared. To the side, Marya kept casting looks at him, her worry palpable.

Hawkers hollered from the streets, pushing their carts or thrusting their trays under their horses' snouts, while streetwalkers whistled from doorways and winked over brightly painted lips. A few clever-eyed urchins eyed their saddlebags, seeing at a glance how well their horses were taken care of and the glossy sheen to their coats, but one look at the poorly concealed trident was enough to send them away again. The smell of the sea rose, and with it the heavy and foul brackish scent of tepid harbor water. The more Hamasa saw, the more unlike Riyushu Róntraih became: not so orderly, nor so neat and tidy. The cantinas and small businesses were older, many smoke-stained, paint peeling on battered signboards.

And yet, the voices were cheerful and lively. No one looked starving, although many were dirty or missing shoes. Whip-thin dogs chased tattered-eared cats that chased rats bigger than Hamasa's foot. Children in clothing both tattered and new chased them all. Some children held toy lances the size and length of broomsticks and painted blue. Others wore wooden masks; crude approximations of snarling red dragon faces. A few masks were grey, and fewer green or black.

Hamasa swallowed hard and stared at Nerva's mane under his hands. He didn't want to look closer. He didn't want to see which poorly made dragon's face would stare back at him with laughing children's eyes.

"There," Valerius announced suddenly. He reined Nerva to a halt and nodded towards Marya to do the same.

A large galley rocked on the wake with ropes almost as big around as Hamasa's waist holding it to the docks. The wood gleamed gold in the sunset and the sails were tied up and only a half dozen men and women roamed the decks with mops and buckets. At the prow, a water sylph was carved lovingly and painstakingly into the dark wood. Her hair swirled and foamed like waves around her shoulders and trailed down her figure to hint at the curves she might have. One hand cupped her mouth, open wide and somehow smiling, while the other hand pressed to her chest. Singing to enchant men and women alike to the depths of the sea.

Along the port side, the beautifully carved and gilded words *Siren's Call* were writ. A tall, broad-shouldered person was hanging upside down from the deck, feet hooked around the banisters dangerously, as they carefully repainted the words in glistening gold paint. Their blonde hair was braided and flopping around their head like a lifeless tail.

"What by the Sun is that moron doing?" Arash asked, eyebrows high. His nostrils flared and the tip of his tongue tasted the air. "Not a mud ape, though."

Marya stared at Arash. "You can tell what someone is by looking at 'em?"

"Smelling them. You humans rely too much on sight." Arash rolled his eyes and easily dodged Marya's kick in his direction. Marya yelped as the too-fierce movement almost jerked her out of the saddle and she barely clung on to her seat.

Hamasa gnawed on his lip. He wanted to do something, say something, but he knew where most of Arash's rudeness stemmed from. How, in the end, it was yet another thing that was his fault. Behind him, Valerius swung out of the saddle and Hamasa stared down at his hands. Two big hands grabbed his waist and lifted him from the saddle. Instinctively, Hamasa reached out to grasp Valerius' shoulders, trying his best not to tangle his legs anywhere or kick Nerva accidentally. The Lance was lowering him to the ground, the mare's massive body blocking them from the view of their two travelling companions.

Hamasa gulped hard, hands lingering on Valerius' shoulders and temperature rising as he stared where the kimono folded over his chest. His eyes lingered where that gaping wound had once been, remembered the stark black thread that had stitched the man together until a better potion could be bought. Valerius set him gently on his feet and Hamasa was all too aware of the knight's hands on his waist.

"I... uh," Hamasa croaked out sounds that were supposed to be words. Clearing his throat, he said, "I can dismount on my own. Now."

"How are you holding up after another day in the saddle?" Valerius glanced cursorily up and down, not bothering to look Hamasa in the face.

He wasn't disappointed. Hamasa didn't want some other explanation for why Valerius had helped him down. Or why his hands still rested on his waist. "I'll make do," he said quickly, stepping back and grunting when his back thumped Nerva. The horse huffed loudly, her ear flicking back towards him.

"You're getting better."

Hamasa blinked and tilted his head in confusion. Valerius glanced away, a hand coming up to cover his mouth. But not fast enough for Hamasa to miss the beginnings of a smile. How did his heart beat faster more at that than Valerius' hands on him?

"Riding. I think the daily exercise has helped you recover, too."

"Yes, I'm sure that you have very altruistic reason for demanding I do all those stretches and punches and... things," Hamasa replied, one hand sweeping through the air.

"I already told you my reason. Your faster recovery is an extra benefit," Valerius said.

Hamasa huffed and met Valerius' eyes. In a strange opposite reflection their usual places, Hamasa crossed his arms over his chest and raised an eyebrow. Or tried to. He struggled with it, both eyebrows rising, dropping, his mouth twisting to the side as he squinted.

"What are you doing?" Valerius asked incredulously.

"How do you—? With the eyebrow!" Hamasa demanded. "You and Marya both do it so well!"

"I have no idea what you're talking about, my lord," Valerius said. Just barely, that twitch returned to the corner of his mouth.

"You're joking again! You're teasing me!" Hamasa exclaimed,

pointing an incriminating finger at the smile that wasn't quite there.

"What are you two doing?" Marya asked as she came around the Nerva's front. Next to her, Arash narrowed his eyes, a look darting between Valerius and Hamasa.

The smile dropped as if it had never been, and Valerius nodded once, his face stoic and business-like already. Hamasa tried not to feel stupidly bereft, hands falling to his sides as he watched Valerius turn away. He followed, wringing the poncho's hem, and took his place between Marya and Arash.

They followed the knight and his mare, Valerius' sure hands holding the reins to lead Nerva towards the docks. Hamasa's eyes met Arash's briefly from under the fringe of his hair. The questioning lift of Arash's pale brow had Hamasa's resolve hardening, and he nodded discreetly. Blue eyes rolled upwards in exasperation, but he didn't say anything aloud. So he was still willing to help. Which was what Hamasa wanted.

Obviously.

"Hamito, you look kinda pale. You feeling good?" Marya asked worriedly. She clasped Hamasa's shoulder with an affectionate squeeze.

Hamasa dredged up a wan smile. "It was a long ride. I'm still tired from all those abdominal exercises this morning."

Marya cast her eyes to the sky. "Ay. *Those*. If I never have to use my stomach for anything other than eating ever again, I'd be a happy girl."

"Don't you want a body more like the knight's? You always complain about not having arms like his," Arash drawled.

"D'you think I could get there?" Marya lifted the arm not leading her horse and flexed her bicep. She had already been wiry and strong from farm work, but there was definitely more mass to the shape of her arm now.

"I have no doubt. Eat more meat," Hamasa suggested. Marya beamed and punched his shoulder lightly. Or what she thought was lightly.

"Mm, meat," Arash agreed, then slowly began to frown. "Are we going to have to eat fish while we're here? Fish is not meat."

"Ay! It's Valerius! And he's not head to toe in metal!" The foursome looked up to see the upside-down not-human-person waving frantically down at them. Valerius scowled uncomfortably upwards and refrained from waving, but the person just grinned wider. "Duby, get over here."

"No, you will not call me that, Teyo." The voice that replied was serious and obviously annoyed, and shortly followed by a figure leaning over the banister near where Teyo was hanging. The man was as tall as his companion, but his hair was dark and short, and a dark goatee surrounded his mouth.

"You're no fun, Duby."

"What did I just say?" The dark-haired man gave Valerius a short salute of a wave without looking at his shipmate. "Teyo makes a good point. It's not often you're without your armor, Sir Emerens Valerius, Lance of the Realm."

Emerens. Hamasa inhaled sharply. Hearing it said out loud, by someone else, so suddenly and out of nowhere, knocked the breath out of him. Struggling to hide his reaction, Hamasa closed his eyes and clenched his hands into fists like Valerius had spent the past two days teaching him. Next to him, Marya leaned in close.

"Emerens? Is his name *Emerens*?"

"Don't, Marya. In Riyukezu tradition, only family and close friends call each other by their given names," Hamasa warned.

"Huh. Really?" Marya propped her fist on a hip and watched Valerius walk down the dock closer to the galley. "I wonder how many people call him that."

Hamasa's mouth pressed into a thin line.

"I'm here to book passage for my travelling companions and our two horses. As soon as possible," Valerius said brusquely, ignoring pleasantries and explanations.

"Not even a hello?" Teyo teased. Teyo put the paintbrush between their teeth and, in an awe-inspiring bout of athleticism, managed to twist and pull themself up onto the deck without spilling a drop of paint from the bucket.

Definitely not human. Hamasa couldn't have pulled that off without magic to help.

"We don't do deals without a mug of michalad to smooth it along. It's a rule, right, Duvhan?" Teyo told them with a grin at the dark-haired man. Duvhan sounded like a real name, and he didn't protest it this time.

"The only rule you actually care about," Duvhan said dryly. "We'll be down to negotiate terms. Do you need a recommendation for a cantina?"

"Or hostal. If you wouldn't mind," Valerius agreed. Duvhan nodded and turned to speak softly to Teyo, who whooped and bounced away.

As Duvhan stood to his full height, Hamasa caught sight of a strange, bulky fur wrapped around his narrow waist. It had a strangely wet sheen to it, but the man didn't look wet. Hamasa leaned in close to Arash to nudge his arm, lifting his chin at Duvhan's back. "Is he…?"

"Not human? Yup." Arash gave him a wry look. "You could've figured that out yourself, rafiik."

Hamasa opened his mouth to protest and then froze, eyes on Arash's profile. Arash had never called him that before. Something warm and soft blooming in his stomach. They had been the only ones their age, two born within months of each other; an occurrence so rare that they'd been raised side by side. By the time either of them would've thought of choosing a singular gender, Arash had already made more romantic intentions known.

This was different, it felt different. An acceptance of Hamasa's platonic feelings and a step forward between them. Hamasa was smiling over at Arash as they walked towards the gangplank, outright grinning when Arash's human body betrayed him. Frost grew along the tips of his pointed ears and down his dark skin like glittering lace.

"What's with the ice?" Marya asked from Hamasa's other side in a much too loud to be an actual whisper kind of whisper. Arash snarled, but refused to look at her.

"Don't worry about it," Hamasa said as Teyo and Duvhan approached.

The Others were taller than all three of the weary, dirty travelers by more than a few hands' span. The captain, with his dark hair and pale skin, was the sort of ethereal beautiful that many humanoid Others had, especially those from the sea. His eyes were the most enthralling; at first seeming black, until the light hit them just right and the startling dark blue of the deep ocean gazed back at them. His hands, when he lifted one for Valerius to shake, were webbed, the skin between his fingers so thin and pale it was almost translucent. Hamasa's eyes darted towards the big blonde Teyo, with eyes the same blue as Duvhan's and made darker by the contrast of their golden hair and skin. Just barely, Hamasa could see the same webbing between their fingers when they rubbed their hands together rather gleefully.

"Four new passengers? That's some nice coin we won't say nay to, huh, Duby?" Teyo said, nudging at Duvhan's side with an elbow and winking at Hamasa. He blushed hotly at being caught examining Teyo too closely.

"Uh, I," Hamasa stuttered wildly. *Rude, very rude!*

"What did I say about professionalism, Teyo?"

Teyo made a complicated face that ended in an over-dramatic pout. "If I can't use it, get back on the boat." Teyo smiled winsomely at Duvhan, who raised a sardonic brow.

"I'm not going to ask questions other than, what's your destination and can you pay?" Duvhan looked over the group, lingering curiously on Arash and Hamasa, before resting again on Valerius.

"Riyushu. You know I can. After we get there."

Both of Duvhan's thin dark brows went up incredulously at Valerius' blunt terms. "After the voyage? That's not how *Siren's Call* negotiates, and you know that."

Valerius stared unflinchingly and directly into Duvhan's obviously inhuman gaze without another word. Duvhan frowned. Marya and Hamasa's gazes bounced between the two with increasing concern. With a loud scoff, Teyo broke the growing silence between the two stubborn shipmates. Teyo thumped Duvhan on the back and leaned their whole weight into his shoulder, almost tipping the dark-haired nonhuman off balance.

Ignoring Duvhan's annoyed grimace, Teyo said easily, "We know this guy. He's so uptight he was born with a spear up his rear-end—" Valerius' eyes twitched at the corners as Marya stifled a snort behind her hands and Arash didn't even bother to hide his toothy grin. Hamasa gaped, torn between shock and outrage. "—he'll pay when we get there or die trying. You know that, Dub-*Captain* Róntraih." Teyo rolled their eyes at Duvhan's glare.

Hamasa blinked and shuffled awkwardly. This whole time he had been thinking of him as *Duvhan*, when the proper address was Captain *Róntraih*. Humans and their names and proper order of them; he hadn't thought Others like Captain Róntraih had two—

"Róntraih?" Hamasa blurted, eyes darting to the captain.

"Like the *city*?" Marya asked, boggling at him.

"You could say my people have been around for a long time," Captain Róntraih replied vaguely.

Of course, Hamasa realized, *he's a selkie*. Valerius had told them days ago. Tongue-tied and stupid, he stared down at his toes silently. He should've remembered the story of the selkie who had come to Mekshi from the Dreikstan Islands all those years ago and founded a home for his beloved, their legacy helping to build Róntraih Porto Cuidat into the thriving city it was today. He could almost picture those disappointed and amused blue eyes, the click of her tongue against her teeth as his longtime companion shook her head at his foolishness. *Don't you remember all those books you read, my friend?*

"What names shall I call your companions by?" Duvhan asked, again his gaze lingering on Arash and Hamasa.

"I'm Marya. Marya Garsia," she introduced eagerly. She hurried forward to hold out her hand so their hands could clasp around each other's wrists.

"A lovely name," Teyo said. Their eyes twinkled with mischief. "Do you know its old meaning?"

Marya blinked. "It has a meaning?"

"Of the sea," Teyo said, smiling. Marya's lips parted in surprise before she smiled back.

"I had no idea! I actually never been to the sea before today. I wonder if my mamá knew?"

"I'm interested in these two," Captain Róntraih said with a glance to Arash and Hamasa. He stepped closer to Hamasa, who tried to look anywhere else, only for his eyes to catch on the cloth around the captain's waist. Sleek black fur and the hint of a webbed claw foot among the folds. A pelt. "I've never met someone try so hard to look like no one at all," the captain said quietly. Hamasa flinched and glanced up to see the captain's smirk.

Arash stepped in front of Hamasa and all Hamasa could see was white hair and a patch of white scales across Arash's nape.

"You can call me and him 'mind your own business'," Arash hissed. "You know what I am, just as I know you. You're not getting either of our names."

"You're not very friendly," Teyo said, that smile never wavering. "How about we call 'em Shortie and Shortie Number Two."

"That's not demeaning at all," Hamasa muttered.

"We need to discuss what comes next," Valerius said. He held his arm out in front of Arash before he could hiss with his usual caustic response.

"Yes, we should—"

"To the cantina! For michalad!" Teyo cried.

They wrapped an arm around Marya's shoulders and began to march, one hand raised and pointing down the road. Marya looked around at Hamasa, waving for him to catch up, her dark eyes dancing. Captain Róntraih shook his head and gestured for Valerius to walk with him, Nerva already clopping up to Valerius' side.

Trailing after the mostly exuberant group, Hamasa didn't bother trying to listen to whatever conversations they began. He held the stolen horse's reins, pressing his face to the pale shoulder, breathing in the scent of horse and leather, heart pounding to the clipping of hooves. Over everything, though, was the scent of the sea. He couldn't escape it or its continuous roar. Reminding him painfully of the home he'd had for seventeen years, and left behind in the dead of night. There was a nudge to his arm and he glanced at Arash. The dragon jerked his chin towards the wharf where there were many ships all a-bustle, crews running to and fro on the decks and shouting orders and warnings while large nets filled with barrels and crates were being lifted and lowered into ships' holds via pulleys.

Cold trailed over his back and Arash moved away. His blue eyes, shining too brightly, gazed at Hamasa's chest.

"It'll last a few minutes. You better go now."

Hamasa stared, his already thumping heart leaping to his throat. Arash's gleaming eyes raised and his icy hand held Hamasa's. Unlike the shadow spell Hamasa had wielded all those days ago, he could see his own hand in Arash's grip. But the crowds around him parted without looking, gazes slid over his features and passed on without meeting his eyes or acknowledging him. Arash let Hamasa's wrist go.

"*Just go, Hamasa. Get it over with,*" he whispered in Draconic.

Hamasa dropped the reins of the horse, pulse jumping, stomach churning. Past Arash's carefully blank face, Hamasa looked towards Marya, where she grinned and chattered a league a minute at an equally cheerful and talkative Teyo. Already she had a new friend. And towards Valerius, whose face was in its usual serious frown, those dark intense eyes never leaving Captain Róntraih' profile. What did it matter if he snuck away from Valerius? Whether or not he was the child named Emerens, Valerius had kidnapped him. Marya though... Marya had been nothing but kind and trusting. Who whispered her dreams under a woolen blanket and worried they were too selfish. She didn't deserve Hamasa sneaking around and lying.

Hamasa gulped down the stone in his throat and forced himself towards the shipyard. He stopped, glanced back at Arash, watched him take the reins of the stolen horse and walk after the others. Never looking back.

28

HAMASA SUNK into the crowd, unnoticed and ignored, while his gaze jumped from ship to ship. Many were easy to pass, when he realized they were unloading cargo and unlikely to be leaving anytime soon. Others were filled with passengers with multiple gangplanks leading to different layers, which made Hamasa's hopes rise. Hamasa dithered at the end of the docks, eavesdropping on conversations to hear when the ship would leave. It was then, as a poorly dressed man whispered urgently to his partner, who was holding up a weary-eyed toddler, about how much money they had after paying for passage, that Hamasa's stomach began to sink.

Money.

He forgot he didn't have money. The few coins that weren't in Valerius' money pouch were in Marya's pockets. Hamasa looked back down the road, but the group he had been with had long since been swallowed by the crowd of sailors and traders heading into the city. He licked his lips, and began to keep looking and listening in, the wheels spinning in his mind. It seemed as if passengers were being separated by how much they could pay, and the poorer passengers, who were walking onto the lower decks of those massive ships, were paying in silver. Marya did have a few silvers, but not many, and it would mean sharing his room with maybe a dozen strangers for the entire journey. Surely no one would notice his oddities if they didn't have a cause to look closer... right?

Maybe a ship with *less* passengers would be a better idea. Although it meant he would have to do something far more unforgivable than just asking a friend for a few coins.

Dusk had spread over the horizon and Cantina windows lit up with welcoming torchlight while the first strains of music filled the air. His body heat was rising, his heart thumping, and desperation clenched a fist around his throat. Finally, he paused at the end of a dock as his eyes travelled over the obviously older, more weathered vessel than the *Siren's Call*. Sea salt and sea air had faded the wood to a silvery grey, the sails a dingy off-white, and the ropes were a little more frayed than he was completely comfortable with, large though they were. Two men were standing on the docks watching the heavy loads being lifted high overhead. A woman's voice rang out moments after a full net was lowered *into* the ship. There was another flurry of motion on board before more than half the heads disappeared below decks. The two men, one rather tall and lean and the other shorter and stout, began to walk up the gangplank.

"Wait!" Hamasa shouted, running forward. The spell slid off him like water off a duck and the countdown began to the moment when his group remembered to think about him.

The men paused to watch as he approached. The shorter one looked curious, but impatient, his heavy black beard twitching around his mouth trying not to frown. The other was completely inscrutable, or perhaps Hamasa was too distracted by hair a shocking hue of black and iridescent green: it was soft and thin and ruffled like a bird's feathers in the wind off the bay. Just barely, Hamasa could smell that tang of Other from the green-haired man, tasting it on his tongue when he inhaled deeper.

"Who's the bairn?" the shorter man asked. His accent was

heavy and strange, and his slang confusing.

Green-hair raised an eyebrow at him. "You think I know him?"

"H- Masa, my name is Masa," Hamasa said, quickly correcting himself. "I need to know where you're going," he begged in a rush.

"Where... aren't ye supposed to tell us that?"

"Shamus, quiet for a moment," Green-hair interrupted, not quite sharply. His eyes were a gleaming yellow that pierced Hamasa's. He swallowed nervously, but refused to step back under that gaze. He needed a ship. "We're heading to Dreikstan Islands."

"When?"

"Are you assuming you'll be on board?" Green-hair asked with a smirk.

Hamasa clenched his jaw even as his knees knocked. "Hoping."

"We're not coming back this way 'til next trading season, so we're not taking passengers," the man called Shamus replied. His eyes darted towards Green-hair, though, as he frowned. "Not that I know of."

Green-hair kept his eyes on Hamasa, still smirking and unreadable. "We're leaving at first light. And it's two silver coins when done the proper way."

"Calum, we have to ask the Cap before you offer her boat," Shamus said with a frown. The full, thick beard and bushy brows made him seem even angrier.

"I can be here. With two gold coins if you could forget the proper way this once. Please... please take me with you," Hamasa asked, just shy of begging. Or maybe actually begging. His gaze darted between them as he gnawed on his lower lip.

"He's small enough. Margita'll never notice," Calum said

with a wave of his hand.

Shamus groaned once and rolled his eyes heavenward. "All right, but you're telling her. And you," he pointed both his gaze and an index finger at Hamasa, "you will be here 'fore sun gets above that horizon, or we won't let you on for *five* gold."

"We'll definitely let you on for five gold coins. Margita likes gold more than she cares about another hammock in the berth," Calum said with a smirk. "But try not to be late. Masa."

Hamasa pressed his hand to his chest, unconsciously holding down the beating of his too fast heart. Both men were already heading up the gangplank, Shamus throwing bemused looks at him. Hamasa quickly shook his head and took a step back, looking around to memorize the neighboring ships and get a look at the name of this one. *The Squall* was carved deeply into wood that looked newer than the planks around it. And at the prow...

With another startled step back, Hamasa barely kept in the surprised gasp. A dragon snarled with all its teeth bared at him from the prow. In wood almost black with age, an approximation of the First Shield had been carved crudely, the expression more savage and dire due to its harsh lines and sea-weathered curves. Two thin whiskers trailed down from its snout, and a round pearl was clamped between its splintering teeth. The legends didn't quite get it right, but the sight of that wooden pearl had Hamasa's fingers, already pressed to his chest, clutching at loose folds of wool. Slowly, he retreated down the dock, eyes darting to the two sailors walking onto the ship above his head, and then to the figurehead.

A carving of a Storm Dragon of yore and a pearl that wasn't even real shouldn't be making that icy chill run down his spine. He licked his lips, breath leaving his mouth shakily, and turned. He had a jog ahead of him and a story to concoct.

Guilt curdled in his belly.

The crowd thinned the darker it got. He rushed to the last place he saw his group and torch posts were lit one by one by city lamplighters. Spheres of light spilled out over the dirty cobbles and lit up the faces that laughed and caroused outside the buildings. Sailors smoked from every doorway and alley, and the scent of burning tobacco tickled his nose and damp lips. He stopped in the street, frowning thoughtfully, eyes darting from sign to sign, head jerking towards every horse he saw.

"Asa!"

Relief warred with the guilt that still curdled. He turned, raising a hand, and promptly had his arms full of Marya. The fresh scent of sweat and road-dusty hair blocked out the cloying odor of tobacco and decaying kelp and the dozens of different meals being cooked in the cantinas and hostals around them.

"Marya," Hamasa greeted with a weak smile.

"Getting lost already? C'mon, you better stay close to me. I swear, Wally was about ready to run down the crowd on horseback to find you," Marya said.

"You really shouldn't call him Wally."

"It suits him better than Emerens. Anyway, we're up here at the Wharf's Mouth."

***

Marya shook her head in condescending amusement and completely missed Arash's dark stare in Hamasa's direction. Hamasa sunk further against the wall and drew his knees up to his chest, bare toes curling into blankets. The room Valerius had paid for had two beds (one of which Hamasa currently sat on) and a little table with a basin and urn. Steam curled gently from the surface of the basin and water sloshed over the sides as Marya rinsed most the road dust and grime off her face and neck. Hamasa dropped his eyes and traced the rough linen of the blankets beneath him with the tip of his index finger.

"Got lost in less than a second after you got on your own two feet in the city. You're lucky if Valerius don't keep you tied to the bed for the next two days we're stuck here," Marya said with a laugh muffled by her small towel.

Arash scoffed lightly. "Unless he has a pair of those disgusting cuffs, he won't be able to keep Hamasa tied anywhere."

"Arash," Hamasa sighed, voice tinged with warning. Arash rolled his eyes and crossed his arms over his chest.

"I guess he's right. If you could get your spells working right. Maybe you should try to do a giant blast like you did on my farm? Actually that might be too much. A little blast? Distract 'em long enough to make a run for it?" Marya suggested, wrapping the towel around the back of her neck and frowning pensively.

"Giant blast?" Arash asked, eyebrow rising. "Just what do you think Hamasa is?"

"Arash, please," Hamasa groaned wearily.

"No, Hamasa, I really want to know. What excuses has she made for you? Or did you make it all up yourself?" Arash asked. Hamasa's lips pressed together thinly.

Marya looked between Hamasa and Arash. There was a flicker in her dark eyes, and something tight and thick twisted in Hamasa's chest in response. His pulse sped up, eyes widening, wondering what would come out as her mouth began to open. Then, the moment broke and Marya grinned, wide and guileless, while rubbing at the side of her nose.

"A wizard, yeah? Not a very good one, but you need enough to make a boom! A *little* boom," Marya emphasized with some concern.

Hamasa looked away and licked his lips. Was that really what she'd been thinking, what she'd been about to say? The weight of her honest lie was a yoke around his neck. Arash snickered and Marya glared at him.

"I really hate when you act like you know more'n me," she snapped.

"I'm a dragon. Of course I know more. Not that it's difficult to know more than you."

"Arash, stop," Hamasa interrupted loudly. Arash's teeth clicked and his jaw tensed.

"Hamasa—"

"No, just stop. Both of you," Hamasa said before Marya could continue. "This fighting needs to *stop*. Both of you are my friends and you're going to have to figure it out!"

They stared at him. Marya broke first, rubbing the side of her nose sheepishly.

"Sorry, Hamito." She tossed the towel aside and grabbed a relatively clean shirt from her bag. "Want me to get you something from downstairs? You can stay up here. I know you don't like crowds."

Hamasa dredged up a smile, ignoring the sting in his eyes and nose. "Yes, that w-would b-be nice."

Perching on the edge of bed, Marya leaned forward to pat his head and brush hair away from his eyes. "It's been a long week, but we're gonna be all right, Asa. We'll figure it out, even if it takes 'til we get to Riyushu to do it."

Hamasa buried his face against his knees and nodded mutely. He hated it. Hated himself. Hated his choices. His running. His lie after lie. Marya's hand, warm and friendly, left his head, and the door scratched the floor on her way out.

"Hamasa." He twitched, squeezing his eyes shut tighter at Arash's voice. The same hoarse voice from their reunion in the stable. Whatever Arash said next would be the last thing Hamasa wanted to hear. "You can't expect any of them to be truly your friend if you aren't truly yourself. I'm not even sure I know you anymore."

Hamasa flinched. "I don't know either," he admitted.

Cool air brushed his bare arm and he immediately heated in response. An even cooler hand touched his back, fleeting and brief. Kind in a way Arash only was with him.

"You think you're making choices, but you're not. You've just been reacting blindly for seventeen years," he said quietly.

"I thought… I thought if I tried… maybe I could be like my father. But I'm not, Arash, I'll never be like him," he whispered. The stinging in his eyes burned and finally they fell, slipping down his cheeks and drying instantly on his flushed face.

"If you know that, stop *trying*, Hamasa."

Hamasa sniffled and his arms tightened around his shins. A faint sigh whispered over his head and the chill of Arash faded away. The door shut soon after. And Hamasa let them come for real. Falling fast and thick down his face, so much that they couldn't dry fast enough and dripped to his lap. Downstairs, Marya would order something spicy and new, she'd laugh and sing and make friends, excited for every part of the adventure. Arash would sneer and refuse to eat fish, but he would probably give in. Hamasa chuckled wetly imagining Arash's face when he tried spicy Mekshan food for the first time. Valerius would pay for some of their ship's passage with gold that wasn't his, and the two Others would try to pry the full story from him. Tight-lipped and too serious, Valerius would never say a word more than he needed, but soon enough they would be on that ship. Heading towards Riyushu, towards *her*. To the person he betrayed first and most terribly. Not even Arash knew how far he had sunk in his cowardice.

He would never be his father. Except maybe in death. In the

end.

Hamasa lifted his head and rubbed at his face with the heel of his palm. He scuttled off the bed, going for the pack with the armor wrapped and fit neatly inside it. It wasn't locked or magically protected in any way, nor were he, Marya, or Arash in possession of the room key to lock the door. However, if a thief got into the room and then into the pack, seeing the crest on the armor inside would have the would-be thief backing off. No one stole from the Lances of the Realm. Rather than fear, Hamasa had to swallow down his own guilt at the thought. Lingering long enough to brush his thumb over the crest, the white lance on a blue shield with a three-peaked top and gently curving sides to the single point at the bottom.

"The day he was knighted... he gave up his inheritance," Hamasa whispered to himself, frowning slightly.

A loud crash and glass shattering out on the street made him jump sky-high, a yelp barely suppressed behind his hand. Then, an awful, off-key singer wailed a jaunty, ribald tune. Shaking and moving quickly, he dug past wool and steel to the mostly empty leather pouch beneath. While Valerius carried enough on his person in a smaller pouch to get by day-to-day, the rest of the gold Kelso had thrown him was here, in Hamasa's hands.

Wincing and mouth dry, Hamasa counted out five gold coins. Bile burned his throat and he placed one back. Uselessly. He was nevertheless stealing four gold coins. He wanted to promise himself he would give it all back one day, but that wasn't the plan. He wanted to leave Mekshi and never return. He couldn't return to face all these people he was about to let down. Whom he'd already let down. His hand curled around the coins, the blunt, round edges digging into his palms and fingers.

This was what he wanted. This was his goal three weeks ago. To never see Mekshi or Riyushu again. Never see Marya. Never

THE COWARD'S EMBLEM

see... *her*.

Blue eyes shined in his mind's eye and he shook his head wildly to get rid of them. Only for those eyes to be replaced with Valerius'. Dark and honest and certain and seeing right through Hamasa in every way.

No, not every way. Valerius didn't know... not really.

Hamasa's mouth tightened, knuckles whitening. He shoved the coins into his pockets, two to each so they fit into the deepest, narrowest point. Once he was sure they wouldn't rattle, he checked over the pack to make sure everything was back exactly as it was before he dug through it. Satisfied, Hamasa got to his feet, dusted off his knees, and moved towards the door. He would eat one more meal with Marya and Valerius. Arash would forgive him eventually and find him one day. They could relearn what it meant to be friends, rather than whatever Arash thought, or used to think, they were meant to be.

29

The cantinas and hostals they had been in so far hadn't been the classiest or newest establishments. They had all been different degrees of worn down and rough around the edges, but they had always been well taken care of, loved by patrons and owners alike. Places of rest and refuge and some measure of luxury after spending days mired in toil and hard labor. This place, though, whatever place the *Siren's Call*'s captain had brought them to, was *not* of that ilk. The stairs to the bottom floor creaked with every step, no matter how lightly or carefully he stepped. The walls were stained by years of torch smoke and grubby hands. Splotches were splashed along the floor that could be anything from food or drink stains to bodily fluids. Hamasa's hand hovered over the greasy rail of the stairway, then he tucked his arms under his poncho and tried to rearrange his expression into something more neutral.

He hadn't turned his nose up at the Garsias' hut with its dirt floors and glass-less windows. Although the very idea of comparing Irmen Garsia's tidy home, with the colorful rugs and stainless, albeit shabby, furniture to this grimy place made him want to immediately apologize to the woman who had cared for him so well. Her lovingly neat and comfy home deserved better than that.

The cantina on the ground floor of the Wharf's Mouth was

definitely at its best when the sun was down and the only light was the unsteady orange glow of fire light. People of all kinds sat around uneven tables, some vaguely circular and others square in shape, and none of the chairs matched. Hamasa saw people tall and fair haired, small and dark like most of Mekshi, even the raven black hair and golden skin of Riyukezans; rough-spun tunics and trousers, kimono of cheap cotton, some tucked into repeatedly patched hakama, and, most surprising of all, the loose draping linen of a Harenese toga over poorly cut tunics with squared necklines. He probably shouldn't be so shocked. Even in war merchants would trade, and the war hadn't truly begun. Whispers and rumors and the occasionally abrupt street fight do not a war make. And the Harenese had mines of gold and jade and diamonds in their borders, one of the many reasons they had been kept as a closely monitored territory of the Riyukezu Empire years after the first rebellion. People would always hunger for precious gems and metals, especially if war was coming and fortunes teetered.

However, Hamasa kept his eyes on the table full of Harenese merchants, looking for two particular faces, and edging around the walls of the common room. His attention was finally broken when he walked past the small dais built near a large stone and clay fire place. A single woman sat there, hair so blonde it would put Harenese gold to shame and eyes the color of bright amber. She looked… shinier and brighter than everything around her. In the thin wisps of her hair, Hamasa caught the sight of feathers so fine and white they were almost invisible. She tilted her head when she saw him, eyes unblinking as she stared, and he froze. Then, she smiled and her gaze dropped to her lap where she had placed a large, gleaming, golden wood vihuela. The case by her feet was battered and frayed, but the vihuela was pristine, the tune that strummed beneath her fingers clear and perfectly in tune. Cheers erupted, followed by shouts for songs, and Hamasa hurried towards the table where Marya, Valerius, and, another surprise, Arash sat. The *Siren's Call*'s captain and first mate were already gone to Hamasa's relief.

"Didja see her?" Marya breathed out the words, chin on her hands and eyes over his shoulder. Hamasa turned to see the dala, smiling silently and tuning her instrument. "She's the most beautiful woman I ever seen."

"I thought you admired the Sovereign?" Hamasa couldn't help teasing. Marya blushed and she stuck out her tongue at him.

"I can't exactly flirt with an Sovereign, can I? But her, I can buy her a drink at least. Do you think she likes tepacha? Maybe she only drinks sangria or sakki..." Marya frowned thoughtfully.

"Perhaps you should leave her to work," Valerius suggested.

"Just because you've got a stick up your bum, doesn't mean I do," Marya retorted.

Arash laughed out loud and Valerius sighed. Hamasa dropped his face in his hands with a groan.

"We have food coming soon, my lo—" Valerius broke off, scowling so fiercely Hamasa began to worry it would become permanent. "Hamasa."

"It definitely doesn't look like saying his name hurt the same as a sword in the gut," Marya said with a nod and a glint in her eye.

"Mm, yes, very discreet," Arash agreed.

"Is this the only time you two will get along? Teasing Valerius?" Hamasa demanded.

Marya and Arash exchanged glances, grimaced at each other, and then turned to Hamasa.

"Yeah, sounds right."

"There's no other reason to get along."

"My sanity could be another reason," Hamasa replied. And

then more seriously, "I care about both of you very much. I'm sorry about getting upset upstairs, but I do want you to get along."

"Ay, such a little peacekeeper," Marya cried, wrapping an arm around his neck and pulling him close to ruffle his hair. Hamasa gazed at nothing and waited for the wrestling to end, a smile threatening to emerge. "We'll team up against Wally more."

"Not that it gets much reaction, so it's less fun for me. But anything for you, rafiik," Arash said, tipping his head to the side.

"I didn't mean for that to happen," Hamasa told Valerius quickly, eyes wide.

Valerius' chin bobbed. "I've endured worse in my squad. It's nothing."

Arash's blue eyes gleamed — a cat seeing a mouse dart close. "A challenge."

A woman came up to their table with a large tray balanced expertly against her hip. Her skirt barely made it to her shins and was a bit frayed, but the stripes were still vivid and bright, and her white tunic was clean and stain-free under the long black and red vest she wore. She nodded at them without a smile and set the dishes on the table with a clatter of fired-clay on wood.

"Fish," Arash said with a slight curl of his lip. "That one isn't even cooked." He pointed to a dish of finely chopped fish, shrimp, octopus, tomatoes, onions, and sweet yellow corn, glistening in juice and dotted with chilies and herbs.

"I never seen shrimp. It looks good," Marya said, sniffing appreciatively and leaning over the dishes. "And the cervicha's marinated in limón, so it's not *raw* raw," she explained. She pointed at another one, a shallow long dish with a row of tortiyas wrapped around a filling of corn, plump shrimp, tomatoes, chilies, and cilantro, drowned in red sauce and all covered with mounds of crumbled white cheese and fresh salsa. "And this is encheladas."

"I've had that. With beans," Hamasa said eagerly.

"And helped make the tortiyas," Marya reminded him, nudging his arm.

"Red snapper," Valerius said, pointing to the last dish where a fish so large it filled the entire platter and its tail brushed the table. It was covered in tomatoes and sauce and shining green capers and olives. The aroma drifted through the air and tingled at their noses. A bowl of roasted vegetables sat beside it. "It's popular in Riyushu. Though, I've never seen it look like that."

"The lady said this is how they cook it in Róntraih," Marya said.

Hamasa looked up to see Arash leaning over the table, nose twitching and his tongue tasting the air. Their eyes met over the platters, and Hamasa slid the platter of snapper closer. Arash gave him a Look, his head tilting and his mouth twisting to the side.

"It's fish."

"Yes, and you're a human now. Give it a try," Hamasa said.

"I'm not gonna wait around for you to figure yourself out," Marya said. She dug into the encheladas, humming happily and thumbing away salsa that oozed down her chin.

Arash picked at the snapper with a blunt wooden spoon that had one side a little flatter than the other. The look on his face at the first mouthful—the swiftly widening eyes and sharp inhale through his nose—had Hamasa grinning and picking up his own spoon for a bite. A sudden loud coughing from his other side interrupted him. Valerius pressed his fist to his mouth, his pale face ruddy and eyes watering. The spoon that still had traces of red salsa on it hung from his limp hand.

Marya burst into laughter, barely catching it behind her hand. Hamasa jumped to his feet to smack Valerius' back.

"It's *spicy*. Why is the fish spicy?" Valerius gasped hoarsely.

Arash sighed and reached over to tap Valerius' reddened lips with a single fingertip that flashed white. Flowers of ice spread over Valerius' mouth and tongue and, when he exhaled, his breath was glittering mist. Valerius exhaled again and stared at Arash. The dragon merely tried a mouthful of the cervicha without meeting anyone's eyes. The next bite Valerius took was tentative, a slight frown on his face. The ice barely crackled and Valerius' shoulders slumped in relief.

"That's a nifty trick," Marya said. She waved towards the bar to catch the bartender's eye. There was a jerk of a nod and the woman turned away. "But tepacha or fruit water helps better and only costs a few tin bits."

"Is there tea?" Valerius asked. Marya stared at him. "Never mind."

The first song of the night began to play. Almost immediately the entire cantina burst into applause and cheers, the applause becoming claps and foot stamps set along to the rhythm. Marya joined in, snapping her fingers with one hand so she could keep eating with the other. The dala with her vihuela began to sing, her voice a crystal clear tone that trembled at the highest pitch in a way that had a shiver running down Hamasa's spine. Marya sang along, stopping sometimes to quickly explain something Hamasa and the other two didn't quite understand. The food and drinks disappeared without Hamasa realizing how fast it went, his mouth buzzing and his whole body warm and drowsy. From under heavy eyelids, Hamasa watched Marya, Arash, and Valerius all talking or singing or eagerly encouraging each other to try something else at the table. He smiled sleepily, pulled one leg up onto the chair, and wrapped his arms around his shin. Another round of drinks was brought, but he was too comfortable and full to reach for it.

"I didn't think humans could make music like that," Arash said as yet another song began to play, quieter and more melancholy as evening turned to true night. "Though, she is a dala. That must explain it."

Marya groaned and punched his shoulder. Arash stared at her in affront, rubbing the spot she'd dared to touch. "It's still a *Mekshan* song, and a human made a vihuela."

"Innovation does stem from mortality," Arash allowed with a one-shoulder shrug.

"Why do you hate humans so much? Others, like dalas and chanaces, don't live much longer than humans do," Marya demanded. "What's with all this 'mortals' this and 'mortality' that."

Arash narrowed his eyes at her. A brief flash of ethereal blue and slitted pupils there and gone again. "Do you know how long dragons live?" he asked in an oddly casual voice.

"You said millennia... so a thousand years?" Marya guessed, rather nonplussed.

"Millennia is more than one. They can live up to four thousand years that I know of," Valerius said.

"Yes, that's what you know. There have been dragons that have lived ten thousand years. Do you know how long an Sovereign's Shield lives?"

"Arash," Hamasa blurted, horrified, sitting straight up in his seat. Arash ignored him, his gaze pinning Marya to her chair as her chin lifted in defiance.

"No, I don't."

"Guess, human, *guess* how long a being that should live beyond what you could truly fathom lives once they've attached themselves to a puny, insignificant speck of a human life," Arash hissed.

"They can live on after their Sovereign has died," Valerius

said, low and sharp.

"Sure they can, but how many do? The first dragon in Mekshi, the Stormwrought? She was one of the most powerful Greys that had ever lived. She Chose her Sovereign, started an invasion and destroyed armies to give him a kingdom. Then, one hundred and fifty years later, within an hour of her Sovereign breathing his last after her *soul* kept him alive all that time, she died. She could've lived for thousands of years more, but she lasted less than two centuries after becoming a Shield."

"What? But..." Marya stammered.

"That's different," Hamasa argued. He licked his lips when all their eyes turned to him. "She loved him. She only retook her true form in times of strife and lived as a human most of that time. They had children, human children, together. Not all Shields and Sovereigns have that kind of... of story. Most of them don't."

"That's where the dragon blood comes from," Marya realized, thumping her fist on her opposite palm. "The Sovereign's, they all say she's got dragon blood and special magic."

Hamasa exhaled in relief. "It's true. She has innate magic, like an Other, because she's descended from the Stormwrought."

"And he's right, most Shields don't marry," Arash agreed. He leaned back in his chair and crossed his arms over his chest, those narrow eyes on Hamasa now. "The Scarlet Dread—"

"Arash, don't."

"—was more than three thousand years old. Had a dragon lifemate. Even bred and had a kit."

"A kit? Is that what you call a dragon baby?" Marya asked. She tried to grin, but her lips were too taut and the corners falling as if she couldn't quite keep it up.

"Dragons don't breed often, or much. Why do we need to? We live basically forever," Arash said with a hand wave. "Kits are precious. Rare. But he decided the next great deed he'd do was become a Shield. Something no Red had done before. And he died eighty-five years later."

"Eighty-five? That's the… that's how long the reign of the last Sovereign was…" Marya said quietly.

"Yes, it was. He didn't die for love, as the Stormwrought did. He died for honor. For his Sovereign, the damned human he Chose to protect. Dragons live forever until humans kill them."

30

Hamasa couldn't make himself speak. Couldn't so much as open his mouth. He stared at Arash, eyes stinging, hands curled into tight, shaking fists on his lap. Across the table, Arash gazed back. His jaw was tense, ice curling down the jut of it, hands clutching at his biceps a little too tightly where he crossed his arms. Is this how Arash felt when Hamasa had left without a word? Was this what it felt like to be betrayed rather than betray? There was a sharp wound in his chest, different from the emptiness, cutting deeper the longer the words hovered between them. Already said and unable to be taken back.

Arash looked away first and Hamasa gasped, heart pounding crazily in his ears.

"Why? Why would a dragon wanna be a Shield? If it just means they'd die?" Marya asked with a voice that shook at the end.

"He already explained why. For duty," Valerius answered. He glanced towards Hamasa, but settled his gaze on Arash last. Scowling, more in thought than anger, as Arash curled his lip and raised an eyebrow at him. "What's the point of living thousands of years without a purpose? You can't judge them for choosing a life that gives them meaning."

"I can judge whoever I want!"

"Would you want someone to look at your life and think what

you believe to be most important is trite foolishness?" Valerius asked simply. Arash's teeth clicked together. "Everyone and everything dies. Human lives aren't insignificant because they're short, and the Shields' lives aren't unimportant because they've been made shorter by duty."

"So is your life only meaningful because of how you die?" Hamasa whispered.

"I didn't—"

Hamasa cut him off with a watery glance. "I know. I know you didn't." Neither of them looked away, Valerius' mouth in a softer line, parted slightly, as his eyes stayed locked with Hamasa's.

"I... I don't know if I understand everything going on here," Marya started slowly. Arash snorted and Hamasa's gaze with Valerius broke. "But I do know that life is more than just duty and dying. Maybe there's something more to being a Shield, and who they Choose, that we just don't get 'cuz we aren't there? We're not Shield or Sovereign."

"I suppose you're right," Valerius said with a nod. She grinned, although it wasn't quite as wide or bright as usual.

"Whatever you want to think," Arash muttered.

Silence fell, awkward and tense. Hamasa pressed his cheek to his knee and breathed deeply, eyes closed to hold it in. Hold it back. His last night with them was ruined. Because of course it was.

"So, Arash, I got one more question," Marya said after a long moment.

"What."

"Dragons can choose what they look like. And they can be with humans, make babies, too. Like the Stormwrought did, because she fell in love with a human man," Marya said, scratching her cheek.

"Yes, I hear being the opposite sex makes breeding with

humans easier," Arash said dryly. "Though, I'm sure they could've figured something else out if they really wanted to."

"So *why* are you a boy?" Marya demanded, slapping a hand on the table. Arash blinked. Hamasa choked on a surprised chuckle, smothering it with his knee. "There are too many boys. *You* can change. So you should change."

"I... I'm not just going to *change* because you want me to!" Arash exclaimed.

"But you'd make such a *pretty* girl. Like the dala over there, you could look like her. She's much prettier than you now."

"I don't... being pretty isn't—No. I'm not doing that!" Arash protested, hands up as if to fend Marya off as she leaned over the table at him. "I can't change into a dala, or any other kind of Other, anyway!"

"Ay, I said to *look* like her. What if Hamito wants it? Hamito, you want him to be a girl, yeah?" Marya asked, rounding on Hamasa and shaking his shoulder.

Hamasa burst into laughter, unable to control or smother it anymore. It was too much. After *that*. Too ridiculous. He quickly covered his face with a hand, trying to muffle his volume and hide the tear tracks at the same time.

"No! I never said that!" he gasped between laughter.

"You're no fun. Wally, wouldn't he be a pretty girl? He has blue eyes just like the Sovereign, too!"

" ... yes. Very pretty."

"You shut up!"

"You're so boring. I'm gonna go talk to a pretty girl," Marya said decisively, throwing up her hands. She stole Hamasa's untouched sangria and then did exactly that. She made it to the stage and handed the cup to the dala woman. She smiled at Marya so beautifully and shyly, amber eyes hiding under a flutter of fair lashes, that Marya's face burned red. She almost fell over leaning against the dais.

"At least she doesn't bluff," Valerius said dryly.

***

He hadn't been able to sleep that night. Next to him, Marya snored into the pillow, a soft snuffling sound that was more hypnotic than obnoxious. Or perhaps he was used to it now. Carefully, trying his best not to jostle her awake, Hamasa pushed up onto his hands. The candle had long since gone out, and the sun hadn't yet risen, and across the room Valerius was a long, unmoving lump on his narrow bed. He grit his teeth and moved over Marya's sprawled limbs. The coins in his pockets shifted, not quite a jingle that had Hamasa freezing in place, wincing. Marya snuffled louder and buried her face deeper into the pillow.

When he managed to stand in the middle of the room, Hamasa stopped, eyes darting from bed to bed. *Go, just go, you've done it before!* But he couldn't make his feet move and he lingered. Neither woke. Did he... want them to? Did he want them to wake up? For Marya to demand to come with him, or Valerius to throw him over another horse? Hamasa exhaled heavily through his nose and wrung his hands. Closing his eyes and tensing his jaw, Hamasa shuffled his foot over the ground near the bed and found his discarded sandals.

They didn't wake.

He tiptoed backwards, hands finding the door behind him, and then the latch and knob. Too silently, he unlocked the door, lifting it so the bottom wouldn't scratch the floor, and slipped through the narrowest possible opening. He froze, hand on the inside doorknob, as a body shifted on a bed. But nothing else happened, and Hamasa let it close with a quiet *snick*. With a tremble to his lips that he licked away, he pressed his forehead to the door. Then, Hamasa hurried down the stairs, grimacing at every creak and rattle. The common room was empty, the tables and chairs weirdly shaped shadows he dodged. In the far corner, near the small stage, the large fire was banked and the coals a low, dark red glow that left tendrils of warmth in the air.

Outside Wharf's Mouth, the street was eerily empty. There were only a few carts—some dragged behind livestock, some behind a person—that rattled down the patchily cobbled road. An unconscious figure lay slumped in the darkened doorway of a cantina down the road. It was actually cold this close to the sea and so late in the season. Or maybe the cold was on account of how close he was standing to the person leaning against the outside wall of the hostal, arms crossed over his chest, and one ankle crossing the other. Even in the gloom, the white of his scales and the blue of his eyes shined.

"You're off?" Arash asked. He didn't bother to wait for an answer, straightening off the wall and onto two feet. "You know what you're doing, don't you? Leaving it here behind you?"

Hamasa glanced away and rubbed his wrists. Yes, he knew. The night after Ristahe, the Harenese with their unexpected arrival and ready bindings that glowed pink and burned. That alone was worse than the distance he was choosing to go now.

"I'm not going to apologize. For last night." Arash wouldn't meet his eyes, staring towards the sea and the unending horizon. "Stormwrought's kin or not, the Sovereign is still human."

"You shouldn't have... you shouldn't have talked about the Scarlet Dread, but I'm not... I don't need an apology from you," Hamasa said. He licked his lips, then stepped forward to press his forehead to Arash's. His breath stuttered out of him and the chill of it fluttered over Hamasa's chin. "And I'm sorry... I've *been* sorry. I missed you the whole time."

"Well... at least you missed me. rafiik."

"rafiik," Hamasa agreed, stepping back and smiling shakily. "I have to go now. They leave at dawn."

"I'll find you again after a while. When I'm not angry at you," Arash said, adjusting Hamasa's poncho, brushing it as straight and smooth as possible.

"You'll stay here that long?" Hamasa asked, eyebrows rising. Arash scoffed.

"Of course not. I'm going to go leave as soon as you go. I'm going to find it, your rohh, before someone else does."

Hamasa grabbed his arm. "Um, could you... stay and tell them? Please?"

Arash scowled and hissed between his teeth. Hamasa waited breathlessly.

"Fine. Yes. I'll tell them."

"Thank you, Arash."

His hand fell from Arash's arm. Arash watched him, his gaze heavy, so heavy Hamasa felt it on his back when he turned. Felt the weight long after the cantina, and Arash, were out of sight.

His sandals didn't so much as slap his heels as he hurried towards the docks. The sky began to lighten into pearly grey. Heart speeding, Hamasa picked up his pace. A forest of ropes and masts creaked and hulls knocked against dock pilings. *The Squall* loomed ahead, his desperately searching gaze leaping from prow to prow, figurehead to figurehead. Sailors called out to their shipmates, and torch lamps were being put out one by one, faster than the stars blinking out. His footsteps shuffled to a stop, stare locked on *The Squall*'s dragon as he approached the ship at last. The pearl mocked him from between the Stormwrought's fangs.

"So you made it then, sonny?"

Hamasa startled in place. Shamus, the bearded man, stood at the end of the dock. His thick, burly arms were crossed over his chest and his light eyes looked Hamasa up and down. Hamasa grimaced under the searching gaze, trying not to cringe into something smaller and shapeless under the folds of his poncho.

"Y-yes. Yes, I made it. I have the gold," Hamasa stammered, digging into his pockets.

"Keep it. You'll hand it to Margita herself. It'll soothe her ruffled feathers when you come aboard," Shamus said with a single hand lifting.

"Soothe ruffled feathers?" Hamasa asked.

Shamus grinned, his teeth bright white against the dark of his beard. "We'll be leaving the persuasion of letting you on board to *you*, sonny."

"Me?" Hamasa squeaked.

"C'mon on, if you're sure," Shamus said. He turned towards the ship, shouting up at the deck with a voice that boomed in an unfamiliar language.

"If I'm sure?" Hamasa repeated quietly. Slowly, so slowly, he looked up again and stared into the snarling wooden face. As if waiting for the Stormwrought to leap to life and tell him what to do. What would the Stormwrought think of him?

Smirking thin and sharp, Hamasa knew exactly what she would think. It was because of her that the Riyukezu came to Mekshi at all. More than half a nation had come with her, trailing in the wake of her zeal and passion and her complete belief in her Sovereign. Hamasa clasped a handful of wool over his chest. He couldn't even believe in himself. Not in his own friends, people that had left everything behind for him.

There were louder shouts. A man's voice cracking through the air to call everyone on board. Hamasa flinched, but his eyes stayed on the figurehead.

A hand touched his shoulder, and Hamasa flinched again, jerking away. When he looked up, Calum was there. The dalo with green and black feathers and yellow eyes that saw too much. The predawn light glistened on his hair and lit his eyes into dragon's gold.

"I scared you."

"Just startled," Hamasa said quickly. He glanced back to the figurehead. "Why her? Why the Stormwrought?"

"Did you choose us because of her?" Calum asked. His fingers ruffled and smoothed away the feathers that blew around his head in the breeze coming off the harbor.

"No... I didn't know. I just wanted the first ship leaving," he admitted.

"Margita is the captain, but *The Squall* didn't start as hers. It's had other captains, other names, and it'll have other captains after us. If we can take good care of her," Calum said. His hands tucked behind his back and he looked up, head tilted to the side. "Having the spirit of a storm dragon for our ship, it seemed fortunate. We sailors can be very superstitious."

Hamasa smiled and ducked his head. Only to be drawn into looking up again.

"Calum!"

The bulky, short silhouette of Shamus stood at the railing high over their heads. Next to him, a taller, slender figure with hair a wild curly mass, as bushy and wild as Marya's out of her usual braid, leaned over the railing. At her hip, a long, thin sword hung from a wide belt.

"The captain calls," Calum said, setting his fist to his heart and double-tapping with a short bow, as if to the Sovereign. The captain's head flung back and she barked out a harsh laugh. "She's not a patient one."

"Dreikstan Islands. Is it the sort of place to get lost in?" Hamasa asked, licking his lips and following Calum.

"Any place is the kind to get lost in if you try hard enough.

You would know that," Calum answered.

Hamasa's eyes closed and he inhaled slowly. "You knew immediately."

"We can always see Others. Especially when they're right under our nose."

"I've done a very bad job getting lost," Hamasa whispered. He wrung his fingers together. "I keep getting found no matter what I want."

Calum stepped onto the gangplank. Stopped and turned. "Ever thought about why?"

"Bad luck?" Hamasa said with a snort.

"Has it really been bad luck?" Calum asked, eyebrow rising.

Hamasa's mouth wrenched open, scowling, remembering every bruise and sore muscle, every moment slung over a saddle, the magicked cuffs that burned, the acid searing across his back and the scars that stretched over his skin.

Then, his teeth snapped shut.

Meeting Marya, finding Arash again (or, well, the other way around), Valerius — no, Emerens with lips frosted in ice, and the golden eyes of the páhalebra... *What are you waiting for?*

"What are you waiting for?"

Hamasa shook it all away and followed the voice to the speaker. Calum was watching him from the top of the plank, his shining cormorant feathers fluttering in the breeze. Hamasa's mouth opened, and shut, and he stepped back. A memory of needle-sharp teeth on his neck and blood oozing between his fingers and Marya's face pale and wan. Hamasa stared at the prow of the ship. Beams of sunlight broke through the predawn haze and the *The Squall* and its figurehead was etched in shadow and light.

"I... can't," Hamasa whispered in amazement. The churning in his stomach, the writhing guilt he had been unable to shake for weeks, abated. Just a fraction of it sank lower, banked like the fire at the end of the night. He stepped off the gangplank. "I can't go."

"If you're sure?" Calum called down, leaning one arm on the railing.

Hamasa licked his lips, his eyes darting over the ship. His way out.

"Thank you, but no! I mean, yes! I'm sure!" Hamasa shouted with his hands cupping his mouth.

"I'm not sure I need thanking. You got there on your own," Calum said with a smirk. He pressed his fist to his heart and bowed. Then, he motioned behind him and two sailors rushed over to lift the gangplank.

Hamasa didn't wait to watch them pull it up. He ran back the way he came, breath panting, heart thumping. His poncho flapped behind him like a cape and the slapping of sandals echoed through the morning air. Faster than a horse, he zipped over uneven cobbles and around carts. Terrified that if he slowed down his fear would catch him up, Hamasa ran so swiftly it nudged up against that empty space inside him. Choking him, but not enough to slow him.

31

THE WHARF'S MOUTH was right ahead, and the scene outside it had him skidding to a stop at last. Three very familiar people stood by the door. Marya and Valerius looked distinctly ruffled and unkempt, as if they had dressed quickly and run straight out. Marya had both her fists wrapped in Arash's tunic, lifting him up onto his toes and growling at him. Arash's hands were around her wrists, but, other than that, he wasn't trying to get away or say much. Valerius stood at Marya's back, talking quietly while he scanned the street with dark eyes. His eyes met Hamasa's. Time stopped. Hamasa's breath caught. Then, a crowd passing down the street broke the stare and Valerius' gaze followed the crowd with a scowl.

A second later, his attention snapped back to Hamasa. He looked him up and down swiftly and his eyes widened. His mouth moved and Hamasa saw *my lord* form. Marya dropped Arash to crane past him with equally wide eyes.

"Hamasa!"

She barrelled across the street to fling herself on him. Hamasa grunted, bracing his weight on his back foot, arms around Marya's waist. Immediately after, she shoved him away and shook him like a dusty rag.

"What were you thinking? Why did you go without me!?" Marya demanded.

"I wasn't thinking. I was... reacting," Hamasa said, meeting Arash's eyes over her shoulder. Arash's mouth tipped up on the side. Hamasa yelped as Marya pulled him into another too tight embrace.

"You could have gone," Valerius said lowly. "I let my guard down. He said the ship would leave at dawn." He gestured at Arash. "But you returned."

"Why'd you come back?" Marya whispered, squeezing him a little tighter. Hamasa coughed. "Sorry." She stepped back and raised her hands. "You could've gotten clean away. From everyone!"

Hamasa ducked his head, staring at his toes. A series of images that had pulled him back and the easing of guilt in his stomach made for poor excuses. Putting it into actual words, that his answer to a question had drawn him back here, it seemed simple and stupid and... His lips curved up while trembling, and his eyes pricked with tears.

"You're m-my," Hamasa rubbed under his eyes and laughed softly. "You're my friends. What's the p-point—What's the point of finally having friends just to leave them all behind? I couldn't do it, I guess, not after everything."

"Hamito," Marya punched his shoulder, making him wince and laugh. "Idiot."

"I'm sorry, Arash," Hamasa said, meeting those cool blue eyes. Arash's eyebrow rose. "I should've... sooner than now—"

"Stop saying sorry," Arash said roughly. He smirked a little as the sheerest layer of ice frosted the tops of his ears. "Stop doing things to be sorry for."

"I can try," Hamasa said with a smile. With a deep breath through his nose, he looked up at Valerius. "I'm not going with you to Riyushu."

Valerius scowled, but his mouth parted, one eyebrow

twitching upwards. "The Sovereign needs her Shield. Why did you come back if not for that?"

"When are you gonna get it through your empty head!?" Marya started, stomping her foot and raising a fist.

"No, wait, Marya. I am."

Marya stared, her fist hovering in the air, her jaw dropping. Hamasa smiled weakly.

Arash rolled his eyes. "After all this trouble, this is how you say it?"

"I am. Or, really, I was. Kana'iro the Red... that's me," he whispered. "I lied. I lied a lot. I'm sor—"

"Shut up," Marya interrupted harshly. Her hand pressed against his nose, flat over his face, to stop him. She closed her eyes, huffing loudly through her flaring nostrils. The hand at her side curled into a tight fist and she exhaled again, louder than before, her thick black brows knitting into a fierce scowl.

"We should get off the street," Valerius said, one hand on Hamasa's shoulder to steer him.

"But the middle of the road makes it all so much more dramatic," Arash drawled. Hamasa glared at him from behind Marya's hand.

"You shove off, we're talking." She smacked Valerius' hand away, grabbed Hamasa's elbow, and marched towards the hostal.

The door swung in under the slap of her palm. It swung so quick, it hit the wall and bounced off, but Marya had already dragged him past. They made it up to the room without a word between them. She let him go with a huff and began to pace, leaving him standing by the door.

"I'm not stupid, you know!" she finally barked out, spinning on her heel and pointing at him.

"I know," Hamasa said, his words barely getting out.

"I didn't actually *care* whatever your real story was," Marya said. She stopped and propped her hands on her hips.

"I know you didn't," Hamasa agreed.

Marya twisted her mouth to the side, lips pursing. "But I still feel stupid. I knew you were lying, but I didn't think you were lying that much. A dragon? I thought you were something, but a dragon? *The* dragon?" Marya buried both her hands in her hair and ruffled it wildly, curls tangling every which way. "Why would you run away? And why do you look like that? Arash showed up looking like a dragon first."

"I... I was scared," Hamasa whispered. He chewed on his bottom lip and wrung the hem of his poncho. "I've done a lot of things I'm not proud of all because I was scared. It's okay if you... if you want to go. I put you in a lot of dangerous situations, I took advantage of your and your mother's kindness, and, worst, I think it's the worst part, I made you feel stupid for defending me. I don't... I'm a horrible friend, Marya. It's okay to go."

She didn't say a word. The sounds of the street outside crept in through the cracks in the window and she didn't say a word. Marya's feet appeared in Hamasa's lowered line of sight. Then, her hands wrested the rumpled wool from his shaking hands. Of course, she would want it back. It was too nice to leave with him. But her hands grabbed his.

"What's it mean? To be a Shield?" she asked, echoing her words from the night before.

Hamasa's mouth screwed up and his eyes squeezed shut. Despite himself, his shoulders were shaking and his voice hitched as he choked out, "I don't know. I thought I did, but I really didn't. I let her down, my father, you, and Valerius. I'm letting everyone down."

"Ay," Marya whispered.

She tugged him close and tucked his face against her tunic. Hamasa squeaked, blinking rapidly as tears streamed down his face. Earthy, warm, and human, the comforting familiar scent wrapped him tighter than her arms. He inhaled shakily, hands shaking at his sides.

"You don't have to," Hamasa said breathily.

"I know. Must have a weakness for dragon tears," Marya teased. Hamasa chuckled wetly. "You came back today, Hamito. You didn't leave me. So you didn't let me down."

A knock sounded at the door, and Arash and Valerius came in right after. Hamasa and Marya quickly stepped apart. Hamasa wiped at his eyes with his poncho and Marya turned away to clear her throat loudly and not so subtly swipe at her eyes with the back of her wrist. Valerius cleared his throat awkwardly, closing the door. Arash plopped on the bed Hamasa and Marya had claimed and crossed his legs with a loud huff.

"You can't just run off with him when we all need to talk about what comes next," Arash said.

"Whaddaya mean 'what comes next'?" Marya asked, sniffling and pretending like she wasn't.

"He has to go back to Riyushu," Valerius said. Hamasa met his eyes and the knight frowned at him. "People are finding you, and they'll keep finding you. Someone is going to eventually capture and use you against the Sovereign. You have to uphold your duty."

"Who cares about his duty to some human, to any of you? He needs to get as far away from the Merciless as possible. You can't let that monster find you again, Hamasa," Arash snapped. Hamasa flinched. "You should've gotten on the stupid ship."

"You didn't want me to go!" Hamasa exclaimed.

"I didn't want you to go without me!"

"Wait, *wait*. Did you say 'again'? Find you *again*?" Marya asked with wide, red-rimmed eyes darting between them.

"The scars…" Valerius murmured, aghast. "They were made

by the Merciless?"

"But they're all over him!" Marya protested, hands covering her mouth. "They're all over his back, his arms, his neck... how could...? What happened?"

Hamasa swallowed hard. Hands flexed at his sides, barely refraining from touching the scars on his face or neck. Suddenly, they were itching, itching enough to drive him insane.

"How much do you know about the Stormwrought? The part of the story of how she Chose her Sovereign?" Hamasa asked.

"Really, you're going the long way around this," Arash sighed.

"It was... in a river?" Marya said, glancing at Arash for a moment and then frowning at Hamasa. "Her pearl. She told the prince that he would be Sovereign if he found her pearl in a river. What's that have to do with any of this?"

"But it wasn't a pearl. That was a mistake. When the story was told in Mekshan, there were some translation problems," Valerius corrected. His jaw ticked and he crossed his arms. "The Emblem. You don't have it. That's why you wouldn't change no matter what happened. It wasn't only to keep up the lie."

Hamasa nodded jerkily. Bile surged up his throat and only keeping his mouth shut kept it down.

"What emblem? What isn't a pearl?" Marya demanded.

"An emblem is what you call it. We call it rohh. It's our soul made into a stone. That's how a Shield Chooses an Sovereign. A dragon has to give them their soul," Arash spat. His fingers clawed into the blankets beneath him.

"Your soul?" Marya shouted. "You can just give it away?"

"No, you can't just give it away!" Hamasa protested. He swallowed, and swallowed again. "You have to trust them and... match them. No one and nothing can take an emblem away from a dragon, it's something only we can Choose to do—"

THE COWARD'S EMBLEM

"Unless the rohh is already lost and someone finds it," Arash pointed out harshly.

"*Lost?*" Valerius repeated, Marya's same response louder and still baffled.

"The Merciless... when it happened..." Hamasa licked his lips. He could say it. Get rid of that last lie. Come completely clean. It hovered at the very tip of his tongue about to fall.

"Of course you lost it after what happened to you. They're called the Merciless for a reason," Arash said, blue eyes narrowing.

"You lost your soul... and then you landed in my field," Marya whispered. "We should all go. We should all go find it right now. Hamasa, you're in danger, and so's your soul, or your emblem, or whatever it's called!"

"She's right. Your emblem must be found. If those Harenese centurions can find you, they could find your emblem, too," Valerius said.

"I think... I think they might have sensed it once," Hamasa forced past the lump in his throat. One more secret as yet locked away. "The token they had, something they said. But the longer it's lost, the harder it will be to find. It's more stone than soul."

"But it can be found," Arash said. "As long as Hamasa doesn't have it, he can't be who he really is. Can't be *what* he truly is."

"So we'll find it. We'll find it first," Marya said fiercely. Eyes gleaming, she held up a fist and grinned. "We can do it together."

"I should have realized it sooner. My lord, of course finding your emblem is the most important thing we could do," Valerius said, bowing low. Hamasa's mouth dried.

"Oh, do I have to call you...?" Marya asked, curling her lip in distaste.

"*No.*" Marya snickered at Hamasa's swift and vehement reply.

"He's only saying that because he wants you back with his

Sovereign. You're useless to them without your rohh." Arash sneered at the crown of Valerius' head.

Valerius' head snapped up to scowl darkly at Arash. Marya stepped in with her hands up between them.

"You both are done now. We need to plan what to do next. Hamasa, what do we need to do first?"

Hamasa looked at each of them in turn. The farmer-turned-hero, the ex-knight, the dragon... and him. Going back, going anywhere near the place where his nightmare had been enacted and ended so badly, had him shaking. Terror warring with relief. No one had left. For the first time, the choice he made felt right. He swallowed down the lump in his throat one more time.

"I think we'll need a map."

***

That day and the next day in Róntraih Porto were a blur. The *Siren's Call* left without them. Meanwhile they stayed at Wharf's Mouth to plan. Although Hamasa was somehow in the middle of it, he was more like the eye of a storm than the storm itself. No, the storm was Marya. A whirlwind of activity, she chivvied him and the other two to prepare for the trek ahead of them. She repeatedly shoved a map under Hamasa's nose, dragging details out of his hazy memories and asking Valerius to help her pinpoint their directions. The Réo Largo, the great river that flowed down the Ajul Mountains and across the plains to the south until it broke into the many smaller branches of a delta, was the clearest memory. That and the mountain range itself. It was a lot of ground to cover, and magic wasn't quite so predictable that they could narrow it much further based on Hamasa's fall into Elorra.

Other than map searching, they filled up their supplies,

taking a few blissful hours on their second afternoon there to forget the time running against them. Marya had never been to a city before, and she lit up in excitement as they perused the shops and stalls. Strange foods and fruits she had never seen that she convinced Hamasa and Arash to try with her, languages and peoples she had never heard or seen, the bright fabrics and brighter gems and accessories she never could have imagined. They lingered outside the blacksmith, faces heated to red by the strength of the forge, and Marya, and of course Valerius, looked over the weapons and armor inside, although they couldn't afford or didn't need anything there.

They were walking slowly towards the Wharf's Mouth on their last evening, finally ready to leave by dawn. Marya was telling Arash all about the dala woman she had shared her evening with the day before, once again teasing him about becoming a woman, while Hamasa and Valerius hung back. Sunset gilded the buildings in orange and rose, but the market area was still flush with people and scents of cooking and people.

"It's good we're leaving tomorrow. We don't have many funds left," Valerius noted.

"I'm sure. Marya demanded a lot of fruit — Oh, um!" Valerius' eyebrow rose, and heat burned over Hamasa's face and down his neck. "I took some, um, some coins. I put them under my pillow after... I forgot about it."

His second eyebrow rose to join the first and the corner of Valerius' lips curved upwards.

"Keep the gold. If you're brave enough to steal from a Lance, I suppose you've earned them," he said.

Or perhaps teased? Was he teasing? Hamasa's jaw dropped. The smile faded as fast as it appeared, dissolving into Valerius' usual pensive frown.

"I've taken enough freedom from you, my lord. You should

have something in case we are separated."

"Um, thank you. I'll... I'll make sure Marya has them in her bag," Hamasa said slowly. He tugged at the sack he carried full of hard breads and dry beans.

Valerius reached over to take it, but Hamasa thoughtlessly smacked away his hand. Valerius startled, yanking his arm back as he stared wide-eyed at him. Hamasa pressed his lips together and glanced at his own hands.

"It's not heavy and I don't need you to treat me like I can't carry a sack for a little while. I might not have my emblem, but I'm not... I'm not weak."

It stretched between them, an awkward silence that had warmth sneaking up his face. Valerius cleared his throat. Hamasa peered up from under his hair.

"I spent most of my life wanting to serve you. It's hard to change after all this time." Valerius huffed under his breath, the awkwardness breaking with his unexpected humor. "I suppose I should follow Marya's example here, as well."

"Marya is one of a kind," Hamasa agreed. He swallowed painfully, but the words came easier than he meant them to. "You didn't... you didn't act like this before. When it was just us three."

"I wasn't quite ten. I didn't understand what was appropriate," Valerius said stiffly.

"I'd rather be a friend than someone's lord. I don't deserve the familiarity anymore, but she never stopped being Anneki, and I was always Masaki to her. As long as the council wasn't around to hear us." Hamasa chuckled softly. A dagger in his chest twisted at the memory of how they had grown up together and how much they had relied on each other.

"I'm not your Sovereign," Valerius said quietly.

"But I'm always going to be your Shield?"

There was a stirring of commotion ahead, a sudden crowd of people that Arash and Marya made their way into the thick of. Rather than fighting the crowd, they both stopped. Hamasa looked up so his eyes could meet Valerius'. Instead of cringing under the intense, dark-eyed glare, Hamasa lifted his chin. Valerius was not the only one influenced by Marya's nerve.

"I'm Hamasa. I'm not just a symbol. If Marya can see me as *me*, then so can you."

Valerius exhaled roughly, brows scrunched close together, jaw ticking. As he straightened, mouth parting on whatever reply he had, Marya rushed towards them, hissing their names. Shocked by the tone, they turned to her in unison. Hamasa's pulse ratcheted up seeing the wild-eyed girl and the ferociously frowning Arash next to her.

"What is it?" Valerius asked, a little too sharply.

"The Merciless," Marya said hoarsely.

"What?" Hamasa whispered. His vision dimmed, cold spilling down his body, from the crown of his head to his toes. Or was it a heat that seared so hot it numbed him?

"Not here," Arash said. "But down south. On the border."

Valerius blanched, eyes like pits in his ashen face. "What town? Do you know?" he asked hoarsely.

"Somewhere south. We didn't stick around for too many details. All the Lances are being called back to the Capital," Marya said. Valerius' knuckles went white he clenched his fists so tightly. "And some local Arm here in Róntraih are being called down, too."

"All the land routes down south are heavily patrolled. There's no chance Harenae would send a front through Sangsierpe. Even that madman would know better than to go through there," Hamasa said, voice thin and high. "That country is a death trap."

"Riyushu is vulnerable by sea. Attacking from the land

route could be a ruse," Valerius said quietly. "Either to see if the Shield's been found, or as distraction."

"If *you* know that, then surely your Sun-blessed Sovereign does, too," Arash said.

"Surely she does, but she doesn't have much choice since the Shield hasn't come back," Valerius pointed out. Hamasa's gaze dropped to the cobbles beneath his sandals.

Arash let out a loud *oof*, clutching the sack Marya shoved into his chest. She walked up and grabbed Hamasa's shoulders.

"We're going to find your rock—"

"*Rohh*," Arash muttered.

"—and we'll help her together. I'm not gonna toss it in your face and dance off," Marya told him. Hamasa inhaled sharply and looked up. Marya grinned, that same fierce grin she made when she declared she'd help him find his emblem. "You're not gonna have the whole country on your shoulders alone." She leaned down and pressed her forehead to his, the same way Arash did. Hamasa froze like a statue, eyes wide and surprised. "Your only meaning doesn't have to be duty or death, Hamito," she whispered.

"M-marya..." Hamasa gasped. His bottom lip trembled, but he bit down to hold it in. Slowly, he cupped her elbows and pressed his forehead to hers a little firmer. "You're twice the Shield I've ever been."

They stepped away. Marya chuckled and rubbed the side of her nose.

"We shouldn't wait for tomorrow," Valerius said. They looked over at him, but he was staring towards the crowd that whispered and cried out in shock, growing steadily in size. "We should leave tonight. Immediately."

"But in the dark?" Marya asked with a frown.

"He's right. If the Merciless is attacking in the south, near the mountains…" Arash said.

"My emblem," Hamasa said. The word shredded the inside of his throat, pupils pinpricks and skin heating. "They must've realized… when I fell and they couldn't sense me anymore. If they have a mage from Harenae helping them… Those centurions already had one token that sensed my emblem. The Merciless and a mage could easily get another one."

Marya nodded, black eyes flashing and narrowing. "Then, we head out tonight."

32

WITHIN AN HOUR, perhaps two, the group had left Róntraih Porto Cuidat. Although urgency had quickened their exit, the horses kept an easy trot rather than racing. Many times over the next few days, Arash darted ahead, his restless energy bursting out of him until he stopped to wait for their slower mounts to catch up. Their anxiety was so thick, they barely managed conversation during the first days out of Róntraih. Their movements and silences were tense, and the training between Marya and Valerius more fervent than before. Hamasa did his best to join them, but he spent most of their limited rest times with Arash in quiet discussion about what spells would work best finding the emblem. He talked Arash through trying a few obscurer ones a few times. The hills and low brush of the west become the sparse woods of the southeast. Woods that gradually grew thicker and blazed with autumn golds and reds. When the gleaming blue ribbon of the Réo Largo appeared on the horizon, they veered east. The Ajul Mountains loomed ahead; the range bisected the entirety of the continent, Mekshi on the west, what once was Sangsierpe on the east, until they crumpled into rocky hills between the Harenae desert and the Riyushu bay.

One of the last standing cities at the base of the mountains was Vallepidras. It was one of the few cities Hamasa had visited in the past, with the first true university built upon the ruins of the old Mekshan capital. The Serra Falls became the mouth of the Réo Largo there, as well as carving the beginning of a path through the range into Sangsierpe. Something that sent shivers of dread through all four of them as they stared down at the map. For the past few years, more and more people were leaving Vallepidras, the city too close to the shadows of Sangsierpe's tragedy. Mists crept through the blocked mountain pass and left dozens ill in the darkest months of the year.

They stopped to rest outside Vallepidras on the banks of the Réo Largo. This close to the mountains the river was rockier and swifter and more dangerous than the wide, slow thing it was farther downriver. As they crowded around the open map for what felt like the thousandth time, the wild rushing roared in Hamasa's ears. His skin prickled with bumps and the hair on his head rose. He couldn't tell if was it the sound of the river that reminded him of the night he fell because he'd been near it, or if it was the roaring that reminded him the Beast that had stalked him.

"Are we sure that's the best place to go?" Marya asked while rolling up the map.

Arash and Hamasa glanced at each other.

"I don't remember being that close," Hamasa said quietly, "but if I was flung so far north..."

"There's a chance the emblem was thrown as far in another direction," Valerius finished. Hamasa nodded.

"I think there's a good chance it's in Sangsierpe," Arash said with a low, tired hiss. "I still can't feel it and I *should* be able to feel it."

"Shouldn't Hamasa feel it?" Marya asked glancing between them.

"Maybe not," Hamasa said, the creases around his eyes pulled tight as he tried to smile. And probably failed. "It's been weeks and my own magic is tied to the emblem."

"Which is why you used that old Mekshan spell, using the natural magic you told me about," Marya said. Hamasa nodded.

"We'll find it," Valerius stated firmly. Hamasa's expression relaxed into something a bit more sincere. "It's time for spear practice, Marya."

"We'll set up lunch," Hamasa offered.

"I guess I'll help. The faster it's done, the faster I can try locating the emblem again," Arash said with his own short huff.

Setting up lunch was just unpacking a few bits of ready dried foods and a bit of cheese and fruits that hadn't spoiled yet. Arash lingered long enough to press his forehead to Hamasa's, and then went hunting for himself. Once his shadow slipped out of sight, Hamasa closed his eyes and wrapped his arms around his legs. The only people they had met on the Great Road during the times they actually travelled on it had only been talked about Harenae, Harenae, *Harenae*. And of course, the simmering worry about the Sovereign's Shield still missing. Rumors of ships that were seen sailing from around the northern tip of Mekshi, *and* coming in from the west, *and* coming up the southwestern coast; ships with three banks of oars and painted bloody red. Harenese battle ships closing in on every side. It looked more and more as if the would-be King of Harenae would force a war before winter, with or without confirmation of the Shield's death.

Hamasa shuddered and pressed his eyes to his knees.

War. War was coming. The Merciless with it. How could he leave *her* to face it alone? But how could he face it? He had already lost. He'd already done irrevocable damage and if anyone found out... His last secret beat against his teeth and choked back to save her. His selfish cowardice would get her killed. It was delayed only marginally by this last secret.

Next to him came the sound of quiet footsteps. They paused,

and then the body attached settled on the ground beside him. It could only be Valerius, with that height and breadth. Hamasa peeked to the side with one eye. He was looking down at him, silent and pensive and dewed with sweat. Marya finally giving him work to do, it seemed. Hamasa smiled and ducked his head against his knees, sighing softly at the gentle, warm-but-cool touch of Valerius' bare hand to Hamasa's shoulder.

"You've become more withdrawn since we left Róntraih," Valerius observed.

"Mekshi is huge," Hamasa said, voice muffled by his thighs. "I was flung clear across it when I... when I was separated from my emblem. For all we know, it was flung into the sea and now it's sunk to the bottom completely out of our reach. None of you can be the First Sovereign of Mekshi and dive to the bottom to fetch my pearl." Hamasa snorted softly.

"Wasn't that a mistranslation?"

"Pearl, stone, emblem. It doesn't matter." But he was smiling crookedly where it couldn't be seen.

"Of course it matters. Your soul matters," a beat, "Hamasa."

Hamasa's lips trembled. "What am I supposed to do, Valerius? I... I'm not even sure I *want* to find it."

It wasn't a lie, but it also was. He wasn't unsure, he was *certain*. But how would anyone understand not wanting your own soul?

Valerius remained silent. Choosing his words carefully? Or dumbstruck? He picked up the sounds of Marya murmuring to the stolen horse, petting and bribing the gelding with pieces of apple and cane sugar far from where they sat. It wasn't like her to not be nosy.

"No one wants to face a war," Valerius said at last. Hamasa jerked a little. "No one wants what happened to Sangsierpe to happen again. Wanting won't delay the inevitable, though. You made a vow. I made one, too. Part of that vow is to protect all the people living under the Sovereign's protection. People such as Marya and her mother, and all those innocent Others we saved outside Ristahe. That little girl and her mother the candy seller."

"And the Salvatropas?" Hamasa asked, teasing just a bit. Ignoring the ache that all those people created in him. People he didn't want hurt. People he didn't want to suffer. The Merciless was out there, and their devastating ability to destroy the very air everyone breathed, the land everyone stood on.

"Even them," Valerius admitted. The admission was blunt and forced, making Hamasa chuckle. It died away quickly and he raised his head slowly.

"If I don't go, all those people, their lives will be on my hands. If they die... it'll be my fault," Hamasa said woodenly. Valerius' sharply refined features blurred into mush. Is this how Valerius Kaecus saw the world? "If I do go back, if I fight and fail, they'll still die. It'll still be my fault."

"My I—Hamasa—"

"Let's say I go back. I fight. I somehow triumph against the monster that killed *my father*, and we win this bloody, stupid, *horrible* war, won't it just mean more dead on account of me?" Hamasa's fists curled tight. "You can label them enemies, but whatever they're called, they're still people. And the Merciless? Another dragon. The idea of killing a dragon..." Hamasa shuddered all over, gulping down the taste of bile. "It's against all my instincts to kill my kind. It's what makes them a Beast. Do I have to become a Beast, too?"

"We don't always have a choice," Valerius said. "Sometimes to protect and defend, this is the only thing we can do. Fight and kill, or fight and die."

"For what? Why?" Hamasa snapped, eyes flashing angrily. "This isn't what I wanted! This isn't what I thought would happen! I just wanted..."

He closed his eyes. In his mind, it happened all over again. The breaking of his heart as fresh now as seventeen years ago when he heard of his father's death; snuffed out like a candle instead of the fiery inferno he'd been for thousands of years. His mother's scream of grief rending the endless skies with flame. And finally, the call of that tiny voice that needed him. A tiny child's hand reaching out to touch the too-hot golden spike on his snout and the overwhelming relief when she didn't burn.

"I never should've thought I could be like him," Hamasa whispered. Tears filmed his lashes and his bottom lip trembled.

"I don't understand what you are saying," Valerius said after a moment. Hamasa hissed through his teeth. "Whatever the consequences, you have to fulfill the vow you made. You don't have to be your father to be strong enough."

"What if... what if I don't want to?" Hamasa asked, voice quavering.

"It doesn't matter what you want."

Hamasa flinched and laughed, harsh and short. "Don't you ever regret choices you've made?"

"I don't let myself. Regret is useless," Valerius stated with a conviction Hamasa had never felt. "You can't change the past."

"What about being a Lance?" Hamasa asked, his scowl almost matching Valerius'. It was better than crying again. "You gave up your right to head your house, your place in line for the throne, lost your friends—" He broke off and swallowed hard.

"I would never regret it." Valerius said quietly. Hamasa looked up through his bangs, heart thudding to the words: *You will. You will.* "My motives to be a Lance have always been less than altruistic."

Hamasa blinked, absolutely bewildered. "What?"

"My motive was always to serve you, my lord."

"But why?" Hamasa sputtered stupidly.

"You were hope, you *are* hope," Valerius said. He looked over Hamasa's face, lingered on his scars, his eyes, his nose. As if trying to memorize it. "Mekshi was at its darkest moment. Everyone thought no dragon would come and no Sovereign would be Chosen. The Empire was going to crumple under the weight of the infighting and desperation. I was only ten and I could feel the fear everywhere I went. When you came, the fear was gone and the Empire was safe. I knew I could never be you, and I could never be Chosen. But one day... One day I could be strong enough to be someone's hope. I could fight fear itself."

His lips curved into a real smile as his eyes fell to his hands.

"Emerens..." Hamasa choked softly. He pressed his mouth shut, hand yanking back from where he'd reached out to touch Valerius' arm.

"You don't have to be your father, because you're you."

Hamasa couldn't speak. There were no words to reply. How could he argue that Valerius' duty, his entire purpose since he was a child of ten, was shallow and empty? Based only on an ideal of a thing, not even a person. How could he argue, especially because... for a moment... Hamasa wanted to be that thing up on the pedestal. Be the hope that inspired someone like Valerius. Fighting fear itself.

His fingers curled in the air, his hand dropped, and he stared at the dirt. A shadow passed overhead and frost followed in the wake of it. It would be time to go soon. Valerius moved to stand, one hand on the ground next to Hamasa's. Large and fair next to small and dark.

"No matter what happens," Hamasa blurted. Valerius stilled and Hamasa licked his lips. "I believe you're a good man, a better man than Kana'iro the Red and the Shield deserved. It's all I have to give you for all your faith in me."

THE COWARD'S EMBLEM

"Have faith in me in return and in this country you Chose. As Marya says, we'll fight together."

Hamasa watched Valerius go, afternoon sunlight shining on his hair, heart thudding agonizingly. There was nothing else to say.

***

Continuing on towards Vallepidras sunk Hamasa's already worn down spirit further. The Great Road, which they'd left for some of their journey to ride as the crow flies, was slowly filling with other travelers. All of them heading away from the city, many of them families. Wagons and carts, donkeys and shaggy-furred horses pulling them behind, took up the width of the Road so much that the three riders got down and walked the horses. Which was quickly proven a smart choice as the Road became pitted and rutted, each step a second of inattention away from turning an ankle.

"There are so many people leaving," Marya whispered, leaning towards Hamasa.

"It'll have been ordered by the local Sicho. The pass is blocked, but the city is very close to the Harenese border. Some of these people are coming from farther south, too," Valerius replied, obviously overhearing her remark.

"It's the only thing they can do without a Shield, and two dragons being allies with Harenae," Hamasa muttered.

"Not every continent on this filthy mudball has dragons in it to fight their wars for them. You're not a weapon," Arash said sharply. His gaze cut towards Valerius with a curl to his top lip.

"He made a vow. He has a Chosen," Valerius said, just as sharp.

Hamasa licked his lips and ducked his head.

"We'll get into the city before nightfall," Valerius continued. His eyes were back to scanning the finally thinning out crowds. "I haven't been here since I was a squire, but I remember enough."

"And tomorrow we'll go straight into the mountains?" Marya asked.

"This close, there's a spell Hamasa and I can try. I wanted to wait to save Hamasa," Arash told her.

"Save Hamasa from what?"

"It's tiring," Hamasa answered quickly, his mouth drying and his eyes on Arash. Warning him for silence. Arash scowled, but his mouth stayed shut. "The spell goes on until the object is found and I'll be tired while it goes."

"We could make a token and use my magic," Arash grumbled.

"Rubies aren't free here," Hamasa sighed.

"Here? Are rubies free somewhere else?" Marya exclaimed with wide eyes.

Fortunately, the hazy shape of the city began to form into real shapes and Marya was distracted by the city unfolding in front of them. Their first glimpse of the city was two towering crags that cradled the city between them, the Manos Sagradas. Then, a wagon moved past and the tall spires of the university of Vallepidras rose over the horizon. The rest of the city's roofs sat at less than half the height. At the highest peaks of the university were a half dozen spires with a rounded shape at the very tip—the encircled "pearl" of the Empire, Hamasa remembered. All the buildings gleamed a buttery warm tan with brownish-red tiles on gently sloping roofs. They almost melted into the sunset, the Great Road becoming a golden main avenue through the center to the university itself. Outside the city, trees were growing in long, even lines, the smell of citruses and avocados and rich loamy earth filling the air. If the shadow of the Merciless wasn't hounding their heels and the sight of the evacuees wasn't on every side of them, the grand city of Vallepidras would've been uplifting.

A thrill ran down Hamasa's spine—the bad kind. The snap of pennants, the rattle of iron and steel, the constant thundering of the ground under his feet as horses marched in eerie unison. He spun around, breath catching, and stared at the tall poles held upright in stirrups and horses that looked nothing like the long-furred, stocky breed of the locals. And looked a lot like Nerva and the stolen silver horse that walked on either side of them.

"Lances!" Marya said, some of her farm-girl enthusiasm leaking through.

Valerius tensed, so still and silent he didn't seem to be breathing. His hand curled into a fist at his side.

"What's going to happen if they see you?" Hamasa asked. The feeling from before, of missing something important, like taking a step and only finding air, returned. "Kelso said…"

"I'm a deserter. I'll be arrested," Valerius said, fist clenching harder, jaw taut.

"Hamasa doesn't have his soul rock yet. He can't prove you were right!" Marya said, horrified. "Your… knightliness, you'll lose it."

"You care about this now?" Arash asked. "You care about *him* now?"

"Ay, but… he's… Valerius is…" Marya stammered, eyes darting from Valerius to Arash to Hamasa, brows pulling low and close.

"They're not stopping. We should think of something," Hamasa said, gnawing at his bottom lip and staring down the road.

"Why should they even notice? Just duck your head," Arash said with an eye-roll.

"I don't know if that'll work," Marya said. "The horses…

they're too nice."

"And Valerius is too obviously Riyukezan with an obviously expensive weapon, too," Hamasa said, waving towards the canvas-wrapped trident.

Valerius grasped Hamasa's shoulder, startling him at the abruptness of it. "It doesn't matter. You need to go on to find your emblem. Her Imperial Highness may be lenient," Valerius said quietly. Hamasa's abused lip slipped from between his teeth as he gaped. "I failed already. I did it all wrong."

"What? No, it's fine! It's *fine*. I was the—"

"We don't have time for this if we're gonna do something!" Marya hissed, grabbing Hamasa's arm and shaking him.

"It's going to be too late. We're not exactly hiding now," Arash said.

Hamasa and Valerius' eye contact hadn't broken. His hand was still on Hamasa's shoulder. Valerius would be fine. He would be arrested for a short time, but Aneya would remember her cousin. If he even made it that far. Hamasa knew how slowly it worked. All the levels and subordinates and politics of the Riyukezan courts, let alone the local Mekshan government that struggled to keep control of their regions. Valerius could be pardoned right away, or he could languish in prison for a year or more. The war would only make the process slower and more difficult.

And he was only here at all, only at risk for arrest, because of Hamasa's lie.

Hamasa frowned, vision sharpening into shades of red and orange and yellow—"*Hamasa, no!*"—and he raised a fingertip that shined like the heart of a ruby. Valerius stepped back, eyes widening, but Hamasa was already drawing lines of runes from right to left across his chest. They flickered like living flame. Hamasa gasped, fire burning inside his veins, yanking the breath and magic out of him. The emptiness he'd prodded *tore*. Gritting his teeth, Hamasa slapped his hand against Valerius' chest so hard the knight grunted, falling back to knock against Nerva's side. The fiery words burned through him. As Valerius grasped the front of his kimono, Hamasa reached past and traced the same onto Nerva's hindquarters. The mare shuffled in place and snorted loudly, tossing back her mane with a strident whinny under Hamasa's palm as the runes burned.

"**Don't look, don't hear**," Hamasa intoned in the language of his home. Suddenly, the writing was gone.

He stumbled back, gulping down air and head reeling. A cool arm slipped around his waist and a hand over his thundering heartbeat. The chill pierced him as surely as Marya's spear.

"What'd you do? What was that?" Marya demanded shakily. "Your eyes, they're all gold, Hamito."

"Put it away, Hamasa. Cut it off now," Arash growled. Hamasa shook his head, grimacing.

"No, not until we get in the city," he protested.

"What have you done?" Valerius asked, holding up his hands. Nothing looked different. He neither blended into his surroundings, nor disappeared from sight.

"It's an aversion spell. Let's go, now. The longer he holds the spell, the worse it is," Arash said, shoving Hamasa into Marya's arms and snatching Nerva's reins. "Get on your damn horses. All of you."

"An aversion spell?" Marya asked.

The stamping and rattling of the approaching squad of Lances was all but on top of them. Arash hissed and shoved the ex-knight towards the saddle. Marya stared, jaw dropping, at the squad moving around Valerius and Nerva without a second glance. Water parting around a rock. A few nodded at Marya and Hamasa as they passed, a few scowled and muttered in rude

Riyukezan about country bumpkins in the way. And then they passed, heading into the city ahead.

"What... in the world?" Marya wheezed.

"Get him on the horse, ape. The longer he's holding onto the spell, the worse it is," Arash snapped. He glared poisonously at Valerius. "Are you here to help him or not, *knight*?"

Valerius stared at Hamasa, who weakly smiled back.

"It was the only thing I could think of," he said.

Valerius' expression crashed, scowling black thunder. In the next moment, he swung up into the saddle and gazed at the city silently.

"C'mon, Hamito, let's go," Marya murmured in his ear.

Embarrassingly, it took twice the time and effort it normally did. Marya had to half-drag him up with a hand on the back of his poncho as the stolen horse restlessly shifted. The moment Hamasa was sitting up behind her, Valerius tapped Nerva into a run. The silver took off after him immediately, Marya and Hamasa biting back yelps at the suddenness. Arash ran beside them, one hand on Hamasa's leg, chilling him straight to the bone.

33

It had been easy to find a hostal with a vacant room and stables. What hadn't been easy was walking through a veritable ghost town. Building after building, shop after shop, doors barred and windows painted over. The few remaining citizens, a mix of Mekshan and Riyukezan and Harenese, moved quickly from building to building. Market-goers were rushed, the customary chitchat and haggling brusque.

The hostal was a single story sprawling place with an inner tiled courtyard. Limón, guava, and orange trees in their own small areas with stone benches encircling them for shade. In the middle there was a wide, shallow pool with tiles glazed white, red, and turquoise creating the shape of hands cupped in prayer. Reflecting the Manos Sagradas that held Vallepidras at their base. Incredibly, wonderfully, a group of pure blue añhana fluttered and danced over the fountain's surface, their translucent wings sparkling like stars. They all stopped in the middle of their guileless playing, watching with luminescent eyes as the group crossed through to find the owners. Unfortunately, the room they chose had a window that faced the street, not one facing the courtyard, and brightly embroidered curtains they kept closed. Marya peeked past the flowers and parrots to the street. It was already as dark as midnight in Vallepidras, thanks to the shade cast by the mountains.

"I don't see any of 'em. They must've settled in somewhere," she said, dropping the curtains and turning back to the room.

Hamasa sighed and slumped against the wall on one of the beds. He wanted sleep, and fruit water, and meat. Was it possible to do all three at the same time?

"You idiot," Arash muttered.

Hamasa flapped a hand at him. It was caught mid-air and his eyes sprang open to look right into Valerius' glaring face.

"You shouldn't have done that."

"I helped you. Again!" Hamasa said and jerked his hand away.

"You should have let me be arrested. What I did in Elorra, I betrayed you and the Lances that day," Valerius told him, eyes flashing.

"That's ridiculous!" Hamasa shuffled off the bed to glare up at him. He wobbled on his feet and shook his head. "I betrayed you first. I lied from day one. To you and Marya."

"This isn't a competition of who acted worse," Valerius started. Hamasa scoffed loudly. "Because of my mistakes, you're in danger. You keep putting yourself in danger for me."

"You want me to fight a war! Why should me helping you be a problem? It's my duty, isn't it?"

"Of course we're going to help you," Marya added, coming up to stand next to them. "We need you now, Valerius. You travelled the farthest, you know how to teach me, you know about Harenae and Sangsierpe, too."

"Not if it it comes down to me or him," Valerius snapped. Marya rocked back on her heels, but Valerius was already back to glaring at Hamasa. "I didn't forget that using magic will tire you. You were unconscious for almost an hour last time and you used it for a few seconds."

"That was mostly those magic cuffs. And I didn't forget that you gave up everything for me," Hamasa retorted. "You gave up your family for me to be a Lance. And then you gave up being a Lance for me even though all I did was lie and try to hide. You're going to lose everything for me and I don't want that. I'd never want that!"

For a moment, the anger broke. Valerius' eyes widening and he stepped back, no longer looming over Hamasa and making him feel tiny. Or like he was arguing with a giant tree. It didn't last long, Valerius immediately scowling again, although the looming didn't return.

"My duty is to serve you. Finding your emblem, keeping you safe until then, that's the most important task. You should have saved your energy for that," Valerius said, not quite softly.

Hamasa saw red. Not literally, but in the way humans meant it. Actual anger warring with that churning horrible guilt. He didn't ask for this. He didn't want someone like Valerius who would rather lose everything, sacrifice himself in any and every way to protect Hamasa. The weight that sacrifice made, how it dragged down his shoulders, his heart, a leaden lump in his smoldering stomach. He closed his eyes, fists clenching at his sides, his whole body shaking.

"My duty is what I choose! That's the whole point!" Hamasa shouted. "If I choose to save you, then say thank you!"

Hamasa's hands curled and uncurled and curled. There was only the sound of their shared breaths, the pounding in Hamasa's head, and the distant voices of the hostal's workers and few guests somewhere outside.

"I think that's the sum of it," Arash said dryly.

Hamasa startled and jerked his head up. In front of him, Valerius had turned away, eyes on the ground. Without looking towards them, he strode out the door. It closed on silent hinges with a click. Hamasa flinched as if it had been a slam.

Marya came over and grasped Hamasa's shoulder. When he met her eyes, she grinned at him. "You did good, Hamito. He knows you're right."

Hamasa's lips wobbled into a smile and his shoulders slumped. "Being right doesn't really feel good."

"Give it a minute," Arash said as he dug through a pack and pulled out an orange. "It'll feel great once the shock wears off."

Before Hamasa or Marya could worry, though they came very close to it as the minutes passed, Valerius returned. He held a tray of dishes and a jug sweating with condensation. He remained silent, expression blank, and set the tray on the only small table in the room. Food was doled out and eaten woodenly, all of their eyes drawn to the window. The night deepened and moonlight snuck through the cracks in the curtains. After cleaning up and taking turns in the bathing rooms, they sat on their beds, or, in Arash's case, on the floor and propped against the wall with his head tilted back. Hamasa closed his eyes and slumped back. Marya *tch*ed under her breath and tucked her arm around his shoulders. He tensed, only to lean against her, head on her shoulder, and slipped gratefully into sleep.

Sunshine filled the room when he opened his eyes again. The smell of eggs and beans made his nose twitch and his stomach grumble loudly. It was as if he hadn't eaten for days, rather than only hours, but at least he wasn't groggy or out of it. He woke, stretching like a cat and hands clawing at the air, and rolled over to stare at the still barely steaming platter.

"You look a lot better now," Marya said.

Hamasa shrieked and tumbled off the bed, grimacing against the floor as Marya laughed. He pushed himself up and found her by the door, squatting by the pile of their packs and yanking strings tied.

"Ay, where are those dragon senses at? Little ol' me scared

you?"

"I've never really been good at being vigilant," Hamasa admitted, rubbing at his arm. He slipped back onto the bed and pulled his breakfast close. "Where are Arash and Valerius?" His mouth twisted to the side at the thought of those two alone somewhere. It was not a happy picture.

"Wally is getting the horses ready and Arash is snooping 'round town, looking to see where those Lances ended up. Valerius didn't seem... excited about sneaking outta town, but he didn't say nothing."

"Did he say anything at all since...?" Hamasa trailed off, watching egg yolk drip off his spoon.

"Since you told him off?" Marya asked, grinning even wider. She hefted the packs up with a grunt and shrugged. "He said, 'I'll see to the horses.' Don't think he's said anything else. Do you think he sulks? If my mamá saw him, she'd say he's sulking."

"Dragons in their thousands sulk. A twenty-seven year old could definitely be sulking," Hamasa muttered. "You don't... you don't think I went too far?"

"What?" Marya paused, one hand on the door.

"Last night. Yelling at him. Maybe I went too far."

"Are you joking? He had it coming. You shoulda done it a long time ago. With a punch to the nose," Marya said while holding out a fist. Hamasa huffed, shaking his head. "Finish up. Once Arash is back we're outta here."

"All right." Hamasa scraped the plate, noting in some surprise it was almost clean. Confused, he glanced back to the door when he didn't hear it open.

Marya stood there, lips pursed, nose scrunched, and brows pulled together.

"Do you..." She spun around, starting slightly when she saw him already staring at her. She recovered swiftly and said, "Do you want to go back, Hamasa?"

The spoon clattered to the dish. Food turned to paste on his tongue and coated the inside of his mouth.

"You don't want to go back, do you? That's why you kept lying..." Marya said. She came up to the bed and sat down next to him, the pack dropping heavily between them. "I kept asking myself why wouldn't you just tell me? After Valerius showed up, after those Harenese attacked us, after Arash came, you coulda told me any of those times."

"I didn't want to lie. I hated it, I really did. You deserved better—"

"Hey, we're past that. Way, way past it now," Marya interrupted, clasping his shoulder. "I guess I'm a *little* mad 'bout the lying. But you have that Merciless hunting you and that's just the beginning. I get it, as much as I can, not being the Shield myself and all. I hope, yanno, you can trust me now?" she asked, rubbing the back of her neck.

"Of course I trust you, Marya. Could you ever trust me?" Hamasa asked.

Marya met his gaze, eyes serious. "I trust you, Asa. I know I can trust you to do the right thing. You might take a long road 'round, but you get there."

Hamasa ducked his head. "I guess so."

"Does that mean you wanna go back?"

Hamasa bit his lip and turned back to the flames. "I don't know. I made that promise... I made that promise when I thought it was over and the Merciless would never come back." His mouth twisted ruefully, fingers touching the scar tissue on his cheek. "Now they're back, and I'm supposed to fight them, and stave off a civil war, at a quarter of my father's age and *none* of his experience."

"What do you want to do? Keep running?"

THE COWARD'S EMBLEM

"*Yes,*" Hamasa exclaimed breathlessly. "All I want to do is run. Pathetic."

"Doesn't seem like it. Using your magic, shouting down Valerius, searching for your emblem," Marya leaned back on her hands.

"It took me the long road around," Hamasa said licking his lips. "But I know it's the right thing to do. I'm scared and I want to run and I want to vomit almost all the time," Marya barked out a laugh, "but I need my emblem. I need to go back to Riyushu. If anything, to tell her I'm sorry. Sorry for... everything."

"Her, that's the Sovereign," Marya said and Hamasa nodded. "Ay, I can't believe it. You know her. You know *her.*"

"Like a sister," Hamasa said, smiling sadly. "And I left her behind. Alone." *More alone than anyone knows.*

"So you've gotta go back for her. For your sister," Marya said quietly.

"For all my choices, her being the Sovereign? That wasn't a mistake. I saw it seventeen years ago, the greatness in her. It reminded me of what my father said about the last Sovereign. How it shined from within and my father just knew this human was a great one. Capable of amazing things. And maybe I thought, without realizing it, that we could grow up together."

"How old *are* you?"

"I know I'm older than you," Hamasa said, laughing, rubbing at his eye. "Not yet four hundred. Real young for my kind. Too young to be a Shield probably. But I'm fast. And stupid. I got here first, not that many wanted to come. Merciless being summoned like... like a creature to be enslaved, then turning on our kind and... um, killing m-my father. That doesn't happen. Dragons don't kill dragons. But the Merciless did. None of the other dragons wanted anything to do with Mekshi. The Empire was never supposed to be here anyway. It was never supposed to leave Osekai."

"But the Stormwrought fell in love and brought her Sovereign here," Marya remembered.

She breathed heavily through her nose and tipped over to knock her head against his temple. Hamasa smiled at the dragonness of it. Then, Marya got to her feet, stretched her arms over her head, and slung the pack over her shoulder.

"All right, it's time to go. Don't forget to drink your fruit water. I got you guava. You'll like it." She ruffled his hair, snickering at him batting her away, and left the room.

Hamasa finished off what was left of the food and started tidying up a bit, guzzling guava infused water as he did. They needed to get out of the city fast. But before that, there was still that spell to do. Hamasa frowned, lowering his cup and touching the front of his chest. The aversion spell had not been pleasant and the locating spell would be worse, and last even longer. He slipped his feet into his sandals and grabbed the poncho from the peg on the wall. As soon as his head poked through the neck hole, he smoothed down his hair and glanced around the room, making sure nothing was left.

His skin pulled taut with small bumps and his eyes widened.

Terror sliced through him, an overpowering dread that stole the heat from his very bones. He knew this feeling. This utterly consuming fear. The entire hostal shook as the air broke around a roar. Knees hit the floor and cracked against wood. Hands braced on a flat surface and eyes stared blankly at the door in front of him. His knees, his hands, his eyes.

"The Merciless..." he whispered hoarsely from a mouth that was wrong. Flimsy and soft and defenseless. Like the rest of this useless body.

34

THE DOOR OPENED and feet pounded against the floor. Hands, cool-but-warm large hands, grasped his shoulders. Flinching, Hamasa looked up with dim, blurry eyes. Valerius had somehow gotten up the stairs faster than Arash, who was right behind him, frost crawling over his cheeks. Next to him, Marya was ashen, eyes too wide and mouth hanging open. Valerius shook him, forcing Hamasa's blank gaze back to his dark, intense one. He was the only one in the room that showed no fear, only fierce and determined focus.

Hamasa leaned into Valerius' hands. Breath shook out of his throat at last.

"Hamasa?" he demanded curtly. Hamasa blinked at Valerius and gulped down air. For a moment, that façade broke to show relief, then the mask of the Lance slammed back into place. "We need to get out of here. We'll do the spell later."

"You think that monster won't sniff Hamasa out? The distance and the missing rohh might throw them off, but they're on top of us!" Arash snapped, pupils slit like a cat's and glowing.

"I have to go arone," Hamasa said, lips numb and words hollow, eyes on Marya, then Valerius. "G-give m-me a horse and I'll ride until he catches m-me."

"That's out of the question," Valerius said hoarsely.

Hamasa stared, shoulders slumped and the all too obvious

tautness of his face and trembling lips. Valerius scowled and got to his feet, dragging Hamasa up with him.

"We're going to the horses. Now."

"W-wait, b-but..."

Another roar shook the city and Hamasa let out a wispy, horrified whimper. He slapped a hand over his mouth, eyes closing, swallowing it down. All of them were running down the outside corridor and through the courtyard, ignoring the screams and shouts from the people still inside the hostal. In the stables, Nerva and the silver were already saddled and ready, shuffling and tossing their manes as their eyes rolled. Marya ran for the door as Valerius dropped Hamasa's arm and went for the horse stalls. Her stream of loud curses had them all turning.

"Lances. They're running towards the Great Road," Marya told him, eyes still too wide.

"They're going to protect the city from the Merciless," Valerius said, jaw tensing. He led Nerva out of her stall and stared past Marya's shoulders. "I should be with them."

"We already went over this! We need you!" Marya shouted at him.

"Do you serve Hamasa or not?" Arash snarled. Valerius cast a cutting glance at him. Slowly, he nodded.

"But all those knights, they'll..." Hamasa stammered.

"It's what they're trained to do," Valerius said.

"It doesn't matter, the Beast is here for me. They'll raze the city and everyone in it!" Hamasa said.

"You're right," Arash said. His eyes closed and he took a breath, slow and deep. "I can hold him off for a few minutes, but you have to get out of here."

"W-What? Arash, you don't mean—" Hamasa gasped. An arm wrapped around his chest from behind and pulled him back.

"The sense of you is really weak. I'm a lot stronger, and a

whole lot bigger. They'll come after me first." Arash turned on his heel, claws growing from his fingers and the white patches on his skin spreading.

"Arash, no, you can't fight them on your own."

"Get your rohh, Hamasa. I can handle this."

Marya stared as Arash walked past her and out of sight.

"Get on the horse, Marya," Valerius snapped. Marya jumped.

"Right, coming," she yelped, rushing forward.

"He's gonna die. Arash's gonna die. I have to—" Hamasa babbled, hands scrabbling at the arm holding him. His skin began to heat and Valerius adjusted his arm away from any bare skin.

"You can't change, my lord, so what can you do?" Valerius demanded. "The faster we find your emblem, the faster we can help Arash."

Hamasa immediately slumped, head bowed and shoulders shaking. The hold across his chest wasn't tight enough to hurt, but Hamasa couldn't breathe. The vise kept squeezing tighter and harder. He wheezed and gasped, his whole body scalding and eyes stinging, and he couldn't breathe.

The Merciless was here. Here.

And Arash was alone, risking his life for a selfish coward like Hamasa.

His knees were on the ground again and Valerius' broad hand lay against the middle of his chest. Desperately wheezing, Hamasa grasped Valerius' wrist, a hiss of someone else's pain nothing more than a shuddering echo in his head. He curled around the hand on his chest and panted hoarsely. Gradually, the low rumble of Valerius' voice made it through the raspy sound of Hamasa's poor excuse for breaths.

"Slowly, Hamasa. Keep breathing in, and hold it-" Hamasa realized with groggy surprise that his body automatically did as Valerius directed. "-good, breathe out. Slowly. Try one more time."

Hamasa closed his eyes, humiliation spreading like a rash under his skin. Once more he inhaled, held it, and exhaled in time with Valerius. He couldn't force himself to raise his eyes. A screeching roar of fury broke overhead and with it the shouts of the Lances outside, the screams of the citizens, the clattering of hooves on cobbles. Hamasa's breath hitched. Suddenly he was on his feet, Valerius shoving him into Marya's arms.

"Get on the horse, ride towards the mountain away from the Road," Valerius ordered.

"Didn't we talk about you staying with us?" Marya asked furiously.

"I'm not following Arash," Valerius said, scowling. He opened up a saddlebag and Hamasa caught sight of canvas and raw wool. "I'm not going out there without my armor. On the other side of the university, there's a gate leading towards the old mountain pass and the Falls. Meet there and get out of here."

Marya's chin jutted out as she frowned. But she glanced at Hamasa's wan face, and he stared back, mouth working around words he should say. Instead, Hamasa stood swaying in place, all his senses in the air above his head and beyond the ceiling. He could hear the beating of wings. The screaming of horses chilling his blood.

During the moments Hamasa stood fixated on the sounds above, Marya swung up onto the silver horse. He choked in surprise when her hand gripped the back of his poncho and yanked him up. Hamasa grabbed the saddle and heaved himself up behind her, letting her do most of the work. Marya snapped the reins with a shout. They barrelled out of the stables, ducking below the eaves. Hamasa twisted in the seat to stare behind him at Valerius tying thigh guards around his waist.

THE COWARD'S EMBLEM

The silver's ironshod hooves clopped over the road. The stragglers rushing through the streets dived out of their way. They were clutching bundles to their chests or holding on desperately to the person who ran beside them, adult and child alike. Birds of every color and size and lohas with their glittering gossamer wings streaked overhead. While the people were heading to the university and its sturdy walls that had stood for centuries, the birds and Others were heading towards the mountains.

"Are you all right, Asa?" Marya shouted over her shoulder. He swallowed dryly.

"Yeah, I'm all right," he said.

But she was staring past him, upwards to the sky, and with a sinking feeling in his gut, Hamasa did the same. His guts twisted into knots at a massive black form blotting out the sky. Below it, the early morning sunlight glittered on the armor and weapons of the knights. From the very heart of the sun, a blinding white form dropped out of the sky. With a screech, Arash landed on the pitch-black dragon that roared and frothed green liquid from their maw. Arash looked fierce and beautiful in battle, as he always did, but he was also so small. Not even half the Merciless' size. Hamasa gripped Marya's vest in shaking hands, eyes and nose burning and breath too shallow.

The Merciless was a monster in comparison. Huge and menacing, with claws that glinted as brightly as Arash's white scales even as far away as they were. A wingspan that could envelope the entire hostal they had stayed in. Scales so black they seemed to absorb the very light from the sky, darkening the city below impossibly. The Merciless. Unrelenting, pitiless, and stronger than Hamasa could have imagined. Phantom pains slithered over his arms and back and legs, across his right cheek and temple. A piercing ache that bubbled and hissed over his body in jagged lines and smears.

"Shit!" Marya bellowed. She kicked the silver's side and the horse leapt forward. Hamasa pressed closer, clinging like a limpet, teeth rattling in his head.

An agonized scream rent the air and the ground shuddered under their feet. The thundering crash and rumble of a large body hitting the ground, destroying the buildings under it, had Hamasa spinning back around and gasping. The Merciless hovered in the air, roaring in glee as Arash shook off rubble and forced himself into flight. He raced away, jagged white lightning that disappeared into the bright sun overhead, the Merciless in hot pursuit.

"Arash..."

"*Ow, ow*, leggo!" Marya exclaimed, slapping at his arms around her waist and making the horse under them lose its step. Marya quickly grabbed hold of the reins and hissed between her teeth. "You're hotter'n soup bubbling over. Hold on to the saddle!"

"I'm sorry!" Hamasa immediately grabbed the saddle under his butt. He didn't even know how long he had been hot enough to burn. A shiny pink welt wrapped around a wrist sprang to mind. Valerius' hand pressed to his chest and refusing to move away.

Just barely, Hamasa made out Marya's voice, "I don't like it."

He leaned forward, ears straining, and caught sight of the frown on her dark, heavy-browed face. Luckily, Marya didn't flinch away, so he must have gotten his body temperature under control. Before Hamasa could ask what she meant, Marya continued,

"They're guleros, both of 'em, but I don't like leaving them behind. I should be fighting *with* 'em. I'm not this kinda person. I don't leave the fighting to others while I run. I've never done that."

THE COWARD'S EMBLEM

With those words ringing in his ears, Hamasa stared at what he could see of Marya's face. All these weeks, all the things he'd learned and done, and here he was. Back at the beginning. Running. He looked ahead, watching as the university reared up in front of them. Unconsciously mirroring her, his jaw tensed, his brows pulling tight, eyes flashing as the sunlight broke through the mountains. In the distance, there was another roar, and the mists behind the tallest spires were banded in flickering rainbows. The front gates, massive cast iron things, were wide open, but Marya veered the silver horse around the side, following the walls that encircled most of the campus grounds. Giant cypresses swayed over the top of the walls, the rushing and roaring of water drowning out the cacophony of terrified Vallepidras citizens behind them.

They looked up to the peaks that seemed to curve overhead. The summits were already white with snow. As they rounded the university's walls, they finally saw the Serra Falls in all its glory; the thundering spill of icy white water from the peak hundreds of leagues above to the frothing foam that ruffled the glassy sheen of the lake at the base. The avenue they clattered down was lined with the same enormous cypresses that grew inside the university walls and sloped upwards towards the bridge that led out of the city over the shallow but turbulent mouth of the Réo Largo. Marya and Hamasa gasped at the same time, their necks craning back and back, staring up the sheer majesty of the Falls, tasting the snowmelt on their lips as the mist dewed the air all around them. They could only stare in awe.

"Oh, órala," Marya breathed. The roar of the Falls was so loud, so insistent, that her words were almost swallowed up by it. "I never seen a waterfall."

"That is the largest one in Mekshi. You'll never see another one like it," Hamasa told her, heart thumping against his sternum.

Marya pulled the silver horse's head gently around to look back. She *tch*ed loudly, hands tightening and loosing repetitively around the reins. "That gulero better catch up fast," she burst out. She fidgeted and the horse shuffled under them with her, ears flicking back and forth. "What about that dragon? That was them, right? The Merciless?"

"Yes."

"Shit, shit, shit! Are they gonna sniff you out? Like Arash said?"

Hamasa inhaled sharply, fingers curling around the edge of the saddle. "He was right about being a distraction," he answered slowly. "If we make it into the mountains, that'll hide us a bit more, but we should—"

He broke off as the horse beneath them shook its head, snorting and hoofing at the ground in agitation. Marya grunted as Hamasa bumped her back hard enough for them to wobble. When they straightened with matching puzzled frowns, Marya tapped her heels at the silver's sides.

"Ay, hold now. Hold! Is this 'cuz of the kick earlier? I'm sorry 'bout that. I panicked. I promise not to kick you again," Marya said, patting its neck a little hesitantly.

The horse's ears flicked forward. With a suddenness that had both riders crying out and clutching desperately at whatever they could reach, the horse threw itself forward, returning down the avenue and deeper into the city.

35

THE MARE ZIG-ZAGGED through the side streets, ignoring every command Marya tried to give, snorting and iron shoes striking sparks on cobbles in its haste. They both shouted, barely clinging on, as the horse galloped down an empty street lined with shops filled with books and writing utensils of every kind.

"What's happening?" Marya screeched.

"How should I know!?"

The horse stopped and pranced a bit in place, shaking its head and snorting. Hamasa and Marya looked all around them, twisting in the saddle this way and that, looking for any answer or movement. Down the street and several doors down, a dark brown horse came into view from behind a shop with calligraphy brushes of different sizes hanging in the window. On his back was the centurion with the *smile*. On another horse, this one dappled grey, the fairer, blonde-haired partner followed with that glowing pink token hanging from his fist on a leather string.

"Running from the fight again, Kana'iro? Leaving your new friend to die for you?" Gaius asked, leaning forward, arms crossing on the saddle horn.

"He must've gotten his horse trained like Valerius," Marya sighed roughly. She reached down and slipped the spear free from under her leg along the horse's side.

"That looks like a real weapon," Flavius noted, slinging his crossbow forward. "Although, that doesn't mean she can truly wield it."

"Maybe from their Lance friend. I wonder if he's already dead," Gaius said with that teeth-baring grin.

"Stop talking about me like I ain't even here," Marya snarled, pointing the spear towards them like a lance. Her rage seemed to seep into Hamasa, bubbling in his blood as his eyes narrowed.

"You're nothing. Insignificant, really," Flavius said as he reached into the quiver tied to his saddle.

"Thank you for your help, though," Gaius said, still lounging on his saddle horn and smiling.

Marya scoffed. "What help?"

"That mouth of yours. You really should be careful who you run it off to. Not every pretty girl is a friend," Gaius said, smirking. Marya stiffened, her fist clenching around the haft of her spear. In a split second, Hamasa remembered the pretty amber eyes of the dala in Róntraih Porto Cuidat. How carefully they looked through him, how entranced Marya had been. "All we want is—"

The silver under them leapt forward, Marya crying out in shock. Hamasa lifted the foot he had just dug into the silver's side, and its mane whipped against his hands. Across the street, Gaius and Flavius' eyes widened, but they were too well trained for surprise to hold them for long. Gaius pulled free his gladius and rode towards them with a laugh. Flavius slipped the first bolt into the crossbow, frowning as he pulled it back.

"Knock him out of the saddle, Marya!" Hamasa shouted. The sandal slipped into his hand and he flung it with a yell. Flavius raised his crossbow and shot as the sandal smacked it to the side. The bolt zipped harmlessly wide and far.

Marya leaned forward in the saddle, gripped the spear under her left arm, and pulled a hoarse, ringing shout from deep in her chest. Gaius knocked the spear tip aside without effort, smirking. But Marya already held the other side, twisting at the waist and slamming the staff of the spear across his chest with a growl. Just barely they caught sight of his too-wide brown eyes, spittle flying past his lips, his body falling back and to the side; and they were riding past. Flavius had another bolt in and he squeezed the trigger. Hamasa grabbed the reins, chest molding to Marya's back, and jerked them to the side. The horse whinnied shrilly, iron shoes striking sparks, and the bolt grazed Hamasa's shoulder.

He hissed, and hissed again when a whistle cut through the air and the horse halted under them. The thud of the saddle horn into Marya's sternum rocked through her so hard, Hamasa gasped with her.

"We gotta get off this horse!" Marya wheezed.

There was another twang. Eyes glowing, Hamasa turned and raised a hand. "*Stop.*"

The very tip of the bolt dug into his palm. He and Marya stared, panting harshly. Hamasa wrapped his fingers around the bolt thrumming with its delayed momentum, and slowly turned his hand over. And opened his hand. Released like a too tightly strung wire, the bolt zipped through the air right back at the archer.

Flavius grunted, the next bolt he'd readied going wide when his body jerked with the impact.

"Asa... *what?*" Marya whispered.

"Let's go," Hamasa panted, clutching his chest and slithering to the ground. He hit the cobbles too hard, one foot bare, and fell to a knee.

"Aren't you hiding yourself, little Red?" Gaius said, his voice a little breathless and hoarse. Unfortunately, he wasn't unhorsed, though the saddle was crooked under him. "Or is this just part of the plan for saving your own skin?"

"I don't owe you an answer for anything," Hamasa retorted. Coughs, sudden and raucous, burst from his mouth, his body heaving with them. When he opened his teary eyes, they no longer burned gold.

Marya dropped beside him, feet planted and legs spread, spear in front of her. She levelled it, spear tipped towards the centurions and sunlight sparkling on copper bead and iron alike.

"You ain't getting those cuffs on my friend again. Try it and find out what happens," she warned, black eyes as bright as fire.

"Cuffs? Oh no. We gave you the chance to come with us," Gaius said.

He swung down from his horse, and with casual and obvious practiced ease, spun and flourished his sword as he sauntered towards them. He slowly lifted the gladius, the blade worn and well-used, the tip sharp and pointing towards them at the end of his extended arm.

"The King doesn't give second chances. He wants you dead, Kana'iro the Red. We'd hate to disappoint our King again. Not when he has an Empire to topple," he said with the carefree smile.

Marya inhaled sharply, a sound of horror scratching its way out of her throat. Hamasa's stomach dropped, the one card he might've been able to play gone. No bargaining, and no way to run unless he expended too much magic. Just thinking about using enough to carry him and Marya away made his knees knock.

How big a price would he pay for what he'd done already? His lips pulled back far enough that the slightly too sharp incisors were bared, and the world burned in shades of red, orange, and yellow. To the side, Flavius pulled free the bolt in his shoulder. The same moment it clattered to the ground, blood splattering over cobbles, Hamasa got to his feet and set his hand on Marya's arm. His index finger traced words over her shivering skin.

"Message received," he whispered. If it had worked with dogs...

Hamasa took a deep breath, nostrils flaring as Gaius neared and Flavius tied off his shoulder. The words on Marya's arm flickered red. It tore out of him from deeper than his belly, torn out of the very roots and origins of him. A roar that shook the cobbles under their feet, that rattled the glass windows in their panes, that stopped Gaius in his tracks, that had Flavius' hand slipping on cloth. Eyes dilated in that all too human fear at the sound of *predator* gazed from three different, ashen faces.

"*Go! Run!*" he roared, blood and stomach acid burning his throat. He gagged, curling forward, but the words had gotten out.

Trained as they were to be accustomed to a dragon, a direct command was too much. The horses screamed their blood-curdling way, reared and stomped, eyes rolling. The silver and the brown horses raced out of sight, manes and tails cracking through the air like whips. The dappled grey reared and screamed, but Flavius' white-knuckled grip on its reins kept it in place, riding its bucking and rearing like a ship on storm-tossed waves.

Hamasa pressed down on Marya's arm and his palm slipped away. The runes sunk into her skin, where every hair was standing straight up from his roar, and disappeared. Her whole body vibrated with the same tension as the caught crossbow bolt.

"Now, Marya," he wheezed. He wiped at his lips with his wrist before she could see the blood filling his mouth.

Marya stared at him, pupils dilated and face ashen. Then, she blinked. Her mouth pressed into a thin line. And she nodded. She lunged towards Gaius, moving as fast as a dragon. Her spear flashed in the air, and Gaius barely managed to knock it aside.

Hamasa threw himself to the side, running towards the horse that still tugged and twisted under Flavius' control. Seeing Hamasa, Flavius cursed and jumped from the horse, raising the crossbow. His wound in the opposite shoulder bled sluggishly, red dripped down the cuirass to stain the ground. Hamasa dropped to the ground the moment after the trigger was squeezed, then rolled to the side as the bolt struck cobblestone. He scrambled to his feet and flung himself forward again. Flavius swung and Hamasa ducked, hair ruffling in the breeze that followed the crossbow over his head.

With a grunt, Hamasa tackled Flavius around the middle, driving his shoulder into bronze armor. Unlike the last time, Flavius kept standing and there was a crack. Stars bloomed in Hamasa's vision as he fell like a stone to the ground.

"You can't surprise me the same away twice," Flavius said. Calmly, so calm and cool.

Hamasa's brain was agony, shrieking in pain that streaked hot ice down the back of his neck. Feeling it more than hearing it, Hamasa rolled over the cobbles, bits of rocks flying past his cheeks as the crossbow cracked stone. He got his hands under him, pushed up, only for the world to tip and spin and that agony to shriek. Vomit and blood splattered, and he hacked and wheezed. Something glittered in front of his eyes. A crossbow bolt was aimed at him, at his aching, ringing head.

Fear seized every muscle.

It was over so fast.

The crossbow shook. The bolt left the bow. It struck the cobbles and more bits of rock sprayed his face. Above him, Flavius' eyes widened and, slowly, looked down to the side, hand rising. Touching the bloody spear point that had erupted from above his collarbone like a flower. Hamasa scrambled back on his hands and feet, eyes wide and shaking, hot tears streaming down and drying on his horrified face. Flavius shouted wordlessly, grabbing the spear point, only to drop it with a hiss as both his wounds pulled.

Hamasa stared past him, mouth gaping. Marya stood down the street, her chest heaving and arm still extended from the throw. Their eyes met, both terrified, desperate, and he glanced past her.

"Marya!" he shouted, holding up a hand.

It was only thanks to the speed spell that she was able to evade being stabbed through the back, through the heart. The gladius sliced through skin and muscle, and Marya stumbled back, her hand wrapping automatically around the gushing wound. Gaius snarled, none of his charm or false cheer on his face. The gladius flashed and chopped through the air, and Marya darted and dodged as blood ran down her arm.

Hamasa quickly turned back to Flavius, eyes darting to where he'd dropped the crossbow. The centurion was already reaching for it with the less wounded arm, ignoring the pain with a grimace that twisted his once beautiful features into something grotesque. His flaxen hair was damp and sticking to his skin, lines etching deep into his skin around his mouth and eyes, his nostrils white as he bull-huffed. Hamasa's leg moved without thought; pain spread over the top of his foot and the crossbow sailed far out of reach before Flavius could grab it.

"Damn you, Kana'iro," Flavius seethed, reaching for the gladius he too wore.

Hamasa pulled back his leg, gritted his teeth, and kicked with all his strength with a shout. His bare heel crunched cartilage, and the centurion jerked back, clutching at his face with one hand. Hamasa crawled to his knees, curled his hand into a fist, and when Flavius' hand fell, punched, throwing all his weight behind it. Flavius dropped first, Hamasa tumbling half on top of him, his hand still clenched in a fist.

Mind sloppy and dizzy and pounding, he looked up and saw Marya on her feet. She was wobbling, her arm bleeding heavily, and one side of her face bruised purple and puffy, but she was standing. With one more look at the unconscious and bloody-nosed, black-eyed centurion, Hamasa forced himself to his feet. He heaved, hand to his mouth, and breathed in deep. Faltering and slow, he ran towards them. Gaius' head jerked up and his suntanned face paled.

"Flavius. How did you—"

"He's not dead, but he will be if you don't get him help *now*," Hamasa rasped. He looked towards Marya, who grinned weakly back at him, slumping against a building.

Gaius glanced past him, but his gaze snapped back. "Flavius knew the risks. For the King."

"He isn't a king!" Hamasa retorted fiercely.

"He will be!"

The gladius flashed, and Hamasa blinked rapidly to clear the sunspots, and suddenly Gaius was on him. Hamasa jumped back, his brain sloshed, and the ache became a sharp, piercing stab. He reeled back, falling to the ground with a grunt, and Gaius' sword thrust through the air over his head. Gaius corrected swiftly, chopping down, but Hamasa was dragged back, choking slightly at the tight neckline, and Marya huffed behind him.

"You won't win this. I'm clearly your superior in every way," Gaius hissed between gritted teeth. "You're delaying the inevitable."

"Talk, talk, *talk*," Marya drawled, though the effect was almost lost by how shaky her voice was. "You're worse than my donkey."

Hamasa kicked at Gaius' knees. Gaius merely swept Hamasa's

legs away and kicked him in the stomach. Hamasa cried out, curling into a little ball, arms over his head. With a annoyed *tch*, Gaius cut at Marya. Marya dodged out of the way, eyes wide and following the blade as it arced, but Hamasa peeked past his elbow and watched Gaius' arm. With a burst of speed that Valerius would be proud of, Hamasa leapt up and wrapped both his skinny, useless, human arms around Gaius' thicker, wider arm. Gaius raised a fist, but Marya had darted in. Her large hand lifted from her wound and caught his fist with a grunt.

Hamasa, head woozy and strength gone, stared at the expanse of bare skin, the gladius still in Gaius' hand. He felt and saw the muscles flex, the wrist twist, and knew his own weight would be nothing to this warrior. Snarling, Hamasa used the only weapon he had left: he *bit*.

Gaius yelled, flinching and trying to yank his arm away. Marya bared her teeth, growled past her curled lip, and slammed her shoulder on her wounded side against Gaius' chest. She screamed, as much in fury as in pain, as the centurion gasped. Her feet slid over the ground, then planted, her hand twisted in the front of his shirt. Hamasa fell and rolled away and Marya heaved. Gaius flipped over her head and, with a bitten off gasp, slammed to the ground on his back. He coughed, turned to his side with a groan. Marya ran over and kicked his sword. It skittered over the ground, then clattered against the base of a building somewhere.

Gaius pushed himself up on to his hands, grimacing. His head raised and he found Hamasa sprawled in front of him.

"This isn't over, Kana'iro. As long as the King and the Merciless—"

Marya dropped on him, elbow first, right in the middle of the back. He grunted, his forehead smacked stone, and his body went lax. Hurriedly, Marya turned him over and held her hand over his lips. Her eyes fluttered closed as she sighed in relief.

"Alive?" Hamasa croaked.

"Yeah. What about...?" She swallowed and looked over to where Hamasa had left Flavius behind.

"I... I don't know," Hamasa admitted softly. "He was when I left him there."

Marya swallowed again, lips trembling, teeth chattering, until she clenched her jaw. She stomped over to Flavius, leaned over him, and Hamasa glanced away. His stomach heaved, but he forced himself to his feet. An object caught his eye and he huffed an incredulous laugh.

His sandal.

"He's alive!" Marya called out as Hamasa limped his way over to his lost footwear. "Ay, I don't think taking my spear out is a good idea," she added shakily.

"I wouldn't, no," Hamasa agreed. He slipped his foot into the sandal and turned to see Marya searching for something with one hand. Hissing through his teeth, he made his way to her. "I can stop the bleeding and not much more," he said as he knelt besides her.

"Huh?" Marya gasped, wheeling around. "Oh. Yeah. Probably should do something about that." Hamasa smiled weakly at her, and set his finger on her arm. "Wait, wait, not more magic. They had bandages, right? That horse is just over there. We'll wrap up the human way."

"Are you sure? You might become weak very quickly, and you need stitches," Hamasa protested.

Marya grinned and rubbed her nose. "Nah, I'll make it 'til we get outta this damn city or find Wally." Her grin fell. "I'm so sorry about... I didn't think Pali would... I'm sorry, Asa."

Hamasa wrenched bandages from Flavius' pouch. The centurion had never gotten to tie up his own wound, but Hamasa remembered seeing him with the white cloths in his hand. Jaw tense, Hamasa began to wrap her arm.

"Marya, if I couldn't forgive you for letting something like that slip, when they would've found me eventually anyway, then you might as well just leave me here for the Merciless." He waited for her eyes to rise, to meet his, and he smiled at her. "I'm going to do this friend thing right."

Marya sniffed hard, and smiled back. "Doing good so far. And I got something that might help our other friend." She held up her fist. From it dangled two things; a centaur's braid with copper bead and a pink token hanging on a leather string. "Time to find your rock."

36

THEY BANDAGED each other the best they could. Hamasa was much better at magical healing than this. The mess made it hard to see just how bad some of the wounds were. But terrible patching up done, they stole yet another horse. The dappled grey resisted a bit, but it might've been the smell of them more than anything else. They plodded down the road, both of them grimacing with every jostle. They barely made it to the main avenue when the sound of a horse's thundering gait met their ears. They froze, staring ahead in terror, only for the familiar sight of Nerva's buckskin hide and black mane to come barrelling around the next bend. Nerva and Valerius astride her, his face intense and grim.

"Valerius!" they exclaimed at the same time. Relief and hope bloomed in Hamasa's chest, an exhausted smile curving across his lips.

"Where did you—*What happened*?" he demanded, shock and horror spreading over his face.

"The centurions," Hamasa said, his chest suddenly expanding on a breath he didn't realize he hadn't taken.

"The centurions? Where are they?"

"Back thatta way," Marya sighed, thumbing over her shoulder.

"We need to stop and bandage her up probably. And I need something to eat. A lot of something to eat," Hamasa said, even though his stomach rebelled at the idea.

"What?"

"I have this," Marya said, holding up the token. Valerius' eyes widened again. "It's time for the spell, but he already used up some magic."

"I think I have a concussion, too," he muttered.

Valerius' jaw ticked. Gently, he took the reins from Marya's hands, and, clicking his tongue to his teeth, let Nerva set a steady, slow pace towards the bridge and the Falls.

***

They sat below the cypresses swaying in the mist of the Falls that roared through the too-still autumn afternoon. It was beautiful, tranquil despite the thundering Falls, the world a blaze of gold and red and a few hidden gems of green among the branches, and Hamasa barely saw it. There, in the rippling glassy water that lapped at the sandy riverbank, they had washed up as best as they could. Now, Marya sat patiently through Valerius carefully bandaging her, wan and pale after the knight's crude, if effective, stitching. Hamasa gnawed without appetite on a stick of dried goat meat, the last of what he needed to choke down for energy. He was already washed up and had changed into clean clothes, though it had been a wrench to admit saving his poncho would be impossible. He almost missed Marya and Valerius finishing up and making their way towards him. The second Marya got within earshot, she began,

"We get this spell done fast. It's been maybe an hour since Arash led 'im off. We can find the rock and go help him before sunset," Marya said eagerly.

Hamasa got to his feet, swallowed painfully, and turned. "No, we won't."

Marya stared, mouth falling slack. Valerius scowled.

"You can't change your mind. This is the only choice."

"I'm changing my mind because this is the only choice," Hamasa interrupted. "If we go after my emblem, Arash will die."

"What are you saying, Asa?" Marya whispered.

The undigested food in his belly writhed, his knees knocked, and his voice shook, but he lifted his chin and licked his lips.

"We're going after Arash now. We know the direction they flew, and I can feel Arash if I try. I don't need a true spell for that, just concentration," Hamasa said, fists tightening at his side. "Just like he could find me. We're... we've known each other our whole lives."

"That's a death wish," Valerius exclaimed. He stepped forward and grabbed Hamasa's shoulder. "You couldn't face him with your emblem. You can't go after him now without it."

Hamasa closed his eyes, inhaled deeply, and let it go on a sigh.

"My emblem is too far away. No matter what Arash tried, he couldn't sense it, which means it's probably on the other side of the mountains. The Serra Falls pass has been impassable since they collapsed it after the Merciless destroyed Sangsierpe," Hamasa said slowly, clearly.

"We'd have to climb the mountains to the other side, and then climb back," Marya realized, eyes widening. Hamasa nodded at her.

"It's why Arash and I decided to come here before using me as a focus for the spell. It'll take days, at least, to get through. And that's if we can beat winter. Then, it could be more than a week. Arash doesn't have that kind of time right now." Hamasa choked, but he forced out, "This is what a Shield is meant for, right?"

Valerius spun on his heel, stalked a few steps away, and

stared out at the natural golden beauty around them. It was hard to believe it was still morning, it felt like eons since Hamasa had watched Arash drop from the sky. Blinding. Brilliant. And dead, if they didn't go back now.

"The Merciless is thousands of years old. Their power is indescribable. Arash isn't even four hundreds years old and he's not as fast as I am," Hamasa said, lips trembling and voice quavering. He met Marya's terrified eyes. "I can't do it again. I can't leave him behind, not to die for me. What kind of person would that make me?" His eyes turned to Valerius, traced the rigid lines of his shoulders, down to where his fists shook at his sides. "What kind of Shield?"

One long, horrible minute longer, Valerius said nothing. Stood silently, his back a wall clad in metal for the first time since the first time they met him. Then, he turned. His black eyes were fathomless, his Lance's expressionless mask in place.

"What is your new plan, Hamasa?" Valerius asked.

Swallowing, Hamasa nodded.

"Marya, you have something that can help," Hamasa said first. Marya started, gaze snapping to his.

"What? You mean...?"

"No, not the token. The Salvatropas gave you a boon. Remember?"

"Oh, yes!" Marya dug in her pocket. Both braid and token were pulled free.

"All right. You head out first, use the boon and find Sitlal, or the first Salvatropas you can find. Do you remember the way Arash flew?"

"Of course, to the southwest. But I should come with you!" she protested.

Hamasa smiled; she could barely stay upright, she was paler than he'd ever seen her, the dark hue of her skin a sickly grey, and her eyes deep pits in her face with darker smudges under them. The bruise had discolored her entire cheek and it had puffed so badly she could only squint. Her arm hung uselessly at her side and her spear might still be in that centurion's shoulder.

"Marya, you're too injured. Go and follow after us as fast as you can. If you need to, follow the token to find me," Hamasa said, smiling ruefully. Marya gulped and nodded.

"And I, my lord?"

"I'm sorry," Hamasa whispered, wringing his fingers as he turned to Valerius. "I need you to... I need you to come with me. I'm sorry." His chin dropped, eyes closing, shame and loathing clawing their awful talons deeper. "I can't do it alone."

A hand, wearing a metal gauntlet, set heavily on his shoulder.

"It would be my greatest honor, Hamasa."

He choked, laughed a weak, damp laugh, and gasped when an arm flung around him. The smelltaste of medicine and blood and wool, the brush of curls over his nape and ear.

"I'll bring them to you. Just hold on, you and that icy lizard," Marya vowed fervently.

"I have faith," Hamasa whispered, peeking up to smile crookedly at the knight and farm-girl.

Plan set, they hurried to their horses and mounted. Marya swung up first. She wrapped the token around her neck and tucked it out of sight, and then lifted the braid. She scowled briefly with narrowed eyes.

"Sitlal, I need you, please, Sitlal, help me," Marya finally begged.

She blinked as it began to glow. A shimmering dark blue, the same deep blue of the Réo Largo, burst from the copper bead. It lifted off Marya's hand, hovering in front of her eyes, and rocketed away. Heading west.

"Sovereign's luck! Don't die!" She whooped and tapped her

horse's side. She and her horse thundered out of view. Distantly, they heard the clatter of hooves over the bridge, and then she was gone.

"Hamasa."

He startled and spun. Valerius stood at Nerva's side, reins wrapped around a fist, and his other hand held out.

"More riding," Valerius said quietly.

Hamasa huffed, mouth twitching. Squaring his shoulders, Hamasa stepped up and... hesitated. He licked his lips and bit his bottom lip before slowly raising his eyes. Past the trees, the Serra Falls still roared. The iridescent rainbows still flickered in the mist. And even farther, higher, the Manos Sagradas reached towards each other. Hands protectively cupping the enduring and unfeeling beauty of Vallepidras and the Serra Falls. He closed his eyes and reached out, stretching as far as he could, for the other half of him.

There was nothing. Only that emptiness inside of him that had ripped open a little wider.

His hand grasped Valerius', the metal reassuringly solid rather than foreboding. Hefting him up, Valerius set him in the saddle and swung up after him, as easily and neatly as he did without the layers of steel.

"We'll come back for it, Hamasa."

"Yeah," Hamasa muttered.

And their own journey began. Southwest. In the wake of shadow and ice.

***

Vallepidras was devastatingly easy to ride out of. The Lances had already gone, the bloodied and torn up field they'd fought on outside the city was the last vestige of them. Instead of following the Great Road, Valerius guided Nerva into the forest. Through the trees, Hamasa had seen the crowds and lines of people trekking north, perhaps even saw a flash of blue of a Lance's banner. Then, they were too far from the Road to see it or its travellers. They rode on for hours, trying their best not to exhaust Nerva, but never quite stopping. The sun rose overhead and beat down as hot as summer until at last they found the wake of the dragons. Entire swatches of forests destroyed. Frost dripping from shorn branches or crunching under Nerva's hooves. Massive trees centuries old toppled to the ground, smoking and hissing, the rancid smell of something not quite burning, not quite rotting rising all around them. Hamasa's fingers dug into the leather of the saddle between his thighs and he closed his eyes. And like below the Falls, he reached. It wasn't the same, it was harder, because it wasn't a missing part of himself out there.

But Arash was his friend. His sibling. His family. Arash could always find Hamasa.

Baring his teeth and hissing in annoyance, Hamasa flung his awareness farther and further. Reaching out for the hand that always reached back. *I'm coming. We're coming.*

White. Shining and alive and bright white light. Hamasa gasped.

"He's ahead. Keep going, head more west. He must've been trying to stay away from Riyushu," Hamasa breathed, elated.

Valerius nodded and did as Hamasa directed. They would catch up. And Arash was still alive, still flying, maybe they could — The ridiculous burgeoning of hope died a swift death before it could be fully formed. The enraged and triumphant roar of a monster that had caught scent of its quarry at last rattled the trees around them. He hung on as Nerva reared up, neighing wildly, backing away from the predator's cry.

With a lowly muttered curse, Valerius held Nerva in place.

He lifted the canvas-wrapped trident, his scowl as fierce as ever, and yanked the canvas off. The prongs glinted in the noon bright rays of the sun filtering through the trees. And then it came. The shadow, immense and overwhelming, a dragon of the grandest kind. If they weren't so terrifying, Hamasa would've been awestruck by their majesty. Valerius cursed again and Nerva shuffled side to side while backing up.

But where's Arash?

A streak of white darted through the sky. Hamasa let out a cry as the familiar and beautiful and so small body slammed into the Merciless' side. Ice crackled and popped in the air, falling like hail as green slime hissed and spit against Arash's ice breath and dazzling white hide. Both their teeth and claws glinted like swords, tearing through scales and the softer vulnerable flesh beneath. Arash definitely looked worse, bloodied, as he snarled and frosted the very air around him. Wings snapped open wide and snow flurried around him just in time to catch the worst of the green, frothing liquid the Merciless spat from their maw. It sizzled and burned, dripping like rain to the ground, and made it past the flurries to splatter over shining white scales. Arash's scream had bile rising in Hamasa's throat.

"Stop it, *stop it*!" Hamasa shouted, almost falling off the horse as he leaned forward.

"They're too far to hear you," Valerius said, gently holding him in place. When Hamasa looked back, Valerius was pale and frowning. His hand tightened around the trident's staff. "We can't let him fight alone."

"We need to hurry," Hamasa agreed. Valerius spurred Nerva, who fought back before plunging forward with a desperate whinny.

The Merciless lived up to their name. One powerful ebony wing spread wide, knocking Arash away. As Arash reeled back, an enormous claw swiped with breathtaking speed. Blood splattered over the trees from the slash across his breastplate, almost the base of his long throat. Shock fell over them, the sound of Nerva's hoof beats matching Hamasa's heart beats. Arash's wings stilled, his flurries whisked away in the sunlight, and the Merciless' long black tail, spikes gleaming at the tip, whip-cracked through the air and hit exactly where they'd clawed. Arash plummeted to the dirt without a sound leaving his throat. Steam from his cold body in the warm autumn air rose around him, frost flowering over the grass and dirt, crawling up the trees, unchecked and uncontrolled. Nerva skidded to a stop, and Hamasa saw ice filming Arash's jaws and eyes.

"Arash!" Hamasa shouted.

Without waiting for Valerius, he jumped down and ran. The sheer cold slammed into him like a wall, tears freezing on his lashes and cheeks. He would've pushed through, forced the innate warmth of his frail human body to fight Arash's encroaching end, but the sky blackened over him.

Like a mouse under the eyes of a cat, he froze, arms over his face to block the chill radiating from the dragon in front of him. And another dragon, *the* dragon, landed behind him.

"*I hope this one doesn't die, so he may fight me again one day,*" rumbled the deep, nonchalantly brutal voice. "*Not like you, the spineless mouse that got away.*"

37

Hamasa whimpered, knees turning to water, staring into the trees and unable to move. The rumbling hiss of that voice, in a language written into his bones, a language of comfort and home, was a slap in the face. A nightmare that stank of blood and poison. His skin bubbled and a scream echoed through the air, ringing, ringing, *ringing* as his heart ripped open.

It's not real. It's not now, Hamasa thought. In vain. It would take just one opened maw, one roar, for it all to come back. All that pain and fear and helplessness.

"It's not often my friend compliments anyone or anything. Your champion was indeed a creature to be reckoned with," said another, much more human, voice.

The unexpected remark in strangely clipped Mekshan managed to break through Hamasa's spiraling mental state. He spun on his heel, hands slowly curling into fists at his sides and body shivering violently. A cloak as black as the dragon's hide slithered over scales to fall around the man that stood there. Sun-bleached ashy brown hair hair fell in waves around a thin face with a long, blade-thin nose and high cheeks. A slow, faux-kind smile stretched over his mouth. The sight of it, the pretense and condescension of it, made Hamasa want to hiss. But he only trembled, lip rising to bare his teeth.

"So I'm at last able to meet you officially. The mouse," the man greeted.

"Not my champion," Hamasa muttered.

One sardonic brow rose. "Hm? What was that?"

"He's... Arash is not my champion. He's my friend, my family. And you might've killed him!" Hamasa exclaimed. His eyes finally found the Merciless and ignored the nameless human. The Merciless' head tilted and their vivid green eyes met Hamasa's. Their frilled head-crest made them look even more massive, their head on its own bigger than Hamasa's entire diminutive human body. Inky black talons scratched at the dirt restlessly. "How could you do this again? How could you want another one of us to die?"

"He fought well. If he's strong enough, he'll live," the Merciless replied indifferently. Whatever respect he had for Arash did not include sympathy.

"Is that how you felt when you killed my father? When the Scarlet Dread died, did it mean nothing to you?" Hamasa demanded through gritted teeth.

The Merciless rose up, wings shifting restlessly over their back, long spike-ended tail swiping across the dirt. At their full height, standing on their back legs, they towered over the trees. On their thick, black hide there were nicks and scores left behind, ice still crusting along the deepest cuts. None of them fatal. Only a few trickling starkly crimson blood.

"I seek only strength. Your sire was weak and died. That is all."

"You're a monster," he said, eyes on the ground and jaw clenched.

"Says a coward," the Merciless said without so much as a cringe.

"We're not here for passing banter. Either you come with us to Harenae, useless as you are, or you die now," the cloaked human man said, voice pleasant and drawling, mouth smiling kindly.

THE COWARD'S EMBLEM

"The King prefers not to waste powerful tools, so you might still live."

"I'll never go to Harenae," Hamasa forced out past numb lips.

"The only bit of courage you have, I suppose. What a waste," the man said on a bored sigh. There was a glint and the man's hand flicked. Hamasa tensed, ready to jump.

There was a loud clang. Metal on metal. Hamasa jerked back, staring at the trident in front of him and the dagger sunk deep in the dirt at his feet.

"Who are you?" the Harenese man demanded.

"Another champion," Valerius answered shortly.

"Ah, yes. A Lance of the Realm, so that report was true. How disappointing for you that the one you swear to is nothing more than this," the man said, a smug smirk on his face when he looked to Hamasa.

"*He has good eyes. Like the White,*" the Merciless said, indifference replaced with growing, eager excitement. They dropped to all four once more and the ground rumbled under everyone's feet.

"I know you want a fair fight, Merciless, but even with his nice eyes, that Lance is merely a man. He'll be dead in seconds," the man said with a bored eye-roll.

"*You always underestimate true fighting spirit, Mureno,*" the Merciless replied dismissively. The man, Mureno, grimaced and shrugged.

"Stop playing with your food and get it over with," he said sharply. The Merciless rolled an impressively bright green eye towards Mureno, who scoffed and raised his hands. "Fine, fine. Take however much time you need."

"Are you... are you a *Chosen*?" Hamasa blurted in bewilderment and, with something like offense or horror, shoved the disgusting idea away. How could they speak that way? How could they so clearly despise each other? They both ignored Hamasa's outburst.

"Hmph." The Merciless turned to Hamasa and Valerius. *"Prepare yourself."*

"No, don't!" Hamasa shouted, horrified.

"This is why I'm here, my lord," Valerius said softly. He hefted his trident to point it at the man and dragon both.

Fighting fear itself.

Hamasa gripped the tunic over his chest.

A shadow moved and Valerius raised his trident. Obsidian talons sparked against the steel with an ear-splitting screech. Before Valerius had completely recovered, the Merciless' head darted forward, green-tinged saliva dripping down their jaw. Hamasa grabbed the back of Valerius' obi and jerked them back. They stood together, staring up at the dark height of the Merciless. A void growing, spreading, in the midst of the forest. And Valerius had only his steel armor and trident to fend off a dragon's blows and acid that could sear through dragon scale to flesh. Hamasa's finger flew over Valerius' back, fiery lines flickering over steel under his ruby-red fingertip.

"My lord, what can you do?" Valerius asked, eyes calculating.

"I can make things hot and fast?" Hamasa said uncertainly. He pressed the back of his free hand to his mouth to force down a stronger urge to vomit. His moving hand didn't falter.

"Hn. Force the Merciless to expose any weak spots, then retreat," Valerius ordered.

"I can do my best."

"I know you can."

Valerius and Hamasa exchanged a loaded look; Hamasa pale and shaking, Valerius resolute and stern. A whistle cut through the air. Hamasa's clawed hand batted aside the first dagger; the second struck him in the shoulder. He gasped, eyes widening, and Valerius turned with shocked eyes. The Merciless' jaws opened wide and green sprayed over them like rain. Just as flames leapt around Valerius' body, and Hamasa's hand fell from his back. It sizzled and hissed against the flames that enveloped Valerius. Acid burned to vapor that stung the eyes and throat and withered the grasses around Hamasa where he lay.

"I'm fine, go on," he muttered, rolling to his side and grimacing through the feeling of the blade shifting inside him, grinding against the edge of his collarbone where it met his shoulder.

Valerius' mouth tightened, eyes glinting like onyx in the fire surrounding him. Then, the ground shook and the Merciless' tail swung through the air, cracking like a whip. The knight ran forward, closer to the Beast and away from the wide arc of the tail. Hamasa stayed low, air rustling his hair, and rolled away, pulling the dagger free with a short scream as he searched desperately for the human. Fire licked at the wound, knitting it with candle-weak flame.

He didn't need to search. Purple streaks of magic raced over the ground, wrapped around his ankles, yanked him off his feet to drag him, clawing at the dirt, his wound half-healed. The attack ended as abruptly as it had started, leaving Hamasa winded and baffled. Then, a low purple glow enveloped him before withered grass burst from the ground and wrapped around him. Transforming into a net that held him fast. Mureno loomed over Hamasa with grasses knotted between his fingers and glowing the same deep, twilight-bruised purple. He set a foot on Hamasa's chest, pressing down all his weight as he leaned closer. Hamasa's ribcage creaked and his lungs flattened, unable to fill as he wheezed under Mureno's foot.

"I know what it's doing to you, little mouse," Mureno all but purred. A blade appeared in his hand. "You should let me kill you now, rather than whittle your life away."

The very tip of the blade lifted his chin, traced the line of his throat and paused where his pulse beat too swiftly. Hamasa flinched, eyes squeezing shut, heat rippling over his skin.

"They'll all kneel in the end. Long live the Sovereign."

It sparked in his belly first. The magicked ropes smoldered. The tip of the dagger burned cherry red, steel softening to putty. Mureno made a sound, arm jerking back, and Hamasa's throat burned. It roared out his mouth, charred his lips, and the weight on him gone with a terrified human shout. Hamasa rose, ashen bits of rope falling to the ground, and the spout of flame followed the dark shape scrambling back. The fire choked and sputtered away, and Hamasa twisted around to spit and cough, blood sprinkling his torn lips. He wiped at his mouth, trying not to swallow, trying not to breathe, as the inside of his throat and mouth seared. Slowly, he got to his feet, wobbling, vision flickering from red and orange to blurry human hues.

"So you'll die, Kana'iro the Red, like your sire, writhing in pain," Mureno said icily. Two daggers, one from each hand, streaked towards Hamasa.

The wound inside him tore, and Hamasa darted forward. Protected by a shimmering wave of heat so intense the daggers cracked against it and fell uselessly to the ground as though it were solid. Hamasa planted his feet in the dirt, crouching low in front of Mureno, whose arms had risen with the daggers in his hands forgotten as he cried out at the sheer heat still pouring from Hamasa's body. He jabbed twice, right then left, picturing Valerius' up-raised palms. Mureno grunted and gasped and stumbled a few steps back at the solid impact of each punch to his chest.

The heat snapped, shimmer gone, and Hamasa punched with all his weight behind it. Mureno's hand barely managed to knock it aside, and Hamasa's eyes widened in surprise. In the other hand, the dagger rose and slashed towards Hamasa's face. Dodging back so fast, the dagger's edge a hair's breadth from his nose, Hamasa lost balance with his arms pinwheeling wildly.

From that moment, Hamasa could only dodge. Backing up, ducking, twisting, almost dancing to escape each slash and thrust of the daggers. Mureno all but tread on Hamasa's toes, the daggers gaining speed until they sang through the air. Hamasa licked his lips, searching desperately for an opening… and dropped. Mureno stared where Hamasa had just been standing, a second too slow to see Hamasa braced on his hands. He kicked *hard* at Mureno's knees, wordlessly shouting from his ruined throat.

This time, it worked. Mureno fell to a knee with a shout. Snarling, lips pulled back and teeth bared, Hamasa swung his leg across Mureno's face with all his puny human strength. Mureno's head jerked to the side and he slumped to the ground with a muffled groan. Hamasa scrambled closer, raised a fist, and, with narrowed eyes, punched just where Valerius had struck those men at the temple. All tension left in Mureno's body went slack.

Hamasa struggled to his feet and chanced one more look at Arash, licking the air. It was slightly warmer, but more obviously, thankfully, the ice was retreating from Arash's face and mouth. Hamasa wobbled in place and turned back to his nightmare and his knight, immediately stumbling from shock and a bout of dizziness at once.

The fire armor that Hamasa had managed to make was barely a thin sheen of sparks and flickers around Valerius' body. Sweat poured down Valerius' sickeningly wan face, patches of his clothes and skin burned away, hair falling from its tie. Most of his right vambrace had melted, a shiny red welt covering his entire forearm. The Merciless swiped at him, roaring in frustration when Valerius dodged with a nimble roll that looked almost catlike for a man his size and thrust under the Merciless' jaw. The dragon barely dodged, tail swinging around to force Valerius to retreat hastily. Just under one bright eye, the dragon bled profusely from a deep three-pronged scratch. Valerius hacked a cough, body rocking with it, and Hamasa realized the very air was green.

Hamasa swallowed down the nausea and ran. The Merciless pulled back their head, maw opening, and Hamasa darted in. His heated fist, the air around his knuckles glossy, slammed into the hollow under the pitch-black jaw. The Merciless reeled back and Hamasa fell to the ground, heat gone again, stomach heaving with bile.

Valerius suddenly stood over him, thrusting his trident forward. Hamasa spat and hacked hoarsely, and watched the trident screech over scales, leaving behind three faint cuts in the slightly softer scales under the foreleg. Then, the tail whipped down and they both leapt in opposite directions as arm-length spikes gouged the dirt. The Beast shook their head and shuffled back, wings kicking up debris and dust. They backed away, farther from one another, with arms up to block the worst.

Across the distance, Valerius and Hamasa's eyes met, squinting through the churning dust. Claws struck down, breaking their gaze, and Valerius' trident met them. His jaw tensed, arms shaking, spine unbending. Hamasa clenched his fists and, head splitting, ears ringing, jabbed one fist forward. A ball of fire flung from his knuckles, smacking the Merciless' jaw so hard it shook the dragon's entire head. They turned, green eyes pinning Hamasa in place. The trident struck, aiming for the hinge of their jaw and scraping against the thin scales before the Merciless pulled completely away. Their talons slashed at

THE COWARD'S EMBLEM

Valerius, knocking him off his feet so hard Hamasa felt the thud of his body under his feet, but the knight rolled away before he could be struck again.

Hamasa planted his feet and raised his fists. Again, he punched forward, this time twice in succession, a ball of fire leaving with each strike. The Merciless skidded over the ground, body shuddering with each blow, fire catching along the edges of their scales and smoldering. Poisonous froth dripped and slavered between silvery fangs, and Hamasa opened his hands with flames growing around his fingers.

Something small gleamed through the air. Struck one glittering emerald eye.

The scream that tore through the air had Hamasa cringing back, flames wisping into nothing. Blood and acid sprayed over the ground, ate away at the bark of trees, and the Merciless shook the dagger out of their eye with a snarl. Valerius stood with trident ready as the Merciless struck out with their razor talons.

"Valerius!" Hamasa shouted, or tried to. His voice barely whispered past his blistered lips.

The Merciless bellowed fury and pain, and the dangerously spiked tail snaked through the air. From under the cage of claws pressing down on his raised trident, Valerius' eyes widened. As if the steel were merely paper, the spikes on the Merciless' tail sliced through the chest guard Valerius wore. The tip of a spike caught Valerius' side, snagged in the metal, and flung him over the ground with a choked shout.

38

A LOW GROAN, and then a twig cracked under a boot. Hamasa whipped around to see Mureno struggle to his feet. There was a fine trickle of blood from his lip, and half his face was puffy and bruised. He fell to a knee again, staring towards the bloodied, frenzied Merciless.

Hamasa stared at his fingers digging into the dirt, body shuddering and overheating as he heard Valerius — *Emerens* — groaning in pain. Taste-scented blood mixing with his own in his mouth and the lingering bite of wintery frost against his lips.

"You keep struggling, but you'll lose in the end, Kana'iro. You'll take all your pathetic believers down with you. The poor little girl you Chose put her money on a bad gamble," Mureno panted, taunting across the clearing.

Hamasa bared his teeth. *A bad gamble. Was it* her *gamble that failed? It hadn't been a gamble! It hadn't even been* her *Choice.*

She had been just a girl with sad, blue eyes framed by black hair falling like a waterfall of silk around her tiny shoulders. There, in her eyes, he had seen every unnameable emotion that had filled him. When her tiny, soft hand had touched the smooth plate of his snout, she had smiled. *We'll do this together, Hamasa. We won't just be Shield and Sovereign. We'll be family.*

Teeth grinding, Hamasa shook all over, a quaking that began so deep inside him he hadn't been sure there had been anything left in there to quake. It rose up, hot and bright, burning through the darkest, most frightened parts of him, ripping that wound larger, a chasm inside him. *My friends' lives are not at the whim of a bad cast of the dice.*

"No." It rasped and wavered out of him. He licked his lips and looked up into that single green eye. "No. My Choice was not a gamble. My father's had not been a gamble."

Mureno frowned, but the Merciless laughed, acid dripping from their jaws and sizzling around their claws. Thick, viscous, ruby-red blood pooled on the dirt and shined on bony scales.

"*Strong words, mouse.*"

Hamasa got to his feet, eyes shining a bright gold, two tiny suns, pupils slitted like a snake's. Like a dragon's.

The Merciless, the Beast carrying the shadow of his father's death, lifted their head. The green eye gleamed poisonously and oozed blood, and the lipless mouth pulled back to bare nearly every single fang in a parody of a grin. The snakelike tongue darted in the air and that laugh came back—grating and harsh and jarring. Heat rippled from every inch of Hamasa's frail, human body. The edges of his clothing began to smolder at the heat shimmering around him once more. It washed over them all, a wave of heat that made the grass crackle and burn and the hoarfrost melt into soupy muddy puddles.

"*That's it, little Hamasa, son of Abdolla. Show me your killing rage!*"

The words boomed and shook the forest. The Merciless stood rampant and spread their wings, ignoring the blood that continued to trickle from their wounded arm and icy cuts and spilled from under their eye.

"I don't want to fight!" Hamasa shouted. Sparks flickered in his hands and the very air around him glowed, a soft flickering yellow slowly getting brighter and darker. "I don't want to die. I don't want my friends to die. I don't want to kill you, either. So just... *leave me alone!"*

Both his hands rose and opened, the flat of his hands aiming towards the Merciless, the Great Beast.

The fire roared out of him, a wave of crimson flame met by a wall of green gas. It hissed and crackled and popped, a noxious fume rising before the fire completely overwhelmed the poisonous vapor. There was a shocked and pained bellow. And a living blanket of flame covered the Merciless' immense body. Twisting and writhing, flames scattered and flung to all sides around them, burning the trees, catching on every leaf, the very dirt.

A small figure of gold and crimson darted forward.

He flew through the fire like it meant nothing, swatches of his clothes burning to ash as he yelled wordlessly. When he raised his hand, it wasn't a human's fist. Gold claws glittered, so sharp their tip was too fine to be seen by the eye. He thrust his claws forward, throwing every bit of himself right where Valerius had struck. Dragged his golden talons through the bloodiest part underneath the foreleg. The shriek that tore from the dragon's throat had Hamasa's skin prickling with bumps and his hair rising. Mureno struggled to his knees, gasping and arms wrapped tight around his bruised ribs.

The Merciless rose and fell backwards, black scales burning and front leg hanging uselessly. It buckled under their weight and the dragon thudded to the ground, hissing and wheezing as the flames ebbed. Hamasa shone bright red, eyes a brilliant gold, until he stepped back and stumbled. His arms hung in front of him, fingers black and pain so deep it was painless sizzling up his arms.

"*A Red that can be burnt,*" the Merciless croaked in amusement, fire smoldering over their body and the terrible wound pouring.

A large, dark patch spread over the ground that had Hamasa's stomach rebelling.

"A Black that can kill their own kind," Hamasa retorted harshly, panting.

The Merciless shuddered and shifted, forcing themselves to their other three legs. Hamasa stepped back, jaw clenching and eyes flashing in warning.

"I'm not done, Red."

"If you make me kill you, your Chosen will die. You will die. Just surrender!" Hamasa croaked.

"The fool has served its purpose. I wanted only to find you," the Merciless snarled. "I'll finish what I started. Death is nothing to fear."

Horror and disgust had the ground reeling under Hamasa's feet.

"Fight, mouse! Kill me now or I'll kill you!"

"No," Hamasa gasped, voice shaking.

Roaring with fury, the Merciless rose, wings stretching wide. Hamasa blinked, eyes burning but skin too hot for tears to fall, and raised golden claws and burnt black arms, flames flickering as acid bubbled in the Merciless' throat.

Impossibly, Valerius ran forward. *Emerens.* His ruined chest guard gone, his thigh and shoulder guards as bright as Grey dragon scales, his black hair a banner streaming behind him. He planted his feet and he threw. The trident flashed, bronze lightning streaking through afternoon sunlight, and pierced where Hamasa had clawed the Merciless open. It pierced deep, its prongs sunk out of sight, and the Merciless screamed. Mureno screamed with him, his hands clawing at his chest, eyes bulging. The Merciless' head lowered, acid spraying, but Valerius had already lifted the shocked Hamasa off his feet and flung them both behind a tree.

"Valerius—" Hamasa gasped, staring up at him. His torso

was soaked red, his kimono torn to shreds, but the wounds themselves weren't as deep as he'd feared.

"Finish it," Valerius muttered, wincing and holding an arm around his abdomen.

"I can't. I can't just—" They both cringed, flinging forward onto the dirt as the tree they hid behind was ripped in half by the blow of a spiked tail.

Hamasa crawled around the stump, staring at the dragon curled around their leg that was barely a leg anymore. The tail whipped again and Hamasa flung up a wall of flame. He skidded over the dirt, and the flames scattered into sparks, but the tail fell back harmlessly.

"I won't kill you! You can't make me be you!"

The Merciless roared, shaking the trees. Hideously, horribly, they tried to rise. Teeth gritting, Hamasa raised a hand and flames flickered at his fingertips.

And then, to both their shock, an arrow blazing bright yellow whizzed between them.

The arrow struck the Merciless on the shoulder at the wing joint on the mostly uninjured side. The scream of rage and pain knocked Hamasa to one knee while the Merciless spun towards the source. Only to topple once more to the ground on their bad leg.

Hamasa glanced over his shoulder, catching sight of Valerius staring at him rather than anywhere else. Through the trees, Hamasa saw them. Cabadonas, holding up their swords and spears, pointing their arrows from every kind of bow. They ululated and whooped, the cacophony of their voices echoing around the trees. Arrows glowing a myriad of colors whistled through the air like the dazzling fireflowers of old Osekai. All aiming for the Merciless' massive black body sprawled over the ground. Dozens of shining colors striking deep and dangerous into the Merciless' hide.

"We have to go!" Mureno exclaimed, running and stumbling towards his dragon.

"*We must fight*," the Merciless said. They forced themself to their three good legs, facing down the horde coming their way. Hamasa almost respected the utter audacity the Black dragon had.

"We'll lose this fight! We have to go or we'll fail the mission," Mureno argued hotly.

The Beast rumbled in displeasure. "*Your mission, human, not mine.*" They opened their mouth wide and sprayed the newest barrage of arrows with caustic yellowish green slime. A few made it past, striking their body so solidly the Merciless slid back.

"You're not going anywhere!" Hamasa gasped, stepping forward.

"You can't even lift your arms, fool," Mureno spat at him.

Hamasa hissed through his teeth, eyes flashing and fire flickering at his fingertips. A movement caught his eyes, and suddenly Mureno was yanked back. Valerius was behind Mureno, one arm around his throat, his other hand behind Mureno's head, pulling back so Mureno's chin raised, effectively pinning the man against Valerius' unyielding chest and cutting off most of his air.

"Which of you will die first?" Valerius rasped.

Hamasa gaped. A rumbling growl broke his shock and he looked back to the biggest problem. The arrows had not stopped raining down, and the Merciless' wing swiped over their head to guard the dragon. They dragged themself forward, snarling with pain and spitting frothy bubbling acid towards the cabadonas that had begun to spread out to surround them.

Hamasa panted hard and raised his burnt hands. His vision was fuzzy, all the reds and yellows dull and faded. A single shaking finger raised and the golden claw glowed red. Lines and dots traced in mid-air, flickering the same weak yellow of a candle.

"W-with fire I hold y-you," he stammered and slapped his palm over the hovering words.

The Merciless turned, wings snapping to their full span, knocking trees aside and roots pulling up from the ground. But it was too late. The words had sunk to the bloodied ground at the Merciless' feet. Flames, scarlet and gold, sprang from the embers glowing among the black scales over the Merciless' body. The flames leapt high to wrap around every limb and *yanked*. The Merciless screeched, thrashing and bleeding and burning, but pinned by the flaring scarlet flames.

A low whistling sound shredded the air. It took too long for Hamasa to realize it came from him, the rasping of his too fast, too high breaths through his burnt and battered lungs and throat. The chains of fire flickered wildly, barely reining in the Merciless' increasing struggles. Bile surged in his throat, choking him, but he held his fists tightly. His knuckles whitened where his skin wasn't charred black and his golden claws dug into his cracking, burning palms.

"Don't let go," he whispered fiercely. "Don't let go."

Cabadonas surrounded them with stamping hooves and tossing manes. Bronze chest guards, arrowheads, and swords gleamed, none of them with the bright flash of something new or ornamental, but with the dull sheen of weapons well-used and kept always at the ready. And every point aimed at the tied-down dragon. One large figure was coming straight for Hamasa. When it got closer, he could see it was actually a horse, shaggy-furred and small, and on its back: Marya. Beside her, of all things, Nerva the mare. He blinked, wondering if perhaps he had lost his mind.

Marya's hair was as wild and free as a horse's mane, curling in every direction. Someone had given her a bronze chest guard, a new spear, and boots. Her grin beamed like a beacon through the dust and ash and drifting greenish vapors.

"Asa!" she whooped, whirling her spear over her head. Hamasa's lips trembled upwards.

Goosebumps beaded the back of his legs and up his spine and arms. Every hair on his head stood at an icy chill. White caught the edge of Hamasa's eye and a gasp tore from him.

The tip of an icicle, glassy sheer and wet from heat, pointed at the pounding pulse in Mureno's throat under Valerius' elbow. At the other end was a tanned brown hand, fingernails deadly white claws.

"You'll give me... the rohh. Or you'll both die... before you can blink... *ape*," Arash seethed through fanged teeth.

"Arash!"

A small, flat, black gem appeared between Mureno's fingers. At a distance, the jagged edges and smooth, uneven surfaces made it seem a mere chunk of obsidian. But Hamasa could feel the power emanating from it even where he stood. It fell from Mureno's hand into Arash's waiting palm.

Hamasa's shoulders slumped, raised hand dropping. He was falling with no way of catching himself, his fists clenched so tight golden claws snicked bone and blood dripped down his knuckles.

"Hamasa!?"

"Catch him!"

A roar shredded the air. Wiry arms and the familiar smell of dirt and sweat lingered on his tongue. The Merciless roared again, their one eye rolling madly as they twisted and writhed, craning their long neck to snarl and snap. *At Mureno*. Ashen and pale, Mureno was only saved by Arash and Valerius' last minute reflexes pulling him away.

Acid sprayed, burnt to useless sizzles by the fiery chains Hamasa held.

"*How dare you! HOW DARE YOU, wretched filth! How dare you live and hand away my soul!*"

Arash blew over the emblem in his hand, disgust in every line of his face. The roaring ended abruptly and a frozen wind lashed through the trees. Mureno slid unconscious to the ground at Valerius' feet.

His fists opened uselessly. Gold eyes flickered to brown, then rolled to the back of Hamasa's head. A quiet exhale left him as his mind slid blissfully into nothing.

39

He was definitely sleeping on the ground. It was softer than it should be, his palms cautiously running over familiar, coarsely-soft fabric, each individual thread gliding under his sensitive skin making him shudder. He would never grow accustomed to such a thin outer membrane. A long moment of slowly surfacing awareness taught him that the silken hairs were really a large amount of wools piled high and wide, his small human body completely covered and tucked in. His tongue traced over his bottom lip, wincing at the dry cracked skin, the remnants of healing scabs and dry air. Dry and smoky air. The taste of burning applewood was heady and comforting. The warmth of several small smoldering fires around him blanketed his body as surely as the blankets. Sweat and fatigue on human skin that still smelt of well-oiled steel lingered on his tongue.

Hamasa's eyes popped open. He scrambled to throw off the heavy wool blankets while his entire body protested the too-quick movement. Hands on his shoulders also protested it.

"Calm down, we're safe," Valerius' low voice rumbled.

Hamasa jerked under his hands and twisted at the waist to look up at his impassive face. There were bandages and healing burns and bruises across his face and hands and arms, covering too much of the skin Hamasa could see. But he was moving easily, gently coaxing Hamasa to sit against a high bank of pillows. Remembering, Hamasa looked at his own arms and saw there was barely a slight discoloration of his brown skin to show where the newer burns had been. When he twisted his arms slightly, the older, pinkish scars were still there, unchanged. His fingers reached up to touch the ridges of scar tissue on his cheek. At least there wouldn't be more to mar his already small and imperfect body, he thought despondently.

"Whe—" Hamasa broke off to cough. It was more like hacking, phlegm and dry tongue choking him. Valerius pressed a small cup, made of clay and handle-less, into his hands. He gulped down the liquid eagerly, sputtering and gasping around each gulp of sweet juice. When he finished the first cup, Valerius refilled it with clear fresh water that Hamasa sipped more sedately.

"Where are we?" he croaked. "Is Arash...?"

Valerius nodded, and Hamasa quickly cut himself off with another sip. "We all lived and are safe here. You've been asleep for two days."

Hamasa stared at him, jaw dropping and fingers trembling around the cup. "The Merciless? Mureno?"

"Arash is only waiting for you to wake to send that Beast back to... where you come from, I believe. He said either you wake to help him, or he recovers enough to do it alone, whichever comes first. Mureno is on his way to receive the Sovereign's justice in Riyushu."

Hamasa nodded. "And Marya? The Salvatropas?"

Valerius smirked. "We were very fortunate. Most of the Salvatropas have been tracking the Merciless for weeks. Marya caught them an hour or so outside Vallepidras and came right after us."

"Really fortunate," Hamasa agreed, still a little raspy.

He sipped the last of his water while looking around the tent he sat in. The cloth walls were tied down so well they didn't even flap, and several small braziers filled with embers of applewood sat around the small space. It gave the whole tent a red glow and a warmth that reminded Hamasa fondly of his early life with his mother.

"Is that... is that where we are? With the Salvatropas?" he asked when his cup was empty.

Valerius held out his hand. "They're hoping to meet you."

Brown eyes darted to the callused hand waiting patiently for his. Hesitantly, Hamasa lifted his own and, flinching only once, set his hand in Valerius'. Gently and patiently, Valerius helped Hamasa stand, his free hand quickly cupping Hamasa's elbow until he could steady his wobbly legs under himself. The skin of his arms twitched and pulled, and he hissed at the rough calluses of Valerius' hand scraping over his skin.

"Thanks..."

"Don't."

Hamasa's eyes widened and he stared, *gawked*, at Valerius' frowning face.

"What? I mean, don't do what?"

"Don't say thank you." Valerius scowled darkly, looking away with a jaw so tense it looked made of stone. Hamasa waited, breathless and baffled. "What you did, how much you hurt yourself... I've never felt so furious." His dark eyes met Hamasa's widening ones. "Or so guilty."

"I don't understand..." Hamasa trailed off, frowning.

"I don't believe your death has more meaning than your life, Hamasa. I don't believe a Shield is meant only for sacrifice," Valerius said, so fervently it had Hamasa's heart drumming wildly in his throat. "I've never thought that, and what you said then..."

"I shouldn't have!" Hamasa blurted, skin overheating and

prickling uncomfortably. "It was petty and mean. I was just... I was so scared for Arash, scared of *everything*, but I shouldn't—"

"Hamasa!" The tent door flapped open and Marya rushed in. Hamasa squeaked and stepped away, flapping his hands in the air defensively. Fortunately, Marya didn't seem to notice as she bounded across the tent area to wrap both wiry arms around him. "You just swooned to the ground and then didn't wake up for *days*. Don't scare me like that, idiot!"

Marya punctuated that last demand with a full-body shake that had Hamasa stammering apologies.

"We weren't interrupting anything, were we?" said a female voice, teasing and light.

Hamasa blinked and looked over Marya's shoulder to see a cabadona holding open the flap of tent and leaning through. Her hair was the blue-black of deep twilight, shaved to a thin shadow on both sides of her head, and a dense cap of curls on top. Her skin was dark, almost ebony, muscles lean and hard. She wore only a stiff, tight, linen tunic, her arms bare except for archer's bracers made of several wrapped layers of that same stiff linen. Her lower half was dark brown and shaggy-furred, hooves black and unshod. She smirked at him, teasing and mischievous, pale amber eyes dancing from Valerius' rigid stance to Hamasa's flailing everything. Hamasa spluttered and flushed hotter. Marya yelped and finally released him, flapping her arms and blowing on them.

"I'm sorry?" he asked, voice pitching high and thin.

The cabadona only grinned wider. "I'm Huimitl. I guess I'm the leader of this gang of outlaws." She glanced towards Valerius, whose usual stoic frown had returned. "You're welcome as guests, just keep your hands to yourself. Or we'll cut them off," she said it with a pleasant smile and a dark glint in her eye. Hamasa gulped. A second later, she chuckled behind her hand.

"Though, we won't need to worry 'bout that from you, seems like."

"No, of course not," Hamasa agreed, a little bewildered.

"Well, you're awake enough. Get some clean clothes and come on out. You're just in time for dinner, sleepyhead," Huimitl said with a wink before she ducked out of sight. The tent flap swung down to leave the trio alone.

"You better clean up good," Marya suggested, clapping Hamasa's shoulder with a smirk. "You smell like ash and, well, disgusting."

"Eh?! I do?" Hamasa asked, sniffing at himself, tongue licking over his forearm. He immediately cringed. "Ugh, I do."

"Two days asleep," Valerius reminded him quietly, then ducked through the flap. Hamasa stared after him, frowning as his heart twisted strangely in his chest.

"Hamasa, hurry up. Are ya sleeping with your eyes open now?"

"Oh, right, of course. I'll be out soon."

Marya waved and snickered before leaving, too.

Hamasa hurried to find the water, tepidly warm from the enclosed air of the tent and the dozens of braziers, and scrubbed himself down quickly but efficiently. Satisfied he tasted of fresh herbal soap and nothing else, he ducked his whole head into the water to wash the matted nest of hair on his head. It was a long time before he managed to sidle out of his tent at last, dripping hair hanging over his eyes and shoulders. It had gotten a little longer in the few weeks he had been in this body and he wondered if he could tie it yet, like Valerius did. He had found and donned a pair of Marya's old, patched trousers and a well-worn but well-cared-for blue tunic. He plucked at it, face hot enough to dry any lingering dampness. It probably wasn't one of the Salvatropas', not when all the fabric he had seen so far seemed be more natural colors, nothing much dyed. And it was too fine to be Marya's.

As much as his mind skittered around it, he finally admitted to himself that it smelled overwhelmingly like Valerius. He hooked the collar over the bridge of his red nose, breathing fast and deep through his mouth, as he slunk through the shadows of the camp towards the loudest area. He got close enough for him to make out and grin widely at Marya dancing like a lunatic with several other equally wild-looking women. Then, a chill seeped over the ground and his sandalled feet. He stopped, head jerking up and tongue swiping over his lip. He automatically switched directions and headed for a tent far removed from the festivities. The grass around it was yellow and dead, and liberally covered with frost. The heavy material of the tent was crusted with beautiful icy flowers blooming almost to the top of the peaked roof. He shoved the stiff flap open, shivering slightly as his breath steamed out of his mouth in an ironic mimicry of a dragon's breath.

Arash sat cross-legged next to the entrance, arms crossed over his chest as well. One eye peeked open and a smirk curled the side of his mouth.

"Rafiik, you're alive."

"I've been alive!"

"Not for long."

Hamasa frowned and shifted awkwardly. "Not *as* long."

Arash scoffed and got to his feet, his movements heavy and slow and very unlike his usual graceful self. His injuries and holding the prisoner in place must be taking their toll. Hamasa reached out and gripped his arm before tipping forward to press their foreheads together.

"I'm so glad you're alive, Arash," Hamasa said fervently, voice vibrating with his earnestness. "Thank you for risking your life for my sake."

Arash treated him to a rare *real* smile, his blue eyes brighter and his cheeks frosting. "You did the same for me."

"*If you're going to stand there being emotional, just kill me.*"

Hamasa jumped, that instinctual fear kicking in until he fought it back.

A massive body sat tied to a pole in the middle of the tent with ice locking them in place. They looked more bestial than human, but also so far from a dragon that it was horrifying. As if they had been stripped down to something naked and vulnerable. Hamasa shuddered, shoulders high and taut, and heart thudding too fast. The Merciless' skin had a pale, greenish tinge, but teeth and nails and patches of scales larger than Hamasa's hand were all pitch black. Turning towards them, the Merciless bared silver teeth in a fierce grin with green eyes glinting through the shadows falling over their face. Their entire left arm was encased in ice, hiding the horrid mangling Hamasa and Valerius had done from sight.

"*I can taste your fear, Red. Where did those flames go?*"

"Akhris!" Arash snapped. Ice crackled and bloomed around the now chuckling, though thankfully silent, monster.

"Where's Mureno? Valerius said he was going to Riyushu, but how?" Hamasa asked haltingly. The Merciless' smile twisted into a bloodcurdling snarl.

"Some of the cabadonas are dragging him to that city and your female Chosen," Arash grimaced at the word.

"Without Valerius or me—"

"You couldn't be moved," Arash said with a shrug. "Plus, I hear you're still missing something important."

Hamasa stared down at his hands. "I couldn't leave you to die," he whispered.

Arash raised an eyebrow. "We should hurry and deal with this."

They both turned to stare at the shadowed monstrous profile.

"The Elders won't imprison them there. There's no such punishment at home," Hamasa said, biting his thumb.

"True, but they won't force me to give *this* back any time soon, either," Arash said, holding up something small and black and gleaming. Hamasa cringed away from the emblem he held so casually. He could tell by the way Arash refused to actually look at it, he wasn't as casual as he was acting. "We send them back and they'll spend the next few centuries trying to find the damn thing. I know how to hide things well."

"*Get it done with.*"

Hamasa hesitated. "You know even though they won't imprison you, they will not make your existence easier once you're sent there," he said.

"You killed dragons, and tried to kill two more who aren't even fully adult yet. You'll be lucky if they don't keep you from finding your rohh for the rest of your very long life, keeping you trapped like *this*," Arash added, emblem once more out of sight and arms crossed.

"And you... you turned on your *Chosen*. Why did you even have a Chosen?" Hamasa whispered, shuddering at the very idea.

The Merciless merely tched and spat sickly green saliva to the side. It was slower now, less potent in that body, and a few seconds more passed until it started to dissolve the frost it touched. Hamasa hadn't really expected an explanation, but it was disappointing.

"We need your name, Beast," Arash demanded with a hiss.

The body in front of them shifted, then they grunted with a negligent toss of their head. "Jaser."

Arash glanced at Hamasa, frowning in concern. "Can you... without it?" he asked quietly. "We can wait an extra few days so

I can do it alone."

"No, it isn't safe. What's a few more months?"

"It'll be several years for a transportation incantation!" Arash retorted angrily.

Hamasa smiled sadly and shrugged. "I'll outlive them all anyway. No one will be bothered but me."

"And *me*," Arash said fiercely. He turned away with a scowl, but knelt on the ground and began to write. A soft white glow emanated from the lines of runes, and Hamasa quickly mirrored him.

Red and white filled the tent as they intoned the words aloud and watched as the runes flickered and glittered beneath their fingertips. At the crest of the spell, Hamasa's eyes flashed gold and Arash's an unearthly blue. Jaser's head fell back, both relief and irritation mingling in a quiet sigh. They disappeared, sent back to the land of their birth, as the spell ebbed to an end.

When trying to stand, Hamasa wobbled dangerously. Arash's quick, icy-cold arm around his waist was the only thing keeping him on his feet.

"Let's get some food in you, idiot," Arash said fondly.

Hamasa's mouth twitched to hear Marya's word in Arash's mouth. By the time they made it outside, all the ice was completely gone, not even a puddle left behind, and Arash's body was only slightly cool to touch.

40

THE WALK TO the center of the tents wasn't too long, though perhaps it was more because there weren't too many tents. There were more pavilions; canvas draped over pillars and filled with woolen blankets and pillows larger than Hamasa's body. As they stepped past the last line of them and into the bright glare of the fire, heads swiveled in their direction. Some of the women around the fire were on two legs, though a good number of those two-leggers moved with an awkward jolting grace of a body that didn't quite fit; something Hamasa could pick out too easily. Most of them were still on four legs, hooves cutting through turf as they laughed or sang or chatted closely together.

Arash kept an arm around Hamasa's waist as they walked closer to the fire. Hamasa smiled blithely at a few of the more blatant stares in his direction. One cabadona, on all four legs, turned his way and winked. Tepin, Hamasa realized with a surprised smile. Which grew into a real grin at Marya's too-exuberant waving from where she stood with a mixed handful of two- and four-leggers. A movement caught his eye and that same cabadona from the tent was in front of them, arms crossed over her chest. Her dark face was expressionless, light brown eyes snapping in the flash of fire.

"We felt the magic. He's gone then?" Huimitl asked, glaring them down, one hoof scraping at the dirt.

"Yes. Sorry, I didn't think to warn you!" Hamasa exclaimed, suddenly horrified at his rudeness.

Huimitl's façade wholly cracked and she grinned. "I'm glad that beast is gone. Hopefully, for a good long while!"

Around the camp, hoorays and huzzahs echoed and cups clanged in toasts. Arash and Hamasa were quickly led close to the fire; bowls and spits of meat were shoved into their hands, or even straight into their mouths. At the looks of distaste on the women's faces, he had a feeling meat wasn't something often cooked at that campfire. It was... an unexpected gesture of kindness from strangers, and it had him smiling at his hands.

Unlike many Mekshan commoners, these women held no awe for dragons, but instead a measure of respect and genuine interest that most people hadn't shown for decades. For more than five hundred years, only Imperials, those who claimed the blood of Riyukezu, were ever Chosen; never common folk or those native to Mekshi (or Harenae, like Mureno had been). Dragons had always been either fearsome or awe-inspiring. Not something or someone real. Hamasa smiled at these carefree human women and dalas and cabadonas alike with their wide grins and welcoming personalities, treating him like a person, like one of them. No wonder dragons used to come to the human world in droves and wearing human disguises. They had once been so eager to share and learn from the myriad of peoples and creatures with their quicksilver lives. So easily welcomed among people like these. Too soon, Arash met Hamasa's eye. Hamasa licked his lips and raised a hand, and Arash smirked, eyes gleaming in the firelight. Then, he slipped away into the darkness.

Marya joined Hamasa soon enough, face greasy from olive and tomato juices, hands filled with thick brown bread and hard white cheese. The warmth of her, the sound of her laughter and clapping hands, was reassuring and grounding. A touchstone in this raucous party. But still... he felt his attention pulled away. Turning to see Valerius sitting quiet and contemplative and apart, eyes on the fire and hands clasped between his knees. As if sensing his gaze, his dark eyes lifted to meet Hamasa's. Across the flames and shadows and people, their glance held.

Awkwardly and with much shuffling and swaying, Huimitl knelt between Marya and Hamasa, nudging them further apart with her knobby knees and wide front end. Marya tumbled to the side with a yelp and flail of legs while Huimitl leaned in close to Hamasa. Her long ears twitched forward and her mouth dropped open slightly.

"Oh, you're warm. I mean, I knew it, but also didn't," she said, tone surprised and a little self-deprecating at the end. She looked towards the stars and pouted, finger tapping her chin. "Arash mumbled something about you needing fire, but Valerius was the one that rounded up all those braziers and the wood for you."

"Yeah, he never let 'em cool down. I dunno if he slept more'n a few minutes," Marya agreed, popping up and leaning around Huimitl.

Hamasa stared at them speechlessly.

"Your dragon friend left," she said, tilting her head to where Arash had been minutes ago.

"What!?" Marya squawked. "Where'd he—he didn't *go* go?"

"He had another job to do. He'll come back," Hamasa assured her quickly.

Marya pursed her lips and twisted her mouth to the side. "Damn, really? I thought we were done with him at last."

"Marya," Hamasa groaned.

"I know, play nice," she said, grinning.

"So, you're a dragon, with a dragon friend, which is new

according to Sitlal," Huimitl began slowly, leadingly, "a farm girl, and a Lance. And you got tangled up in business with the Merciless of all creatures. If I was judging from the Lance part of your company, I'd say you're the missing Shield of the Sovereign. But everyone knows he's dead." She said it cheerfully, a bright and innocent smile on her face. Hamasa choked on his wine and Marya spluttered loudly.

"We were just in the wrong place at the wrong time," Hamasa said quickly. Too quickly, if that sly look she gave him meant anything.

"Oh, yes, the power of coincidence," she said sagely with a small nod. Hamasa's cheeks heated and he hid behind his clay cup.

"And you?" she asked, rounding on Marya. She squawked in confusion. "What's your lie, hm? Got a better one?"

"Is it really a lie, though?" Marya asked, trailing off into an awkward laugh and rubbing the back of her neck.

Huimitl and Hamasa stared at her, unimpressed.

"So, *not* the missing and probably dead Shield of the Sovereign," Huimitl started with an arch look at Hamasa. "Just where are you heading?"

Hamasa froze, eyes widening. He dropped his gaze to the dregs of fruit water, sloshing it slowly. "I'm not sure…"

"We know exactly where we're going, right, Asa?" Marya said stoutly. "We're heading back east."

"Yes… East." Hamasa murmured. Still that emblem to find. Still that duty to fulfill.

"Not to Harenae?" Huimitl asked sharply.

Hamasa shuddered. "*No.*"

"It's a nice place for a good tussle," she said, cracking her knuckles with a smirk, "but it's no place for a dragon. That man is insane about them. Gotta collect 'em all or something. At least dragon-hunting never caught on here."

"Thank the Sun," Hamasa said fervently.

"I dunno, Wally did a good job dragon-hunting you down in Elorra. You should keep an eye on him," Marya teased.

Hamasa frowned. "You shouldn't even joke about that. Valerius is nothing like those murderers."

"Real devoted fella, ain't he? That friend of yours," Huimitl noted innocently, though her dark eyes glinted. "I offered a tent to each of you. We got some extra supplies to lend for a few nights, normally we don't even bother. It's more comfortable on four legs and under the stars. When we've got some interesting guests, though…" She winked at them. "But the Lance turned us down. Spent every night next to you."

Hamasa steamed at the ears. Marya huffed in annoyance and rolled her eyes. Huimitl looked at him, that glinting gaze sharp and curious.

"Him and his stupid duty this, responsibility that. He doesn't trust nobody but himself to take care of Hamasa," Marya grumbled under her breath.

The strange apology in the tent, before Marya had burst in, replayed in Hamasa's mind. No… He didn't think Marya was quite right this time. Or at least not right in the way she thought she was.

"Mm, I'm sure that's it," Huimitl agreed airily. She stood, Hamasa and Marya swiftly moving out of the way to avoid hooves or knees, and stretched her arms over her head with a small groan. "I gotta make sure my girls don't play too rough. Go get some sleep, wee kiddikins," she said, leaning down to pat both their heads like a grandmother.

He rubbed his head, still flushed and hot, and stared at her back in bemusement. "Kiddikins?"

"She's right, you know. Go get some sleep."

THE COWARD'S EMBLEM

"I just woke up," Hamasa protested. Only to yawn a second later. Marya laughed.

"Yeah, but then you went and did big magic with shit bucket," Marya said, ignoring Hamasa's sigh of 'Arash'. "You aren't even all healed up and you're doing good deeds."

Hamasa shifted awkwardly. "It was the logical next step, not so much a good deed."

Marya shrugged and leaned back on her hands. "You coulda waited, or let Arash do it on his own. I know how much it takes outta you to do magic when you're like this. Sounds like a good deed to me."

"Thank you," he whispered. *But you don't know just how much.*

Marya smiled crookedly and tilted her head back to stare at the stars and the moonlit sky. It was so strange for Hamasa to sit there, mostly healed, arms wrapped around his knees, and realize two days had gone by. It felt like just seconds ago he had held the Merciless to the ground with fire, fists clenched tight and desperate to hold hold *hold*. That he was still somehow living, that his friends were, and that the Beast was gone, was unbelievable. A war still loomed, a promise and secret still churned sickeningly in his stomach, but for a moment, next to a young woman who wanted nothing from him, he felt... safe. Relieved.

"I'm so thankful that I met you," Hamasa said quietly. "I know I made so many mistakes, but in the midst of them I met you. Perhaps that's what Valerius meant when he said regret is useless. If only I could be braver, stronger, I wouldn't be so scared."

"You're plenty brave, Hamasa. What you did to save me, and Valerius and Arash, too," Marya said stoutly. Hamasa ducked his head, pleased, as his ears burned.

"There's still more I should do, more I should be..." Hamasa scratched at the wool blanket under his hand.

"Ay, but the Merciless is gone. The worst of it is over, right?" Marya asked. "If you show up in Riyushu, you'll scare off that stupid war-hungry whoever in Harenae."

"I don't think that's how it works," Hamasa said with a small smile. "The Merciless... I don't know exactly why they joined Harenae, maybe it had something to do with that man, their Chosen. Or maybe there was another reason altogether, but it wasn't the war with Riyushu that the Merciless wanted. My returning alone won't stop it."

"I don't want a war, either," Marya admitted. She scooted over and bumped their shoulders together. Hamasa glanced over, and she smiled at him. "You forget about my papi? About what happened to him in the end? I don't want anyone else to go through what he did, or what I did."

Hesitantly, Hamasa raised an arm and wrapped it around her waist, squeezing lightly. Marya dragged in a deep breath.

"But you're ready to face it, in his honor. If the call came, you'd go towards it, not run from it like I did," Hamasa said softly. "I've twice the power you have, I'm almost four hundred years old, but still I ran..."

"We'll be together," Marya said. "You didn't run this time, you went after the Merciless. You had us, Arash and Valerius and me. Being brave ain't always about facing fears alone. That's just the stupid kinda brave that gets people killed."

Hamasa laughed again. "I guess you're right."

Marya crossed her arms over her chest and preened. "A'course I'm right. Look, now you've got friends that'll fight with you. You don't have to protect the country and the Sovereign by yourself. You can be brave with us at your back."

"You're pretty smart. Don't listen to Arash," Hamasa told her. Marya rolled her eyes.

"I never listen to Frostbite." Marya clapped his shoulder. "Now, go get your beauty rest, and tomorrow we can go looking for your bloom or rock thingy. It'll be a fun adventure, right?"

"Emblem. The word is emblem, not bloom."

"Yeah, yeah," Marya waved off irreverently. "You get outta here before I tuck you in like a mamá."

"I'm going," Hamasa said, throwing up his hands in surrender. "Thanks, Marya, for everything you've done for me."

"I know, I know," Marya said, rubbing the side of her nose with a shrug.

Hamasa walked away, shaking his head and chuckling softly. The walk back to the tent being lent to him was serene and hushed. Most of the noise was behind him at the big fire-pit. The singing and laughing and whooping only occasionally echoed down the crooked rows he sauntered through. Yawning wide enough his eyes teared up, he wiped them clear in time to recognize the tent ahead. It helped that the Valerius was already standing there, an obvious and imposing figure with arms crossed, familiar scowl on his face, and his trident strapped to his back.

"It's strange," Hamasa said, coming to stand in front of Valerius and lifting his gaze upwards. The quiet grunt the Lance made encouraged Hamasa to continue, "I haven't seen the sun in two days? Three days? I've never gone so long without the sun."

"You'll wake to it, my lord," Valerius replied simply. Hamasa nodded and ducked his head, nose scrunched and a chuckle escaping.

"You've called me Hamasa, often now." He glanced towards Valerius' profile, but the knight's expression never wavered.

"You kept your side of the deal."

"The deal? Oh, the compromise?" Hamasa said, eyebrows meeting his hairline.

"You told them all you're the Shield," Valerius said.

"Um..." He realized between one beat and the next that Valerius had been waiting outside his tent, even though Hamasa had awoken and was mostly healed. "Were you going somewhere? Or did you need something?" he asked rather bemusedly.

"I saw you leave and came this way," Valerius answered. An eyebrow slowly rose and the next words had Hamasa's face heating. "I thought perhaps you became lost. I was about to search for you."

Hamasa barked a quick laugh. "I was just taking the long way. What is it? Did you not get a tent of your own? Huimitl said—"

"You're well enough to leave now," Valerius said, interrupting him abruptly and stepping closer.

He reached back to pull free the trident strapped to his back. Hamasa blinked rapidly, nonplussed at the action and wondering when Valerius had gotten it and why. He hadn't had the weapon at the fire-pit. Then, Valerius lowered himself to one knee and lay his free arm over the other knee. Hamasa scrambled back a few steps, eyes wide and hands shaking. The trident Valerius held at his side stood tall and looming over them. Valerius bowed his head and Hamasa's breath wheezed from his chest.

"I wanted to request properly this time."

"Request?" Hamasa squeaked.

"I swear my fealty once more to you, Shield of the Sovereign, Kana'iro the Red. Allow me to accompany you on the quest to retrieve your emblem and return to the Sovereign. It is your quest and not mine. This is how it should be done."

Hamasa's heart stopped. And then broke. Both hands clutched at the blue linen over his stomach. This brave, honorable man believed in him still. So completely. All of them did.

And Hamasa was still a Sun-cursed *liar*.

41

"I can't... I can't accept. Please, Valerius — *Emerens*, please stand up."

Valerius' face tightened, dark eyes hooded and jaw ticking. He got to his feet heavily, all grace gone.

"Of course. I am unworthy of your trust. I should have—"

"No, nonono, you are *not* unworthy of trust. I already told you," Hamasa gripped his arm, quickly let go, and stepped back. He hadn't felt himself move, hadn't felt himself reach out, until the smooth weave of Valerius' kimono was already under his hand. Instead, Hamasa reached for the edge of his poncho, which he obviously wasn't wearing nor had replaced yet, and began to twist his fingers together. "It's me. It's *me* who's unworthy of trust. Of yours, of Marya's, even Arash's. I've been the liar all along."

"You had a reason, my lord. Without your emblem how could—" Valerius broke off at Hamasa's sudden, inexplicable laughter; harsh, grating cackles unlike any sound he had made before. Valerius' eyes widened, darting over Hamasa's twisting expression.

Hamasa buried his face in his hands and muffled the wretched sound of the laughter that wasn't.

"You keep believing in me. In the dragon you think I am! Why won't you stop? Why can't you understand? That's. Not. Me."

Hands settled on Hamasa's shoulders. Warm, for a mere

human, solid and real, thickened with calluses that scratched against the beautifully woven linen Hamasa wore. He swallowed and looked up, willing himself not to cry. He didn't deserve it, didn't deserve the relief or Valerius' sympathy.

Valerius' forehead touched his. A gentle bump and the silken brush of hair across his temples and cheeks. Over scars that he shouldn't be able to feel so minutely. Hamasa's breath knotted in his throat, choking on the words, the last confession. Against his better judgement, Hamasa let himself be swayed. His eyes slid closed on a hiccupped laugh, rocking up on his toes so Valerius wouldn't have to lean so far down. Valerius' hand stroked up and down Hamasa's arms, past the short rough sleeves to bare skin. When his hands stopped, everywhere his hands weren't, was suddenly cold. Colder than he'd been moments ago.

"I know that. You're Hamasa, not just Kana'iro, not just the Shield," Valerius said. He'd always been quiet, but this was *gentle*. Hamasa's heart thudded, raced, shuddered in a chest that felt too small and too large all at once. "Hamasa, the Red dragon that chose us, chose Mekshi and everyone in it, and the one that chose his friends over his soul, that's the one to who I pledge my loyalty. Allow me to make right my mistakes."

The grass whistled around their ankles. An autumn breeze too cool to be comfortable stirring their clothes and whipping loose strands of their hair. In the distance the Salvatropas still sang and danced, the bonfire still crackled and burned. Valerius' scent was linen and sweat and horse and spices he must have hated eating. And under it all was something uniquely *him*, something that this body Hamasa wore would never truly taste or smell. A part that Hamasa was missing, would always be missing, because of what *Hamasa* had done.

He slowly fell back on his heels. His forehead left Valerius'. And he stepped back. For a just one second, almost imperceptibly,

THE COWARD'S EMBLEM

Valerius' hands tightened. Held on. And then let go. Fell to hang, unmoving, to his sides. Hamasa hissed in a short breath and raised his eyes. In the dark, far from the fire, Valerius' face was masked in impenetrable shadows. The last thing, the *very last thing*, Hamasa wanted was to speak to the young man suddenly closed off and silent in front of him. More lies, or truth, neither would be what Valerius wanted to hear.

"I stole it."

It dropped and hit the silence like a pin to glass. Clattering, ringing, ebbing back into silence. A silence waiting with bated breath for Hamasa to continue, to *finally finish.*

"I stole my emblem back from Aneya. While she slept."

"No, you—" Valerius started, stopped.

Hamasa barrelled on. "I knew the Merciless was coming back. I could feel it, that presence they have, it echoed through Mekshi the moment they took flight. War was already coming, I was already so scared, so horrified at the idea I'd have to... that so many were calling for death, they *wanted* it, Valerius. So many were eager for it," Hamasa whispered, the words falling out faster and faster, eyes widening and hands shaking. He gripped the loose fabric in front of his stomach, wrung it tight in both fists, and stared into the darkness beyond Valerius' broad shoulder. "I couldn't... I couldn't do it. I couldn't think about it. In the middle of the night, when I knew she'd be sleeping, I snuck into her room and stole my Emblem back. *I stole it back.* I rejected my Chosen, and I left."

"You can't just... She's your Sovereign, your Chosen," Valerius said, stepping back and shaking his head. He dragged a hand through his hair and glared at the ground. "You called her sister."

"She's not. Not my Chosen. She hasn't been for... for a while," Hamasa whispered. Valerius' eyes closed, his nostrils flaring. Rather like Nerva, Hamasa thought stupidly. But it made him want to smile, if he didn't feel like throwing up. "I didn't go looking for the Merciless. I was running away. The Merciless found me running. I was alone, and terrified, and ran right into the very thing I was trying to avoid. And then I lost."

Hamasa could feel it again. The burning of acid on his back, his wings, dripping down his legs and tail and face plate. The shrieks that rent the air torn out of his own mouth. He had been too much in pain, too terrified, to call on flame.

"This can't be true," Valerius snapped shortly. Caustically.

"For the first time, I've never been more honest," Hamasa said hoarsely. Valerius turned away, his shoulders bowing as if under a weight he couldn't shrug off. "When I realized I couldn't win, I tore it out myself. I ripped my soul out of my own body and threw it. I rejected my soul the same way I rejected *her*. I Chose her, and Mekshi, seventeen years ago. But I threw them all away, threw myself and all my power away, because I'm a coward. A lying coward."

Valerius' hands curled into fists. His head dropped. There was only the shuddering inhale, exhale, of each breath, the lifting and falling of his bowed shoulders.

"You don't need my forgiveness, Emerens. Whatever mistakes you made, whatever choices you made, you made them out of loyalty. You are more a Shield than I have ever been." Hamasa's gaze dropped to his toes, bare and chilled in the grass. "And I won't ask you to forgive me."

"Then, I won't."

The reply was whipcord thin and stung as badly. Hamasa flinched, shoulders drawing close to his ears, head ducking low. Exposed without his wings, without even his thick alpaca wool poncho.

"You warned me and I didn't listen. Kana'iro the Red never

existed. Who knows what you are."

Hamasa cringed again, teeth baring in a silent hiss, hands digging into the soft give of his belly through his tunic. There were footsteps in the grass. Footsteps that moved farther and farther away.

Hamasa stood outside his tent long after the footsteps faded. Long after the bonfire died and the songs ended. The sky began to lighten and the first weak, trembling, grey rays of dawn's sun spread over the grass, up his bare shins, up to his lowered face and closed eyes. And he still felt cold.

This shame hurt worse than fear, piercing straight into the deepest wound inside him where a soul used to lay.

When it was truly dawn, and the grey wisps of light had become autumn gold and the sleepy-eyed Marya stumbled towards him through the maze of tents and pavilions, Hamasa hadn't slept a wink. Hadn't even sat down. He trudged to the center clearing behind Marya. His feet stopped at the sound of Nerva's huffing and click and creak of saddle tack, but his eyes didn't raise. Couldn't rise. The acid churning in his stomach grew, writhed, bubbled, and his gaze stayed on the grass crushed beneath hoof and boot alike. He didn't need to look up to see Valerius' face turned away. His broad shoulders and back were already the last sight of him Hamasa would see. What would looking again do?

"Do we gotta go so quick? Arash the Wonderful isn't even back yet," Marya complained around a yawn. "I'll get my things."

"Don't. I'm going to Riyushu alone."

Hamasa didn't so much as grimace. Marya, though, inhaled sharply. Her gaze on the side of Hamasa's face was a physical weight.

"Wha? But Hamasa's emblem...? And you're not a Lance, not really, won't you get in trouble if you go back without Hamasa?"

There was a grunt and leather creaking against leather. Nerva huffed, hooves shuffling over dirt and immediately stilling.

"Okay, something is going on. We were good yesterday, we were celebrating! Hamasa, you fought the Merciless, you saved all of us! And Valerius wasn't demanding we drag you back to Riyushu because I thought... I thought you were gonna go, we were all gonna go, together. When we got the emblem back." Marya stammered to a stop when neither of them spoke.

Hooves came from behind and Hamasa finally looked up. Huimitl stood there, one hand lying easy and lax on a quiver hanging from a belt across her waist. One elongated ear twitched as wind whistled through the beaten-down grass and the surrounding forest of their large tent-filled clearing. Her startling amber eyes moved over Hamasa's face, and, deliberately obvious, she looked towards the knight packing the last of his things. Hamasa dropped his chin, eyes on the ground again.

"This is an interesting development," Huimitl said mildly.

"I don't understand what's happening!" Marya exclaimed, throwing her hands up and letting out a wordless shout right after.

"I'm returning to Riyushu to face the consequences of my actions. I never should have forsaken my duty," Valerius said flatly.

There was another wordless exclamation from Marya, somewhere between rage and confusion. Although he saw her body turn towards him from under his hair, Hamasa didn't bother lifting his head.

Why doesn't he just tell them? Tell them I'm a fraud?

Valerius swung himself up off the ground as a quiet sound of disdain escaped Huimitl and the saddle creaked.

"Marya Garsia, I underestimated your worth and your strength many times since I've met you. I sincerely offer my apologies."

THE COWARD'S EMBLEM

"Wh—uh, do you—? Are you serious?" A pregnant silence. "*Ay*, all right, yes, thank you. But why are you leaving?!"

"Take care of yourselves. Don't get killed."

Hamasa flinched.

"Wait, you can't just go like this—Valerius!"

A quiet click of tongue against teeth, and Nerva shot forward. Grass and dirt flew from under her heavy, iron-shod hooves. Hamasa stared at his feet.

"Asa, *what happened*?" Marya demanded, grabbing his shoulders and jerking him around.

He cringed away from under her hands. Her touch dropped immediately, but she moved to stand in front of him again, not even a full pace away.

"Hamasa?"

"He's doing what he should've done weeks ago," Hamasa said at last.

"That doesn't make anymore sense..."

"It was frustratingly vague," Huimitl agreed.

The strange pitch and stress of her tone made Hamasa look up. She was gazing down at him, light eyes boring through him like a beam of sunlight controlled by a glass lens, and smiling. That crooked smirk of a smile. She looked down on him with that infuriating smirk on her face. Knowing more than him, seeing through him. He never disliked anyone as much as he did in this very moment, meeting her stare for stare. He wanted to hiss or snarl or shout. Anything to wipe that look away.

But that sounded exhausting just in his head. So he kept staring back, too tired to frown, to smile, to raise an eyebrow. He looked until her eyes pulled away. Towards Marya, who was speaking again.

"Ay, we don't need him anyway. We've got each other. And the shiny lizard whenever he gets back," Marya said, reaching out to grasp his shoulder, only to quickly change direction and ruffle her own hair.

"Marya you don't... you don't have to stay either. I can find it on my own. Or with Arash when he—"

"What, you don't need me anymore now you've got your dragon friend?" Marya demanded, fists on her hips and black eyes flashing.

Hamasa sighed, lips curving upwards gradually. "No one can replace you."

Unlike Hamasa's pitiful excuse for a smile, Marya's fairly outshone the sun. For the first time since Valerius walked away outside the tent, Hamasa felt warmth trickle into his heart, responding involuntarily to Marya's joy. She scratched her cheek and pretended like her face wasn't rose red.

"You're damn right." She clapped her hands together and met his expectant gaze. "I still have that token. We'll go find that emblem ourselves and we'll go down to Harenae and find that ancient Green dragon. Between us, we'll convince them to stop the war. We can do it, I know we can."

His smile spread a little wider and a little thinner. Her enthusiasm and hope was so contagious, filling up so many empty spaces inside him. But he also knew how small a shot they had. How uninspiring he himself was. The emptiness she soothed was made by himself, by secrets he still hoarded like dragons of ancient fable. Secrets he had given away which had been thrown back in his face. As he deserved.

But... She was holding out her hand.

His champion. His friend.

He reached out, clasped her large, farm-calloused hand in his, and forced his smile to be more: more real, more hopeful, more bright.

"If anyone can stop a war before it begins, it'll be you, Marya

THE COWARD'S EMBLEM

Garsia."

And he told himself he believed it as she gripped his hand tight enough to hurt.

"I think this will be a fun little adventure. Averting a war? Finding a single rock lost in the mountains? Saving the Empire? Sounds like a good song for the storytellers."

Hamasa and Marya started, hands dropping. They shared another quick smile before turning back to Huimitl.

"We'll come back and tell you all about it," Marya promised.

Huimitl shook her head oddly, tossing back her head and snorting. "Oh no, I wouldn't miss this for the world. The Salvatropas could do with running themselves without me for a time."

Hamasa and Marya exchanged a glance.

"I'm sorry, are you offering to come with us?" Hamasa asked hesitantly.

"I don't think she's offering, Asa. I think she's telling," Marya muttered from the side of her mouth.

The knowingly horrible smirk was back and Hamasa barely kept from hissing. Not at the offer. Just at that *smile*.

"You just lost your knight," Hamasa cringed, "and your dragon hasn't come back yet. You need someone with experience to help you. Not to mention someone to keep up your training. If I don't come, you'll both end up dead before you find the emblem."

Marya scowled. "I don't think we'll end up dead. I'm doing a lot better with the spear and Hamasa can do magic again—"

She broke off at the soft dissenting sound that left Hamasa's mouth unbidden. Marya turned to him, but he looked away, hand over his mouth, his brows low.

"Perhaps he can, but it takes a lot out of him. He's still recovering and it's been three days," Huimitl pointed out.

Marya's eyes widened.

Hamasa shrugged. "It was a lot of magic. I can wield smaller amounts and human spells without much backlash."

"Will it really be better after we get your emblem back?" Marya asked, eyes darting over Hamasa's face and overall posture. Cataloging all the little hints of his unwellness for herself.

Hamasa smiled at her. "Of course."

"Which makes you vulnerable until you find it or your dragon friend gets back," Huimitl said, arms crossing over her chest, one hoof cutting turf. Marya glanced at her with pursed lips, looking frighteningly similar to Irmen. "And though you have improved with the spear, you are still a novice and require a teacher if you want to protect your friend and yourself. Unless Hamasa could take the knight's place as an instructor?"

"No, I couldn't," Hamasa admitted. "All my knowledge comes from observation. Nothing practical."

"I wouldn't mind you coming," Marya said slowly.

"Kind of you," Huimitl said wryly. Marya laughed.

"But it's not my quest, it's yours, Asa."

Hamasa glanced between them, at Marya's concerned frown and Huimitl's damnable smile. He held up a hand and shook his head.

"No, this isn't my quest. If anyone's the hero, it's you, Marya." She beamed, that rose red blush back. "Do you want her to join us?" Hamasa asked.

"Well... she's right. About being sitting ducks and needing help. And I like her," Marya said stoutly.

The smile on Huimitl's face softened into something real and pleased. "I also like you. In fact, I like you both."

Hamasa narrowed his eyes at her. He had a suspicion her feelings towards him were more amusement than actual liking. But... he did believe her about liking Marya and he couldn't protect Marya, or teach her martial arts, the way Huimitl could.

"We're honored by your offer and humbly accept," Hamasa said, hands at his thighs as he bowed.

"Thank you." Huimitl bowed in return, one foreleg curling under her body. "Are all dragons as polite as you?"

Marya burst into loud, rollicking guffaws with arms wrapped around her torso. "Definitely not!"

"You've only met three," Hamasa said with a small laugh.

"Yeah, and one's a gulero and one tried to kill us all. I've got a pretty good idea." Marya flipped her hair over her shoulder as Hamasa laughed again despite himself. "Now that *that's* settled, we've got a long road to walk."

"We'll spend today preparing and resting. Tomorrow at dawn we'll head out," Huimitl said firmly.

"We should head out right away. The Lances were called back to the Capital days ago. The war is coming fast!" Marya protested.

"Rest is important. As you said, the road ahead will be long. We need rest when we can get it. We can't run out with a wish and a can-do attitude. I also have duties and responsibilities to discuss among my companions."

Marya opened her mouth, brows pulled tight and low, but Hamasa cleared his throat.

"I could use a little more sleep." *Or any at all.*

Marya's mouth snapped shut and she squinted closely at him. "All right. Tomorrow at dawn."

He gestured for her to walk ahead with Huimitl. He, however, stayed behind. He turned slowly towards the Great Road. And the south. He would be going back soon. For a moment, one nonsensical moment, he pretended he could see a tiny pinprick in the distance.

Dramatis Personae

LEADERS

Riyukezu Aneya : Sovereign of the Mekshi and direct descendant of the First and the previous Sovereign

Kana'iro the Red: the Shield of the Sovereign, a Red Dragon and the offspring of the previous Shield, the Scarlet Dread

Huimitl: leader of the Salvatropas and cabadona (half-horse, half-woman)

(NAME UNKNOWN) King Commander of Harenae

MEKSHI

Arash- a White dragon

Emerens Valerius (Kaecus)- a Lance of the Realm and son of the Baron of Saig'shu

Irmen Garsia- the mother of Marya, lives in Elorra

Marya- a young Mekshan farmer woman from Elorra

Hamasa- young-seeming man on the run

SALVATROPAS

a group of outlaw women who protect Mekshi

Eluya- a cabadona (half-horse, half-woman)

Sitlal- a cabadona (half-horse, half-woman)

Tepin- a cabadona (half-horse, half-woman) who rides with the Salvatropas, a group of not-quite-outlaw women that protect Mekshi

HARENAE

Flavius- a Harenese centurion and mercenary

Gaius Tarcinius Varro- a Harenese centurion and mercenary

The Merciless, the Beast- a Black dragon corrupted by events that took place 17 years before the start of 'The Coward's Emblem'

Mureno- a Harenese man and Chosen by the Merciless

About The Author

Alex D Guier is the author of the Emblem Series of fantasy novels. The first book, *The Coward's Emblem*, will be published in 2022. She is an English teacher currently living in Wuxi, China. She has also lived in Fujian province, China and Jinju, South Korea.

Born in Modesto, Alex has run a book club in every city she's ever lived in and writing is her passion since she was 13 years old and posting Dragonball Z fanfiction online. Vast amounts of Dungeons & Dragons, Star Wars, and multiple fantasy series or films have helped shape every character Alex has ever created. And it is from the characters that her stories spring.

www.ingramcontent.com/pod-product-compliance
Lightning Source LLC
LaVergne TN
LVHW030313070526
838199LV00069B/6466